HEART
QUEST™

HeartQuest brings you romantic fiction
with a foundation of biblical truth.
Adventure, mystery, intrigue, and suspense
mingle in these heartwarming stories of
men and women of faith striving to build
a love that will last a lifetime.

May HeartQuest books sweep you
into the arms of God, who longs for you
and pursues you always.

Freedom's Promise

Dianna Crawford

HEART QUEST™

Romance fiction from
Tyndale House Publishers, Inc.
WHEATON, ILLINOIS

Visit Tyndale's exciting Web site at www.tyndale.com

Check out the latest about HeartQuest Books at www.heartquest-romances.com

HeartQuest is a registered trademark of Tyndale House Publishers, Inc.

Edited by Kathryn S. Olson

Designed by Jackie Noe

Scripture quotations are taken from the *Holy Bible*, King James Version.

Scripture quotations marked NLT are taken from the *Holy Bible*, New Living Translation, copyright © 1996. Used by permission of Tyndale House Publishers, Inc., Wheaton, Illinois 60189. All rights reserved.

Library of Congress Cataloging-in-Publication Data

Crawford, Dianna.
   Freedom's promise / Dianna Crawford.
      p. cm. — (HeartQuest)
    ISBN 0-8423-1916-6 (sc)
    1. Frontier and pioneer life—Tennessee—Fiction.   2. Women pioneers—Tennessee—Fiction.
I. Title. II. Series.
PS3553.R27884F74 2000
813′.54—dc21   99-051692

Printed in the United States of America

05   04   03   02
9   8   7   6   5   4

*I dedicate this book to my forefathers, who
walked the same trails in search of their dreams
as did the characters in* Freedom's Promise, *and to my husband, who makes it
possible for me to walk my own trails.*

Acknowledgments

I would like to acknowledge several people for the invaluable assistance they graciously rendered during the writing of this book: Frances Young and Robert McGennis, who work with the McClung Collection at the Knox County Public Library System; Shelly Thacker at the reference desk of the Palm Springs Public Library; Rachel Druten, Mary Firman, Sally Laity, and Sue Rich, my critique partners; along with Denise Bean.

1

Charlotte, North Carolina
June 1786

"'Scuse me, ma'am!"

Annie McGregor caught her balance—and the unwieldy round of cheddar she carried—as a young man in a great hurry careened past her on his way out the door of the mercantile.

Mr. Jewett, the storekeeper, as openmouthed as Annie, watched the fellow race away. Then a smile cracked his sparse lips. "Reckon I'd be as excited as him, iffen I was still spry enough to go chasin' overmountain into Tennessee country for some of that cheap land."

Cheap land? Annie's pulse picked up at those words. "How cheap?"

Recognizing a receptive audience, the storekeeper continued. "You ain't heard, have you? Isaac Reardon, of the Salisbury Reardons, has built a fort on some land him and his brother got for fightin' the war. A purty little valley, he says, out past Henry's Fort. Ike Reardon's here in town, lookin' for settlers to take back with him. Says they've planted enough grain and vegetables to winter thirty people and their livestock. And all he's askin' is fifty cents American an acre."

Fifty cents? I could have ten acres for five dollars . . . plenty of land
to start her own dairy—land out of reach of her pa's greedy hands.
And she'd still have four dollars and two Spanish bits left over to pay
for ferry crossings and such. Could this be God's answer to an entire
year's worth of prayers? No, it sounded too good to be true. "Why
would Mr. Reardon want to be so generous?"

The hollow-cheeked storekeeper chuckled as if Annie'd said
something amusing. "It's more crafty than generous. He's come
home to fetch the workin's to a gristmill that won't make a profit if
he don't have no folks comin' to him to have their corn ground. And
I think maybe he likes the notion of foundin' his own town, too . . .
one with his own religious bent. Comes from a family of Baptists.
That's why he's over to the smithy's right now. He's lookin' for a
minister, and it seems the German what works there used to preach
all that dunkin' baptism business back where he come from."

Though a Presbyterian herself, Annie had naught against the
Dunkers. She'd heard they didn't hold much with drinking hard
liquor and dancing, but after her seven years of servitude to Mr.
and Mrs. White and one more as their hired dairymaid, Annie had
never acquired a taste for those worldly pleasures anyway. And it
could even work in her favor. If she were allowed to travel with
folks bent on keeping to their beliefs, she wouldn't have to worry
about being bothered by any of the men. A trickle of hope skittered
through her. This truly could be God's answer. Her way of escape.

"Please, Mr. Jewett," she said, handing him Mrs. White's gro-
cery list along with the cheese she had brought to trade, "could you
be quick with this? I have other business that needs tendin'."

❧

Sweat beaded Isaac Reardon's forehead. It tracked into his sun-
bleached brows and ran down his temples. The heat was intense.
But for once, he was glad for it, because he was standing in the
middle of a busy four-man blacksmith shop. He'd spent most of

the past few years a good three days' ride from the nearest smithy. When the flintlock broke on his Pennsylvania rifle last fall, he'd lost a week's work just going to get it repaired.

And now he'd be taking one of these tradesmen with him back to his own valley.

Ike walked past two workers in heavy leather aprons to reach Rolf Bremmer—the stocky German blacksmith he'd come to see. He stopped a couple of feet shy of Bremmer's ringing hammer and flying sparks, waiting to gain the busy man's attention.

Just then young Ken Smith burst through the wide double doorway of the barnlike building, his face flushed as if he'd been running for his life. Pausing only a second to let his eyes adjust to the dimmer light, the strapping lad charged straight for Ike and grabbed hold of his shoulders. "Mr. Reardon!" he shouted out, breaking into the biggest toothy grin Ike had ever seen. "She agreed to go! My Betsy. She said yes!"

"She did?" Ike took hold of the young man's arms and gave them a squeeze, as relieved and pleased as Smith seemed—if that were possible.

"Alleluia!" boomed Rolf Bremmer, waving a tong-held piece of fiery red iron as if it were the new American flag. "Anodder family is coming *mit* us," he added in an enthusiastic mix of German and English.

This was a day for rejoicing. As young as Kenneth Smith was, he'd been raised by a barrelmaker and had spent several years as an apprentice to a wheelwright. With those skills added to Brother Bremmer's and with the mill machinery Ike himself was bringing, they would have a great start for a settlement. Three other families had also pledged to complete their business and dispose of their property in time to relocate to the Reardons' holdings when he returned for them next spring. One even talked of starting a settlement store.

Ike's dream—most of it, anyway—was taking shape.

3

For the next few minutes, he reveled in the pleasure of answering questions about the distance to his valley, the challenges they might have crossing the rivers and mountains, the slim chance of any hostilities with the Cherokee or Creek tribes. Even the Chicamaugas—as a group of renegade Creeks and Cherokees now called themselves—had not been on the warpath for more than a year.

Bremmer and Smith were eager to get started. And Ike was glad to hear it. "How about a week from today? We'll meet outside the smithy's next Monday morning, ready to roll."

When the other two heartily agreed, Ike turned to tell his partner, who'd come into the smithy with him. Jigs, who'd been nicknamed in accordance with his love of dancing the lively jig, hadn't even been listening. The much shorter man stood several feet away, staring at the doorway and grinning as if he had no sense.

Then Ike saw why. A young woman stood silhouetted in the opening. Leave it to Jigs to notice her first.

Taller than most women, she wasn't just skin and bone like so many women her height, but nicely fleshed out. She took a step, then stopped and checked the tuck of her plain shawl collar before coming forward.

As she moved into the muted light of the shop, Ike saw that, though her eyes were unusual—gold-rimmed jade—her complexion was darker than one would expect. On closer inspection, he realized she'd not kept herself sufficiently shaded from the sun's rays. Adding that to the coarse homespun of the woman's attire, he surmised that she was some poor farmer's wife sent to have a tool repaired. A simple, hardworking young woman. Certainly not someone his former betrothed would deign to have to tea, now that she'd become mistress of her fine new house.

Sour grapes again. Would he ever get over his intended's betrayal? Or his own lack of good judgment? The fact that he'd believed her when she'd said her dream was the same as his had shaken his confidence in his own intuitive abilities. Why hadn't he seen through her beguiling lies? Sylvia had known when she accepted his proposal that, as the third son, he had inherited no land from his father—only mill machinery. She'd also known the new congress could not afford to pay his back army wages and had cashiered him out with acreage of his choosing west of the Tennessee River.

"Gentlemen," the woman began. "I'm searchin' for a frontiersman by the name of Reardon. Would one of you be this man?"

"Ain't you the woman with the cheese?" Ken Smith asked, a strange expression accompanying his question.

"Aye. Could you tell me where I might find Mr. Reardon?"

"That's me." Ike turned to fully face her. Perhaps the woman had come on behalf of her husband, seeking information about the planned trip. "What can I do for you?"

"I'm here about the land you're sellin' in Tennessee country. Is it true that the askin' price is fifty cents an acre?"

"Aye."

"I also heard it's in a valley. Does that mean it has good-growin' bottomland?" There was nothing coy about the straightforward gaze she maintained from beneath her simple straw bonnet.

"The best."

"And is the money to be paid before or after folks get there so they can take a look for themselves?"

Ike quirked a one-sided grin. The woman was downright suspicious of him. As calloused of hand and lean of body as he was, he was amused that she could think he might make his living as a shiftless flimflammer. "After we get there and after we agree on the parcels, then I'll take their money. If I might ask, for whom are you inquiring?"

She straightened her capable-looking shoulders, shoulders without the fashionable slope to them. "For myself, of course. Annie McGregor of Mr. Vernon White's dairy farm. We're the only maker of hard cheese in two counties. And we keep European bees."

"Excellent. But I'm afraid you've come to inquire at a very late date if you wish to go with our party this year. We're leavin' next Monday. Could you and your husband conclude your affairs and be ready to travel in so short a time?"

An eager smile transformed a merely pleasant face into a thing of beauty. "Yes, yes. I've been preparing for this day for almost a year. You're the answer to my prayers."

"Wonderful. Cheese makers. We're glad to have you along." Why couldn't Sylvia have understood the thrill of building something of one's own all from scratch? Or Smith's wife? Or Bremmer's, for that matter? They'd both been reluctant to come along. Only his brother's betrothed had displayed an eagerness, and Ike suspected Lorna Graham's enthusiasm was due more to a desire to escape her father's eagle eye than in anticipation of their destination. "Will you be bringin' honeybees, as well?"

Her smile relaxed into one no less pleasant. "Yes, indeed."

"But be advised that the valley is several days' ride from the nearest settlement store, so you must carry everything you'll need with you. I'll be takin' care of business here in Charlotte until this evenin'. Have your husband seek me out, and I'll provide him with a list of things he'll require for the trip."

She glanced away. Then, leveling her gaze on him again, she took a deep breath. "I fear you misunderstood me. This trip I will make alone. I have no husband."

Ike's head jerked up. *No husband? Alone?* Poor thing. Most likely she'd lost her man to the war, like so many other young brides. Nonetheless. . . . "I am sorry, ma'am. But it isn't possible for you to accompany us . . . 'lessen you have someone to take charge of seein' you safely there and settled."

"No, I have no money to spare for such luxuries. But I assure you, I'm quite capable of takin' care of myself."

6

She certainly didn't lack determination, just good sense.

"Ma'am, it is my responsibility to see that all who travel with me arrive safely, along with all our goods, and I take that responsibility very seriously. Without someone who is capable of lookin' after your outfit and who knows how to use a rifle if the need arises, I simply cannot allow you to join our party."

Ike had forgotten that the other men were listening until Jigs intervened. "Aw, let her come if she's so set on it." The dark-headed charmer turned to the McGregor woman and doffed his tricorn. "I'd be real pleased to offer the lady my assistance and my protection."

Ike grazed the rake with a warning glower. "You'll already have your hands plenty full. You have a wagon loaded down with mill-works to get over those mountains, remember? Trails to be widened, rivers to cross."

"Mr. Reardon is right," Brother Bremmer added in his thick accent. "Is not goot for da voman to make da long chourney alone."

The widow's gilt-edged green eyes took on a bleakness, erasing the beauty that had lit up the sooty furnace-hot shop only moments before. "Is that your final word?"

Ike had no choice. "I'm afraid it has to be."

$\sim$

"Why, God?" Annie cried out, once she'd driven her horse and cart far enough from town not to be overheard. "In your Bible it says I'm to have joy and peace. Night after night, Mr. White has read that you're a loving and merciful God. Yet, when my one chance comes, you let that man shut the door in my face. Is it just me you don't love? Is there something so wrong with me? I've tried. You know how hard I try to be good." Her last words came out on a strangled sob as hot tears spilled down her cheeks.

Feeling sorry for yourself again, aren't you? Pressing her lips tight, Annie swiped viciously at the evidence of her weakness. Just because that frontiersman wouldn't let her go with his party didn't mean she couldn't go somewhere. But where? With only nine American dollars and two Spanish bits, where else could she buy ten acres of her own? Certainly not here in North Carolina. She'd have to go over the mountains for land that cheap.

If she was ever to have anything of her own.

She couldn't fault Mr. and Mrs. White on that count, though. They had been more generous than any bond servant had a right to expect, allowing her to keep any tips she received while making deliveries and letting her work the extra year to get her start—or her dowry, as Mrs. White always insisted on calling it. Her elderly mistress assumed Annie was accumulating possessions so she'd have a better choice of suitors. And Annie never had the heart to tell the kind lady that she had absolutely no intention of being enslaved again.

Land of her own was what she needed. She now had two milk cows and a bull to start her dairy. The crates that would carry the chickens Mrs. White promised her were already built. And bless Mr. White—he was giving her a hive of domesticated bees. Honey was liquid gold since almost everyone had a sweet tooth.

For two years now, Annie had been trading and scrounging and scavenging—seeds, tools, household goods. So she could tote all her property, Mr. White had given her an old hay cart, along with a double yoke and chains, for the price of having the axle replaced. Most important, though, Annie had her dog. She'd match Cap against any cow dog in the county.

She was as ready as she'd ever be. It was time to go, past time. She simply had to get far enough away so her pa couldn't find her and drag her back. But she couldn't just take off alone. Desperate as she was, she wasn't that much of a fool.

What could she do? She bit her lower lip, studying on her predicament.

Then it hit her. The answer was so simple. Why hadn't she thought of it before?

~

Annie could hardly contain her excitement and her trepidation as she and plump-cheeked Mrs. White, both in their mobcaps and fresh aprons, rose to clear the evening meal's dirty dishes from the kitchen table. Annie could almost see her galloping heart bumping against the fabric of her gray linen bodice. Yet the moment when she planned to ask her elderly master if he would release her a week early was still a quarter hour away . . . after Mr. White's nightly sharing of a Bible chapter.

Once they were all settled, Mr. White put on his spectacles, then carefully opened the old book to the place he'd left off the night before, marked by a satin ribbon. It would be in the Psalms. He'd been reading from those chapters for the past couple of months.

Tonight it seemed as if he was taking a deliberately long time to set the ribbon aside and smooth the pages with his gnarled and weathered hands, but Annie knew better . . . her impatience merely made it seem that way.

"Chapter sixty-one," he began at last in his rumbling, lumbering monotone. "Hear my cry, O God; attend unto my prayer. From the end of the earth will I cry unto thee, when my heart is overwhelmed: lead me to the rock that is higher than I. For thou hast been a shelter for me, and a strong tower from the enemy."

Mr. White continued to the end of the psalm, but Annie heard nothing past those first verses. It was as if God was speaking directly to her. She rolled the words over in her mind, in her soul. *Hear my cry . . . attend my prayer . . . my heart is overwhelmed. Lead me to the rock that is higher than I.* Oh, yes, she prayed silently, *for these past eight years, Lord, you have sheltered me. Now it is time for me to be led up to that high rock. I thank you, O Lord. You have answered my prayer. On the very day I needed it. And gracious Lord, I ask your forgiveness for my lack of patience, and most of all for doubting that you care.*

After finishing the chapter, the farmer closed the Bible. Taking a sip of the tea left for him, Mr. White wiped his mouth and grizzled beard on his shirtsleeve and started to get up.

"Sir?" Annie reached across the table. "I would have a word with you, if you please." Annie's mouth went suddenly dry. Everything depended on her making the old couple understand. She swallowed. "I spoke to a man in town today—a Mr. Isaac Reardon. He's guiding a group of settlers overmountain into Tennessee. He's offerin' good bottomland for fifty cents an acre." She swallowed again. "I'm set on goin' with 'em."

"You? A girl alone? Nonsense." Mr. White scooted his chair back.

Annie sprang to her feet. "Please, I beg of you. Hear me out."

Her master hesitated, his strong fingers gripping the edge of the table.

"When I went home last Christmas," Annie said in a rush, "I learned my younger sister had married."

"That's a good thing, dear," Mrs. White said. "And there's no reason to think you won't find a husband, too. Especially with the dowry we've been helping you gather."

"No, Mrs. White, I'm afraid the marriage was *not* a good thing. No dowry was settled on her so she could make a mutually pleasin' match. Instead, my pa gave her to a widower who has five children still at home. Or should I say, Pa sold her. The man traded him a crib of corn and two hogs ready for slaughter. My sister never had a say in it. And she doesn't even like the man. I've been prayin' that she'll grow to care for him. But I never saw such a miserable girl as Emma Jane, ma'am."

"Oh, I'm so sorry," Mrs. White sympathized. "You should have mentioned this sooner. We would have prayed for her with you. Wouldn't we, Vernon?"

"At the moment, I'm just praying Annie will come to the point."

Annie straightened and spoke faster. "My pa as much as told me, he'll be lookin' for a good prospect for me, too. And a *good prospect* to him means someone he can profit from. I have no doubt that he will take everything I've worked so hard for—the cattle, the beehive, cart, everything—all for hisself—when he marries me off."

Mrs. White sighed heavily. "I'm sure," she said in a wistful voice, "your father loves you and thinks he's doing right by you."

"He doesn't think about us girls much one way or the other. When my ma finally started givin' him sons—after us four girls—that's all he's cared about."

"The man's still your pa," Mr. White said gruffly.

Annie had anticipated his every argument and knew her next words were vital. "Sir, I feel that my pa sold his rights over me when he indentured me to you. No dire straits forced him to sell his second daughter into servitude. We had food on the table, clothes on our backs, and he already had more land than he could put to plow. He had no urgent need—'lessen you count his greed for more land. So I say, he's already received his 'thirty pieces of silver'. He forfeited any right to sell me again."

"I'd hate to think those pillowcases and napkins I embroidered for your chest wouldn't go with you when you marry," her plump mistress said. "Vernon, I've grown very fond of Annie, and she's worked so hard for us. Don't you think she deserves to find what happiness she can?"

Bless Mrs. White. She was standing up for Annie, pleading her cause. Annie barely restrained herself from kissing the old woman.

"She should have a chance to make a good match for herself," Mrs. White concluded with unusual vigor.

The farmer stared at his wife a long moment . . . then grunted a response in what sounded like agreement.

11

They agreed. Maybe. Annie's spirits soared as she dared to hope she'd interpreted correctly. She pressed her cause. "That's why it's so urgent for me to leave now, get as far away from my pa as I can, whilst I have the chance. He'll be comin' to fetch me at month's end."

"But, dear, you have no husband. No one to look after you on the trip."

"The German blacksmith and his family are goin', and you know what fine upstandin' Christians they are. He's to be given his own church in the valley. I'll be fine, just fine." Annie felt a twinge of guilt. She knew she was deceiving her mistress by leaving out the fact that the leader of the party hadn't accepted her.

Mr. White stroked his beard thoughtfully. "You've always been a fine hand at chopping wood and fixing what's broken. And I suppose you could trade your milk and cheese and honey for what you can't do, like raising your cabin." He tucked his chin and eyed her. "Or did you think you could do that by your lonesome, too?"

Annie held her own. "Like you said, I'll trade for what I can't do."

"Well, you're not going off into the wilderness 'lessen you can load and shoot a musket—*and hit what you're aiming at.*"

"But, sir, I don't have the money to buy a weapon."

"Ye'll not leave here without one."

Annie felt her hope dashed. She'd had no plausible argument when Mr. Reardon brought up the matter of her safety either. But if she used her money for a musket and powder, there'd be none left to get her to Tennessee and settled on her own place.

"I'll give ye mine. Haven't done much hunting the past few years anyway. It'll be my contribution to your dowry," her usually terse master ended with a rare smile.

Unable to contain her joy this time, Annie flung her arms around the old man. "Thank you! Bless you! Thank you!"

Grinning wide now, he unloosed Annie's stranglehold and held her at arm's length. "I'll also be sending along a good supply of paper and ink. We'll be expecting to hear from you real regular."

By now, Mrs. White had risen and wrapped an arm around Annie, hugging her tight against her comforting plumpness. "And my New Testament. You'll need more protection than some old gun. I expect you to put all that reading I taught you to good use." She kissed Annie's cheek. "And we'd better learn you've found yourself a good, hardworking husband before the year's out. You shouldn't have no trouble. I hear overmountain there's ten men for every woman. Plenty for you to pick from."

Annie's eyes stung with unshed tears. No one had hugged her or kissed her since the day she said good-bye to her mother. This childless couple had always shown through their deeds that they cared about her. But now, for the first time, they were surrounding her in an embrace, even Mr. White. They loved her. And, she remembered, so did God.

Now all that was left was to prove to that tall, rangy Mr. Reardon that she had the grit to make it on her own. And that would be easy enough to do. She would simply start out before the others and stay ahead of them until she had trekked so deep into the wilderness that the wagon master couldn't possibly refuse to accept her. Or could he?

2

A white-tailed buck broke out of a tangle of dogwood and ivy and flashed across the trace in a blur of brown, then dove into the thick undergrowth on the other side.

Annie, walking barefoot alongside her yoked milk cows, watched her shaggy-haired dog chase after it. Cap's high-pitched barks echoed loudly in the hollow they traveled up. And for the first time since she'd started out on this adventure, she felt completely, eerily, alone. Not a single person had she passed this livelong day.

With each hour this afternoon, nine days into her journey, the ridges on either side had crowded closer—ridges she could only catch a glimpse of through the verdant forest of oaks and hickory, ash and black gum. So deeply did they shade the path she followed, she couldn't be sure which direction she traveled. Yet Annie knew she was on the correct trail. The cutoff from the Trader's Path to the Catawba Trace had been clearly marked.

The Blankenships, at whose farmstead she'd camped the night before, had said she might not see more than two or three travelers a week now, because the next white settlement wasn't for a hundred miles.

She would be on her own tonight. No more hospitable settlers to shelter her . . . no more helpful recommends to the next farm up the way. This would be her first night utterly alone.

The idea of riding ahead of the wagon train until she was deep into the wilderness . . . was this truly the will of God? Or that of willful Annie McGregor? What if Isaac Reardon still refused to accept her?

Something rustled. Twigs snapped behind her.

Annie swung around to see her tan-and-white dog bounding onto the deeply shaded path again.

Cap stopped in the middle, his ears perked, his body at attention, and he stared intently down the trail from whence they'd come.

"Good boy," Annie whispered as she lifted her musket from the leather scabbard nailed to the side of the cart, then unhooked the powder horn and bullet pouch. Since she always kept the barrel loaded, she merely had to uncork the horn and sprinkle a smidgen of gunpowder into the flashpan and her weapon was ready to fire. Slinging the recorked horn strap over her neck and shoulder, she went to stand beside Cap, her musket couched over her arm, extra paper-wrapped cartridges in her apron pocket in case she needed them.

She then took a calming breath, knowing she had to keep her wits about her.

Her fawn-colored cows ambled only a few feet farther up the road without someone to prod them and came to a stop. The calf ran to his mother and started to suckle. Only Ruben, the young bull tied at the rear of her cart, seemed concerned. He strained against his tether, trying to look behind him.

With the ceasing of her own outfit's noises, Annie now heard what had brought Cap out of the woods . . . the thudding of horse hooves. Quite a number of them.

Indians?

Then came the jangle and creak of metal and leather. A man's voice. Two.

Her heart skipped a beat. It couldn't be the wagon train—she had left three days ahead of them.

The first rider, a clean-shaven man with his three-cornered hat kicked back, emerged from the nearest bend. Behind him came a string of heavily loaded pack horses and two more men, both with scraggly beards, and wearing droopy wide-brimmed felt hats and the fringed leather clothing of frontiersmen.

The leader, a man who in contrast appeared rather prosperous in milled cloth, raised a hand to Annie in greeting while pulling in on his mount's reins. "Whoa," he ordered in a loud voice. "Afternoon, ma'am." He tipped his tricorn. "A real pleasure to see more settlers on their way to Tennessee. Where do you folks plan on lightin'?"

The well-fed man seemed harmless enough to Annie. "We'll decide that once we get to Henry's Fort."

"We've taken to callin' it Henry's Station—sounds friendlier. And I know you'll be glad you decided to come overmountain. It's fine country. The richest soil you'll ever see in the Watauga settlements. Must be half a dozen now 'tween the French Broad and the forks of the Holston."

"That's what we hear." She relaxed her grip on her hefty weapon.

"The name's Keaton. I own the dry-goods store at the fort. You folks be sure to come by when you reach the settlement. I'll ask around about land for you in the meantime."

"Why, thank you, Mr. Keaton." The lead rider seemed an honest sort.

But the two men down the line didn't appear nearly so harmless, particularly the one at the rear. His broad flushed face above his unkempt beard surrounded beady little eyes that were much too interested in her.

"My husband and his brothers," she said to the storekeeper while trying to ignore the other man's leer, "will be purely pleasured to know you'll be makin' inquiries for us."

Lying again, as she'd done all along the way. It didn't set well with Annie, even if she wasn't exactly bearing false witness against anyone. But in her desperation to make this journey, she just didn't see any other way. Once she joined the other wagons—*if she were allowed to join the other wagons*—then the lying could stop, hopefully forever.

Mr. Keaton surveyed the surroundings. "Where be your menfolk?"

"They should be back anytime now. They went after a gobbler. I heard a couple of shots just a few minutes ago. Frank, my husband's oldest brother, never misses, and the others are almost as good."

"That's real important out here. Bein' a good shot. They'll be able to keep meat on the table without you havin' to slaughter your own animals."

Annie was sure Mr. Keaton would have given more reasons, such as defense against bears and wildcats, wolves and Indians, had he been talking to a man. *And scoundrels,* she added to herself, wishing that third man would take his ogling eyes off her. "Aye, 'tis a good thing."

"Well, good day to you. I'll be lookin' for you in a few weeks." He heeled his mount into a walk. The string of pack animals behind him did the same without too much fuss.

The animals, smelling like their natural selves, kicked up a fine silt of forest dust as they veered around Annie at a much greater speed than her own lumbering animals ever moved.

The second man's sour smell competed with his horse's odor as he rode by, touching a long grimy finger to his droopy black hat.

She wanted to avoid the sight of the third man as he passed, but thought better of showing any weakness. By far the most power-fully built of the trio, this grimy one took his time as he led his string of horses by. No gesture of respect came from him, nothing but that sly leer emanating from those sunken blue eyes. And he never took them from her, even after he had to swivel around to stare. Then, just before he disappeared into the curve, he pointed at her and nodded as if he knew she'd lied about being with others . . . as if he planned to return and take advantage of her secret.

In the nine days she'd been on the road, no other man had looked at her in such a disturbing fashion. Why now? On this first night she would spend bereft of any family's protection.

What a fool she'd been to think she could travel alone several days into the wilderness before halting to wait for the Reardon party to catch up. *If they even took this trail.*

Annie shook off thoughts of the dreaded alternative. She couldn't allow herself to dwell on that possibility. Tomorrow she would find a good defensible spot to camp and wait the two or three days before the wagon train caught up to her.

The carved-out features of Isaac Reardon leapt into her thoughts. The man was as tall and sinewy as the raiding Norsemen of old. He wasn't at all like his much shorter friend with the quick smile and roving eyes. And he didn't seem the sort who changed his mind very often once he took a stand. No, this was a man of purpose. Deadly serious purpose.

Reaching over to stow her musket, Annie drew her lips into a hard, resolute line. *So am I.*

$\sim$

"Sorry mine oxes make for da slow valk." Rolf Bremmer, the big German, huffed as he trotted up on foot to Ike.

19

"Can't be helped." Ike, riding at the head of his pack train, glanced back and saw that Rolf had left his ten-year-old son, Wolfgang, in charge of the oxen yoked to the family's heavily laden covered wagon. "Besides, it makes for less wear on the horses. We're doing fine."

"Goot," Rolf said with a nod.

The more Ike got to know the man, the better he liked him.

The two men looked up as Otto, Rolf's youngest, shot past, whooping. He raced up to the top of the rise they'd been ascending for the past half hour.

"Stop! Stop!" yelled Isolda, the eight-year-old in charge of him, as she ran after, her skirt caught up in one hand, her flaxen braids flying. Otto delighted in giving his older sister the slip every chance he got.

Rolf yelled after them. "Don' go far!"

But Otto was already dropping out of sight, as the scamp charged down the other side of the rise . . . with the poor, beleaguered Isolda on his heels.

Ike reined in his mount and swung to the ground. "Brother Bremmer, would you mind takin' my place for a few minutes? I'd like to check the line."

"*Ja, ja.* Give mine feet da rest."

As Rolf rode off on Ike's blaze-faced roan, Ike stayed where he was, eating dust, swatting gnats while checking the legs and gait of each pack animal that plodded past. All were looking fit, including the extra gelding tied at the rear. The slow pace well suited the horses. This string of pack animals he'd rented from Keaton at Henry's Fort were as sound as the storekeeper had promised. Though they were more heavily loaded than when he had taken them east to North Carolina, they'd trudged along the trail and forded dozens of streams in the ten days since they left Charlotte, with nothing worse befalling them than getting a few stones lodged in their hooves . . . nine days of hauling so far, and only the Sabbath to rest.

Still, he reminded himself, this had been by far the easiest leg of their return journey. No more low rolling hills lay ahead. All morning it had been a steady upward climb into the mountains through a dense forest, where an increasing number of pines crowded out the beech and elm.

Pulling the Bremmer outfit, two pairs of beefy short-legged beasts leaned into their double yokes, shoulder muscles bulging in their uphill struggle.

The big rig loaded with the family's worldly goods crushed every rock and root beneath its iron tires and left deep tracks in its path. Bremmer had only one replacement ox, and Ike hoped that would be enough.

Mrs. Bremmer, her freckled nose starting to peel despite her wide-billed sunbonnet, and her oldest daughter, Renate, a young replica of the Germanic blonde, walked at the rear. He nodded to mother and daughter as they passed by. Each carried long sticks to keep after their trailing livestock.

The three half-grown pigs the Bremmers had bought from a settler a couple of days ago were a handful. But the indomitable Mrs. Bremmer would have them whipped into shape in short order—or she'd be serving up some pork chops soon. Of that Ike had no doubt.

Inga Bremmer brooked no insubordination from child or beast . . . except from Otto, her youngest. For some unfathomable reason she let the little towhead run wild, while his sister Isolda was charged with the daunting task of keeping up with him. And always it was the girl, not Otto, who caught the back side of her mother's hand if the boy hurt himself or managed to escape her.

Five-year-old Otto's winsome smile, which he wielded with utmost skill, kept him out of trouble. Ike's patience was growing

21

thin at the injustice of the whole situation—a situation he could not put to voice, though, since it was none of his business.

At the thought of winsome smiles, Ike glanced at his own wagon, taking up the rear behind the newlywed Smiths'. His future sister-in-law Lorna Graham and Jigs were his business, and he would wait no longer to speak his mind to them. Once they were settled for the night, he would take them each aside and this time mince no words.

Returning his attention to the inspection of the train, Ike surveyed the Smiths' team of workhorses. They moved past without much strain as they pulled the smaller, lighter wagonload up the incline. Fortunately, the young newlyweds weren't as yet burdened with an accumulation of years of housekeeping.

Ken Smith had his arm around Betsy's waist as they walked alongside, and it looked as if the robust young man was assisting his fragile-boned wife.

"Almost to the top," Ike said as they approached him. "We'll stop for noonin' soon."

Ken hugged his wife closer. "Good. We could use a rest."

Ike knew Ken was concerned only about his bride's rest. Still, Ike suspected that Betsy Smith—not Lorna—would do most of the work to prepare the noon meal for her husband, Jigs, and himself. Several days ago Lorna had convinced Betsy that they'd each have less work if they shared the cooking chore. And clever Lorna had managed to save herself quite a lot of labor. That girl had a whole bag of ploys and excuses she shamelessly used, with the aid of her theatrics.

Ike's own outfit moved forward, drawn by his youngest brother's inheritance, two massive Clydesdales. He glanced up at Lorna perched on the jockey seat of the wagon while Jigs sidestepped alongside, refastening a rope holding the canvas cover in place. Suddenly, it dawned on Ike that Lorna was not walking as she should have been. Jigs knew better than to put an extra burden on the team going up a steep hill. But it appeared the girl had charmed him out of whatever sense he had.

"Down, Lorna," Ike ordered, pointing to the ground.

"But, Ike, I—"

Her complaint was cut off by Jigs. "Lorna has a stone bruise," he said in her defense.

"Then you help her along. Like I said, Lorna, climb down." Not giving the two a chance to argue further, Ike wheeled around and headed for the front again, more certain than ever that his brother Noah's betrothed would make the poorest of frontier wives. Ike's mother had been right when she said the young woman was unsuited for frontier life. The baby of her family, Lorna was accustomed to using her charm to get what most folks obtained by the labor of their hands. And she gave no thought to the cost or who would have to pay.

At that moment, little Otto came running back over the crest, yelling, "Pa! Pa! Honey! Get me some!"

Whatever the child was babbling about, the demand *Get me some!* came out loud and clear.

Ike glanced back at his own wagon to see Jigs helping a pouty Lorna to the ground and knew he had two spoiled children on this trip—Otto simply hadn't learned to be as subtle in his requests as Lorna.

Ike quickly reached the front of the train, where Otto trotted alongside the quarter horse, tugging on his father's trousers.

"Vat is dis about da honey?" Bremmer asked, dismounting.

"The lady said to bring a scoop, and she'll give me some. Get me a gourd, please." His cheeks red from running, Otto switched to yanking on his pa's shirtsleeve. "Please!"

Bremmer turned his attention to Ike. "You know somet'ing about dis voman, dis seller of da honey?"

"No. There must be some new settlers up ahead."

"Poor land to settle, *nein?*"

"Aye. Too rocky for a plow." Ike untied the lead to the pack animals and handed the leather strips to Rolf, then gathered his saddle horse's reins and mounted. "I'll go check."

After descending the other side of the wooded crest, he didn't have to go far before he left the darkness of the forest for the bright sun of a tilted meadow. Rhododendrons and berry vines covered the upper half, while the greenest of grasses blanketed the lower end upon which cattle grazed. A fast-running stream cut across one corner. And almost out of sight on the other side of the stream stood a cart tucked against a wall of stone that rose several hundred feet up a mountainside.

Ike saw no one save a lone woman who was loading a chicken crate onto her cart. From the look of the outfit, it appeared that she and her people were merely passing through, just as his own train was. He slowed his roan to a walk and cut across the meadow, then nudged him to the far side of the swift but shallow water to reach her.

A big shaggy dog rose from the grass and barked a warning.

"Halloo the camp," he called as he neared. The woman had yet to acknowledge his arrival.

She still didn't turn his way as he reined his quarter horse to a halt. Was she deaf?

The dog made up for her lack of interest by growling viciously, his hair standing on end.

Ike prudently chose to remain in the saddle. "Ma'am?"

She turned then, her dress sporting a starched white shawl collar as if she were on her way to town. And upon her neatly coiled braid of gold-streaked hair sat a prim straw bonnet. There was something familiar about her.

Then it hit him. She was the same young woman who'd asked to come overmountain with them. The widow whose jade and gold eyes were so startling against her sun-browned face.

"Mornin', ma'am," he said, politely dipping the brim of his dark

24

hat. "I see you managed to find someone to take you to Tennessee after all."

She lifted a serious gaze up to him. "I was beginning to think you hadn't come this way. This is my fourth morning waitin' here for you."

"Waitin' for us?" What was she talking about?

"I'll be loaded and ready to go by the time your train reaches here." The good-looking widow brushed past him to speak to her dog. "Cap, fetch the cows."

The dog sprang to his feet. He ran past Ike's horse and flew across the narrow brook as he ran toward the livestock.

"Do you plan to hook up with us?" Ike scanned his surroundings for other life. No one else was in view, but that dog sure was one fine worker. He already had the cattle bunched and headed in the right direction. "I'd be obliged to speak to your man first."

She collected the long double-curved yoke leaning against the cart and swung back to him, her jaw set. "You'll have to speak your piece to me. I've come this far without a man. And I intend to go the rest of the way. With you or without you." Balancing the yoke across her shoulder, she started for the cows.

Ike rolled his eyes skyward and whispered, "Lord, I thought my troubles were over when we sent the British packing." But here he was beset by another woman, and he hadn't yet figured out what to do about the ones he already had.

He reined his horse around and followed the young widow, refusing to give even a passing thought to the way her skirt twisted around her hips after she leapt across the stream. Quickly overtaking her, he moved his mount alongside and used what he considered his most authoritative voice. "Ma'am. You do that, get your cart hitched. That's what you should'a done days ago. Then you take yourself down off this mountain and back to Charlotte. I can't believe any man would bring you this far and then just leave you."

25

Her eyes narrowed as she eyed him. "That's 'cause there wasn't no man. And I'm not goin' back. I'm goin' to Tennessee."

"Well, you sure aren't comin' with us, and I can't let you go it alone. You'd never make it. You'd be prey to every renegade Indian and band of thieves, not to mention the wolves and bears and raging rivers."

"You can't stop me! You don't own this trail."

"Well, I do own an axe, and before I let you go on and get yourself killed, I'll take it to your wheels."

"Try it, and I'll shoot you where you stand."

Threats now. Ike closed his eyes, attempting to regain his temper. "Fine. Do as you please," he grated out. Why was he trying to take on what he had no intention of making his business in the first place? "I wash my hands of you." Not quite controlling his ire, he jerked hard on his reins, spinning his mount away, and sent his roan into a gallop.

But Ike didn't get away fast enough. Sharp as a bell, he heard the widow holler, "That's right, you wash your hands of me. But I'm still goin' to Tennessee!"

3

Annie watched the wagon master gallop away across the meadow and up to the trail, berating herself the whole time. Having been warned by the appearance of the children, she'd known he wouldn't be far behind. And hadn't she rehearsed what she was going to say a hundred times? Yet she'd skipped from *I've been waiting for you* to *I'm loaded and ready to go,* without giving a single one of the carefully worded reasons why he should accept her.

But the lordly way he'd glowered down from high up in his saddle had swept her thoughts away. Those pale gray eyes had seemed as cold and forbidding as the rest of his north-wind features . . . the fact that he was dressed in the fringed linen shirt and leather leggings of a frontiersman instead of the vested shirt and breeches of a town tradesman had only added to his formidable appearance.

And there she'd stood in her Sunday-go-to-meeting hat and starched collar. She even had her shoes on.

To make matters worse, she'd matched the man's stubbornness with her own, then insulted him. What was the matter with her?

For someone who kept bees, she, of all people, should know not to antagonize. Besides, far more flies could be caught with honey than with vinegar. Hadn't she watched Mrs. White turn her husband completely around with a few soft words and a little gentle persuasion?

What was she to do now?

Well, he did flatly proclaim he was washing his hands of her. If he actually meant what he said, he wouldn't try to prevent her from following along behind. She would stay back a ways. Not get too close, but close enough to feel safe.

The distant creaks and rumbling sounds of the wagon train came to Annie from across the meadow. Soon they would be passing. She'd better hurry. Whisking off her hat and collar, she returned them to her linen chest and tied on a workday apron, then shed her uncomfortable shoes and stockings.

Since she'd started loading her wagon at the first sighting of the blacksmith's children, Annie had only the team to hitch and the bull to tie to the back of the cart. The calf she didn't have to worry about. It could always be counted on to stay close to its mother.

Annie was hitched and had the cart rolling across the narrow stream, praying that all would go well this day, when she saw Mr. Reardon riding along the trace. Behind him, he pulled a string of packhorses. And not once did he glance her way.

Fine with her.

Then she saw the two children running across the meadow toward her, the little flaxen-haired boy waving a small half-gourd scoop by its long neck.

"Honey lady! Honey lady! I got the scoop!"

She couldn't help smiling. He was such a precocious imp. He reminded her of Duncan, the older of her two little brothers, just before she'd been sold away from the family. She had lost out on the fun of watching him and baby Charles grow up. Although the boys had been the cause of her banishment, they weren't to blame, and she'd missed them as fiercely as she did the rest of her family. Except for Pa. *Forgive me, Lord, but never Pa.*

Slipping her whip into its slot beside her musket, Annie walked to the rear of the still-moving cart and pulled out the keg of honey she'd left handy for the Bremmer children's return. Her initial kindness toward them had been motivated mostly by her desire to make a good impression on Mr. Reardon and the other adults, but soon her intent was lost in the charm of rambunctious Otto and timid Isolda with her downcast eyes and long white-blonde braids.

An ox-drawn wagon broke past the trees with the burly blacksmith walking alongside, driving the animals. He glanced her way and waved, friendly-like.

He'd always been the congenial sort when she'd taken anything to the smithy's for repair. But today his amiable nature especially touched her. Tears threatened as she waved back.

He then yelled something to Mr. Reardon, but she couldn't quite make out the words. Besides, she had other business to attend.

The two little ones came to a sloppy halt in front of her, panting for breath, their dusty faces flushed and streaked with perspiration on this cloudless summer day.

"Well, Isolda and Otto. I see you made it back," Annie said, taking the halved gourd from the boy's grubby fingers. Wiping it out with her apron, she popped the keg lid and poured some of the thick liquid amber into the scoop, then handed it to his sister. "I think maybe Isolda should carry it back. Take it straight to your mother."

Before Annie could say otherwise, Otto had a dirty finger dipped in the honey. Just as quickly, the digit went into his mouth, and his lively blue eyes closed in his bliss.

Isolda's yearning gaze shifted from the gourd in her hand to Annie, but she didn't copy her brother's lead.

"Here," Annie said, taking her free hand. "I'll clean your finger so you can have a smidgen, too." She walked the little girl next to the covered water bucket dangling from the cart bed and dipped the corner of her apron into it, then wiped the shy girl's extended finger.

Isolda then received her own bit of sweetness and rewarded Annie with her first smile.

"Annie McGregor," came a call across the clearing. It was the smithy. He had pulled his big wagon to a stop on the meadow grass. "Come. Ve talk."

By the time she brought her own outfit to a spot near where Mrs. Bremmer busily pulled out fixings for their noon meal, two other wagons had pulled off into the grass. Ken Smith, the young man who had nearly collided with her at the store in Charlotte, stood by one. Helping a young woman down from another wagon was the cocky fellow who'd tried to plead Annie's cause that day in the blacksmith shop.

At the north end of the clearing and still sitting in the saddle, Isaac Reardon had also stopped. He leveled an angry stare at her. It was obvious he was not at all pleased with Mr. Bremmer's desire to speak with her.

Annie dipped into a slight curtsy as the smithy stepped up to her. "'Tis a real pleasure to see you and your family in good health," she said, not wanting to be the first to broach the subject of her unexpected appearance.

"Goot to see you faring so vell, too." He glanced toward the scowling wagon master. "Ike says you come dis far by yourself."

"Aye. The trail has been easy to follow, and I have my dog to help me." She pointed to Cap, who was sniffing around the Bremmers' oxen. "And I have my musket in case of trouble," she added with a meaningful glance toward Mr. Reardon.

"Brave voman, you are," the smithy said.

His wife, who'd been listening as she worked, stepped closer and snorted her disapproval. "She is da fool, I say. Vat kind of voman no husband has? no family? You fall from grace? Dey drive you out?"

"No, nothing like—"

"Inga," the smithy reprimanded, "Annie McGregor has in Charlotte goot reputation. She is fine, hard-vorking voman, chust like you."

Grateful for his vindication, Annie sensed he was about to make a request. "I vonder . . ." he said, "you bring *mit* you cheese?"

"Aye. I thought it would be good for tradin' along the way."

"You vant to trade for fresh venison Ike shoot yesterday?"

Fresh meat. "Enough for a stew would be wonderful."

"I cut off a chunk right now."

Ignoring Mrs. Bremmer's suspicious stare, Annie returned to her cart to slice off a wedge of the round Mr. White had given her. As she leaned into the cart, she felt accusing eyes on her, not Inga Bremmer's this time but the wagon master's. Peeking past the bowed edge of the canvas cover, she saw him riding toward her. What now? Was it his intent to deny her even some honest trade?

Well, by George, he could protest all he wanted. Refusing to pay him any more mind, Annie lifted the cheese out of her food box, removed its cloth, stabbed into it with a sharp knife, and sliced through it with anger-driven vigor.

She heard horse hooves come right up behind her, an animal's snort. There were footsteps closing in, too, and whispers. But she ignored them all until she'd carefully rewrapped and replaced her cheese and swiped her knife whistle clean. Finally, folding the wedge of cheddar in a corn husk, she turned back, determined to appear unperturbed.

All the men stood waiting, though Mr. Reardon remained in his saddle several feet behind the others. Beyond him, the women and children still tended to their mealtime chores. Nevertheless, they too watched closely.

There was no telling what their leader had told them about her.

Annie looked straight at the smithy and spoke with solid force. "Here's your cheese, Mr. Bremmer. I hope it's a satisfactory trade."

"*Ja,* is goot," he said, handing her a nice chunk of shank in return.

Then she eyed the other men. "If anyone else has come to trade fresh meat for cheese, I'm sorry, but I can use only so much at a time before it spoils. Good day, gentlemen."

No one spoke, but the short, dark-haired man, the cocky one, grinned as if she and he had some secret—a very disconcerting grin. Particularly since Mrs. Bremmer noticed, too, with a raised brow.

Abruptly, Annie brushed past him and snatched her whip from its holder. Snapping it over her yoked team's back, she shouted, "Giddyap!" Who said she had to follow the Reardon party? Let them eat her dust.

Ginger and Queenie, the dear angels, obeyed immediately, lending proof to her capability as she moved out.

"Miz McGregor, I would make a trade with you, too."

Annie looked back and saw the clumsy young Smith fellow trotting after her. "Do you have somethin' besides fresh meat?"

"Aye. Dried apples. If you could use 'em." His expression held the same earnestness it had the first time they met. "The name's Kenneth Smith." He wiped his right hand on his breeches, then extended it. "Ain't you the cheesemonger from back in Charlotte?"

Annie wasn't accustomed to shaking hands with folks, but it made her feel important, equal. "Aye, and I would purely enjoy some dried apples, Mr. Smith."

He squeezed her hand a little too hard, but it was worth it, especially when she saw a muscle jump in Ike Reardon's jaw as he now moved his own mount closer. Things simply were not going his way.

"Ma'am," Mr. Smith continued, "some of your cheese would be nice, but mostly what I'd like is some of your cow's milk."

"*Ja*. Since ve all go da same trail," Mr. Bremmer intervened as he came forward, "maybe you not get so far ahead of us so we could trade for maybe a little butter from time to time, too. Mine female goat give only enough milk for da little ones. *Und* since Ken's Betsy is going to be da mama, she need da milk every day."

"*Betsy's with child?*" Mr. Reardon practically bawled. His control was snapping.

Annie could hardly keep from laughing at his appalled expression—he was undoubtedly the last to know. His jaw almost unhinged as it dropped, the reins fell from his hand, then his head moved slowly back and forth as he looked from person to person. His gaze finally settled on Annie. Closing his mouth, he nudged his mount toward her.

She hiked her chin a notch.

"Very well," he grated out. "You may come along. But if you hold us up for any reason whatsoever, I vow I'll leave you at the first settlement we come to." Retrieving his reins, he wheeled his gelding and rode away toward the stream, undoubtedly to cool off.

Annie could no longer contain her happiness as she turned back to the others.

She met the lazy dimpled grin of the short dark-haired one—that same discomforting expression that offered far too much. Even the way he shoved back his tricorn to let some stray locks fall across his brow showed a devil-may-care attitude. He certainly was the daring sort, particularly since the very attractive woman he'd helped from his wagon, presumably his wife, eyed him with even more menace than Mrs. Bremmer had previously. He would have to be watched.

"Pleased to have you with us, ma'am," Kenneth Smith then offered with a sincerity she was grateful for. "I'll go fetch the apples and a pail." He then turned and went to a very thin, very young girl Annie figured was the mother-to-be.

Small wonder Mr. Reardon had reservations about Mrs. Smith being with child on the journey. She probably gave up playing with dolls no more than a year ago.

All through her musings, Annie felt the heat of the dark-featured one's grin.

He took a step closer.

But the smithy drew Annie's attention by taking hold of her shoulder. He gave it a gentle squeeze. "You haf plenty spunk, *fräulein*. Plenty spunk."

"Thank you." Annie glanced toward the retreating Isaac Reardon, who was guiding his roan across the stream now. She had a strong feeling that Mr. Bremmer had sidestepped Reardon's wishes by approaching her. She hoped the good man wouldn't suffer for it. "You won't regret lettin' me come with you. I promise you, I won't be a burden."

"You come dis far alone. You do fine. I go now, put mine animals to graze while ve haf da noontime. You come sit *mit* us to eat. I introduce you to mine family."

As he walked away, Annie could no longer avoid the grinning fox.

"The name's Jamison Terrell, but everyone just calls me Jigs."

The nickname only added to her distrust of the boyishly cute man. "How do you do?" she said and started to turn away, but he continued to speak.

"In Charlotte I offered my assistance to you. The offer still holds." His tone, like his expression, conveyed far more than the simple words he spoke. "Anytime you need me, I'm at your beck and call."

"I appreciate your offer, Mr. Terrell, but—"

"Call me Jigs. We'll be traveling together for weeks, like one big happy family. Don't you agree, Annie McGregor?"

"I agree that we will be travelin' on the same trace for weeks," she said, a coolness in her tone. "I appreciate your offer. But I think any beckonin' or callin' should be your lovely wife's privilege."

"Wife?" Terrell glanced back at the attractive and fashionably dressed young lady who continued to watch with an idle wooden spoon in her hand. "Lorna's not my wife. She's betrothed to Ike's brother Noah. Ike and I are merely charged with her safe delivery."

This fellow had been entrusted with the safe delivery of a beautiful young woman? Perhaps Annie had misjudged him. No, everything about him reminded her of a workman her former master had hired a couple of years ago. A real sweet-talker, just like this one. The bounder had half the maidens in Charlotte mooning over him . . . until one cold January night he was forced to run for the hills or face the wrong end of a musket belonging to some ruined lass's father.

"Mr. Terrell, you seem to have your hands full with your own chores. But I shall keep your offer in mind, though I doubt I'll be needin' help of any kind." Annie nodded toward Lorna. The young woman had moved to a big black pot on a stone rimming the Smith's cook fire, but she had yet to stop snatching looks at Terrell and Annie. "Now, if you'll excuse me, I do believe one of your chores is waitin' for you."

Terrell tilted his head with one last smiling entreaty, then tipped his hat in departure.

Annie let out a long sigh. In the past half hour, she'd been met with anger, accusations, suspicions, and a too-friendly man probably no more worthy of her trust than the one who had frightened her four days ago. Maybe she would've been better off keeping to herself.

She glanced across the meadow in the direction Mr. Reardon had ridden, but he'd disappeared—her very reluctant, very angry guide.

4

Ike rode across the meadow shelf until he could go no farther, the way blocked by the jutting face of a stone wall in front of him and dense thorny undergrowth on either side. It was probably just as well, since his urge to desert the entire lot of them was almost irresistible.

Thirsty. His anger had given him a powerful thirst.

Dismounting, he led Ranger back to the stream in a secluded woodsy spot just before the frothy cascade tumbled through giant boulders and lost itself in the trees that descended the steep mountainside. He dropped to one knee and scooped up a palmful of water to drink, then swallowed down several more until he was sated—his thirst, anyway. He then splashed some of the icy liquid on his face, hoping it would cool his rage. Finally, a tad calmer, he rose to his feet and found a flat-topped rock to sit on.

He leaned forward, resting his chin in his hands, and closed his eyes, trying to concentrate on naught but the calming pine scent and the sounds around him . . . birds twittering, squirrels chattering, the soft gurgling of the brook. But his mind refused to relinquish what had provoked his ire.

It was bad enough to be defied by that fool of a woman, but to have the men he'd come to like and trust during these past weeks go against him in the matter! Not trust his judgment concerning the wisdom of taking on a lone woman. All too soon, they would all find themselves facing the trials and dangers of the frontier. Soon, none of them would have the time or energy to play nursemaid to some featherbrained female.

This woman, whom he was sure had lied about coming all this way alone.

And Ken . . . what could he be thinking?

Ike really didn't want to believe Kenneth Smith had been aware that his wife was with child before he brought that skinny little thing on this trip. Her condition often brought peril to a woman even in the best of circumstances. Traveling a rough trail through the wilderness was far from that.

He breathed a heavy sigh.

Looking up, he saw that no breeze stirred the treetops, and no cloud cluttered the blue. "Thank you, Lord," he prayed out loud, "for that, at least." He knew the Good Book said rain fell on the just and unjust alike. "But, Lord, I do hope you'll keep it scanty. Leastways, until we get through the passes."

The trail had been mostly dry since they left Charlotte, with only a couple of nighttime sprinkles, so these mountains were due for a good downpour . . . a wheel-sticking, river-swelling, mud-sliding downpour. The kind only he and Jigs had experienced.

Yet his comrade didn't seem to have enough sense to care. Not whenever women were anywhere in the vicinity. Especially unmarried ones. And now there were three—Lorna, the widow, and Renate, if Bremmer's fourteen-year-old was included. And that timid quiet one might as well be. Ike had caught Renate stealing more than her share of shy peeks at Jigs.

38

And, of course, Jigs never had anything on his mind but stirring up a little excitement. That tendency had worked to Ike's advantage during the war, but now, with families to consider . . . and the women.

Women. What a lot of confusion and strife they brought with them. Why hadn't he noticed that before he came up with the idea of starting a township? Or before his fool idea to marry a city-bred lass with hands soft as pudding? From that, anyway, he'd been saved.

Now if he could just get the rest of this mess in hand. For starters, that serious talk with Jigs about his flirtation with Lorna was long overdue. And they'd be having it tonight . . . *if I can calm down enough to even return to the train.*

Ike straightened. He knew exactly what would take care of the rest. He'd prove to everyone that the McGregor woman was a liar. "And, Lord," he insisted, "I'm not just seeking vengeance here, but the truth. The other folks deserve to know she didn't come all this distance by her lonesome."

Leaving Ranger to graze on the sweet grass near the stream, Ike strode back to the fire ring and the tramped-down area of Annie McGregor's camp. Whoever brought her would have left plenty of readable prints, and so would his horse, even after four days.

Surveying the location, Ike noted that he couldn't have picked a better site himself. Obviously, whoever left her here knew enough to set her up in a secluded and easily defensible spot. When he exposed the woman, he'd make her disclose her cohort as well. He, too, should be shown for the hornswoggler he was.

But try as he might, Ike could not detect any human tracks besides the woman's and those he'd made himself. At first he thought her accomplice might have covered his tracks, but nothing looked the least brushed over. The dust lay in equal depth over every leaf and twig.

As Ike looked around in astonishment, the unbelievable idea

39

that she had actually done as she said began to sink in. Had she really traveled the roads and trails alone? Was she that determined? Or that desperate? Who was she running from? Someone who might prove an unpleasant—even dangerous—surprise?

He *would* have the answers.

~

Annie avoided joining the Bremmers as long as she could. She set her chicken cages out on the ground again to allow the birds more time to peck through the slats for bugs and grubs. Then, unpacking a pail and her milking stool, she moved to Queenie's side to milk her.

In puzzlement, the cow turned her head as much as the double yoke would allow—only the calf normally took milk from her this time of day.

Annie stripped no more than a pint or two, not wanting to steal too much from the calf's midday meal. As she rose with the pail, she saw Ken Smith coming, his own husk-wrapped offering—the dried apples—in his hand.

"I'm mighty obliged to you," the sturdy-framed young husband said.

She handed him the pail. "If you set the milk in cold water, it should chill by the time we leave. And it'll give the cream time to rise to the top so you can skim it off."

"No, I'd just as soon she drink the milk the way it is. My Betsy needs all the richness I can get into her. She's off her feed real bad."

"I'm sure that won't last. Congratulations on your baby . . . even if it isn't to Mr. Reardon's likin'."

His guileless sky blue gaze slid past her to the meadow beyond, and he reddened sheepishly. "Ike sure looked powerful mad."

"It'll pass. Don't let him suck the joy out of your blessin'."

He cut his attention back to Annie. "Say, why don't you come meet my Betsy? She's plumb curious about you."

Annie glanced toward the Bremmer encampment where she was expected. Rambunctious Otto and shy Isolda and the two older children were youngsters Annie wouldn't mind getting to know, but she could easily put off into next year another skirmish with their mother. She smiled. "Meetin' your wife would be my pleasure."

Up close, the first thing Annie noticed about Betsy was her eyes. Light brown like her hair, they dominated her thin face and had a downward slant at their outer corners. This gave them a sad expression, even when Betsy smiled as she now did during her husband's introductions. That kind of eyes tugged at the heart even when there wasn't a reason. But with hundreds of miles still to travel, there was ample reason to want to protect her.

"I'm purely pleased to meet you," Betsy said in voice as light and airy as the girl herself. "My Kenny says you're the one what asked to come with us the week before we left. You got a lot more grit than I do. Just the notion of not havin' someone to look after me out here in the wilds is deadly fearsome."

Smiling, Annie shook her head. "I'm not so brave. I guess it's mostly that I just wanted to go someplace where I wasn't under someone else's thumb. I'm wore-out tired of never gettin' to think for myself. Or decide for myself what needs doin' each day."

Betsy offered that sad smile again. "It seems to me, we all pretty much have to do the same things whether we tell ourselves to or let someone else tell us. We still got the same needs to tend."

The insightfulness of the lass's words surprised Annie. "I reckon you're right. I never thought about it quite like that."

Young Smith enfolded his wife with his oaklike arm and hugged her to his side. "My Betsy's real good at sortin' through things. Ain'tcha, sweet pea?"

His Betsy gazed adoringly up at *her* Kenny, and Annie was suddenly glad she'd joined this party, glad that these two would one day be her neighbors.

If Ike Reardon agrees to sell me some land. Annie saw her work cut out for her with him. She would have to make a real effort, not just to stay with the train but to convince him she would be an asset to his new town with her dairy and domestic bees, worthy of buying a few acres.

"Is the stew warm yet?" Smith asked his wife, the light unaccountably gone from his expression. "Ike's comin' back across the meadow."

As Annie turned to stare at the approaching rider, every bit as grim-faced as before he so abruptly left, she vaguely heard Betsy say, "I'm not sure. Lorna was supposed to be lookin' after the pot. Where's that girl off to this time?"

Before Annie had time to fortify herself with more than a couple of deep breaths, the man was upon her, his eyes on her alone. He eased a long leg over his saddle and down to the ground, dismounting in what looked like a relaxed manner, but the knuckles of the sun-browned fingers holding the pommel were white from his grip.

He continued to stare at her for an eternal second before he finally shifted his attention to the Smiths. "Congratulations on the expected addition to your family. It'll be the first white baby born in our valley. A true blessin' from the Lord."

Those were the last words Annie had expected to come from the tall frontiersman's mouth. She suppressed the impulse to gape at him.

Ken and Betsy were no less surprised. Both their faces lit up like the sun breaking from a dark cloud. Betsy flew into Mr. Reardon's arms while Ken pumped one of his hands, both repeating their thanks several times.

Reardon, obviously caught off guard himself, awkwardly patted the young mother-to-be on the back a few times before extricating himself from the couple's enthusiasm. He returned his attention to

Annie. "Mrs. McGregor and I need to discuss some details of the trip. Would you two excuse us for a few moments?"

Before Annie had a chance to correct his error about her marital status, he took her arm almost painfully and escorted her into the shade of an old pine on the forest side of the trace.

Annie was grateful for the shade. It was too warm a day to stand in the heat of the sun while enduring the heat of Reardon's wrath. Nevertheless, she wondered what this was about.

He continued to hold her arm as if she were a disobedient child as he spoke in a quiet—but by no means pleasant—tone. "You've come all these miles alone and gotten your way over me—I'll give you that. But we'll not step one foot from this spot until you tell me what drove you to do something so outlandish. Who's after you? The law? Or your husband? Are you a thief or a runaway wife?"

"How dare you make such assumptions!" The man never failed to jump to the wrong conclusions. "I'll have you know I left my home of eight years with prayers and blessin's."

"Do you expect me to believe that?"

She glanced down at his offending hand on her arm. "Unlike arrogant, all-knowing sorts like yourself, my people love me and understood my need for a fresh start in a new country. This very night after they read the Bible, I have no doubt they'll be praying for my safe passage just as I will pray for them."

Her retort seemed to take the starch out of the man. He dropped her arm, and the rigid contours of his bronzed features softened along with his silver blue eyes. "I . . . apologize, Mrs. McGregor," he said, albeit grudgingly. "Please accept my deepest sympathies."

Before Annie could fathom the meaning of his words, he turned on his heel and strode back to his horse.

Glancing across the trace, she assessed her old cart. It seemed right at home with the other outfits. She counted the folks milling about, taking their noonday meal. Here with them, she could sleep tonight without waking at every little sound. A peaceful night's rest. Her weary eyes, her whole body ached for that.

It wasn't until Mr. Reardon had ridden back to his pack animals that she understood his sudden change of heart. He thought she was a widow who needed to get away from her sad memories!

Well, if it would make him treat her with more kindness, did it matter if that's what he thought? It wasn't as if she herself had told him such a thing. *Lord, I ask you, what possible harm could there be in letting the man think I'm a widow? At least till I'm on my own land.*

Then she remembered. The blacksmith knew she was naught but a servant girl.

5

There was nothing left for Annie to do but walk over to the Bremmers' campsite. She found the family of six seated on a large patchwork quilt spread in the shade of the nearest oak. As Annie approached, she noted that they shared warmed-over beans, fried venison, boiled grits and carrots, and thin slices of the newly acquired cheese. The kind of vittles that "put meat on your bones," Mrs. White had always said.

Otto saw Annie first. Chewing on a mouthful, he bounced up on his knees and mumbled some garbled nonsense as he beckoned her with both hands.

The rest of the square-headed blonds turned toward her, all wearing simple homespun clothing and friendly smiles, except for Mrs. Bremmer, which was no surprise.

The blacksmith patted an empty space beside him. "Ve haf plate vaiting for you. You eat *mit* us, *ja?*"

"Thank you, Mr. Bremmer, but I already ate before you folks came." She dropped down between him and his oldest son, a lad of eleven or twelve, and tucked her bare feet beneath the folds of her skirt.

"Coffee, den." Bremmer's large block of a hand grasped a soot-blackened pot from a stone behind him and poured dark brew into a dented pewter cup. The table settings were all practical, wood or metal, nothing fancy. Handing her the cup, he pointed to his oldest daughter, who had a charming halo of braids atop her lowered head. "Dis is our Renate. She is big help to her mama. *Und* you haf met ever'one else, 'cept Volfie."

"Wolfgang," the lad corrected as he sat a little taller.

"*Ja,*" his pa said, flashing a grin. "And dis here is Annie McGregor. Ve meet ven she bring sickle *und* hayfork to smit'y for repair."

"When you repaired the axle to my cart, too," she added. "And, please, since we're goin' to be travelin' together, just call me Annie." She heard an almost inaudible disapproving grunt from Mrs. Bremmer, but no one else seemed to notice.

"Mama is making corn bread for supper," Otto piped in. "And we get to put the honey on it. Ain't that so, Isolda?" he added, elbowing his shy older sister's ribs.

She flinched but said nothing.

"That'll taste real good," Annie answered, relieved that Mrs. Bremmer was keeping her own counsel—so far.

Renate, who looked to be the height of her mother but still girl-ishly slim, leaned forward. "I have never heard of anyone doing what you did," she said, scarcely above a whisper. "Things happen, and women sometimes is cast out, but they never just go off on their own for no reason."

"*Ja,*" Wolfgang piped in with much more force. "Even in Bible days when God still talked out loud to his people, Hagar only went off alone because she was banished. And she had her son with her. And Papa says Ishmael was older than me so she really wasn't alone. Still, without a man, God had to come and save them."

46

Out of the corner of her eye, Annie saw Mrs. Bremmer cock her head in a manner that dared Annie to contradict his reasoning.

In a fleeting prayer, she asked God to bring to her memory the details of the story. "Uh . . . when Abraham sent them into the desert, he gave them food and water. But if I recollect right, Hagar didn't have a plan as to where she was headin'. The Bible says she just wandered about. I know where I'm goin', and I've brought provisions that should last until I get there—just as Ruth did when she and her mother-in-law left Moab and crossed the wilderness alone to reach Bethlehem."

"*Ja,*" the older woman said, her expression unyielding. "But dey vas going home from da heeden land, going to Naomi's people—da chosen of Gott. You go *from* your people to da land of heedens."

"Chust as ve do, Inga," Mr. Bremmer said, coming to Annie's defense. "You *und* me, ve Annie's people now. Togedder, ve all take Gott *mit* us to da heeden land."

His wife shrugged and took in a spoonful of beans as if she had no more interest in the matter.

But Annie knew better.

"The reason Annie wasn't afraid to come," Wolfgang said, as if he alone knew the answer, "is because she has her own gun. Papa was makin' me a rifle in his spare time," he said to Annie. "But he sold it for cash money just before we left." The lad's disappointment was evident in his tone and the downward curl of his mouth.

"I make you anodder rifle, Son, ven ve settle again."

His father's statement did little to lift Wolfgang's expression. The straw-headed lad returned his attention to Annie. "What kind of gun is yours?"

"It's not one of our American rifles. It's a Brown Bess like the British foot soldiers used. But it shoots true."

"Can I try it sometime?"

Annie glanced at his father. "If it's all right with your pa."

47

"Papa don't mind. Do you? Maybe Ike or Jigs could take me huntin' with it. I could hunt for Annie's table."

"You're askin' the boy to hunt for you?" A gruff voice came from behind.

Annie twisted around.

It was Mr. Reardon. And his glower was back.

"Is Volfie's notion." The kind blacksmith again spoke in her favor. "Da boy is trying to talk himself into da borrow of Annie's Brown Bess."

A snorted chuckle replaced Isaac Reardon's scowl as Wolfgang continued. "Aye. I figured I could go huntin' with you. Learn to track and such. And anything I shoot I'd give to Annie for her lettin' me use her gun."

The wagon master clapped a hand on Wolfgang's shoulder. And for the first time since Annie had met him, he smiled enough to show his teeth . . . a smile that testified to the fact that the man did have a sense of humor, *and* that his usually too-serious expression could transform into one that was strikingly appealing.

Annie found herself smiling, too, when he turned to her. "That's up to Mrs. McGregor. If she allows you the use of her musket, then I reckon you can come along."

Reardon had said *Mrs.* McGregor in front of the blacksmith! Before she'd had a chance to speak to him alone. Holding her breath, Annie shot Mr. Bremmer an anxious glance.

The German studied her a moment, then winked. "Annie asks us all to call her by da Christian name, now dat she part of our little family."

"Well, then," Mr. Reardon said directly to Annie, real friendly-like, "I suppose *Ike* gets it said a lot faster, too."

Annie could have kissed the hulking smithy for not correcting the wagon master's error. "Well, *Ike,* I shall give Wolfgang the loan of my rifle when he's with one of you men. If it's agreeable with you folks."

"Brudder Rolf am I." Bremmer turned to his wife. "Inga? About da boy, is dis goot *mit* you?"

Her expression ominously unreadable, the woman glanced from Annie to her son. *"Ja."*

Annie let out a breath and took her first sip of steaming coffee. Maybe even Mrs. Bremmer would start to trust her soon. As long as Brother Rolf didn't divulge Annie's secret to his wife. Otherwise, Mrs. Bremmer would surely conclude that a ruined reputation was what had sent Annie packing.

"You haf coffee, Ike," the freckle-faced woman ordered—not asked—then rose from the quilt to fetch him a cup from the back of their wagon.

"Maybe half a cup," he agreed, squatting next to Wolfgang. "Then we need to get a move on."

"So," Wolfgang said, leaning around until he was in Ike's face, "when are we goin' huntin'?"

Barking a laugh, Ike shoved him away. "Tomorrow, kid."

The man was acting—*and looking*—more human all the time.

"Mr. Ike," Renate called softly, drawing his light gray eyes to her—a color that looked exceptionally pleasing against his sunbronzed skin. "We been traveling for days and days now. How much farther is it to your valley?"

He chuckled again, a pleasant deep rumble this time. "Renate, girl, we just begun. We been skirtin' 'round the mountains to the southwest, and now we're turnin' north to go up into 'em. Like this." With his finger he drew the bottom half of a circle on the quilt.

Wolfgang again took over from his quieter sister. "But why? We should have cut straight across."

"Couldn't. 'Specially not with wagons. There's no through passage. But from now on, we'll be going pretty much in the right direction."

"Preddy much?" Mrs. Bremmer echoed, a frown pinching her brow.

Silently, Annie concurred.

"Mine vife," Brother Rolf cajoled, "da passes twixt da mountains don' follow da straight line."

"Try to enjoy the beauty of the mountains and valleys we'll be passing through," Ike said, including everyone. "Soon enough you'll be planted in one spot again."

His words didn't help. Renate looked as if she were about to cry. "With nobody to go see, no one to come calling." The flaxen-haired girl cut her glance toward the woods, her blue gaze turning even more forlorn.

Following her lead and looking toward the woods, Annie saw Jamison Terrell come walking out of the trees, and she understood Renate's true concern. The girl feared she'd have no young man to come courting.

Ike must have understood, too. "More folks are movin' over-mountain every year. Besides, there's a good-sized settlement west of us where the Natchez Trace crosses the Cumberland River. They call it Nashville. It's an easy two-day trip downstream by canoe. Lots of young fellas there to pick from."

Renate's eyes flared wide, just before she cast her gaze down to her hands, and a blush crept into her lightly freckled cheeks.

At that awkward moment, Inga returned with Ike's cup.

Cap set to yipping. A chicken squawked.

Something was amiss.

Flinging her skirts to the side, Annie leapt to her feet and ran around the Bremmers' wagon just in time to see Cap out in the meadow running back and forth, madly trying to herd in her black-and-white-speckled chickens. They were loose. Wings flapping hysterically, they ran in every direction.

But how did they all escape? Annie had three separate cages.

Ruben, the bull, bellowed as he tugged at the rope tethering him to the rear of Annie's cart. Beneath his belly, Annie—to her horror—found the answer.

Little Otto was scrambling between Ruben's massive legs, chasing after the rooster. The child could get himself killed!

Annie sprang forward in a mad dash to reach the five-year-old. Someone behind her screamed, spurring Annie to greater speed.

The rooster flew under the cart, and Otto dove between the bull's hind legs after him . . . and by a hairsbreadth escaped a kicking hoof.

"Thank God," Annie cried as she, too, dove past a wheel and captured the youngster under the cart. She sat there holding him close as she caught her breath. Then she noticed that everyone in camp had also come running in the wake of the chicken-squawking, dog-yipping hullabaloo.

Inga reached the cart first. With a horrified expression twisting her face, she reached under and pulled the child up into her own arms. "Mine Otto, mine Otto," she choked out as she hurried away with him, casting a scathing glance over her shoulder at Annie, as if the whole incident had been her fault.

"Look!" came a cry from another quarter. Wolfgang. He pointed to the sky. "Chicken hawk!"

Before Annie could crawl from under the cart, she heard the swishing sound of her musket being pulled from its leather scabbard.

Wolfgang had her weapon. A chill of fear skittered up her spine as he raised it toward the heavens and fired. The kick of the musket knocked the lad off his feet. He obviously hadn't expected a load packed with enough powder to kill a bear.

And he missed the hawk. It swooped toward one of the frightened hens. But her gun was now empty.

Flapping her apron and shouting, Annie ran into the field.

Startled, the predator veered up and away from its prey but continued to soar overhead, waiting for another opportunity. The

51

chickens were so scattered, Annie didn't know which direction to run next.

A second shot exploded.

And the hawk plummeted to the ground.

Annie swung around to see Ike handing off a smoking long rifle to Brother Bremmer.

Then his tyrannizing gaze landed on her, his expression as grim as she'd ever seen it.

All the ground she'd gained with the man this past hour was lost.

Not far behind him stood the pretty miss with the fashionable clothes and shiny black ringlets. Her hands were on her hips, and a smug grin splashed across her face.

Annie's mind grew deadly still as she realized the young beauty had thoroughly enjoyed the crisis. Lorna Graham bore watching.

6

When the wagon train reached the glen Ike had scouted out earlier in the afternoon, he sighed with relief. It'd been a long hard day, what with Annie McGregor popping up out of nowhere. Learning that the Smiths were expecting a baby had also added to his list of concerns.

With no more than an hour of light left before dusk, Ike raised an arm to signal a halt. He guided his string of packhorses off the trail and through a gap in some firs now casting long shadows across a grassy area near a mountain stream. Mostly spruce and dogwood walled in the glen, while chestnuts lined the bank down to the water. The seclusion of the spot had a cozy feel to it, but he knew better than to be seduced by a sense of safety in this wild country.

Ike glanced back to see if Brother Rolf's oxen and wagon would make it between the trees and saw little Otto riding his pa's shoulders.

Otto. The only time that scamp didn't have to be watched was when he was asleep.

Ike then spotted Isolda at the rear of the wagon, her white-blonde head downcast as she chased after the piglets with the rest of her family. As usual, she'd paid the price for yet more of Otto's mischief. Her cheeks had been beet red since her mother gave her a tongue-lashing more than an hour ago. Ike's chest banded at the thought.

He couldn't understand why Brother Rolf allowed it. The pastor always had such good common sense in everything but his two youngest children. *God in heaven,* Ike prayed, *why is your faithful servant so wise yet so blind when it comes to his wife's unjust treatment of those two?*

Ike shook his head, knowing he had no right to say anything to the Bremmers. He'd have to continue to bite his tongue and leave the matter to the Lord.

But there was something he could do. Tonight he'd start whittling on a play-pretty for Isolda. A doll. One like her, with long braids and coltlike legs. He'd get Lorna to make it some clothes. That girl had certainly brought enough lace and satin fancies that she could spare a little for the child.

For the first time since the chicken incident, Ike's spirits lifted. Yes, he'd get a piece of hickory from Ken and start on it tonight. And from now on, he'd make a point of saying a kind word to the child whenever he passed her . . . no matter what his mood was.

Behind the Bremmer outfit came the widow's. She'd easily kept pace all afternoon with no problems. With the aid of her whip and that quick dog of hers, even the young bull tagged behind without balking more than a time or two. Ike had to hand it to her—she seemed to have as much grit as any man he'd ever come across. Leastwise, he hoped she did—that today's performance wasn't just a show.

Once the Bremmer wagon reached the center of the glen, Ike unhooked his pack animals and rode over to Rolf and Otto. "With four wagons we can square up an enclosure to help keep in the smaller animals. So take your outfit over there," he said, motioning in a wide arc.

The man's beefy face folded around a grin. "*Ja.* See? Is goot t'ing ve haf da cart of Annie."

"And her honey," Otto chimed from above his pa's head, his grin a replica of Rolf's.

It was hard to stay mad at the imp. So Ike jokingly echoed Rolf's, "*Ja,* is goot."

The last wagon to be given direction was his own, with Jigs and Lorna up on the jockey seat.

Lorna, who usually lavished her charms on Jigs, favored Ike with a disarmingly friendly grin. With a lavender blue dress setting off her flirty eyes of almost the same hue, Ike forgot for an instant that she belonged to his brother. He soundly reprimanded himself . . . just before an uneasiness crept into his bones. That feeling he got when he sensed he was being stalked. What was Lorna after?

∼

Leading her cattle just outside the square of wagons to graze, Annie saw Isolda coming toward her, both hands clutching her little brother's arm, dragging him after her. The squirming but mute child obviously objected.

Isolda stopped in front of Annie, but didn't quite look up at her. "Mama says we have to tell you we're sorry for Otto letting out your chickens."

Otto kept his head turned away, but Annie heard a tiny, mouse-like, "Sorry."

Annie pulled his resisting chin around to face her. "I accept your apology, Otto. But you must promise to never touch any of my belongin's 'lessen I give you permission. And that goes double for my bees. They won't run from you like the chickens did." She lightly pricked his arm with a fingernail. "Have you ever been stung by a bee?"

"Ja." His eyebrows crinkled close as he remembered. "Right here," he said, pointing to his neck.

"Well, if you bother my bees, a thousand of them will fly at you and sting you. So don't even get close to their box. Not even with a stick," she added for good measure.

He looked up at her with those innocent round eyes. "Do you like me again?"

"If you leave my property alone."

"I will."

"Then I surely do." She bent down and pecked him on the cheek. "And, Isolda, I never was mad at you." She ran her hand over the misused child's head before kissing her too.

"Can I have some honey? Just for me this time?" Not a speck of Otto's hesitancy remained. Such an imp he was.

"Not right now. I have to get my animals tended and my supper on before dark."

"We can help. Can't we, Isolda?"

The little girl nodded, her expression brightening somewhat. They both wanted a taste of honey real bad, Annie realized with a smile.

But their mother might not appreciate Annie's taking up their time, and she didn't need any more reasons for the woman to want her gone. "I think you'd better go help your mama first."

"She don't need no help," Otto objected stubbornly.

Annie's own tone matched his. "Before you two can help me, you must ask your ma if you can."

So this time it was Otto dragging Isolda as they ran back to their own camp.

Chuckling, Annie called her dog out to the pasture to keep an eye on the cows. Then, as she turned to walk back, she saw Jigs coming with those magnificent workhorses, so huge that they'd make three of her cows.

"You should have waited for me to unhitch your animals," Jigs

said with a smile that reminded her of the one Otto had just bla-
zoned when he asked for honey. "It'd be my pure pleasure to help
out a fair young widow wherever I can." As before, his eyes and
tone insinuated more than he actually said.

Annie was sure Mrs. Bremmer was watching. And probably Ike,
too. "I thank you, Mr. Terrell, but—"

"Call me Jigs, please."

"—Mr. Jigs, but these simple chores I can do real easy by
myself. I'm sure your partner would prefer it if you helped with the
unloadin' of your pack horses."

A body would think she'd turned down a proposal of marriage
from his overly dramatic look of disappointment. "Very well. But
my offer extends to other chores, too. Like, say, me helpin' you after
supper to take your dishes down to the stream for a good washin'."

The man had absolutely no respect for her at all.

But this was the price, she supposed, for striking out on her own.
"I'm sure you'd like that a lot." Hands on hips, she leveled her
most deliberate stare on him. "But I'm not lookin' for that kind of
help. Good day to you, sir." Brushing past him, she stalked away.

"Well, then, good evening . . . for now," he called after her, hope
still ringing in his voice.

Perhaps letting this one think she was a "lonely widow" might
not be such a wise idea. Lies always did seem to end up being more
trouble than they were worth.

But even a godly man like Brother Bremmer was going along
with this one. Or was he? How much did he really know about her?
Did she dare risk the asking?

～

Ike, carrying a large sack of seed over his shoulder, watched his
partner meander toward him in no particular hurry. But then, Jigs
was never in a rush to work when there was an available woman
within twenty miles.

Ike dumped the barley sack under a spraddle-limbed spruce. Then, rubbing a kink from a neck muscle, he observed Annie McGregor walking back to her outfit. From Jigs's theatrics out there with her, Ike had no doubt his comrade had been lathering on the charm as thick as butter on bread. Annie's returning smile, though, had seemed no more than polite.

But with everyone in camp watching, even a simpleton would've known not to act too interested.

Everyone except a flirt like Noah's betrothed.

Well, for once Lorna was hard at work at the Smith's camp, peeling turnips instead of chasing after Jigs.

Annie, quick in her movements, pulled those blasted chicken cages out of her cart and onto the ground again—those chickens that had been the cause of such commotion at noon and cost them a half hour travel time. Then he watched her cross to the edge of the small clearing. He'd stolen glances at that long-legged stride of hers all afternoon as she walked beside her cows. There was no hint of a simpering swish about it. And, of all the grown females here, she was the only one not wearing a sunbonnet to protect her complexion.

A body would think she didn't have the slightest interest in catching a man's eye.

But somehow she still managed to do just that. The widow couldn't begin to match Lorna's beauty, yet here Ike was, his eyes riveted on her as she stooped to gather deadfall for a fire . . . and, in all this time, Jigs had yet to reach him, because he, too, gaped hungrily at her.

Ike started to yell out to Jigs, then thought better of it. Encouraging Jigs to switch his attention from Lorna to the widow might not be such a bad idea. If Jigs became too amorous with her, Brother Rolf would be here to see the two of them decently married.

That was food for thought. If they wed, she'd have a husband to see her safely to the valley, clear her a piece of land, and raise her cabin. Ike's worries would be over on her account.

Jigs finally reached a packhorse. Whistling some nameless ditty, he began unlashing the load. No care in the world seemed to affect him, anymore than society's strictures did. Ike realized there was no way Jigs would stay "tied to a woman's apron strings," as the bounder liked to put it. Married or not, he'd leave her flat, first chance he got.

Lifting a large box from a horse's back, Ike glanced back at the widow, who had already collected half an armful of sticks. She was no slacker. Maybe Jigs wouldn't be able to walk away so easily from that one. She wouldn't sit home whining over her loss. No, she'd set out after him, track him down, her and her trusty Brown Bess. Ike grinned at the thought.

"Glad to see you're in a better mood," Jigs called to him from down the line. "You been grouchy as an old bear lately."

"And you," Ike said, his smile now gone, "are actin' like a fox in a coop full of young hens. And you know what happens to them foxes when we catch up to 'em."

"Well, this fox has always managed to dance circles around narrow-minded goodies and still give 'em a merry chase."

It had always been useless to reason with Jigs about women. Falling into silence, Ike finished the chore of unloading the animals.

Jigs, never one to volunteer when it came to menial tasks, started gathering up all the horses' leads. "I'll take the horses down to water 'em."

It took Ike no more than a glance toward the stream to see the reason why. Annie McGregor and the two little Bremmer kids were heading that way, one child carrying a tin pail, the other, a bucket.

Annie's dog tagged along behind until the widow turned around and waved him back to the herd, though Ike could not make out her actual words.

The dog sprinted off like a flying bullet. He was worth his

weight in gold. And truer to his mistress than a dozen Jigs Terrells would ever be.

"I'll see to the horses. I'm real thirsty." Ike gathered the reins from Jigs before he could protest. "You go brush down the Clydesdales."

With fairy-tale beauty, the last rays of sun danced off the widely spaced layers of chestnut leaves as Ike paused to search for a wide enough path to lead the horses down to the gently murmuring brook. He loved this time of day in the mountains. On the cool breeze, the smell of pine needles mingled with woodsmoke. He heard a child's chattering—Otto's piercing pitch—then saw the trio upstream a stone's throw away.

"I killed three spiders today. *And one snake.*"

Through the thinly branched greenery, Ike saw Annie lift her skirts and step a trim foot out onto a flat stone, a water container in each hand.

"It was not a snake, Miss Annie." Those childlike words came from serious little Isolda. "Otto just likes telling whoppers. It was a big pink worm he found under some leaves."

"*Ja,* and I got it right here in my pouch. You wanna see?"

Ike almost laughed out loud, and would have, if he hadn't been more interested in viewing the young woman's reaction.

"Maybe later," he heard her say, no sign of repulsion in her voice. "But, Otto," she said, dipping the wooden bucket into the stream, "if you'd let the worm live, you and your pa might'a caught a fish with it this evening for your supper."

The woman didn't rattle easily. Ike admired that about her. Then, recalling the incident with Otto between the bull's legs, he also knew she was quick to act in a crisis. The more he saw and heard, the more he appreciated.

Yet here he was, gawking at her from a distance like a Peeping Tom. He started through the trees with his string of horses, their twig-crushing hooves making too much noise to be drowned out by the sounds of the stream.

"Look! Here comes Ike," Otto cried, pointing.

Reaching the bottom of the bank, Ike dropped the horses' leads, giving them their heads. Then, waving a greeting to the trio, he maneuvered along the rock-and-root-cluttered edge toward them.

Annie McGregor nodded a silent and wary greeting, but not Otto. "See what I got," he cried and dug two halves of a squashed worm from a leather pouch hooked to his suspenders.

"Nice worm." Ike winked at Annie. "Too bad it's stopped wigglin'. We could'a gone fishin' with it."

The conspiratorial wink caught her off guard. Her lips parted, and she almost lost her footing on the slick stone.

"Reckon you're right," Otto said, taking a last look at his pathetic glob before tossing the pieces into the stream. He wiped his grimy hands down the front of his linsey-woolsey shirt. "After supper I'm gonna catch me a whole bunch of lightnin' bugs. Mama says I can have a bottle to put 'em in, so we'll have light in our tent all night. Isolda's scared of the dark, you know."

"No, I didn't." Ike shifted his gaze to the little girl.

She stopped trailing a stick in the water but didn't look up, causing that same pitying hitch in Ike's heart.

"I get scared in the dark sometimes myself," Annie said, though Ike doubted if much of anything scared her.

"If you give me a bottle," Otto said, puffing out his pint-sized chest, "I'll catch some lightnin' bugs for you too, then." He looked up at Ike. "I'm helping Annie, you know, cause she ain't got no man."

Ike couldn't resist giving the wagon train's latest addition a smug look. "Yes, I know."

She stiffened. "Otto wanted to earn a spoonful of honey. So he and Isolda are carryin' water for me."

Ike checked the buckets in her hands and saw that they were no more than a quarter full. "I saw Jigs talkin' to you awhile ago. I thought maybe he'd be carryin' your water for you this evenin'."

Annie's expression turned to stone, and she just stared at him.

What possessed him to say that to her? "I apologize. That was totally uncalled for."

Her stance eased a bit. "But you are right. He did offer to help. He strikes me as the sort, though, to expect more in return than I care to give." She hopped back to shore, handing each child one of the water carriers. Then, with fingers splayed across each youngster's spine, she started them up the eroded bank. "Good evening, Mr. Reardon."

She was back to calling him Mr. Reardon. Watching her help the little ones up the steep incline then disappear from sight through the trees, he reckoned 'Ike' really was harder for her to say . . . especially since he'd made a habit of blurting out the wrong thing every time he spoke with her.

But maybe it was for the best. He shouldn't get too friendly with someone he might have to leave behind at the next settlement.

7

The sultry July heat lost much of its grip as the last glow of day-light faded away. Ike was almost as grateful for that as he was to finish brushing down the last horse. Dropping the currying tool into his wooden grooming box, he headed for the tree-shrouded brook to wash up for supper.

Passing a scraggly old oak, he saw something strange up among the branches—a solidly built box. Suspended on a rope flung over a sturdy limb, it was tied off around the trunk.

The bees. The widow had the good sense to relocate the smell of honey away from their camp. Another surprise in a day of surprises all around. Having a bear ripping through the wagons after its favorite treat was one surprise he could do without.

By the time Ike made his return trek from the stream, the hob-bled livestock and the wagons were nothing more than silhouetted forms. The inky darkness was pierced only by the tiny flashes of lightning bugs and the pools of light made by lanterns and camp-fires. As he strode closer, he noticed that the widow had no tent.

She'd been trying to prove how self-sufficient she was all day, but he really hadn't expected her, a woman, to be that unconcerned about her privacy. Or that brave. The night could bring anything from rain to snooping raccoons to one of those roving bears.

As he drew nearer, he noticed canvas curtains skirting her cart and realized she planned to sleep beneath it. She might be brave but not foolish. To her credit, she'd also dug a small ditch around the perimeter of her cart to divert the rain in case the starlit sky changed to storm clouds during the night.

The limited space below a wagon was a bit too close for him, but if it rained, both he and Jigs would be crawling under theirs, too, since Lorna had his tent.

Near her campfire, Annie McGregor placed a wooden bowl of food before her dog. As he dug in, she patted him on the head. Then she abruptly straightened. She'd seen Ike closing in from out of the darkness.

He stopped a few feet short of her. "Evenin', ma'am. You set for the night?"

"Aye. We're doin' fine." She swatted at something near her face. "Except for the mosquitoes. But I suppose there's nothin' to be done about them."

"Move closer to the fire. They don't like smoke."

"Thank you. I appreciate that." Though she didn't actually smile, he heard the hint of one in her low, restful voice and saw it reflected in her flame-lit eyes.

He caught himself staring, and not for the first time today—or even the tenth. Fact was, feasting his eyes on her was getting to be a habit he'd better curb. And fast. "We'll be movin' out first thing in the mornin'."

"Don't fret. I'll be ready." Her tone had a slight edge to it now.

Too bad she'd read more into his words than he'd meant. "Evenin' to you, then," he said, turning toward the campfire he, Jigs, and Lorna shared with the Smiths.

"Good night," she replied softly, treating him once more to a voice that could soothe any savage beast . . . be he man, dog, or one of those hulking bears.

Skirting the outer side of the Smiths' wagon, Ike reached the dwindling cook fire between his and the Smiths' outfit. Everyone was eating, with Lorna and Betsy on camp stools and Ken on the grass beside his wife. Jigs leaned back against the wagon astraddle the vehicle's tongue.

"Venison stew again," Betsy Smith said without enthusiasm. "Left over from noonin'."

But Lorna smiled warmly as he passed her on his way to pluck a trencher off the foldout table. A suspicious greeting. She usually had a store of daily complaints ready to rattle off at the supper hour. She hopped up from her stool and took the wooden trencher from him. "Let me get your food for you. Go. Sit. You've worked hard all day."

Don't look a gift horse in the mouth, he told himself as he eased down on the grass and folded his legs beneath him Indian-style.

Lorna returned with his wooden plate heaped with stew and biscuits, and coffee, enriched by a generous portion of cow's milk. Anyone would've thought she was handing him a birthday present—her smile was that generous.

No doubt about it, with those coal black ringlets curling around her perfectly shaped face and framed by the ruffles of her pristine mobcap, not to mention her deeply dimpled cheeks, she was about as pretty as any girl he'd ever seen. Taking the plate, he thanked her.

But Ike knew something was up. And he knew exactly what it was when Lorna darted a menacing glance at Jigs. The two must have had a falling-out, and she was trying to make Jigs jealous.

Using her intended's brother to make another man jealous. Unbelievable. They both needed to be set straight. Soon.

65

"Lorna, dear," Jigs called in a teasing lilt. He held out his dented tin cup. "Would you mind pourin' me some more coffee, too?"

Shooting him another glare, she sucked in a breath, then went to fetch the coffeepot from a stone next to the fire. Lorna was incredibly childish. What kind of wife would she make for Noah?

Since Ike was too late for the communal Lord's blessing over the food, he lowered his head over his plate and gave his own thanks in silence; then he added yet another request for patience and wisdom.

Ken clambered up from the ground. After taking both his and Betsy's trenchers to the work table, he snagged a lantern handle, then offered his wife his hand. "Me and Betsy's goin' to bed now. It's been a long day."

Ike couldn't agree more. "Sleep well," he mumbled around his first bite of food.

"Oh, and thank you, Lorna," Betsy said, her voice as thin as the rest of her, "for doin' the dishes for me tonight."

Ike had to concentrate to keep his mouth from falling open. Lorna had actually volunteered to do dishes by herself?

Lorna offered a brief, lackluster smile to the couple retiring to their tent. Most likely, she regretted her offer.

Jigs, on the other hand, happily whistled some gay tune, never taking his eyes off the voluptuous lass as she came and poured his coffee.

Upon finishing, she immediately whirled away and turned to Ike with a smile that looked forced. "Did you have a good day?"

Another first from the usually self-absorbed girl. "I've had shorter," he said, then returned his attention to the safety of his food.

"I imagine so," she gushed sympathetically. "All that extra bother you were put to because that *questionable woman* joined our congenial little group."

Jigs stopped whistling. "I'd rather think of her as a *mysterious lady.* I say we invite her over. Get to know her a little better."

"I think not!" From Lorna's indignant tone, a body would think the man had suggested inviting Delilah or Jezebel to supper. "You'll not ask some fallen woman to my dinner table, no matter how humble it may be. And it's no *mystery* to any of us why you've been taking on about her all day."

Noah's betrothed wasn't even trying to hide her jealousy. She expressed it quite loudly. Ike glanced toward Annie McGregor's camp, but the Smith wagon blocked his view of it and of her. *Lord, he prayed, please don't let her hear Lorna's words. I don't know if I could deal with two squabblin' females on top of everything else.*

"Lorna," he said in as calm a tone as possible. "Until we learn that she's somethin' other than what she claims, I think we should all extend the widow a little Christian charity. You haven't even met her yet, have you? Why don't you put your most charmin' foot forward and go over there? Extend a welcomin' hand."

Lorna clutched her "welcoming" hands hard against herself. "I've lived near Charlotte my whole life, and I never heard of any McGregor fellow dying and leaving a widow. I say she's a scheming opportunist."

To make matters worse, Jigs burst out laughing. "And, Lorna dear, I think your water is boilin' over."

"I don't have to stay here and be insulted by the likes of you. *Good night.*" With that, she unhooked her lantern from their wagon and stomped off to her tent.

"But, Lorna, your dishwater really is boilin' over!" he sputtered.

No response came from her tent. Just the sound of spits of water sizzling in the nearby fire, along with the *baa* of one of the goats staked within the wagon circle.

And for the first time since Ike sat down to his meal, he latched onto his own bit of amusement. "Well, Jigs," he said mildly, "what with Lorna goin' off in a huff, I reckon the hot water is all yours. Looks like it's you who will be doin' the dishes tonight."

That stupid grin melted from Jigs's face. "Me? I was just havin' a little harmless fun."

"Maybe. But when it pits folks one agin the other, it's not without harm—'specially since we'll all be livin' close for some time to come. I never thought I'd be sayin' this, Jigs, considerin' what we been through together. But if you continue in these 'harmless' flirtations, as you call them, you'll either have to leave the train or choose one of these women to wed."

Jigs sprang to his feet. "You must be jestin'." He came to stand over Ike. "Besides, Lorna is already bespoke."

The lad did abhor the entrapments of marriage. Nonetheless, Ike looked up at Jigs with unyielding eyes. "I'll un-bespoke her."

Jigs cocked his jaw. "You know my mother was the very shrew Shakespeare wrote about . . . except she never got tamed. I'll never be trapped the way my poor pa is."

Ike continued to hold him in his rigid stare.

Jigs exhaled harshly. "Very well. For your sake, I'll try to keep my dealin's with the women down to a low simmer."

"And for Noah's sake, too. He won't take your mischief near so lightly as I do. He might just up and shoot you."

∾

Crowing the dawn, Annie's rooster awakened her after a blissfully undisturbed night's sleep. She rolled onto her back and stretched while she listened to myriad chirpings of birds . . . only to have her dog dive past the canvas curtain and plop on top of her, wagging his tail and licking her face.

Dodging his lapping tongue, she gave the hairy beast a hug around the neck and a pat. "You're right, Cap. It's past time to get up. If I'm going to show Ike Reardon I can be ready quick as anybody, I got to figure out every move. Not let any go to waste." He may have been pleasant enough last night, but he'd also given her fair warning.

More time was used up than she would have liked, though, as she struggled in the cramped confines beneath the wagon to get out of her night shift and into a clean drawstring blouse and front-laced sleeveless dress. But she had no choice, now that she was in such close proximity with two men.

But even that time she'd used wisely. When she emerged into the predawn light, she had her next moves planned. Not even checking to see if anyone else was up yet, she started for the stream, carrying her soap, towel, milking pail, and stool. The latter two items she dropped as she passed Queenie. She'd milk the cow on her way back. Also on her return trip, she would bring the beehive back from the tree where she'd suspended it.

And so her first half hour back in camp she dashed madly about, preparing to leave while snatching nothing but hurried peeks at the other outfits to see how fast her fellow travelers were progressing. She scarcely remembered to greet Betsy Smith when she dropped off some of the fresh milk for the weary-eyed expectant mother.

"I don't know what we have to trade you for the milk," Betsy said as her nose curled at the smell of the warm liquid.

"Don't fret about it. I'll probably be needin' a wheel fixed before we reach Tennessee country."

"How do, Annie," came a child's voice from the direction of the Bremmers' wagon. Otto stood beside his mother at the family's cook fire in his nightshirt, a knotted fist rubbing sleep from an eye. "Want me to come help you?"

His mother, stirring a pot suspended over the flames, mumbled something to him too low for Annie to hear. And her stony expression didn't look any more neighborly than it had yesterday.

Annie called back. "You better get dressed and have your breakfast. We can visit later."

Turning back to her own business, she assessed her camp. Just

69

about everything was fed or packed and back in the cart. Queenie stood tied at the rear with her suckling calf nosed under her. Ruben and Ginger, still out grazing, would be yoked and hitched when the other folks brought in their own draft animals. She looked around to see if she'd forgotten anything, but nothing remained unpacked excepting her coffeepot, pewter cup, and a trencher holding slices of the venison and dried fruit she'd been given, along with yesterday's biscuits.

Able to relax at last, Annie poured a cup of coffee and picked up her plate. Walking around to the front, she perched halfway up the wagon tongue. But before she could take a bite, Cap was there, tail wagging and begging. He'd already been fed, but she tossed him a slice of meat so he'd leave her in peace. Collapsing back against the front side of the cart, she took a much-needed sip of the steaming brew and closed her eyes as she swallowed the soothing warmth.

A gradual awareness of distant male voices brought her lashes up again to where Ike and Jigs worked together at the edge of the clearing. They were still reloading their pack animals. She smiled. Who was waiting for whom?

Out of the corner of her eye, she caught a flash of bright color. Yellow, as bright as any daffodil, emerged from a tent across the grassy square. Lorna Graham straightened and smoothed out a floral-print day gown with white ruffled undersleeves and a scalloped collar. Even for folks who could afford printed fabrics, they were a rare sight. Having been unavailable during all the war years, they had only recently begun to reappear in the dry-goods stores—at a considerable price. Yet this young woman could afford to wear such a dress for everyday.

Annie eyed her own homespun linen that had been tinted brown with dye she'd mixed herself. Plain. Plain and dowdy.

From beneath a light straw bonnet trimmed with satin roses, just the right number of Lorna's black ringlets escaped a ruffled

70

mobcap that fringed her face. Annie was sure Lorna could have been presentable even at King George's own court.

Sighing, she reached up to swipe away one of her own flyaway strands and, to her horror, realized she had yet to take out her loose night braid and put her hair in some semblance of order.

Stuffing the last of her biscuit in her mouth, she dumped the rest of the food on the ground for the dog, hurriedly fetched her bag of personal items, and withdrew her brush. Turning away from the cart, she saw that from every angle someone in camp would be able to watch her. For a measure of privacy, she moved around to the far side of her conveyance. This was much too personal a chore to perform in public.

~

Ike just wasn't expecting it.

Finished with loading the packhorses, he and Jigs had started walking out into the small meadow when he spotted the long streams of gold flashing in the early morning rays. Every shade, from the lightest gold to the richest bronze, flowed from the woman's head. Masses of hair that put meaning to the words *crowning glory* . . . hair his fingers, his hands, begged to bury themselves in. Her sun-kissed skin added another golden shade as she tossed her head, sending the silky tresses swirling to one side and exposing a tender neck.

He was too far away to see her eyes. Nonetheless, he added their splendor to the picture—those China-green irises rimmed with more gold.

Annie McGregor stopped brushing midstroke. Looking up, she caught him staring.

And Jigs, too, Ike saw.

Jigs had stopped alongside him and now nodded a polite greeting to her, but his leering smile was anything but mannerly.

"Come on, Jigs," Ike roughed out. "We're runnin' late."

71

It took all his willpower to keep from looking back at her as he and Jigs walked away to catch the two Clydesdales. But that didn't stop him from remembering the heart-stopping sight she'd made in the early glory of morning. Her neck, her arms, had such a natural grace to them, as she'd stroked her hair—not studied, but fluid, like when a doe wandered aimlessly through the forest.

Continuing to glance back, Jigs made no effort at good manners, nor did he seem to remember their discussion last night about his flirting.

And for reasons Ike chose not to explore, his partner's unabashed attraction to the widow bothered him far more than the wolf eyes Jigs cast at Lorna.

"Mornin', Annie McGregor," Jigs called as he veered off toward King, one of the Clydesdales.

"Good mornin', Mr. Terrell," she returned.

The lack of warmth in her voice gave Ike a secret moment of pleasure. Throwing a rope over the head of the other Clydesdale, George, he peered beneath the large animal's neck to see the widow walking into the clearing with her own tether.

Her hair was now pulled back tight and hidden within an efficient braid as she came to fetch her last two animals.

Ike had just tightened the slipknot on George's lead and started back with him when a thought stopped him. "Mrs. McGregor."

She turned to face him. "Good morning, Mr. Reardon. Is there somethin' I can do for you?"

"Surely, you don't plan to hitch that bull to your cart."

Her eyes, which had been questioning, turned to shards of green and gold. "Aye, I do. My animals must all take turns."

"It's bad enough that you were pullin' with two milk cows instead of oxen yesterday. But a bull? They can't be trusted."

"I hand-raised Ruben. He wants to please me. But even if he stops fearin' the whip and my dog, I still have that ring in his nose to pull. We won't hold you up."

"Not till one of your cows comes into season. This isn't going to work. Your husband would have known that."

"And you should purely know that without that bull, I will have no dairy." She glanced over at Jigs, then stepped closer to Ike and lowered her voice. "I been puttin' Ruben under the yoke since before I began this trip. And, even though you started out three days after me, I got here four days ahead of you. As the Christian I assume you to be, I expect you to honor your word and give me a fair chance to prove myself."

The woman stood her ground worse than any man. But he refused to let her have the last word. "I suspect the reason you were a day ahead of us is because you didn't stop and give the Sabbath to the Lord, like we did."

Saying nothing, she pressed her lips tightly together, and he also detected an extra tint of red in her cheeks.

He'd bested her.

"You're right, Mr. Reardon. I did travel some that day."

Ike straightened to his full height and looked down at her. "This is a company of Christians." He shot a narrowed glance to Jigs who, not to be left out, had moved closer. "Mostly, anyway." Then he returned to her. "We'll have no ungodly behavior on this trip."

Annie McGregor's face turned red again, but this time with anger. To her credit, though, the impertinent woman managed to keep her mouth shut. At least she had enough sense not to press her luck.

"You're to take your place at the rear today," he said, exerting the leadership he'd had trouble maintaining the day before. "I'll not put the rest of the train at risk."

8

With no more than a light sprinkle or two during the last fortnight, fording the thirsty mountain streams that morning proved of minor consequence to Annie, but centuries of use by man and animal had churned the trail into dust finer than sifted flour. Even though Ike Reardon had placed her at the rear of the train for his own reasons, she appreciated not being trapped in the middle. She kept her outfit a good distance to the rear and, contrary to the wagon master's worries, she had no problem keeping pace. If anything, she had to hold her team back to maintain the distance she preferred from the slower wagon ahead of her.

But the dust wasn't the only reason she lagged more than a stone's throw behind the preceding outfit. She preferred to keep a goodly space between her wagon and Reardon's. Although the bowed canvas cover blocked Annie's view of Jigs Terrell and Lorna Graham whenever they rode atop their rig, more often than not, steep inclines required the two to climb down and walk . . . as they were doing at this moment. Their ridiculous behavior was again in plain view of the whole forest.

If Jigs's elaborate farce hadn't all been directed at Annie, it would have been almost comical. He was overtly friendly in his waves and smiles directed at Annie, while Lorna pouted or flounced about in fits of childish anger.

And Annie couldn't be the only one to see it. Surely their zealous leader had, on his regular inspection tours of the train. How could Ike Reardon allow such byplay to go on, particularly if this was the young woman he was taking home to wed his brother? At the very least he should exchange positions with Jigs, send the bounder to the front with the packhorses and stay back with Miss Graham himself.

That picture—Ike with Lorna Graham—disturbed Annie more than the one in front of her eyes.

Before she had a chance to dwell on that thought, a holler issued from the forest ahead. Annie couldn't make out the words—they bounced over each other as they echoed against the sides of the steep, narrow hollow.

Jigs must have understood, though. He grabbed the nearest horse's bridle and pulled back until the giant beasts halted.

Curious, Annie continued with her yoked pair until she closed the distance between the two outfits.

As she did, Ike and Brother Bremmer emerged from a curve in the tree-crowded trail. They strode down the hill, one lean, one stout . . . two tall, powerful men who, unlike Jigs, seemed to have real purpose in their lives. Men who instilled assurance in others. And though she didn't want to be subject to a man's will ever again, she respected anyone who strived to make a better future for himself, just as she was trying to do. A man who dreamed big and acted on it—like Ike.

Annie didn't feel she should join the group uninvited. She did move close enough, though, to hear anything that might concern her, too, as the two men stopped to talk to Jigs. Pausing in a piece of deep shade, with her apron she dabbed at a stream of perspiration trailing down her temple.

Ike spoke first. "Jigs, I need to scout around this afternoon, make sure there ain't no surprises waitin' for us up yonder."

Jigs nodded, serious for once. "Things have stayed quiet all through the spring, but that ain't no guarantee."

"What are you talking about?" Lorna's alarm marred the lovely oval face beneath her fancy bonnet.

Jigs draped an arm around her shoulder, his dimpled grin returning. "Nothin' that you have to worry about, sweet cakes. 'Lessen you want to give us a hand clearin' a rockslide off the trail or maybe take an axe to some fallen tree."

Satisfied with his answer, she shrugged out of his grasp. "You're getting my dress dirty."

Annie wasn't so easily mollified. The uneasiness that had stayed with her those last days before joining the Reardon party crawled inside her belly again. Her thoughts flashed to the vile man who'd ridden with the storekeeper's pack train. Clearly a man of ill intent.

Anyone with a mind to listen had heard tales of traders who'd become vengeful after losing their lucrative trading franchises with the Cherokee and Shawnee after the British lost the war. Considered traitors by the patriots, these men had taken to raiding pack trains of the new settlers and pirating along the rivers.

"I need you to take over the packhorses whilst I'm gone," Ike said, again addressing Jigs. "Can Lorna manage the team by herself yet?"

"Oh, dear me, no," the girl answered for him, her cheeks denting with one of her winsome smiles. "He's simply not a fit teacher." She rested a hand on Ike's arm. "But I'm sure I could learn ever so quickly from you. Why don't you switch places with Jigs for a while?"

In the duel of dimples, only one of Jigs's came into play with his

77

lopsided grin. "Now, Lorna, you're too modest." He then looked up at his much taller partner. "I'm sure if she puts her mind to it, she'll have no problem at this slow pace. If we come across a tricky spot, I can tie off the packhorses and take the wagon over it myself."

Lorna immediately changed her pose to one of indignation. "You are *not* going to leave me back here without protection. I could be carried off by painted savages."

Ike, at least, maintained his dignity . . . no idiotic grinning or childish tantrums there. "The McGregor dog will give plenty of warnin' if anyone tries to sneak up on you from behind. Isn't that right, Annie?" he called, looking over Lorna's head. He'd been fully aware that she was listening.

"Aye," she said, walking toward the group. "Cap won't let anyone surprise us."

Ike turned back to Lorna. "Now that your fears have been put to rest—I'm sorry, but there's just the three of us. And since the trail is getting rougher, you're going to have to start doing your share. And I'd suggest you get out of that fancy dress before it starts smellin' of horse."

"Would you excuse us a moment?" Angry sparks flashed in Lorna's violet eyes as she took Ike's arm and pulled him away, up the trail. But not far enough. Her hissed whispers were still audible. "You never once said I'd have to do men's work on this trip. *This is not what Noah wrote to me in his letter.*" The last words rang out loud enough for a squirrel in the tallest pine to hear. Glancing back at Annie and the other two men, she stepped closer to Ike. "It's bad enough that I have to cook over a campfire—my hair reeks of smoke—and sleep in a smelly old tent . . ." Her hands went to her hips. "Noah is going to hear about this."

"Noah?" Ike seemed to find humor in the mention of his brother. He cocked a one-sided smile. "Yes, Lorna, you do that. You tell him everything that's been going on here. But in the meantime, you *will* be takin' the reins this afternoon. And I better not find either one of the horses with a sore mouth at the end of the day. Or have any broken wheels. Is that clear?"

Apparently it wasn't. Hands still on hips, she raised up on her toes and jutted out her chin. "You never thought of talking to me this way before *she* came." Lorna tossed her curls in Annie's direction. "I will never care so little about my appearance that I start looking like some old plow nag like her. Nor am I some field slave to be ordered about by the likes of you."

He gazed at her with deadly calm. "Fine. But, rest assured, I won't be your slave either. After noonin', you will drive this wagon, or I'll unload all your truck and leave you here where we stand."

She didn't back down one tittle of a dot. *"You wouldn't dare."*
"Try me."

So engrossed was she by the standoff, Annie hadn't noticed that Brother Bremmer had started toward the two. He put an arm around Lorna. "Sometime, mine *fräulein,* ve all haf to do vat ve never t'ink ve haf to. Is da way our Gott chooses to gif us chance to lean on him. Gott is plenty strong. He always sees us t'rough. You chust lean on him, Lorna girl."

She slumped against the minister, the fight visibly going out of her.

But whatever happened henceforth, Annie knew what the girl thought of her. A plow nag she might be, but at least with her in the field, crops would get planted. She'd have food on her table and be answerable to no one.

Touching the brim of his hat, Ike ended the set-to. He turned back to Annie and Jigs, strolling nonchalantly toward them, but the lines of his face had resolute edges.

For once, Jigs had his own expression somewhat in check. His usual smirk was barely noticeable. And he was silent.

Following his example, Annie turned and started for her cart before Ike found a reason to vent any remaining wrath on her.

"Annie," Brother Bremmer's booming voice called, "I need speak *mit* you."

Escape wasn't possible. She swung around as he and Ike approached. "Yes?"

"Up yonder," Ike said, speaking in the minister's stead, "we have a ridge steeper and rockier than anything we've climbed so far."

"*Ja.*" Bremmer nodded with serious blue eyes. "And I haf da favor to ask."

"Of me?" The conversation was taking an interesting twist. *They* needed something from *her*. She glanced at Ike.

He didn't meet her gaze. He looked off somewhere above her head . . . this man who'd said *she* would be the one needing help.

"*Ja.* Mine oxen, I don' vant for dem to vork dis much. And maybe come up lame. So I come to ask da borrowing of da bull. I yoke him *mit* mine extra ox and hook dem on in front of da odders."

"Not one of my cows?" Annie shot a glance up to Ike. "You want my bull?" She couldn't miss this opportunity to gloat. This almost made up for being called a plow nag.

"Cows don' have da big muscles." Bremmer emphasized his meaning by flexing those in his own hefty arms.

"Of course, Brother Bremmer. I'd be glad to make you the loan."

"Goot. *Und* ven ve reach da top, I bring dem back to help you. *Ja?*"

"That would be real neighborly of you, Brother Bremmer," she said, a reminder to Ike more than to the preacher that she wanted to become a permanent neighbor of theirs. "I'll unyoke Ruben and replace him with my extra cow. I'll bring him up to you in a few minutes."

"No. You should not haf to do dat all by you'self. Ve help you. Ike *und* me."

"Why, that's real neighborly of you, too, Mr. Reardon."

Her repeated words forced him to look at her as she'd meant them to. He rubbed his unshaven cheek. "You're enjoyin' this, aren't you?—me eatin' crow."

"I would have to say the pleasure's all mine—if that's the neighborly thing to do." It was a sweet victory after his remarks about her bull that morning.

But she didn't want her triumph to blow up in her face like an overloaded gun barrel. She returned to Bremmer. "I'd better take my dog and go along with you. Ruben might not obey a stranger. You can send Wolfgang back here to keep my cows movin'."

"Ja. Is goot."

"And don't forget, Bremmer," Ike added, while still looking only at her, "to warn Wolfie away from Annie's musket."

He didn't seem to be condemning her for yesterday's incident, but she couldn't be sure. Was she misreading a warmth she heard in his voice? saw in his eyes?

Suddenly, he shifted to Brother Bremmer. "Tell him he'll have time a-plenty with it when we go huntin' tonight."

"Ah, yes." Annie chuckled as a boldness crept into her. "Wolfgang and the musket. My gallant young champion is going out to slay a mighty beast for me this eve. And, I hope, returnin' with a heap of meat for my humble table."

"That's right." A smile played at the edges of Ike's lips. "Going forth into the great unknown with nothin' but your musket and this trusty old scout." He did smile then, a friendly smile, one an honest man shared with a woman. And not a single dimple in sight.

~

As the last rays of sunlight flamed the piney western ridge, Ike waited belly-down in a bed of ferns; the long barrel of his Pennsylvania rifle jutted out before him. He lay upwind of a small pond he'd found earlier in the day. He'd come across it in this little mountain pocket while following two sets of moccasin prints—prints, thank the good Lord, that had crossed the trace ahead of them and continued in a westerly direction . . . away from his northbound party. He'd just as soon not have to deal with Indians on this trip. They were as unpredictable as spring weather.

Stretched out beside him, Wolfie held Annie McGregor's Brown Bess. It didn't have the range of Ike's longer weapon with its spiral-grooved barrel, but in these dense woods, distance didn't count for much.

Neither he nor the lad made a sound as they waited for their prey to make an appearance, which Ike knew would happen. The muddy bank around the pond was heavily pocked with imprints of sharp-edged deer hooves.

A woodpecker began tapping a rapid staccato.

Wolfie jerked at the sound, but for only a second before settling again, his bright-eyed attention returning to the pond below them. The women may not be having a good time on this trip, but the lad sure was.

Women. Life without them was so much simpler. Even before he left camp this evening, he sensed he shouldn't have left them to themselves—particularly Lorna. The good Lord alone knew what mayhem would greet him on his return.

But he'd promised to take Wolfie hunting, and how did one explain to a kid about something Ike didn't really understand himself? He shot a nervous glance in the direction of camp, a good mile away.

Before leaving, he'd warned Jigs again of the consequences of his careless dalliances—for all the good it seemed to do. If he hadn't needed Jigs to stay behind for the camp's protection, Ike would've insisted he come along. Better yet, he should have sent Jigs with Wolfie. But then he would've been left to contend with an irate Lorna.

Ike saw a rustling in the brush across the pond just as Wolfie nudged him.

Out came a raccoon, gamboling toward the deeply shadowed water. At the edge, the masked and ring-tailed creature pulled something from its mouth with an agile front paw, then began to wash it.

Tidy little critters, Ike thought, *'cept when a pack of 'em come tearin' through camp in the middle of the night.*

Wolfie clutched his musket tighter and started to raise it.

Ike placed a staying hand on the barrel.

A coon would provide enough meat only for tomorrow's supper, and the sound of the shot would scare off the bigger game. He needed a deer, at least. Enough meat so he wouldn't have to hunt again for a few days. He always felt uneasy when he ventured too far from the train. It wasn't wise for one of the only two crack shots in the party to be gone more than absolutely necessary.

Perhaps the others should have some shooting lessons. Ike smiled at the thought of Lorna getting her hands on a gun. But then considering how angry she was with him today, it was probably best she didn't learn to shoot.

The smile disappeared, though, as thoughts that had ridden with him all afternoon came back to bedevil him. Lorna had threatened to complain about him to Noah.

The more he'd pondered on that, the more he knew Noah had every right to be upset with him, but not for Lorna's reasons. He'd neglected his duty in protecting her from Jigs because he'd judged her to be unworthy of his brother. Admittedly, he didn't know that much about women, yet he'd condemned her almost from the first roll of the wagon wheels.

Lorna was merely an impressionable young maiden from a small town. How could she know the difference between a harmless flirtation and the wiles of a worldly man like Jigs? A man who'd traversed most of the lands they now called the United States of America and who'd entertained himself in a good many of the taverns dotting the highways and byways—and who planned to keep right on doing so? Footloose as Jigs was, he'd even signed over his land grant to Ike in exchange for a place to stay if ever he needed to hole up somewhere for a while.

This was the philanderer with whom Ike had deliberately left Lorna, while telling himself he was merely testing her loyalty to Noah. Or had revenge been lurking beneath the surface? Was she paying the price for his own disappointing romance with Sylvia?

Lord, help him. He prayed that was not the truth. That he was a better man, a better Christian than that.

But he had to admit, it wasn't until Annie McGregor showed up and sparks started flying every which way that he had done anything to try to stop Jigs. And then only because he didn't like the way Jigs looked at Annie. How very wrong he'd been about that one. She'd turned out to be a woman of hidden beauty and surprises at every turn.

But then, he reminded himself, he hadn't been right about any of the women. He'd assumed Inga Bremmer would be as friendly and kind as her husband was. He'd even gotten angry at Smith's wife because she was with child—the most natural blessing a husband and wife could share. And he'd told Annie McGregor that a lone woman wasn't fit to travel without a man. She was certainly proving him wrong on that score.

He liked that about her. Fact was, he just flat out liked everything about her. A lot.

So? He'd been real fond of his intended bride, Sylvia, too. And thought he knew her mind. But what could a man really know about a person from a few social visits during his rare trips back from the frontier? At those times people always put their best foot forward. Including him. And Noah.

And Lorna did seem amazed that anything was expected of her . . . as amazed as he was with her childishness.

The widow impressed him; he couldn't deny that. But he'd better hang back awhile. Watch. Learn to read the woman—her moods, her secrets, her habits—same as any good hunter studies God's creatures.

Yes, Lord, you can see I'm floundering here. You know that feisty lass tempts me. Help me keep a safe distance. I don't want to make another mistake.

Wolfie elbowed him.

A stag had emerged, his rack of horns barely visible in the dimming dusk. The animal stepped toward the bank, his head turning to and fro, his ears swiveling back and forth even more. He'd come for his evening drink, just as Ike knew he would.

9

The day had been drizzling and cold, unusual for July, but Annie had heard weather up in the mountains could turn chilly even in the summer. She couldn't decide which was worse, being hot and sticky from the sultry heat or damp and shivering.

The rain had washed everything clean, and the air was heavy with the pungent scent of pine. But they'd mucked through some pretty muddy wallows during the morning hours, and now the stony bald she crossed was slick in spots with wet moss, causing the cows to lose their footing much more than usual.

A few moments ago, the clouds had lifted. Annie, placed at the front of the train two days ago, had a clear bird's-eye view of her surroundings. The trail had reached a high crest, and across the emptiness on both sides she saw more ridges, one after another till they disappeared into the gray.

Ahead, the trace led over what appeared to be a narrow stone bridge between two knobby plateaus. Seeing the steep drops on either side, Annie felt a rush of fear. If only the fog would return so she could pretend the cliffs were not there. Especially since the stone she crossed was nothing but layer upon layer of crumbling shale. In several spots, only an expanse of a few feet's width looked stable enough to carry her cart without giving way.

But it must be safe. Nothing had been mentioned to the contrary. Annie would be first to cross. And she could not allow her fears to rule.

Ike had moved her outfit from the rear after he'd been surprised by the sudden appearance of several riders. Although they turned out to be merely a harmless family going east for a wedding, Ike wanted Annie—and most particularly, her dog—to take the lead. Cap could always be counted on to sound an advance warning of any danger.

At that time Ike had also made another change. He'd exchanged positions with Jigs. He now drove the big wagon at the rear while Jigs rode with the pack animals right behind Annie. But no amount of dust her outfit stirred seemed to deter him a bit. There was rarely a moment she didn't feel Jigs's eyes on her from behind—except when the trail was wide enough for him to bring his string alongside her. Then he and his dimples were right in her face.

Raising her whip, she snapped it louder than the crunch of loose rock and started her cows across the bridge, trusting Ginger and Queenie to watch their step. She looked after her own, lest she twist an ankle on the uneven layers of stone or cut her bare feet on a splintered edge.

She was dismayed that Jigs chose that moment to come visiting again. Surely the man could see there wouldn't be room for both her cart and his packhorses on the narrow stone bridge.

But nothing seemed to faze him. With a stick, he beat out a rhythm on the side of her cart as he rode past it. Reaching her, he dismounted and fell into step with her. "See that deep cut down there?" No greeting. He just pointed with the stick as if they were already in the midst of a conversation. "That's one of the upper reaches of the French Broad."

"French Broad?"

"The river. It cuts through the mountains all the way to the other side. Flows into the Tennessee just below Henry's Station."

"It does? That's wonderful. I thought it would be weeks before we reach the fort."

"It will be. As slow as we're goin', another two or three anyway. Lots of time for you and me to get to know each other better." Those infernal dimples played attendance to his ungentlemanly innuendoes.

Ignoring the suggestive glint in his dark eyes, Annie cracked her whip above her cows' heads again and increased her pace across the shale, picking her steps with added care.

"I'm surprised you've gotten this far without shoes," Jigs said, lengthening the strides of his own shorter legs. He didn't give up the game easily. "You really could use a pair of moccasins like mine."

Annie glanced down at his feet. She'd noticed the soft Indian footwear he and the wagon master wore and had coveted some like them more than once. "I have shoes. I prefer not to wear them."

"Hurt your feet, do they? You need to get Ike to make you a pair of these. Over the years, he's gotten right good at it."

Annie suppressed a huff. She had no intention of asking Ike for shoes or anything else, not after she'd practically shoved down his throat that she could take care of herself. "No, thank you. My feet are a sight tougher than that soft leather you wear."

"Even tough leather wears through after a while or gets ripped up."

"My feet are just fine the way the good Lord made them." Annie couldn't resist bringing God into the conversation. It was the only thing that could make him squirm in the least.

89

Jigs didn't lose a single dimple. In fact they dug even deeper. "And is the rest of your body just as fine?"

"Of course," she retorted, determined to maintain her composure. Mentioning her body like that? The man had no shame.

"Well, then, if you see no need to cover your perfect feet, why do you bother to cover the rest of your perfection?"

Taking a tighter grip on her whip, Annie swung to face this insulter of God and women. "Mr. Terrell, you are—"

A crashing thud resounded. A horrendous screeching scrape followed. Ropes snapped with a thwang.

To her horror, Annie saw that the wheel on the opposite side of her cart had splintered and fallen away. The bare axle hit the rounded stony bald and slid sideways, taking the cart down the slope toward the edge of the cliff.

She dashed for the frightened cows.

Bawling, they bucked as the dog yipped and nipped at their heels, and the cart skidded closer to the edge.

Its sudden stop jolted the beehive loose, and it toppled out, crashing onto the stone. It split apart, releasing a torrent of angry bees.

"Stop, Cap!" Annie screamed. She latched onto the team's yoke. "Whoa! Whoa!"

With her in front of them, Ginger and Queenie began to calm. She spoke their names as gently as her panting breaths and pummeling heart would allow. "You're fine—fine. Everything's fine."

Though it wasn't fine at all.

The cart was now on the verge of tipping over. If the axle slid down the slope a few more inches, it would go and maybe take her cows with it. And Ruben, the bull, was tied at the back.

Ruben. He could help if she could leave the cows long enough to get to him.

"Jigs!" She glanced back. Where was he?

Then she saw him hurrying toward her, leading the saddle horse. He'd untied the roan from the pack string.

"Hold on, Annie!" he called. Dragging a coiled rope from a saddlebag, he lashed it to a harness ring, then half ran, half skidded down the shale with the other end, which he looped around the axle on the near side. Pulling the rope taut, he called up to the horse. "Steady, boy."

Beyond the obedient horse, Annie saw Rolf Bremmer come huffing up the hill. "Vat is—" His eyes told him the rest as he gaped at the dangerously teetering cart. "I go. Get mine ox *und* yoke. You hold."

It seemed to take the man forever to return. Meanwhile, Annie hung on to the cows, praying that the bull at the rear of the cart wouldn't take a notion to pull in the opposite direction.

The swarming bees didn't help. Ruben swished his tail at them, flicked his ears, tossed his head. Jerked on his rope.

The cart screeched a few inches. Tilted even more precariously.

Jigs immediately pulled the horse in the opposite direction, and the cart stopped, dangerously close to the precipice.

Annie held her breath. Everything she owned in the world was in that cart. *Please, Lord,* she cried silently.

Jigs, for once, was just as quiet, just as tense.

Almost as suddenly as the bees had been released, they flew away in a swarm, across the bridge to streams of little yellow flowers growing out of cracks in the shale.

"Thank you, God," Annie whispered fervently, then glanced at Jigs.

He rolled those expressively dark eyes of his but didn't move a muscle.

Suddenly, she realized she'd have to thank God for him, too, though most of the time the bounder had little to redeem him.

That last condemning thought would cost her, and though it stuck in her craw, she prayed, *Please, Lord, forgive my uncharitable assumptions about Jigs. And please help me not to be so judgmental toward him from now on.*

Then, thank heavens, Brother Bremmer came lumbering back with an ox and a double yoke over one hefty shoulder. He handed the beast's lead to Jigs, then sidestepped down the steep slope to fetch Ruben.

At that moment, Ike and Ken Smith strode out onto the natural bridge, with Otto, the unpredictable tyke, trotting after.

Annie read disapproval in Ike's face. Her heart sank. After struggling so hard to earn the smallest semblance of respect from him, she'd failed. She hadn't kept her mind on her cart long enough to keep a wheel from slipping into a hole and shattering. Now it would take all of them, with the good Lord helping, to get her cart back up to level ground and the wheel replaced.

The sun, which had been hidden all day, chose this moment to peek out from behind a cloud and turn the honey oozing out of the broken box into gleaming golden glory. Ike couldn't miss seeing this second disaster.

He started barking orders. "Rolf, once you get the extra team hitched, come help Ken and me lift up the cart. Jigs, you keep holdin' the horse steady. Annie, when I holler, start movin' your cows."

"And me," Otto cried. "What can I do?"

Just the thought of Rolf's youngest getting in the middle of things sent a chill through Annie. She started to speak, but Ike beat her to it.

"Boy, you go tell your ma and the other women to turn around and take the wagons back to the flat we just come across. Now, scoot."

Otto took off across the bald on his "great commission."

And Annie breathed again. No telling what havoc he might have set off in this dangerous situation.

With everyone working as a team, the three below putting their backs into the broken side and Annie driving the cattle, while Jigs and the horse steadied their progress, they soon had the cart up on fairly level terrain again.

Only then did Ike turn to her. He wore that unreadable blank expression that always made her uneasy. And today she had more reason than ever to worry.

She braced herself for the worst. *Please, Lord, help me.*

"Is your spare wheel in good repair?"

"Aye."

"Jigs, you unhitch the front team and take them down to the flat along with the pack animals. I'll be down to help you with the unloadin' once everything here is taken care of."

Jigs looked puzzled, but merely shrugged as he walked to the livestock.

Ken spoke, however. "Why unload your horses? It's only been an hour since we stopped to noon. We can have a wheel on this cart in no time."

"The bees. We need to repair that hive so the bees will return to it this evenin'."

Ike was willing to wait for the bees? Annie could hardly believe he actually cared about anything of hers. But she knew better than to read anything extra into this kindness. A couple of days ago, she'd mistakenly thought they'd become friends, yet since that time he'd avoided her as if she had smallpox.

"Besides," Ike continued, "I need to get that foot bandaged and make Annie a pair of moccasins. That cut's bleedin' pretty bad." He pointed.

Annie looked down. One of those feet she'd been bragging about such a short time ago was leaving bloody footprints with every step. Her attention swung back to Ike. A broken wheel, scattered bees, and an injured foot. She'd cost the train half a day's travel. The only thing she hadn't done was start bawling like one of her cows.

This would not bode well for her.

~

Ike shook his head. What a mess. He'd known they'd be crossing this treacherous spot today. He should have anticipated its instability when something as heavy and wide as their wagons started over . . . those iron tires grinding into the shale. He'd shirked his duty by not being up here to see the vehicles safely to the other side.

Disgusted with himself, he strode to the back of the widow's crippled cart. "Annie, where do you keep your clean rags?"

She hobbled toward him, looking almost as crippled as her conveyance. "In the tote hangin' from the rear bow."

Quickly he rummaged through the dangling overstuffed bag until he found a piece of old sheeting. He ripped a long strip from it. Dropping down on one knee, he motioned for her. "Come here."

She hesitated—but for only a second—then came forward. When he patted his propped leg, she lifted her seeping foot and rested the heel just above his knee. But from her awkward stance and heightened coloring, he realized she was more than a little self-conscious about it.

Although his goal was to stem the flow of blood by padding and tightly wrapping the gash, he couldn't help noticing the trim shape of her ankle. Resting against his weathered hand, it seemed almost as fragile as he'd expect frail Betsy Smith's to be. This young woman wasn't nearly as strongly built as she made out to be. Ripping the last several inches of the strip down the middle, he tied the two ends around that smooth, slender ankle.

Setting her foot to the ground, he rose. "That should hold it for a few minutes."

"Thank you kindly" was all she managed before he scooped her into his arms. *"What are you doin'?"* She floundered, then grabbed him around the neck. "I can walk."

94

"Not till we get it cleaned up and dressed proper."

He saw further protest in those green-and-gold eyes of hers, but it remained unspoken. Considering she was a woman, her silence was most unusual. And commendable. Considering she was a woman with a penchant for speaking her piece, it was almost comical. He chuckled to himself.

While carrying her to his saddled horse, he noticed another surprising thing. She was much lighter than he'd expected. Her bulky homespun had conspired with her determination to make her appear a stouter woman. Though she'd never own up to it, she wasn't nearly as strong as she let on.

Ike lifted her onto the saddle, then catching the reins, he swung up behind her. "I'll be back in a few minutes," he called to the other men. Rolf stood by the cart while Ken lay beneath, unbolting the spare wheel.

Then, with his arms encircling Annie, Ike reined the horse around and started off the shale bridge. Her shoulder nested against his chest and her golden head rode just below his mouth.

He breathed in the scent of her . . . and tried to ignore the warmth of her surprisingly slender form resting ever-so-slightly against him. Much too close for him to think about another blessed thing.

10

There was no ignoring the fact that Ike's arms supported her as he guided the horse. All her efforts to keep her shoulder from bumping his chest were useless. No matter how straight she tried to sit, the sway of the horse pushed her against him. Try as she might, all she could think about was the warmth of his arms around her, his breath tickling the top of her head, the comfort of the muscles padding the chest she leaned into.

She finally gave up trying and relaxed, though this was all so embarrassing. Her every bragging assurance came back to slap her in the face. The wagon almost lost, the bees scattered, and now he considered her incapable of even walking. How could she ever look at him again?

Not a word did he speak on the ride back through a scattering of gnarled, stunted pines. She felt like those trees, whose exposed roots wound among the outcroppings of stone in their struggle to survive. Like them, she was barely hanging on. Ike had threatened that if she held him up he'd leave her at the first settlement they came to. At this very moment he was probably plotting exactly when and where he'd rid himself of her for good.

She knew she needed to think of an argument in her favor—though she couldn't imagine what that would be.

The horse stepped into a rut, jogging Annie to the side.

Ike caught her, holding her tighter against him.

The harrowing experience she and her animals had just survived flooded into her thoughts again, and she couldn't help but take comfort in being coddled for just a little while. To feel safe, to be close to another human being . . . needs she thought she'd put behind her when her father ripped her from her family home.

Her eyes stung, and her throat began to ache. Sure as tomorrow, tears would be next. Taking a deep breath, she willed them away. All Ike needed was another sign of her weakness.

The trail slanted off the rocky ridge and down into a fertile bowl-shaped cove. Flourishing oaks and pines were reflected in a pond that had no stream feeding it, only one trickling outward. And those same yellow flowers the bees had flown to abounded in the grassy area around the water. After being out on that bald, the cove seemed far lovelier than when she had passed through it before. Annie now saw its majestic testament to God's creation . . . to life, life that seemed more precious at this moment after almost losing hers.

As they started down the slope, Annie saw that the three wagons had pulled off the trail to cluster in the small clearing.

The women and children all hurried forward to meet them. Of the three women, only Betsy Smith's expressive eyes held any sympathy.

Towheaded Otto broke through to the front in a leg-churning run. "See, Ike," he cried, "I told 'em what to do, and they did it."

As Ike reined the horse to a stop, Lorna rushed up behind Otto, forgetting her usual ladylike decorum. Her scathing violet glance slashed across Annie before settling on Ike. "I told you that woman had no business coming with us. Otto says she almost ran her cart off a cliff and busted one of her wheels in the bargain." This was the closest Lorna had ever come to her—this cat of a girl who'd been waiting for the right moment to pounce.

"Lorna Graham, I presume," Annie replied. Her voice brittle as ice, she let her own manners fly off with the birds. She was as good as banished anyway. "The one who is *supposed to be* Noah Reardon's betrothed. I don't believe we've been properly introduced."

As Lorna took a step closer, the young woman's eyes turned the deepest shade of purple. "What do you mean, *supposed to be?*"

Behind Annie, Ike's chest quivered; then he broke into a fit of coughing.

Inga now pushed her way to the front. "Ike Reardon, I tell you dis morning, travel in da rain is no goot. But, no, you do not listen. Get down. I get you some medicine for dat cough."

"No, I'm fine," Ike said, regaining control. "But Annie, here, needs to have a gash in her foot cleaned up and salved and bandaged. Could you take care of that for me? I need to get back to help Rolf and Ken mount the wheel."

Betsy stepped up beside Inga. "Are you hurtin' bad?" she asked Annie.

"No, really, it's just a little cut. I can take care of it myself."

Behind her, Ike slid off the horse's rump. "Inga, where do you want me to put her?" Then, before Annie could protest, he plucked her from the saddle and carried her toward the Bremmer outfit.

It was too utterly humiliating. Annie leveled her gaze to Ike's collar, concentrated on the weave of his heavy linen hunting shirt, avoiding all the stares. Especially the disdain she knew would be in Lorna's eyes.

Inga's voice was much too near as she said, "You put da girl on da back of mine vagon."

Setting Annie on the edge of the wooden bed, his silvery gaze imprisoned hers.

She held her breath. Would he inform her in front of all these people that she would be left at the next settlement? Even in front of Wolfgang? The lad was the only one who considered her a brave and forthright person, instead of a fool—or worse—a wanton woman.

"You are not to put any weight on your foot today or tomorrow," Ike ordered in a no-nonsense voice. "When I get back, I'll make you a crutch."

"But I have to—"

"No buts. We'll take care of your chores. Then I'll start on those moccasins for you. We'll be stayin' here until Monday. And, in case you've forgotten," he said with a slight lift to one side of his mouth, "tomorrow is Sunday." He turned away. In a long-legged stride, he retrieved his horse and swung into the saddle as Inga, her daughter Renate, and Betsy closed in on Annie.

Lorna, thank goodness, walked away to her own wagon.

Wolfgang crowded next to his sister. "Did your cart really almost go off a cliff? Otto don't usually get his stories straight."

"I'm afraid it did."

"Told you," Otto retorted.

"Da bull done it. Bulls no goot for da pulling of da vagon."

"No. It was my cows. They panicked when the wheel splintered at the very spot where the trail is only a few feet from the edge." Wanting to shift the topic from that frightening moment, Annie turned to Betsy. "It appears that Ken will be payin' me back for the milk sooner than I expected. I'll be owin' everyone milk and honey after this sorry day."

"You shouldn't be worryin' about nothin' but that foot of yourn." Betsy turned to Wolfie. "Find some dry wood and get a fire started for your ma. And Renate, you fetch a bucket of water whilst we get this here foot unwrapped."

Inga hoisted herself up on the wagon. "Isolda, you take Otto under da dry tree. Play *mit* him. I find dat bag of berry root for to boil. Make goot medicine for da cut."

Betsy began loosening the bandage tie. As she did, she looked up at Annie. "Who put this on you?"

"Mr. Reardon."

"He did a real careful job of it. Must'a taken him quite a spell." She smiled then, as if she knew a secret.

Was Betsy insinuating that something other than doctoring had taken place? If so, the young woman needed some doctoring herself. Ike Reardon had only one thing on his mind—getting rid of her as soon as possible.

Nevertheless, a tiny part of Annie reveled in the notion that Betsy might take it into her head that a man of such handsome and strapping proportions could ever be interested in a woman as plain and ordinary as she.

~

The clouds were breaking up, exposing the sun. It warmed Ike's back beneath his damp hunting shirt as he neared camp with Ken Smith riding double behind him. All the animals were grazing except for one pack horse. And Jigs, along with Wolfie, was almost finished unloading the bay gelding.

Ike had expected to return to camp sooner, but the beehive also needed to be restored before any more of the bees returned to it. As it was, he'd been stung twice and Ken once while they worked on the box with the only carpenter's tools they could find in Annie's cart—a dull saw, a hammer with a loose handle, and a small drill. They'd found no nails or wooden pegs, so they'd had to whittle some on the spot. He'd also been obliged to pry off a part of one of the cart's side boards to replace a slat for the hive. But it couldn't be helped.

A large fire licked toward the sky. Surrounding it were clothes and blankets, some strung on rope, some tossed over bushes. The women were drying out their things after the rain.

A large black pot hung over another, smaller fire. Renate, the oldest of the Bremmer children, stirred its contents with a long-handled wooden spoon while the women sat near the flames on folding stools—probably drying themselves out, too. Inga, never idle, was knitting a stocking.

As Ike and Ken rode closer, the aroma of pepper and onions mixed with woodsmoke, causing Ike's stomach to pang. With this much time to cook, tonight's supper should be better than the usual hurried meal. "Howdy, folks," Ike said as he dropped Ken off.

"Vere is mine Rolf?" Inga asked, her face as humorless as it was freckled.

Leaving Ken to explain that Brother Rolf was coming with Annie's cart, Ike reined his horse toward his own wagon to unsaddle. Riding past the Bremmers', he realized that Annie was still sitting exactly where he'd left her a good hour ago. Her feet, one bare, the other rebandaged, dangled a couple of feet above the ground at the rear of the wagon, and she looked just as damp and cold as when he'd left her. Why hadn't anyone helped her to the fire?

Or had the stubborn girl refused to accept their assistance?

Either way, it had probably been for the best, considering Lorna was at the cook fire. That girl hadn't even made a pretense of politeness. But then Annie hadn't let Lorna's spiteful tongue get the best of her . . . anymore than she'd let him that first day. When Annie put Lorna in her place, he'd almost choked to death, trying to hide his amusement.

Squelching a smile that even now tried to break free, he nodded at Annie just before dismounting.

She returned his nod. Nothing more. No smile, no words of thanks for all he'd done for her this day. Annie, it seemed, had no problem giving help, but she sure hated taking it. That widow had too much pride for her own good.

And worse, she reminded him of himself.

When pride cometh, his mother had quoted to him more times than he could count, *then cometh shame: but with the lowly is wisdom.* A hard lesson for him to try to live.

Unlooping the cinch, he dragged the saddle from the horse's back while peeking to see if Annie was watching him.

He should have known better. She stared straight ahead as he tossed the saddle over the wagon tongue, then added the blanket. Nor did she sneak a single glance while he slipped the bridle off the roan's head and hooked it over the wagon brake. Yes sir, she was a prideful woman, that one.

He snagged his camp stool from inside his wagon and marched straight for her.

"Your lips are blue, and you look like a drowned rat. Here, take this," he said, handing her the portable seat to tote, then while her hands were occupied, he scooped her up.

She went rigid, and those jewel-like eyes flashed, but she held her tongue as he carried her to the cook fire.

"Betsy," he said, addressing the only sweet-natured woman in the train, "would you mind unfoldin' the stool so I can set Annie down?"

Betsy's sad-eyed smile was more endearing than ever as she rose. "It would be my pleasure. I'll put it right next to mine, 'lessen you have another place picked out for her."

"No, that's fine." He sure as shootin' didn't want Annie next to Lorna.

"I set a batch of tea to steep," Betsy remarked kindly as Ike seated her. "It'll be ready in a minute."

"Sounds mighty good," Ike answered for the widow, since she was spending an inordinate amount of time fussing with her skirt.

"Soon as I've had some, I'll get started on that crutch, Annie. Me and Ken already fixed your beehive."

"I'm obliged to you," she said, but she looked up at Ken warming his behind in front of the fire, not at Ike. That woman and her brambly pride.

Jigs and Wolfie tramped into the fire circle, coming from where they'd staked out the animals.

"Tell 'em what you told me, Jigs," Wolfie said, excitement ringing in his voice. "About Miss Annie. How she saved her animals and her cart. How they almost pulled her over the cliff. But she wouldn't let go. Even whilst she was gushing blood all over the rocks. Jigs, tell how she talked them cows down, them a-stompin' and a-bawlin'. With bees swarming all around 'em."

Jigs chuckled as he rubbed his hands near the fire. He loved it when he got folks all worked up. "You're tellin' it just fine. Better'n any town crier I ever heard. Ain't that so, Ike?"

"All he needs is a big drum."

The square-headed lad ducked his chin and grinned. At that moment he looked younger than Otto, who never seemed abashed by anything he said or did. "Miss Annie," Wolfie continued in a voice that had turned reverent, "you're a heroine. Just like that Molly Pitcher during the war, taking water to our thirsty soldiers, even with bullets and cannonballs flying all around her."

Ike, along with everyone else, turned to Annie, and she looked more embarrassed than the kid had. But without the grin. "I just done what had to be done." She spoke barely above a whisper, looking only at the campfire. "All I have in the world was fixin' to go over."

Suddenly, Ike realized the story the boy had repeated wasn't one of Jigs's gross exaggerations. She had actually almost been killed.

"Anybody would'a done the same," Annie added with a bit more force.

Ike knew different. As Jigs began filling in the details of her

104

heroic feat, Ike knew none of the other women here would've risked her own life—well, maybe Inga, but only if Rolf was nowhere in sight. Ike's attention gravitated to Annie's injured foot. Now he understood why she'd been unaware it was gashed and bleeding. At this very minute, she could be lying dead at the bottom of that cliff.

And he would be to blame.

He took in a ragged breath, knowing he should've been there, looking out for her, looking after all his responsibilities . . . instead of playing nursemaid to Lorna.

He glanced over at the vexatious girl.

As usual, Lorna had only herself on her mind. She stared at Jigs, and anyone could see she didn't like it one bit that he, like Wolfie before him, was beating the drum for Annie . . . bigger and louder with every word.

But then Ike wasn't sure he liked Jigs's bragging on her all that much either. "Betsy, do you think that tea's about done?" he asked, overriding Jigs's comparison of Annie to those Amazon women of Greek mythology. "Sounds like Annie could use a strong cup about now. I know I could. Please, some tea for Annie and me."

11

The sun crowned the trees in its slide to the west as Annie hobbled on the crutch Ike had made for her. She hop-stepped out to where her cows grazed with all the other livestock. The two youngest Bremmers came with her, Otto carrying the milk pail and Isolda with the stool. Inga had not discouraged them from helping her. Annie didn't know whether the woman was softening toward her or if she just wanted the children out of the way while she and the other women labored over their steaming washtubs, scrubbing their clothes clean.

"Miss Annie," Isolda said, keeping pace, "how long will it take Ike to make you a pair of Indian shoes?"

"It shouldn't take too long. They don't look to have more'n one piece to 'em. But I wish he wouldn't bother. My feet are tough. Gettin' gashed like I did was just an accident. Maybe he'll get to workin' on other stuff and forget about 'em."

"Oh." Isolda sounded disappointed. "I thought maybe . . . I . . . oh, nothing." Looking up from her own feet, she shrugged a thin shoulder.

Annie glanced below the little girl's dress that was several inches too short and noticed a number of scratches on the child's feet and legs. Her brother's didn't look much better. He was forever running off into the brush, with Isolda having to chase after him.

Otto stopped in Annie's path, almost toppling her as she hopped along. "Look. Your calf is nursing from Queenie. Want me to shoo him off?" He charged forth at a run.

"No!" Annie cried before he'd gone more than a few feet, his pail poised to swing. "Shy Baby needs to nurse whenever he can. The little feller is mighty young to have to walk all the way to Tennessee."

"I'm not." Otto's walk turned into a swagger.

"What's your calf's name?" Isolda asked. "I ain't never heard you call him nothing but Shy Baby."

"I reckon I haven't gotten around to givin' him a proper name yet."

"Proper? Is that the same as his Christian name, or a different one?"

Annie chuckled at the concern in those soulful blue eyes. "Aye, it's the same. How about the three of us studyin' on it a spell? Come up with just the right name for him."

As they reached Queenie and Shy Baby, the caramel-and-white calf's big eyes walled toward them nervously. He didn't like being surrounded. Nonetheless, he kept right on tugging at his mother's teat.

"Let's call him Walkingstick," Otto said, banging the bucket down beside the calf.

"*Walking Stick.*" Isolda's voice carried that big-sister disdain. "That's a dumb name. Who'd want to be named after Annie's crutch?"

"No, not that kind." Otto's chin flattened stubbornly. "After the one in my pouch." He spread open the grubby leather container hooked around a suspender and pulled out two or three small stones, a dead frog, and a mangled twiglike insect.

"Yuck." Wrinkling her nose, Isolda stepped up to the calf and ran a hand across his smooth coat—his skin twitching wherever she touched. "He needs a name he can be proud of. His mama is Queenie. He should be named something fit for a prince," she said, lifting her freckled face up to Annie.

"You're right, Isolda. Why don't we call the little fella Prince?"

"*Ja*, I like that. Our little shy Prince." The child bent down and rubbed her cheek across the calf's soft hide.

Annie was tempted to pull the little girl into a hug but knew her mother would not appreciate Annie bestowing attentions.

The calf backed out from under his mother, his long pink tongue licking his mouth.

Annie took the short-legged stool from Isolda. Placing the seat beside Queenie, she managed to drop onto it without putting any weight on her injured foot. Then, with the pail in place, she grabbed the two nearest teats and began the pull-squeeze action.

"Look! A butterfly!" Otto took off after a mauve, yellow, and brown beauty.

Isolda instantly took several steps in her brother's direction. The child knew all too well she couldn't risk losing sight of him. "Oh, shucks. He's heading for the woods. I gotta go get him."

Annie watched the little girl chase after him. Soon they both disappeared into the tangle of brush beneath the trees, and Annie turned her attention to the warmth radiating from the cow on this chilly day and her slow steady breathing. She listened to the ping of milk against the pail, the birds warbling above, insects humming around the animals sawing on the grass.

In the distance, Annie heard the sound of hammering—Ken working on her wheel repairs. She saw Jigs sitting on a downed log, whittling a new flute. He'd been complaining about having nothing to play since his other one had fallen out of his pouch and gotten stepped on by a horse. Down near the pond, the women chatted as Betsy and Lorna shared one steaming tub of laundry and Inga and Renate stooped over another, rubbing their clothes over scrub boards.

All seemed so peaceful this evening in the lovely mountain meadow. She would hate it if Ike made her leave the train . . . even if she did have problems with some of the folks. But if she had to go on alone, she wouldn't let herself be stopped. She *would* reach the rich bottomland of the Tennessee or die trying. It meant that much to her.

Oh, Lord, she prayed, *let me be right.*

Even as she prayed the words, she knew it was a selfish request. But she couldn't see any peace or joy in her life if she didn't get the one thing that could make her dream come true—land of her own, which would ensure her freedom from bondage to any man.

Ike shouldn't have left her hanging without giving her his decree. Not knowing had plagued her every thought this afternoon, even this halcyon moment. Maybe he aimed to save himself from her arguments by not putting words to his decision until they reached the next settlement.

She was afraid that if she pushed him for an answer, he'd be more likely to say those dreaded words. The longer the delay, the better the chance that he might later change his mind. And there was time. Only this morning, Jigs mentioned there was nothing between here and the outskirts of Henry's Station but a few lone cabins. Even the Indians had moved their towns farther west.

Surely Ike wouldn't dump her at some remote cabin . . . would he? *God, please. Don't let him do that to me.*

Then, like a bad penny turning up, Ike rode into camp—he'd been up on the mountain bald studying the best route for the wagons. He rode past the encampment . . . headed straight for her.

Had the awful moment come? Would he tell her now?

Of course, everyone else's attention shifted to her. They all stopped what they were doing to stare.

Just as she stripped the last of the milk from Queenie's udder, Ike reached her and swung to the ground. "I told you to stay off that foot. It needs all the chance it can get to knit 'tween now'n Monday."

"I used the crutch to get here. If I don't keep my cow stripped, she won't make as much milk."

"I told you we'll do your chores for you. That cut foot is serious. The longer it takes to heal, the longer you won't be able to walk on it."

Without so much as a by-your-leave, he reached down and lifted her off the stool and deposited her on his horse. Without so much as a by-your-leave!

The arrogant bully handed her the crutch, then picked up the stool and pail. Taking the horse's reins, he started back to camp.

A body would think she was his own personal sack of meal.

"I'm going to roll out your bed in a dry spot under that spruce over yonder." He nodded toward a giant dense-limbed tree. "And I expect you to stay put for the rest of the evenin'."

If she did as he said, she'd have to be waited on hand and foot—*injured* foot, that was. She glanced at the people busy again at the camp, folks who already had a fair share of their own chores to do each day.

Inga and the other women were now hanging their laundry over bushes and on rope strung between trees to dry in the slanting sunlight, rather than waiting until tomorrow, its being the Sabbath. They'd most likely want to launder themselves, too. And if Annie had gotten Lorna's measure, tomorrow the girl's attire would rival that butterfly Otto was chasing. None of them would be pleased to have Annie to look after, too.

But she knew Ike would have it no other way. She glanced down at his head, hatless after the shower had caused the brim to droop.

111

The rain and wind had ruffled his hair, which was a shade or two lighter than her own and just as liberally sun-streaked. On him, the outdoorsy bleaching looked good, not the blight to femininity hers was. His hair had a breezy softness to it, begging to be touched . . . like the temptation to run a finger over a flower petal or the velvety moss on a tree trunk.

He glanced up, caught her looking.

She pretended she'd been peering past him.

"I checked on your bees. They was buzzin' around the hive again. I'll go fetch the box just before sunset."

"I'm much obliged to you." Another inconvenience he could add to his list.

"No trouble. I'm as partial to a little honey in my tea as the next man."

He sounded as if he meant it. But with him looking straight ahead, Annie couldn't tell for sure.

"First," he continued, "I want to trace around your feet for that pair of moccasins and get the leather cut out whilst there's still some sunlight left."

The thought of his hands on her feet again sent a nervous shiver through her.

And no doubt Lorna and Inga would be watching.

Then she remembered Isolda. "I do have my Sunday shoes I could wear till the cut heals. So, I was wondering, could you make a pair for Isolda instead of me? I'd give you a good-sized wedge of cheese in payment if you did. That youngun's wee feet could sure use the covering."

He stopped. Stared up at her. "I never noticed her feet." He said it as if that, too, was supposed to be on his list of duties. "I've been carvin' her a doll."

The man cared enough to make the little girl a plaything? This was a side to Isaac Reardon she hadn't seen before—this tender kindness. She did her best not to sound amazed. "That's real nice of you. Otto's feet aren't much better. But I reckon he's too busy chasin' after bugs and such to notice."

Ike grinned. "That boy is a caution. Looks like I got more work cut out for me this afternoon than I figured." He stretched into a faster stride. "Three pair of moccasins. Hope I got enough cured leather."

~

Annie sat alone in the dark beneath the spruce where Ike had rolled out her bedding a couple of hours earlier, a long stone's throw from the glow of the nearest cook fire. Except for the last glimmer of fading light trimming the crowns of the hilltop trees, night had claimed the bowl-like cove.

Ike had shown her many kindnesses this afternoon, expended most of his time on hers and the children's moccasins, and now he was off to fetch back her beehive. Yet not a word had he spoken about that which pressed so heavily on her mind—her expulsion from the train.

Jigs broke away from those milling about between two of the fires and started toward her, carrying the flute he'd been working on most of the afternoon—graduated lengths of hollow reed tied together with hair he'd pulled from a horse's tail. He'd stayed away while Ike was nearby, but now the mischievous child of a man regained his boldness.

Stopping before her, he was nothing but an outline framed by the brightness of a lantern someone had just lit. He blew across the reeds, running up the musical scale. "What do you think?" he asked, a smile evident in his voice. "The pitch is nigh onto perfect. Wouldn't you say?"

She looked up from her pallet. "I don't know much about music." She spoke flatly in her attempt to discourage him. Though he blocked her view of camp, she had no doubt everyone was watching.

Jigs was never put off by polite subtleties. "Rolf has *deigned* to let us have a singalong after supper tonight. But only if we sing hymns—*how ever much fun that will be.*" His voice dripped with disdain. "Do you know of any lively hymns? I haven't been in a church since I mustered out of the army. After having to put up with ol' Washington rammin' his religion down our throats every Sunday morning, I been steerin' clear. But here I am, stuck with another pious psalm singer. And with Ike goin' right along, actin' like he never missed a day of church in his life. . . ."

Ike? Who'd as much as accused her of dishonoring the Sabbath? "I thought Mr. Reardon was a Christian."

The outline of a shoulder lifted and dropped. "Maybe he is. But it never got in his way before. But now with Brother Rolf and you women along . . . so, I gotta fall into line myself. For now anyway. So teach me a spry hymn—if there be such a thing. I don't want to give our holy brother over there the satisfaction of findin' out I don't know any."

This was the first time Annie had seen Jigs care about a single thing enough to become upset. Queer that it would be over something so trivial as music. She leaned past him to see the other women busy with their final meal preparations while Rolf and Ken placed two loading boards on barrels—the same barrels that had rolled down them from the Bremmer wagon a few minutes before. Their minister was determined to have the entire party gathered around one table for this evening's meal and for tomorrow's Sabbath dinner. Everyone, even the children who were collecting table service, seemed busy.

She could think of no good reason not to help Jigs. "I reckon I know one or two songs that might take to the flute. Have you ever heard this one?" She lifted her voice in a simple tune.

> *"God moves in a mysterious way,*
> *His wonders to perform.*
> *He plants his footsteps in the sea,*
> *and rides upon the storm."*

"No. Is that the whole song?"

"The first verse."

He dropped down on his knees beside her. "Sing it again."

As she repeated the tune, he did a so-so job of keeping up, quietly, of course, so Brother Bremmer wouldn't know what he was up to. By the third run-through, he was playing fair to middlin'.

"One more time," he begged. "Sing all the verses. Then you can teach me another song."

He was as serious about this as he'd been this afternoon when they almost lost her cart over the cliff. A pure puzzlement to Annie.

Halfway through the song, what little light coming from camp became blocked by an approaching silhouette—a silhouette that could be none other than Ike's tall, lean frame. He'd returned from fetching the beehive without her noticing.

"Appears you two are having your own private little blanket party, sittin' out here in the dark." He sounded condemning.

How dare he! Beneath this drooping-branched fir is precisely where he'd put her and ordered her to stay.

Jigs didn't seem the least put off by his partner's inference. "Aye, as much of a party as a body can have playin' *hymns.*"

"It's time for supper." Ike's response was curt.

"But I only learned one song. Oh, well," Jigs sighed. He took Annie's hands and started to rise with her.

Ike laid a hand on his shoulder. "I'll bring Annie. Lorna wants you to tote her iron kettle to the table for her."

Why hadn't Lorna asked Ike to carry it? The answer was obvious—Jigs required rescuing from Annie's clutches. Just the thought that the beautiful young woman would think she was competition always made her smile, as she did now.

Jigs, however, groaned, then sprang up from his haunches. "Her majesty calls."

Annie turned to fetch her crutch leaning against the tree trunk.

115

"Never mind," Ike murmured—and she was up in his arms.

She was beginning to think the man enjoyed having her there, even if he acted like carrying her was of no more consequence than loading or unloading one of his packhorses.

As for herself, she was undeniably aware of being held close to him. He was still hatless, and her hands were locked around his neck. How easy it would be to trail her fingers through his rain-softened hair. All she'd have to do was raise her hand ever so slightly. . . .

And how crazy. If she ever did allow herself to fall in love, it wouldn't be with a man who thought it was his God-given destiny to be in total command. Her freedom meant more to her than any man ever could.

As they reached the circle of light, Betsy smiled warmly. Too warmly. The bride had the eye of a matchmaker. "Put Annie over there," she said, pointing to a real chair—one of four that must have been unloaded from a wagon.

"No," Annie said, stopping Ike. "I wouldn't feel right, takin'—"

Cap started to bark—wild, shrill barking.

Someone or something was coming. Annie looked up at Ike. "Did you hang the hive away from camp?"

"Aye," he barely put sound to the word as—forgetting to put her down—he strode toward the trail.

"*Quiet, Cap,*" Annie ordered.

The dog ceased, and the sound of horses drifted toward them. Ike stopped.

Annie felt the tension in his arms, his body.

Jigs and Brother Bremmer stepped up on either side. Jigs had his Pennsylvania rifle.

"Sounds like two horses," Ike said, staring up the trail.

Jigs moved his long-barreled weapon to the ready position, one hand near the flintlock. Ken came alongside Jigs with his own weapon, a slightly shorter musket.

Then out of the darkness came a horse and rider, then another horse, this one with two men on its back.

Jigs moved in front of Ike, blocking Annie's view.

"Goot evening," Brother Bremmer called. "Come sit *mit* us. Ve sit down to eat now."

"Why, thank you" came a hoarse-sounding reply. "You sure you got enough?"

"*Ja,* ve haf plenty food."

"I'm mighty glad you do," another said. "I smelt your cookin' half a mile away."

The three men dismounted and, leading their horses, walked alongside Rolf and Ken. In the dimness, Annie hadn't gotten a clear view of them as yet, but as they came farther into the light, she saw they wore old and sagging buckskins.

Jigs dropped behind with Ike, who had yet to relax. Ike's arms around Annie felt like bands of iron.

"You don't have much with you to be so far into the wilderness," Ken, just ahead, commented to the strangers.

"Right ye are, laddie," said one who sounded as if he hadn't been away from England too many years. "We be set upon by robbers."

"We was lucky to get away with our skins," another added.

Ike and Jigs eyed one another; then they moved closer, each stepping up on opposite sides of the group.

Annie really did feel like a sack of meal now as she willed the men to ask where the robbery had taken place. *When? How many culprits were there?* She wished Ike would put her down, since he'd apparently forgotten he held her.

"Where?" Jigs had the good sense to ask as he stepped in front of the men, stopping them. "On the trail to the Watauga settlements?"

"Nay," the English one said. "To the west, several days' ride. 'Twas them heathen redsticks what set upon us."

117

Indians were rampaging across the frontier again? Annie prayed it was not so.

"Cherokee or Creek?" Ike asked.

"Must'a been Cherokee," said the other man who'd spoken before. "We been over on the Cumberland, out past that Nashville settlement, tradin' some Chickasaws outta their beaver pelts and buffalo hides. Comin' back, we was cuttin' across to the Trader's Path when we happened on the Cherokees' old capitol, Chota—the one they abandoned awhile back. Anyways, they swooped down on us, howlin' like a pack of wild animals. They got our packhorses and shot Beckley's out from under him. Ain't that right, Frank?"

Annie clung tighter to Ike's neck. How far away was this Chota? Several days' ride, they'd said. But what if the Indians had followed them? Was a war party closing in right now?

"That's right, Foley." When the farthest stranger spoke, he turned, and his face was illuminated in the light.

Annie froze. It was him! The same flushed face and greasy beard, those same beady blue eyes. This man hadn't been off trading furs; he'd been with the pack train to Henry's Fort. Why was he lying? What were these men up to?

12

Ike felt Annie stiffen in his arms. She stretched up to his ear and whispered, "He's lyin'."

Although Ike had no idea how she could know that, he believed her. To let her know he'd heard, he answered with a quick squeeze.

"Yessiree," the red-faced one they'd called Frank Beckley said, "pert near got m'self kilt."

If Annie was right, danger was afoot. Jigs and the others needed to be warned. Right away! "Beggin' your pardon, gentlemen," Ike said with studied nonchalance, "but I was takin' my injured wife, here, out to tend her needs when you rode up." He held Jigs's gaze, hoping his friend would understand that something was awry.

Jigs stared back, but only a second or two. "Well, then, I reckon you oughtn't to keep your wife waitin'. 'Lessen you want me to take her off your hands," he added with a teasing smile.

"I think not," Ike said, shifting Annie's weight in his arms. He'd been holding her for several minutes now, and she was becoming weightier. "You just save us a place at the table," he added, letting his glance slide across Rolf and Ken, grateful that they, too, showed no sign of either surprise or alarm.

"Come," Rolf said to their questionable guests. "I vill introduce you to mine family."

"Cap! Come!" Annie called to her dog as Ike turned away with her.

The minute flashes of a few scattered lightning bugs made the coal black of the nighttime woods seem all the darker. Ike gingerly chose his steps until he had Annie far enough away from camp for complete privacy. Halting, he asked, "Why do you say they're lyin'?" Although he looked straight into her face—only inches from his—in the deep darkness, he couldn't make out a single feature.

"The man, Frank Beckley—the one who claims his horse was shot out from under him—that didn't happen in some faraway Indian town. He passed me on this very trail no more'n a week ago. He was with a storekeeper from Henry's Station. A Mr. Keaton. And they were headed that way. I don't see as how Mr. Beckley could be in two places at once."

"Neither do I." This didn't bode well. Not at all. "Are you sure it's the same man?"

"That's not a face I'd soon forget. He was ridin' at the rear of the storekeeper's pack train. He looked at me real strange-like till they rode out of sight. Gave me the shivers."

And her out on the trail all alone. Shivers almost seized Ike himself, just thinking about what could've happened to her. He held her all the tighter. "I hope that taught you that a woman can't wander around by her lonesome. 'Specially a looker like you."

He heard her breath catch. "I—"

"Yes? What?" He braced himself for an onslaught of her tongue. The woman always insisted she was as self-reliant as any man.

"Nothin'. Just that this Frank Beckley needs close watchin'."

120

"Aye. And I hope the storekeeper he was with hasn't come to any harm in the meantime. Keaton's a good honest trader."

"From the looks of them," Annie said thoughtfully, "with no provisions, three of 'em ridin' on two horses, it don't appear they took nothin' off of the storekeeper."

"Which means they're probably still on the prowl. Do you think this Beckley fellow will recognize you when he sees you in the light?"

"I'm sure of it. He looked at me even longer and harder than I did him. And he'll recognize my dog. Most likely, he led the others back down the trail, thinkin' they'd find me alone and easy pickin's."

Ike's chest expanded on a sudden intake of air. If he hadn't let her join his party, she'd be in those men's foul hands this very minute. "I think it's time you took sick."

The widow broke into untimely laughter. "That shouldn't be hard for them to believe. You haven't set me down since before they came."

He chuckled, too, as he became much too aware of the woman in his arms. Not good. Better change tack. "That's one way to keep you out of trouble."

Again she didn't answer back to defend herself the way he'd expected . . . this one he held so close that all he heard was the two of them inhaling and exhaling in this cocoon of darkness. Her breath blew warm on his throat . . . fuzzing his brain, until all he could think about was how much he wanted to kiss her. . . . And all he'd have to do was just lean down a few inches. . . .

Just in time, he caught himself. What could he be thinking? She'd given no clue that she'd be receptive to such an advance. Or had she? She did seem quite content in his arms. Or was it just his imagination?

He gave himself a mental shake. This was no time to have his mind on courting. At this very minute, villains were in his camp—villains who needed his undivided attention. "Heel, Cap."

◇

Annie could've sworn Ike was about to kiss her . . . or something. The very air between them had seemed to come alive.

But she must have been mistaken.

He abruptly swung around with her and started back toward the trail. Stumbling in the dark a couple of times, he didn't take nearly the care with his steps as he had on his way into the forest thicket.

Once they reached the trail, the glow from camp was clearly visible, reminding Annie that her silly imaginings were just that. Even if Ike Reardon were to have romantic notions about her, it certainly wouldn't be on this night.

Careful to stay clear of the circles of lantern light, Ike returned Annie to the deep shadows of the giant spruce where he'd laid out her bed earlier. Slowly he lowered her onto her one sound foot.

He was taking such tender care of her, she could think of nothing but the loss she would feel when he let her go completely.

He continued to hold on to her until she had a solid stance; then he started to help lower her.

"No. Please," she said.

"I mean no disrespect," he whispered, but his words were much too close to her ear for comfort. "I just want to help you down."

Why would he presume she thought his intentions weren't honorable? "I'm sure you don't," she said as her heart picked up pace again. "But what I'd like is for you to fetch my crutch. It's leanin' against the tree."

"Don't be a ninny. I can help you down a lot easier than you can manage with that makeshift crutch."

"Of course you can. That's not in question. But, kind sir, at the moment, I need to go and do some of that tendin' to myself you spoke of to the men a few minutes ago."

"Oh, uh, I see—"

She would've loved to see the flustered expression on his usually unreadable face. But, alas, it was too dark.

Still steadying her, he reached around and collected the crutch he'd made earlier in the day, brushing past her too close for clear thinking. Then, handing it to her, he let go so suddenly she almost lost her footing. He swiftly swung away. "I'd better get back to the others now." He swung back. "Stay, Cap," he said to the dog at their feet.

The man was as erratic as her thoughts about him.

But within seconds, his long strides smoothed out, and she knew he would have nothing on his mind but the strangers by the time he reached them.

The thought saddened her . . . even if, when they were back in the woods, he'd as much as accused her of being trouble.

"Maybe so, Cap," she whispered to the dog. "But, he also said I was a looker." That brought on a smile—a long lingering one.

～

Ike slowed his pace as he walked toward the well-lighted table and took measure of the strangers. They were gathered with the others and already eating. The three guests sat in the Smiths' chairs, along with Brother Bremmer.

The man who'd been with storekeeper Keaton looked as if he could take on a half-grown bear—and win. Small wonder he'd frightened Annie. He was built like a block of wood. And from his dress, it was evident he'd spent years in Indian country. He wore nothing but fringed buckskin, and Ike knew he'd have the usual knife and hatchet hooked into his belt, along with fixings for his musket.

The one sitting next to him, a whipcord-lean man, was dressed the same. His eyes were the unfriendly kind. Deep in the socket, they were close-set beneath a shelf of brows and separated by a long, thin nose above a full beard.

Seated at the end, the third man spoke. "'Tis a grand pleasure to be sharing this fine meal with such lovely ladies," he said, his English accent evident. "A very long while it's been. I never would have expected such refinement in the wilderness." Unlike the other two, the Englishman had no beard, and he sported a suit of clothes one might see on a merchant—except his attire looked as soiled and worn as his companions' leathers. There was another, more pronounced, difference. Pudgy of face and body, he seemed almost as feminine in his movements as a woman. Except for his eyes. They darted about as if he were taking inventory, even while he smiled.

"Why, thank you," Betsy replied to his compliment, always polite to a fault. Especially so, considering the dirty men sat in her prized chairs, while she and the others perched on backless camp stools. And they smelled like they'd wintered in those clothes. Betsy also seemed oblivious to the reason her husband hovered so close.

"Niceties aside . . ." Lorna muttered. She sat toward the other end, cloistered between Ken Smith and Jigs. "I want to hear more about the Indians."

The Englishman leaned in her direction. "Aye, those heathen redsticks, miss—you did say your name was *Miss* Graham, didn't you?"

"Aye," Ike answered for her as he moved out of the darkness. The Englishman jumped. The other two merely stared at Ike. They weren't so easily startled.

Ike came up behind the man. "She's betrothed to my brother. And as for the Indians, Lorna," Ike continued, refusing to let these men turn the women into a gaggle of hysterical females, "they moved far to the west, toward the Mississippi River. The ones our guests saw probably just came back to their old sacred town for the remains of some revered ancestor. Isn't that so, gentlemen? They caught you men rifling through their leavings and ran you off." Ike turned to Lorna again. "Chota is a good seventy, seventy-five miles from here across the highest peaks in this mountain range."

"That ain't all they was set to do," argued flush-faced Beckley. "A hatchet whistled right past my ear. Pert near took my head off. An inch closer, and my brains could'a been spread from—" As if suddenly remembering women were present, he stopped speaking and shoveled a spoonful of stew into his oversized mouth.

"Papa, did you hear that?" Renate cried, while the other children, seated between their parents, looked on with just as much fright.

"Even so," Ike countered, "'lessen you killed one of 'em or took somethin' they set a whole lotta store in, they wouldn't trek this far east. Not with the war bein' over."

"You sure about that?" Foley, the wiry one, drawled as if he knew something no one else did. But the man's twisted smirk gave him away.

It was the final proof Ike needed. These men were showing themselves to be the lying reprobates Annie suspected they were. All of them. He needed to warn the others. Now. "Annie's not feelin' well. Betsy, could you fix me and her a plate?" Ike should have asked Lorna to do the chore. But she surely would've balked at doing anything for Annie, and he had too much on his mind without having to deal with her petulance right now.

"It'd be my pleasure, Ike." Betsy rose from the table, smiling as if she, like the foul-smelling hunter, knew some secret. But, unlike his, hers would be a happy one. "And you be sure and tell Annie I'll be prayin' for her foot tonight."

"I know she'll be pleasured to hear that," Ike said, then turned to Jigs at the far end of the long table. "Terrell, before I go, I need you to mend a piece of harness. Would you mind takin' leave of your meal long enough for me to point out the spot to you?"

Jigs lumbered to his feet. "Oh, all right," the born actor grumbled as Ike picked a fagot out of the fire to take with them. "But you don't expect me to fix it by lamplight, do you?"

125

When they reached the far side of their own wagon, Ike lighted a lantern on the pretext of showing Jigs the worn strip of leather, then quickly explained what Annie had told him. "I'd like to expose their game right now. Send 'em packin'. But we don't have any proof they're up to no good."

"And they'd just be out there layin' in wait. Catch us when we can least defend ourselves."

"Aye. If they're gonna do it, it's best to let 'em make their move tonight and get it over with." Ike unhooked the heavy harness and held a piece up to the lamplight. "Make sure Bremmer and Smith are told. Have 'em go to bed like usual, but with all their weapons at hand, primed and ready."

"You don't have to tell me that."

"I know. I'm just anxious, I reckon, what with all these women and children here."

"I'll be layin' right in front of Lorna's tent."

"And I'm stayin' over with Annie," Ike said, hoping he sounded nonchalant about it. "I'll have a better view of the camp and the livestock from there."

"And a cozier time with your *wife,*" Jigs teased.

The remark hit Ike all wrong. He didn't like it any more than the grin that came with it. "I don't want to hear no more of that kind of talk about her. Annie's a decent, hardworkin' woman."

"You know, Ike," Jigs said wearily, "you're turnin' into nothin' but a grumpy old codger. I been puttin' up with this ever since you found out your intended married someone else. And it's gettin' real tiresome. The sooner we get these folks to your valley and I can take off for New Orleans, the better I'm gonna like it."

The mention of his broken engagement caught Ike off guard. Sylvia was the furthest thing from his mind. And had been, he realized, since Annie had joined them. He looked across the deeply shadowed clearing to the tree he knew she sat beneath. Where he would soon go to her. Be alone with her for hours, maybe all night—if the strangers didn't make their play.

But they would.

"Sorry you feel that way, Jigs. But tonight, we'd both better keep our minds on just one thing. The enemy in our camp."

13

Annie heard the livestock moving restlessly. Unsure of the two strange ones in their midst, the horses whickered. Sitting on her bedding, she held Cap fast by his collar, though he strained to bolt free. Her dog was too distinct with his shaggy fawn-and-white coloring not to be recognized by Frank Beckley if the man got a good look at him.

Deep in some mountain hollow behind her, a wildcat screeched, only adding to Annie's sense of impending danger. And all the while, she watched those in the circle of the campfire's light. Ike had just returned to the table with Jigs from what she was sure had been a very enlightening conversation. She'd particularly liked the fact that Ike had come back with his rifle. Did he plan to confront the frontiersmen there and then?

"Our Father, which art in heaven," she murmured aloud—as much to soothe her dog as to quiet her own angst, "deliver us from evil. Though I fear that tonight we, like King David, are walking in the valley of the shadow of death, please, Lord, help me to fear no evil." *And give the men special wisdom, that they might know how best to deal with the intruders.*

She gazed at the outline of her cart, and though she couldn't make out her weapon in the darkness, she knew exactly where the musket was sheathed. If only she had it here with her. But she knew she couldn't hobble over to it without drawing unwanted attention to herself. It was vital that Ike and the others didn't lose their advantage.

She saw Ike take a pair of trenchers from Betsy and move in her direction, his rifle crooked under one arm, a lantern handle hooked over the other.

Two portions of food. He planned to come and eat with her. Annie's heart tripped over itself. *But that's only because he told the strangers I'm his wife,* she reminded herself.

Then he veered away. To her cart.

Annie willed him to retrieve her musket . . . which she saw him do after considerable juggling of his other burdens. It was as if he'd read her mind. Or, she mused, letting another possibility dance across her thoughts, as if the two of them were of like minds, kindred souls.

She had no idea what Ike's plan of action would be concerning their uninvited visitors. But she knew he would have one. Isaac Reardon was a man of principle, a veteran of the War of Independence, a town-starter. He took action.

Moving away from the cart, Ike came toward her. He'd obviously trimmed the lantern wick. It gave only a dim glow. When the overburdened man reached her, he held out both trenchers. "Here, hold mine, too, whilst I shuck the rest of this truck."

The food smelled as good as it looked. Heavily spiced with herbs she herself lacked. The women must have pooled more than just their vegetables for the stew. There was also bread—not biscuits, but Dutch oven–fresh bread—along with the butter she'd contributed. And a fried pie for dessert. A mouthwatering good feast.

Ike leaned their long-barreled weapons against the tree. He carefully set the lantern far enough away so that their faces would not
be exposed to those across the way but close enough to light their
plates. "I thought you might want to see what you eat," he said,
smiling, as he dropped down beside her.

His hand brushed hers as he took his own trencher from her.
Unintentional, she was sure, yet it stirred her blood. Suddenly, she
realized how compromised she must appear to Inga and the others.
Unless . . . "Do the women know the real reason why we're out
here alone?"

His wooden spoon stopped midway to his mouth. "Not yet. Is
your Brown Bess loaded and primed?"

"Aye. I keep it that way." She picked up a thick slice of bread to
butter.

"Good. If trouble comes, pass it to me to shoot."

Annie started to protest, then saw the wisdom in his words. He
would be a much truer shot, and she could be loading his spent
weapon as he used hers.

Before she could ask for his powder horn, his words *if trouble
comes* struck her. "You don't have a plan yet? Surely you're going
to do somethin' about 'em before we bed down for the night."

"No. There's nothin' we can do till they make a move agin us."

She set down her bread. This couldn't be true. "Pardon me, but
aren't you going to disarm them and—"

"*And what?*" His words were scarcely louder than a whisper, but
it was clear he didn't like her questioning his judgment. "We can't
take their weapons from 'em without just cause. That's called
stealin'."

She leaned closer, unintimidated by his glowering eyes. "But
you do have just cause. They're lyin' about where they come
from—at least that Beckley fella is."

"That still don't give us enough reason to take away their only
protection and their means of huntin' for food."

131

"But you know as well as I do that they're up to no good. If it was Indians ridin' in, you wouldn't wait for them to take the first shot."

"Only if they had paint smeared on their faces. You see, Indians are more honest about their intentions. They let you know if they're set on takin' your scalp."

Annie slammed down her trencher. "So all you're gonna do is wait and hope they don't shoot us in our sleep?"

"Keep your voice down," he ground out, glancing across the clearing. "And eat your supper. You need to keep up your strength."

"Aye, it does look that way, doesn't it?" She scooped a heap onto her wooden spoon. "'Specially since I have to stand guard over my property all night."

"*Women.*" Ike slammed down his own plate, the spoon rattling against the hardwood.

"*Men.*"

Annie stared back long enough to show him she wasn't cowed; then she picked up her plate and began to eat, though she no longer had any taste for her supper.

Ike shoveled in his own food as if he were devouring an enemy. Not another word did he utter during the remainder of the meal.

But then what else could he say, if he was going to do nothing but sit around and wait till the culprits shot someone?

~

Ike gulped his food down as fast as a hungry wolf. The sooner this meal was over, the better. The impudent widow had called his very manhood into question. Such gall. Widow, ha! She probably wasn't a widow at all. Any man married to such an obstinate woman would think twice about returning to her after the war. Most likely, he just let her think he'd been killed to get out of her clutches.

132

Their meal finally finished, he took her plate without a word and left her to rejoin the others. He needed to see what the hunters were up to anyway.

The men had all left the long table and lounged on blankets around the dying campfire, while two of the women did the dishes at one end of the table and the others put the clean ones back into the wagons. Ike heard Inga order Renate to put the younger children to bed.

Jigs, never at a loss for words, was carrying the conversation with the visitors. "So, you say you were downriver of the Nashville settlement. Have any of you ever gone as far as the Mississippi? Better yet, all the way down to New Orleans? I hear the French have themselves some real—" he shot a glance at Rolf—"a real prosperous town there."

Ike couldn't tell if Jigs had told Bremmer or Smith the plan yet, so he stepped up behind the German. "Brother Rolf, I was wonderin' if I could make the borrow of your whetstone. I can't seem to find mine. There's a rough spot on my awl, and I need to start punchin' holes in the moccasins I'm makin'."

"Sure t'ing." Bremmer lumbered to his feet. Snagging a lantern from the table, he strode with Ike toward his wagon.

As they did, Ike heard one of the strangers—the skinny one—say, "Your tall friend don't seem none too friendly."

Ken answered. "Oh, that's just his way. He likes to keep to hisself."

Jigs laughed. "Not as much as he likes keepin' his wife to hisself."

When Ike and Rolf reached the Bremmer wagon, the hulking blacksmith climbed aboard and hung the lantern from a hook above.

Waiting below, Ike spoke in a low voice. "I don't really need a whetstone, but find it for me anyway. We don't want them to get

133

suspicious. I'm just here to find out if Jigs has had a chance to speak to you and Ken about the strangers yet."

Without slowing in his search through his toolbox, Bremmer answered. *"Nein."*

"These men are lyin' about where they came from. They're up to no good, and we need to be ready for trouble. Just go to bed like usual, like nothin' is amiss. Then lay at your tent flap with your musket at the ready. I doubt those hunters will wait too long after we're all bedded down to make their move."

"But if I lay me down at da flap, mine Inga, she vill vonder."

"Tell her what you have to, but not until you've blown out your lantern. You know how clear everyone can see your shadow when it's lit. And these men will be watchin' us as close as we're watchin' them. Tell Ken to do the same."

"Found it!" Brother Rolf called in a booming voice. He leaned out the back of the wagon with a small whetstone in his palm.

Ike pretended to receive it and stuff it down the neck of his belted shirt.

As the two returned to the other men, Ike took the lantern from Rolf and started for his own wagon to fetch his cut leather pieces, his awl, and work board. On the way there, he couldn't help remembering how shy Annie had been this afternoon when he'd come to size the leather to her feet. Her cheeks had turned beet red when he'd traced a line around each foot with a charred stick.

A man would think two different women lived in that graceful shape of hers, she was so infuriatingly changeable.

Ike stopped and just stood several yards from his wagon, contemplating her slender toes, the turn of her ankle. Shaking off his unruly thoughts, he hurried on, lecturing himself on the seriousness of this night.

While at his wagon, he also collected his pistol—which he stuffed out of sight in his shirt—along with his moccasin makings.

Then, returning the borrowed lantern to the table, he overheard the frontiersman Annie had recognized.

"Whose dog is that?" Beckley rose up from his buffalo robe onto his knees.

Cap had escaped Annie! And Renate was feeding him supper scraps.

"That's Reardon's dog," Jigs said.

Ike started to call Cap to him but changed his mind. It would only center more attention on the dog—especially if he didn't obey.

"You sure he don't belong to some Scotswoman, a McSomething or other?"

"No," Jigs answered evenly. "It's just Reardon's raggedy old mutt. He's a good one, though. Aside from keepin' watch at night, his nose is as good as any hound's. He can track coon with the best of 'em."

"Do you mean," asked the Englishman, "you lads don't take turns on night watch?"

Picking his way back to Annie's camp in the dark, Ike smiled as he heard Jigs brag, "Don't have to. He's one keen-eared cur." Jigs was giving them what they'd surely think was very valuable information.

Ike's smile faded as he approached Annie.

Sitting back from the small circle of light, she leaned against the tree trunk with her musket in her lap, her expression just as resolute as when he'd left her.

Fine. If she didn't think he could protect her, let her sit there all night.

He dropped down Indian-fashion on the end of her bedding and laid out the deerskin pieces on his work board along with his awl and hammer.

"Surely you aren't gonna work on them Indian shoes now?

Tonight? That lantern needs to go out so we can see through the darkness better."

She was questioning his intelligence again. "Beckley was admirin' your dog," he retaliated in a drawl without looking up at her.

"Cap?" Frantically, she glanced around. "Oh, la."

"Call him to you. He don't need to be over there, makin' friends with 'em." He looked up at her now, daring her to defy him.

Annie's eyes, as always, reflected the night light to perfection. They stared at him a long stubborn moment. Finally, she summoned the dog as he'd asked, and Cap immediately came dashing across the grass toward her.

Ike scanned the men around the dimly glowing campfire in the distance. The other men seemed to be conversing lazily, but Beckley watched intently as the dog came running. Ike was sure he'd heard Annie's voice as she called her dog. Did he recognize it? Whatever, the man had been given something to ponder.

He would make his move tonight. Of that Ike had no doubt.

Cap came flying into Annie's lap, oblivious of her musket. A body would think he'd been gone a year from the eager greeting he gave his mistress.

"Good boy." She wrapped her arms around him and nuzzled his neck. "Lie down beside me. I'd like the company."

Ike was sure her last words were directed at him . . . an accusation that he wasn't a fit companion.

Catching himself falling into those disturbing thoughts again, he picked up his awl and struck it with his hammer. Harder than he'd intended. He controlled the strength of the next tap as he pretended to work on his tanned leather. All the while, he kept his eyes out of the light and on track of the three strangers, listening as their voices mixed casually with the others.

Ken and Betsy were the first to retreat inside their tent. Their lamplight set the canvas aglow, but for only a few moments. Ike wondered how Betsy would react when Ken told her about their guests.

Shortly, Rolf and Inga strolled with Lorna to her tent before they went to their own. It had been obvious that Lorna thought the three men beneath her station in life. Thank goodness she wouldn't have to be told of their true situation. Lorna didn't handle crises well.

Soon only Jigs remained with the men. And, true to his nature, out came his new flute, and he began to pipe a lively tune. Ike heard only snatches of the melody.

One of the men began to sing along.

Ike remembered to hammer again as he watched them.

Another man rose and moved away from the fire.

Ike blew out his own lantern, to see better.

The man headed down toward the pond.

"Where's he goin'?" Annie whispered from behind Ike.

"Probably just out to tend his business. You keep an eye on the others whilst I make sure."

After checking for his hunting knife, Ike moved deeper under the spruce. Hugging the treeline, he followed the man's progress. It was the gaunt hunter. Ike had to make sure the man didn't circle around and get behind Jigs. Or him and Annie, for that matter.

It turned out that the fellow really had just gone to take care of his nightly business. He returned to his companions as Jigs began piping a rendition of "Yankee Doodle Dandy," a song that had become very well known during the war. Originally adopted by the British soldiers to make sport of what they considered crude and uncultured Colonist troops, the song had been turned back on them by the patriots. Ike recalled what fun it had been to sing it whenever they had the redcoats on the run. Yankee Doodles chasing off the world's best-trained army.

Ike noted that none of the men sitting with Jigs joined in singing along with that one. If they'd been traders for the British and Tory supporters as Ike suspected, they wouldn't appreciate a reminder of their defeat.

With scarcely a pause, Jigs went from the lively tune into something slow and lilting. A pretty, lonesome-sounding melody. Behind Ike, the widow began to hum along. Softly, throatily, hauntingly. Ike wondered if the song made her feel as lonely as it did him.

Even if it did, even if the two of them were the lonesomest people in the vast wilderness, she was not the sort of woman a man would want to seriously consider. A woman with such an impertinent attitude was certainly not the kind a man would want to take for a wife. It would be best to just leave her at Henry's Station and go on without her. Let her disrupt the lives of those folks for a change.

Eventually the song came to an end, and Jigs, who'd been entertaining their dubious guests, rose and stretched. After a few mumbled words that Ike couldn't decipher, Jigs left the men for the bedroll he'd laid out in front of Lorna's tent.

Ike, who'd almost forgotten his own vigil during the song, came alert again. The heads of the three visitors dropped onto their pallets, and though Ike knew they'd wait until they thought everyone was asleep before making their move, he didn't like being so far away. It made him anxious. Even though Jigs and the others would be watching from their vantage points, it had always been hard for him to leave important things to others.

Something rustled close by. Annie.

She crawled up beside him. "It's gettin' cold." She wrapped one of her quilts around his shoulders, and another around her own, then settled next to him, her musket at her side. The song must have had the same effect on her as it had on him.

All the anger he'd been nursing disappeared like the morning dew. "Thanks. Get some sleep now. I'll wake you if somethin' stirs."

"How about we take turns sleepin'? Between me and Cap, we won't miss nothin'."

"As you wish." Though he didn't mean it, he didn't want to have words with her again. "I'll take the first watch. I'll wake you when the moon rises."

"Promise?"

"Lie down."

And she did. Wrapping a quilt around herself, she curled up right beside him. So close, there was no chance he'd fall asleep on his watch. No chance at all.

14

A low growl made its way into Annie's consciousness.

Cap.

She rolled onto her belly, her heart pounding as she tried to come fully awake.

Crouched on his haunches, the dog crawled off the pallet toward the wagons. In the moonless sky they were barely visible. Annie spied no movement; not even a single lightning bug dotted the blackness.

The strangers! How could she have forgotten?

Frantically, she reached for her musket.

It wasn't there!

Neither was Ike. Where was he?

He hadn't awakened her, and he had taken her weapon. And Cap was getting away. She stretched out a hand to stop him, but caught only a snatch of tail fur.

Ignoring her, the dog inched steadily forward.

Should she call him back? Or follow?

She spotted a faint outline of movement not far ahead of her dog—someone crawling toward the pasture end of the wagons. It had to be Ike.

But what was happening? Annie scanned the night-shrouded camp. Where were the strangers? What were they up to?

"Halt!" came a shout. "Get outten mine vagon!" Brother Bremmer had spotted the culprits. One, anyway.

"We got you boys covered." That sounded like Jigs.

Something crashed, the sound of splintered wood. A box of supplies?

Cap began to bark, shrill barking.

A flash of light. An explosion.

The gunshot came from camp.

Then shouting. From the left, the right.

"Who shot?" It sounded like Ken.

"Anyone hurt?" Jigs again.

Annie felt so helpless. If only she could see.

Another musket flashed and exploded from the circle of wagons. The ball slammed into wood with a thud.

A woman screamed.

More yelling.

And another burst of light and a blast so close that Annie recognized Ike's grim expression in the flare of gunpowder in his flash-pan. He was on his feet now, running toward the livestock.

Other footsteps, pounding, crashing into things.

Cap's bark changed to a vicious growl. A yelp. Then nothing. *Not Cap.* Annie sprang to her feet and raced for her dog.

"Hurry! Run!" The shout came from the direction of the livestock.

More pounding feet. A shadowy figure sped by, not more than a few feet from Annie.

Out in the pasture, Frank Beckley's face flamed bright with a rifle's flare when he fired.

142

The horses! They whinnied wildly in all the uproar. From the thundering of their hooves, some had surely bolted. But they'd all been hobbled for the night. Beckley! He must have loosed the tethers around their front legs.

Horses galloped past Annie. Three of them. With riders aboard. The outlaws.

Another flash and shot. Ike again.

"I'm shot!" came the amazed cry of one of the bandits.

None of the horses slowed. If anything, they sped away faster.

"Jigs, are you hurt?" Ike called from the pasture.

"No. Are you?"

"No. Ken, Rolf, where are you?"

From opposite ends of the camp, they, too, shouted back that they were unharmed.

"My dog—what about my dog?" Annie cried as she reached the first wagon. "Light a lantern."

Somebody stirred the banked embers of the campfire and lit a stick from the glowing coals. Jigs. He took it to a lamp that had been left on the makeshift dining table.

Almost instantly the darkness was dispelled.

Annie and the men all closed in on the lamplight.

"Is it safe now?" came Betsy's voice from inside her tent.

"Aye, you can come out now, sweet pea," Ken called as he hurried to his wife.

The Bremmer children also peeked out of their tent, along with their mother, German blue eyes all round as full moons.

"What happened?" Wolfgang, the oldest boy, asked, his voice quiet and filled with awe.

Annie didn't have time for explanations. "My dog. Help me find my dog."

"Who cares about your old dog?" Lorna crashed out of her tent in her nightgown, stumbling across a tent rope as she came. "A ball

143

tore through the canvas. It could've killed me! Was it Indians? Were we attacked by Indians?"

Annie didn't wait for Lorna's question to be answered. She grabbed a lantern from her cart, lit it from the campfire, and started searching for Cap.

She found him lying beside the Bremmer wagon. Setting down her light, she dropped to her knees and ran her hands over him. His hairy chest rose and fell softly. Thank God, he was still alive. Just unconscious. A bump on his head, damp and tacky, told her why.

"Renate," she called, "fetch me some clean rags and some water."

Ike came and knelt beside Annie. He placed his hand on the dog's shoulder. "He's breathin' good. He should be all right."

A slap of anger replaced Annie's fear. If, as wagon master, he had done something about those intruders earlier, her dog wouldn't be lying there near death. She shot him her most condemning look.

Ike's expression turned to stone. Abruptly, he rose. "Light all the lanterns," he ordered. "Find out what those pirates made off with. Jigs, let's go see which horses they rode out on."

"Aye," he said, watching Ike and Annie from a few yards away. "They came in on two and rode out on three."

Eventually, Annie's dog began to whimper under the cool compresses she applied with the help of the oldest Bremmer girl and the caressing hands of Isolda and Otto. Cap blinked a couple of times; then he looked up at Annie with those faithfully worshiping eyes of his and licked her hand.

Her trusted friend and helpmate had awakened and knew who she was. Tears swam in Annie's eyes. She turned her head away from the children—she didn't want them to see her weakness. Swiping moisture away, she saw that the lanterns in camp glowed brightly, and the men were taking a couple of them out to the pasture.

From the Bremmers' wagon, Inga complained about a keg of spilled flour. Betsy called out that a sack of cornmeal was missing from her stores. All the while, Lorna kept asking everyone who passed if they were sure they hadn't been attacked by Indians.

Cap staggered to his feet and licked Otto across the mouth.

The little boy gave the dog a hug . . . and Annie knew for sure all would be well with her pet. The anger she'd been harboring against Ike began to dissipate as she rose to her feet . . . and suddenly, she felt a throbbing in the bandaged one.

She'd forgotten to stay off her injury. Limping to the table, she sat down in one of Betsy's chairs. She'd send Wolfie to fetch her crutch when he returned with the men from counting the horses.

A wave of exhaustion overtook her. Almost in a daze, she stared into the rekindled campfire.

Betsy sat down beside her and handed her a cup of tepid coffee. "I will never doubt God's mercy again," the young woman said in her thin airy voice. She placed a hand over the new life growing inside her. "As soon as Kenny told me about the men, I started praying."

"That's all we had left to do, since Ike Reardon refused to deal with those thieves forthwith." Annie's bitterness was slower to fade than she thought.

Betsy placed a hand on Annie's arm and gave it a companionable squeeze—an unspoken yet gentle reminder that Annie would have to forgive him.

The men, along with Wolfie, left the animals and returned to the table.

"They took three of Ike's best packhorses," Wolfie volunteered.

Brother Bremmer set a lantern on the table, then walked directly to Annie. He took her hand and patted it, his eyes sad.

Dread filled her.

"I ask to be da one to tell you, Annie. Da calf is dead. Shot by da stray bullet."

145

First Cap was felled and now her Shy Baby? "You're sure?"

"*Ja*. Ike, he check real goot."

Annie swung to Ike.

He just stood there, a few feet back, staring guiltily at her. With nothing to say.

Her calf had been sacrificed for his stubborn honor.

"Da calf, it is dead?" Inga's words broke into their silent stand-off. She walked up to her husband. "Rolf, you go out dere and gut it now. Hang it up to bleed before it spoils. Tomorrow ve haf special meal for da Sabbat'. Ve haf *veal*."

~

All the next afternoon, Annie's anger grew as she watched Inga, across the expanse of grass, turn and baste the calf on the spit. And now they all were sitting down to devour Shy Baby. Even if she turned away, Queenie's bawling for her missing offspring would still be a constant reminder of last night's direful events that led to the meat being served for today's Sabbath meal.

Since the moment of her loss, Annie had sat under the spraddle-limbed spruce, seething with bitterness and resentment—especially toward Inga, that heartless, greedy woman who saw the calf's death as a boon. Except for taking care of her personal needs, the only time Annie had left her pallet was when she'd gone out to milk Queenie and try to console the bewildered animal with a few sympathetic words.

For the most part, the rest of the company had given her a wide berth. Everyone except Ike. At his insistence, she now wore moccasins on her feet, secured with ties around the ankle and padded with fine muskrat fur. She'd insisted on paying for them with a generous amount of milk, cheese, and honey. She would not be beholden to the likes of Isaac Reardon or any of these people, her resolve now more firm about that than ever.

Ike had finished the soft leather footwear before the Sabbath service . . . a church service she'd also shunned. She'd refused to be a hypocrite and pretend she had love and forgiveness in her heart, when she couldn't bear to look at a single one of the weak-minded men, every one of whom might have acted sooner, rather than costing her calf its life. As for Inga, Annie didn't even want to be on the same mountain with that woman who saw Shy Baby's death only as a special treat for her gluttonous appetite.

Oh, Annie remembered Ike's speech that first day, all right—the one where he'd as much as told her she wouldn't be welcome in their group if she didn't do whatever he or Brother Bremmer deemed Christian. Well, the only way she'd be able to hold her tongue until they reached an overmountain settlement was to steer clear of the lot of them.

A child's pained cry caught Annie's attention. Even at this distance, she caught Isolda's astonished expression as her hand covered her cheek.

Inga had struck her.

And, as usual, Brother Bremmer did nothing but sit in silence. The man shared equal blame for allowing his wife's mistreatment of the little girl.

Annie could bear to watch the whole gruesome scene no longer. Whether Ike approved of her walking on her injury or not, she clambered to her feet and, with the help of her crutch, moved into the cool, enclosing darkness of the woods behind her. She wanted to get far enough away so she couldn't see them or hear them . . . or smell the calf meat they'd been roasting on a spit most of the day.

She didn't return to camp until almost dark—and then only because Queenie needed milking, and she sure didn't want any of those cannibals touching her grieving cow.

Once she'd finished the task, Annie gazed down into the bucket. It held thrice the milk she'd gotten from Queenie yesterday when Shy Baby was still nursing. Annie's bitterness gained new strength. She could almost hear the German woman's accent as Annie imagined Inga's pleasured response to the added milk—another boon the calf's death would provide.

Annie herself would not be able to stomach any of Shy Baby's milk tonight. So after taking the bucket to Betsy—the only adult she could bear to look at—Annie hobbled to her beehive and closed it up in preparation for the next day's travel, then went to her cart. She fed her caged chickens and put them safely inside, and, taking some cheese and biscuits from her food box for her own meager supper, she headed back to her pallet.

There, she noticed firewood had been gathered . . . several pieces arranged inside a ring of stones, ready to put to flame. Someone had also fetched her kettle. It hung from an iron tripod—not hers—and straddled the arranged wood. She wondered who'd done this kindness. Had it been Ike? Her heart softened . . . then hardened. This was just their paltry way of repaying her for the meat her calf had provided.

In a flare of rage, she swung back with her crutch to destroy their measly gesture—

"Annie!"

Little Isolda's voice stopped her just before she struck the tripod.

The child and her younger brother came running across the grassy field, Isolda holding high a flaming stick. They'd been sent to light the fire.

And, of course, she'd let them. No matter how Annie felt about the others, she would never take her anger out on the children.

"I got some of Betsy's India tea," Otto said, proudly holding out a wrinkled wad of paper. "She says it's for your Sabbath."

"Isn't that nice of her," Annie said, taking the offering. "But it wouldn't be nearly so like the Sabbath 'lessen you and Isolda share it with me."

Isolda, jamming the fire stick in among the kindling, glanced sheepishly up at Annie. "You would invite us to be with you after we—" tears pooled in Isolda's eyes—"after we ate Prince?" The last phrase came out in a whisper.

Prince? Who was Prince?

Then Annie remembered. Yesterday she and the children had renamed Shy Baby. Yesterday. It seemed like a month ago.

"I know it was a wicked thing to do. You hate me, don't you?"

"She don't hate us," Otto chimed in. "She knows Mama made us eat him." He grinned up at Annie with a cute, if practiced, tilt of the jaw. "Don't you?"

Annie suddenly realized why Isolda's face had been slapped. It had been because of the pair's refusal to eat the calf. Annie reached out and cupped one of Isolda's round cheeks. "I'd love it if you two would join me for tea. But first, you'll have to go to my cart and fetch my teapot and two more of my pewter cups."

By the time the tea was ready and served, darkness surrounded them. As long as Annie didn't look in the direction of the campfire on the other side of the clearing, she could almost believe that she and the children were enjoying the treat all alone—a treat made even tastier when Otto insisted they all add lots of honey and cream to it.

Sitting in a small circle with the two little ones, Annie nursed her tea while Otto told her of the cave he'd found while out exploring that day.

"A cave so big," he said, "that a whole family of bears could live in it. They'd have a place to eat and sleep and ever'thing."

"My goodness, that is large," Annie agreed as she watched Isolda's head wag in denial. "But I think maybe it wasn't quite that big. And it sounds to me like your wandering' is gettin' a far piece offen the path."

"*No.*" Isolda's blonde braids swung with an emphatic shake of the head. "I never let Otto get past the hearin' of the wagons. We come back to the sound o' your whip a-crackin' lots o' times."

"Isolda. Otto." Brother Bremmer's voice startled Annie, since he'd come within the glow of her campfire unnoticed. "You mama vant you to go get ready for da sleep, *mach schnell.*"

Isolda sprang to her feet in a flash, her fear of being punished evident. Handing Annie her cup, the child bobbed into a curtsy. "Thank you for the tea, Annie." She started away, then turned back. She shot a quick glance to her father, then bent down to Annie, "And thank you for still liking us."

"You're most welcome," Annie whispered back, just for Isolda's ears.

Isolda grabbed her brother's hand and pulled him to his feet. "Come."

"No!" Otto jerked free.

Otto ran to Annie, still sitting on the ground. He threw his arms around her, almost knocking the metal cup from her hand, and planted a sloppy kiss on her cheek.

Such spontaneous exuberance couldn't have been staged. Annie felt as if she'd been given a gift. The child had finally stolen her heart . . . as his sister had some time ago.

"I love you," Otto said, then whirled away and ran on his little windmill legs. "Beat you home," he yelled at his sister who chased after him across the darkened meadow.

But Brother Bremmer did not follow. He stared down at Annie. "Ve need to talk."

Feeling at a disadvantage on the ground, she struggled to her feet. As she did, he took her arm.

"Please, I'd prefer not to be helped," she said, her words more a demand than a request.

The minister immediately let go. "As you vish."

Once she'd steadied herself with her crutch, Brother Bremmer spoke again in his deep, rumbly Germanic voice. "Da day ve find you on da road, I speak to Ike on behalf of you. I know vat is like to be da bond servant. Inga *und* me, ve be da bond servants ven ve come to America. Seven years. So I say to myself, Annie, she is

goot Christian *fräulein*. Hard vorker. I don' say not'ing when Ike
t'inks you is vidow. I leave dat to you. But dis bad blood you haf
for Ike on Gott's Sabbat', dis is bad t'ing. You must go to him, ask
him to forgive you."

He thinks I *should ask forgiveness?* The very idea sent heat rushing to Annie's head. Didn't the man know *she* was the injured
party? "I think you'd better go back to your own camp before I say
things you don't want to hear."

"You haf acted all day like *ve* shoot da calf—not da bad mans. If
you haf anyt'ing to say dat vill redeem you in mine eyes, or Gott's,
say da vords now."

"Redeem me in your eyes? You, a man who will not even defend
your own child from that witch you call a wife? You are not my
minister of God. I will not answer to you." With that declaration,
she stiffened her back.

Brother Bremmer's face darkened. He clenched his fists. For a
moment, Annie thought he would strike her.

He didn't. The hulking man spun on his heel and stalked away.

Watching him go, Annie's conscience assaulted her. She
couldn't believe she'd said such mean things to this Christian pastor who'd always treated her fairly and kindly.

Until tonight.

Heavenly Father, you know I'm right. I am.

Still, no confirmation came to her from out of the vast darkness
above, no comfort.

All she heard was her own stubborn declaration echoing in her
ears.

151

15

In the week following the death of Annie's calf, her foot healed nicely—with the aid of her crutch and the moccasins layered with soft fur. But not her anger. It continued to fester and grow rock hard at its core like a nasty boil. And, as with a boil, she couldn't ignore it. Neither could she ignore the pain of her loss or her conscience as the two warred within her.

Annie, her cart, and her dog continued to be placed near the front of the train as before the accident, but instead of Jigs at the lead, Ike now rode just ahead of her with the pack animals. Annie rarely looked at him and never spoke unless a question was directed straight at her. She would do and say only what was necessary to reach Henry's Station. She'd made up her mind that she would not travel with these people one step farther than that. Not even if they pleaded with her to come to their valley. She intended to find much better neighbors.

She'd also stopped reading the New Testament Mrs. White had given her. Despite what it said about the virtues of Christian charity toward others, she felt wholly justified in her anger over Ike's foolish handling of a dangerous situation, and her ire had spread to the men who had followed him like dumb sheep. Then there was Inga Bremmer . . . this woman, so quick to watch for a splinter in another's eye when she couldn't see the logs in her own.

Cap, who'd been trotting alongside the yoked team, spun around and, tail wagging, ran past Annie toward the rear. Probably to greet Isolda and Otto. Aside from when Ike rode back to check on the other outfits, the children were the only ones who ran freely between the wagons while they were rolling.

Annie recalled that each of the two little ones now wore a pair of ankle-tied moccasins—smaller replicas of her own. She smiled sadly. It was the one good thing that had come out of that cursed day with the outlaws.

Flipping her thick braid off her shoulder, she clutched tighter onto her crutch and increased her step until she reached her bull's side. Ruben needed to be reminded to keep his pace steady whenever her dog was not near to nip at his heels. Annie had no intention of being accused of needlessly holding up the others.

Cap returned within a few seconds, not with the children but with Betsy.

"Thought I'd stroll on up here and see how you're gettin' along." The frail mother-to-be sounded a little out of breath and looked flushed as she brushed some fine brown strands from her temple.

"I'm doin' fine. How are you? Is your baby givin' you any more trouble?"

"I'm keepin' my breakfast down a little better now. And you know what an old hen Ken can be. He won't let me carry so much as a bucket of water anymore. My, isn't it a lovely day?" she added with an endearing smile.

As Betsy glanced to one side of the wooded trail, Annie felt obliged to do the same, although they'd been threading their way through a forest of white-trunked birch for some time now. In stark contrast to the trees' light trunks, a bed of rich green ferns blanketed the ground around them. It really was quite lovely.

And Betsy was her usual lovely balm to Annie's mood, smoothing the prickles from it.

"Aye," Annie agreed. "It's so much cooler down in this hollow than when we crossed that stony field of nothin' but mountain laurel."

"Ike told Kenny last night that if nothin' holds us up, we'll be gettin' to that big settlement along the Tennessee River by the end of next week."

"Henry's Station? Next week?" Only a week and a half more of putting up with these people. Except, of course, for Betsy . . . and even Ken who was too young and inexperienced to know what he should've done. Those two were dears. But the others . . .

"Then on to our beautiful new valley," Betsy continued. "I can hardly wait. Just imagine, to sleep in a bed and have a roof over my head again. And Ike says it don't 'pear as if anybody's ever lived in the valley before. He ain't found no sign of an Indian village, no pieces of pottery or baskets. Just an odd arrowhead or two. We'll be the first people to ever make it our home. The very first. Don't that seem a wondrous thing?"

Annie grinned at this will-o'-the-wisp of a lass. "It won't seem so wondrous when you have to start clearin' that virgin land for plantin'. Some of them old trees might prove awful big."

"Well, I don't want to cut down near all the trees." Betsy surveyed the scene around her. "I purely do hope we have some birches on our land. I love 'em even in the winter." She glanced from the trees back to Annie. "Wouldn't it be pleasurin' to have a grove like this one separatin' your house from mine? And a path comin' through 'em. And lots of birds and squirrels. I want there to be a sight more critters than what's up here in the high country."

155

"Aye, that does sound real pretty. I hope you find yourself a place just like that."

"And you, too, Annie." The timbre of her voice changed, took on more strength. "You *are* comin' to the valley with us, ain't you? Brother Bremmer mentioned this mornin' that you might not be goin' all the way. When I asked why, he just shrugged and walked off."

So that was why Betsy had come up here "just to see how she was gettin' along." "Reardon's valley isn't the onliest one over-mountain. I hear tell there's valley after valley all the way to the Mississippi nobody's ever lived in. And America now stretches as far north as them Great Lakes and down almost to that Frenchy town in the south."

"But, Annie, that don't answer my question. Are you or ain't you comin' to our valley with us?"

"It's best I don't." Annie glanced ahead to where Ike rode at the front of his pack train. He looked as tall in the saddle and as sure of himself as ever. "I fear I couldn't trust my property to Mr. Reardon again. 'Specially if there was danger afoot."

"But Annie, I thought he did a real fine job, chasin' off them bad men. Him and all the other men was so brave. I was real scared for my Kenny—he never been to war or nothin'. But he's so brave. I'll never be a-feared again, long as I'm with him."

"I'm sure that must feel real good. But you didn't have your calf shot dead and your dog pert near killed. I, for one, don't feel all that protected."

"But somethin' like that run-in with them bad men don't happen but once in a blue moon. That shouldn't keep us from bein' neighbors. I'll pine somethin' awful if you ain't nearby. Lorna and me, well, we don't seem to have the same interests. And Inga, she comes from a foreign country with different ways of doin' things."

"Ways I cannot abide."

156

Betsy's lips parted. In her roundabout questioning, she obviously hadn't been prepared for that answer.

Before Betsy could say anything more, Annie continued, wanting to put an end to this subject. "I already said as much to Brother Bremmer when he come to speak to me. He understands, same as me, that it's best I leave the train at Henry's Station. I am purely sorry we can't be neighbors, Betsy. But it isn't to be."

"Oh, Annie, are you sure? Have you prayed about this? Searched your heart? The Bible calls on us to forgive and love our neighbors just like we do our own selves."

"And that's why I can't be neighbor to some people. Believe this, Betsy, my stayin' behind at the settlement is best for everyone." *Except, maybe, for little Isolda,* Annie lamented to herself.

Betsy looked more determined than before. "We all have another week to pray on this." She shifted her gaze toward the front, to Ike, then smiled that sad smile of hers. "Aye, we got so much to pray about."

~

Ike was dripping wet, but even a soaking didn't cool him on this muggy day. Just before dawn, clouds had let loose with what he was sure was every drop they had in them. Now, several hours later, a creek made swift and dangerous from the rain had stopped the train for more than a half hour while the men labored to get the wagons and livestock across. And this was the second such creek they'd had to cross this morning.

Only two or three more days to Henry's Station, he kept telling himself as he stood on the other side of the roaring stream, holding a line he and Jigs had made by tying several ropes together.

Jigs had returned across the river and now stood opposite Ike, beckoning the women and children to start across.

Annie strode down to the water, surefooted now that the gash had healed. She'd tied her moccasins around her neck, and her skirts were pulled up between her legs and tucked into her apron's waistband, displaying a lot more leg than was proper, yet she didn't seem to care one whit.

He wished he, too, could be so disinterested in her bare legs, but he had a hard time keeping his gaze above her waist.

Grasping the line with one hand, she started across as if she had not the least fear of being swept to her death by the boulder-strewn torrent.

Yet, as he watched the lithe figure come toward him, the water whipping all around her, Ike had no doubt of the power of this mountain stream. His wagon and team had been stuck in the middle of it, buffeted and rocked by the raging waters when a hitching chain broke in two. This *after* he'd insisted Annie McGregor wasn't capable of driving her own outfit across. And all the while he'd been down in the water replacing the chain, he'd felt her eyes boring into him from the bank above. Even though he never actually caught her staring. Or, for that matter, ever caught her chatting with the other women.

The obstinate female had refused to mix with anyone on the train since the night her calf was killed.

Annie quickly reached his side. Ike thought he caught a quirk of her lips as she passed him, but he refused to give her the satisfaction of turning his head to make sure.

But his curiosity soon got the best of him. And when it did, he couldn't be sure if the smile she sported was to taunt him or to welcome her dog. Cap, who'd ridden over on her cart, was running to greet her.

Ike schooled his attention on his own business again and saw that Betsy came next. But not one of her toes touched water. Her always-watchful husband was carrying her across.

Inga and her older daughter, Renate, came next. Inga, as stubborn as Annie, tucked her skirts up and came forward without hesitation.

Renate wasn't so brave. Ike couldn't hear Jigs above the water's roar, but he saw his comrade's mouth working quite a lot before the man convinced the timid girl to step into the powerful current. Gripping the line with both hands, Renate still lost her footing as she neared Ike's side. He thought he would have to jump in after her. But she hung on to the line and managed to regain her footing. Then, drenched up to her neck, her face frozen with fear, she stepped onto solid ground.

Ike reached down and pulled the half-grown girl up the bank. "You did just fine," he said to encourage her. "You were very brave."

She attempted a shy smile, and Ike noticed how very much like Isolda's it was. Both girls were so withdrawn—nothing like their rambunctious brothers. Or their parents.

Lorna's turn came next, and she, too, balked. She hadn't so much as removed her shoes, and she refused to budge . . . no matter how much talking Jigs did.

Finally, Jigs tied his end of the rope around a skinny chestnut trunk and scooped her up into his arms and started across.

Watching them, Ike didn't know who was worse—Lorna, who always wanted to be babied and pampered, or Annie, who had asked for nothing except to be allowed to join the train. Oh, but there *had* been that second request . . . her insistence that he deal with the thieves *before* they committed a crime, which no honorable man could do. Despite their losses, he could not have acted any differently.

Yet Annie refused to understand. For some unfathomable reason, women simply did not think logically. Even his own mother. Had Louvenia come along, she could have been a great help with these troublesome women. But, no, his mother had to stay behind to greet a newborn grandchild who would never remember if she was there or not. *Lord in heaven,* he asked silently, *why did you make women so blame puzzling?*

159

Lorna, high and dry in Jigs's arms, looked quite smug as he lowered her onto the bank. "Thank you, Mr. Terrell," she said sweetly. "You were as gallant as Sir Walter Raleigh. More gallant. He only gave up his cloak to keep a lady's feet dry."

This girl used words like they were cash money to buy whatever she wanted.

Jigs wasn't so bad at it himself. He whipped his tricorn from his mop of black hair and swept it before him as he bowed low, oblivious of his own dripping leggings. "Ah, this is a mere hint of my gentlemanly traits. A true lady like yourself cannot help but summon them forth."

Ike stifled a groan. At least Lorna was the last on the other side, and they could be on their way again.

But where were the little ones? Had they crossed inside a wagon without his spotting them? "Inga," he called to their mother. "Where are Otto and Isolda?"

Sitting on a log replacing her shoes and stockings, Inga glanced up and looked around. "Dey haf not crossed?" She shoved her foot into the second shoe and stood up. "Rolf! Is Otto *mit* you?"

Brother Rolf raised up from checking the hoof of one of his oxen. *"Nein."*

Ike strode up the bank to the waiting outfits. "Has anyone seen Isolda and Otto?"

Searching glances were his only answer.

"I'll check in my wagon," Ken offered. "Mayhap they're hiding out in there."

The others did likewise, and all came up empty. One by one, they started calling the children, making enough noise to wake the dead or, at least, to silence every other creature this side of the roaring creek.

Then Annie lifted her whip from its slot.

Surely the woman wasn't so callous as to start off without them.

160

She came toward Ike, that determined expression on her face. Did she intend to use the whip on him for losing the children?

"Stretch out that rope again," she ordered. "I'll go across and see if the crack of my whip will scare 'em up. That's what Isolda listens for when they're too far from the wagons to see us."

Now the woman was trying to take over his job. But she did have a point. The youngsters had most likely gone exploring while the train was stopped. "You stay here, finish dryin' off. I'll see to 'em."

"Here, take this." She thrust the whip into his hand and turned back before he could refuse it. It was bad enough, her getting him to do her bidding, without making him use something of hers to do it.

Jigs must have read his mind, because he gave a mocking salute as Ike started down the bank again. Ike was already several yards into the water, threading his way across, when Wolfgang came slogging after him.

"Wait for me!" The lad held Annie's old musket over his head.

Reaching the far shore, Ike walked a good stone's throw up the path from the noise of the creek. Unable to see more than a few yards into the woods on either side, he yelled the children's names several times. Getting no response, he unfurled the whip. As he did, he noticed how ragged the thin braid of leather was. It wouldn't be much longer before Annie would need another.

He slung it up into the air and flicked his wrist, causing it to snap. Because of its condition, the lash didn't make as sharp a crack as he would've liked. Perhaps he should start working on a new one for Annie tonight.

Am I really that moonstruck? This one would do just fine until they got to Henry's Station. After what Annie said to Betsy the other day, her staying in the Watauga settlement region would be best for them all. He swung the whip up again.

"Watch out!"

Wolfgang had come up behind, and the sight of the musket resting on his shoulder—Annie's musket—irritated Ike more than

161

when she'd given him the whip. "Does Annie think I don't have enough sense to look after myself?"

"I don't know." Wolfie looked confused. "I thought we could shoot off the Brown Bess. The kids would hear that for sure."

Ike cracked the lash again. "Aye. But the sound would be so loud, its echoes would bounce back and forth in the hollows till a body couldn't tell where it came from. It might send the youngsters off in the wrong direction."

After several minutes of cracking the whip and shouting, Ike knew he would have to start tracking. He checked along one side of the trace for children's footprints going off into the forest. It didn't take long for him to find some, but within a few yards they returned to the trail.

He followed several other sets of tracks, but they all circled back to where the wagons had been—Otto was being his typically busy little self.

"What if them bad men circled back and took 'em?" Wolfie said, following along behind.

Ike had avoided that thought until the lad's words forced him to consider the possibility. Though he saw no evidence of foul play, he had to consider the chance that the children had been taken to be held for ransom.

16

"Wolfie, go back and fetch Jigs," Ike said as he found yet another set of child's prints going off the trace into a weedy tangle near the creek, only to return again. "Tell him I need a hand with some tracking. And tell your pa I ain't found no sign of foul play."

"Then can I come back?" Wolfie's face beamed with excitement.

"I reckon. If your pa lets you. Bring my rifle when you come."

To the lad this obviously seemed like a great wilderness adventure. But not to Ike. Worry gnawed on his gut. If those two young'uns had attempted to cross the storm-ravaged creek anywhere around here, their bodies would be miles downstream, battered on the rocks and by now jammed under a boulder or a log.

Ike didn't watch Wolfie go with his message. Instead he began making a wide arc about fifty yards east of the trail, circling toward the creek, hoping to intersect the point at which the children had left the area. He came across some trampled ferns, but saw no footprints. He followed the direction of the freshly broken stems, but stopped when he found only the recent hoofprints of a deer.

He moved again toward the creek, struggling past a prickly patch of berry brambles. The density of the woods seemed to be conspiring with the roar of the creek to hide the children from him. He tried not to think the worst. "Lord, please keep them safe until I get to them," he murmured.

"Ike!" It was Jigs.

"Over here!" he shouted. With Jigs covering the north side of the trace, they would find the children's trail that much sooner.

Jigs wasn't the only one who had returned with Wolfie. Brother Rolf and Ken also tramped their way toward Ike.

He waved them off. "Stay on the trace till we find which direction the kids took."

"*Ja, ja.*" Brother Rolf stopped instantly. After looking at the ground around him, he backtracked, pulling Wolfie with him. "Mine Inga, she frets." His own voice trembled with concern as he raised his worried eyes to Ike. "Ve need to find dem *kinders* soon. She t'ink maybe da bad ones get dem. Or a bear."

"We'll pick up their tracks before long. Jigs, you start upstream of the trace and circle around toward it."

When Ike finally came across two sets of children's footprints leaving the area, he was relieved to see no larger ones accompanying them. But they were much too close to the creek and heading downstream. From the spacing, it appeared the children had been running. Not surprising. Otto ran more often than he walked.

Ike called out several times, then stepped back into enough of a clearing to snap the whip a few times just in case they were within hearing distance.

Neither child responded, but the men did. Their shouts returned to Ike and, within a couple of minutes, all but Jigs had worked their way through the undergrowth to Ike.

When he showed them what he'd found, Brother Rolf turned to his son. "Volfie, go tell you mama ve find da trail."

"Aye," Ken Smith concurred. "And tell my Betsy to just rest up whilst I'm gone. It shouldn't take us long now."

"Oh, all right." Wolfie was clearly not pleased to be sent to the wagons again. "But I'll be right back."

Coming at a lope, Jigs barely dodged the lad's hasty departure. Serious for once, he examined the children's tracks for a few yards, then turned to Ike and the others. "They're following the water southwest. But the trace we're takin' leaves this creek and hooks to the north."

"I know," Ike said. "And just below here, the creek shoots through that narrow-walled canyon."

The two exchanged glances, but neither voiced the fear they shared. God willing, the children were safe, merely caught out on some ledge or boulder, unable to get back. But if that were so, they needed to hurry more than ever. "Spread out. Look for other signs."

～

For the second time, Annie saw Wolfie thread his way across the creek to the waiting wagons, her musket tucked under his arm.

Inga ran down the bank and met him as he charged up it. "Vat? Vat?" she cried, her distress showing more by the second. "You find mine *kinders*?"

Annie couldn't help but feel sympathy for the woman. Inga was wringing her hands like they were Monday morning's wash.

Wolfie kept his distance as he answered his mother. "No. But we found the way they went. We'll find 'em soon." He wheeled away from her. "I only come to get Ike's rifle."

As he headed for Ike's saddle horse, Annie followed him. "Are all the men going looking?"

"Aye," he said hesitantly, suspiciously, as if he thought she was going to make him stay behind.

"Then leave me my musket. We might need it here."

165

"Oh, sure." With a flicker of regret, the lad handed it over, then pulled Ike's rifle from its scabbard. He wheeled around and took off for the water again at a dead run.

Watching Wolfie cross, Annie noted that the current had eased up considerably in the time they'd been waiting—first to get the outfits across and now while the men hunted for the children. Annie was amazed that Isolda had let Otto get so far away that they'd become lost. And as agitated as Inga was, Annie didn't even want to think about the severity of the punishment that would befall the little girl when she did return.

Betsy came alongside Annie. "Lorna thinks those bandits has hid out the young'uns to draw our men away from camp." Her voice quavered. "So they can come and rob us . . . and do whatever else they might have on their minds."

The thought hadn't occurred to Annie. She glanced at the Reardon outfit and saw Lorna seated on the jockey box, the reins to the giant work team in both hands. The girl was prepared to take off at the first sign of danger.

"Ken left me his musket," Betsy went on. "But I don't know how to load it."

"I'd be glad to show you."

"Would you? Kenny always treats me like I'm too weak to do anything. Oh, and don't repeat what I said about the bad men to Inga. She's frettin' enough as it is."

Betsy drew Annie's attention to the German woman, who stood as still as one of the boulders along the bank, her hands clenched into tight fists at her sides.

Renate stood behind her mother. A quiet girl, she, too, watched the far shore. Her blonde profile, so similar to her mother's, made her appear to be a phantom sentinel.

Annie found herself doing the same while she prayed that Lorna's fears were unfounded. But the alternative was just as bad. Had the little ones fallen into the creek? *Dear God, don't let it be so.*

~

The meandering tracks of the children led eventually to the edge of the creek, just before it dropped into the deeply shadowed rock-walled canyon. White foam roiled around the giant boulders that littered the narrow passage. The confined roar sounded like rolling thunder.

Brother Rolf took one look and blanched.

Ike thought the worried father might pass out. He grabbed his arm. "Spread out," he yelled to the others over the turbulence. "You, Ken, go upstream. Jigs, you and Wolfie go down." Shoving Rolf toward Ken, Ike then scrambled up onto a boulder almost as tall as himself. He jumped from it to another one farther out in the torrent and searched both directions and along the banks.

Nothing.

But he did see where a pine had fallen across the creek perhaps fifty yards down, making a natural bridge.

"I found a footprint!" Wolfie called out. "It's pointed downstream."

Ike leapt from the boulders and ran for the log, not bothering to check the print or to look for any others. Reaching it, he found the evidence he knew would be there.

Brother Rolf, huffing for breath, caught up with Ike within seconds. He didn't say anything as he surveyed the narrow log extending across the swirling water, its uneven bark chunked out in places and stubs of branches sticking up. The worry that ridged his brow and his clamped jaw said it for him.

Jigs jumped onto the log and, with no regard for his own safety, darted out over the water. He stumbled over a protruding knot. Tipped. Waving his arms wildly to regain his balance, Jigs dashed on, overstepping all other impediments. Reaching the other side, he remained on the rooted end of the log as he stooped to examine the ground for what Ike desperately hoped was there. Footprints. Small footprints. Or broken twigs. Anything.

Too nervous to just stand waiting on the bank, Ike hopped up onto the log, and though he knew he shouldn't in front of Rolf and Wolfie, he searched the raging waters for bodies, praying all the while he wouldn't find them.

After what seemed like an hour, Jigs yelled, "I found something! Come on!"

Relieved beyond coherent speech, Ike ate up the length of the log as he raced across on his pliable moccasins.

"I was a-feared of this," Jigs told him as Ike dropped down from the large, gnarled root-end of the fallen pine. "They headed into the woods. I know they was thinkin' the trail is over yonder to the west instead of a mile or so to the north. You can be sure Otto had it in his mind to run up on us and surprise us. That boy thought he'd be a-hootin' and a-hollerin', thinkin' he outwitted us."

"Aye." Ike nodded solemnly. "But the squirt wasn't smart enough to see he was wrong soon enough to find the way back to this log—the only way across." Ike checked the slant of the afternoon sun. "They must be real scared by now. 'Specially Isolda."

Not only were the kids completely lost, but the little girl had to know her mama would be waiting to flog her like she'd never been flogged before.

One by one, the others made it safely across the dangerous water, where Ike explained to them what the children had done.

"But find dem ve vill." Rolf's gruff voice had regained its strength. Faith fired his eyes. "Point to me da vay."

∾

Standing at the head of the trace with her musket crooked under her arm, Annie saw that the day was waning. There'd been no sign of trouble. Not a soul had passed going in either direction. Even the wildlife wandering through camp had been nothing more threatening than the squirrels scampering up and down the trees. All looked peaceful.

But all was not as it appeared. The womenfolk were gripped by the strain of waiting and wondering. Annie herself chose to believe that if the men were still out looking, the children must be alive. But as young and small as Isolda and Otto were, so many perils could claim them.

Maybe the men would find that the young'uns had simply seen a bear and climbed into the high branches of a tree and couldn't get down.

Wherever the truth lay, Queenie was mooing now, waiting to be milked. Annie's two cows were still yoked and hitched for travel. She'd milk the one, and if the men hadn't returned with the children by then, she'd unhitch them and put them out to graze with Ruben. Grass was sparse here, but they'd make do.

After finishing the milking, Annie tended the rest of her evening chores, then walked down to the stream where she could wash up and cool off. The night's rain had made the day extra sticky with humidity.

Inga, she saw, still sat alone on a rock above the bank. Mending lay on her lap, forgotten, as she stared across to the other side.

While Annie was careful not to stare, the fair-skinned woman's red-rimmed eyes couldn't be missed. But whatever pity Annie had for her was overridden by thoughts of Inga's treatment of Isolda and her callous disregard for Annie's calf. Annie couldn't help thinking the woman was getting her just punishment.

She knew she shouldn't feel that way, considering that the children might be lying out there dead, but she couldn't help it. The water had slowed to a gentle brook, so after washing the animal stench off her hands, she removed her footwear and waded across to retrieve the rope. The men would be worn out when they returned—too worn out to take care of their own evening chores. She and the other women would need to do them.

The men would be hungry, too.

While Annie untied her apron and sat down to dry her feet, she

169

glanced back at Inga. Her daughter Renate would have to start the Bremmer family meal.

Cap lay under Annie's cart. She called him, and the obedient dog crawled out. He humped his back in a stretch, then trotted down the bank. He rubbed against her leg in a friendly greeting, which she returned with a scratch behind his ears.

"Watch the cows," she ordered as she stood to go.

Cap sauntered down to the stock at the stream's edge. Such a good and faithful companion.

Her thoughts shifted to Ike and the way he'd watched her cross the stream this morning. There'd been real admiration in his silver blue eyes. . . .

Catching herself, she refused to let her mind go down that fruitless path. Instead, she went to speak to the women.

Betsy was off to the side of the Reardon wagon, talking quietly with Lorna and Renate. They sat on their camp stools in a semicircle.

She strode to them. "Girls, it's time to tend your livestock and get supper on. Lorna, if you'll unhitch the Clydesdales, I'll give you a hand unloading your packhorses."

"*Me?*" Lorna's mouth flopped open till her chin hit the pristine lace of her shawl collar. "You expect *me* to unhitch those great smelly beasts?" She swept her rose linen skirt aside as if the very thought might dirty it.

"Very well," Annie said. "You start unloading the packs, and I'll do the unhitching."

Lorna puffed up like a batch of rising dough. "As you can plainly see, I am a lady. Not some backwoods peasant. I don't do such things."

Annie wanted to jerk Lorna off her stool and shake some sense into her, but this useless girl was no concern of hers. Setting this one straight would be her new husband's job.

Turning away, Annie shook her head. Could Lorna really be the sort Ike and his brothers coveted for wives? A useless dress-up doll. Something she herself would never be, even if she had the chance. Swinging back, Annie eyed Lorna with disgust. "I'll go ahead and take care of all the Reardon animals because I can't abide havin' 'em suffer. But you *will* have a good hot supper waitin' for me by the time I'm finished."

Lorna maintained her superior posture. "Have you no feelings? Those of us with the least amount of sensibilities are much too worried to eat."

Those perfectly coiled black curls begged to be snatched from the uppity girl's head. And Annie's fingers itched to do the job. She started for her.

Betsy sprang to her feet and stepped in front of Lorna. "We'll fix one big cauldron, enough for the men, too, when they come back—*with the children,*" she added firmly. "And I'm sure I can get my horses unhitched." Betsy turned to Renate. "You can unyoke your oxen, can't you?"

Renate looked doubtful. "I ain't never done it, but I reckon I can."

Annie grasped Renate's hand and pulled her up from her stool. "Come, I'll show you."

The timid girl glanced back longingly at Lorna but didn't resist. Annie was sure any will of her own had long since been beaten out of her by her mother.

By the time Annie finished for the night, her back and arms ached worse than during those first days of the journey. She never knew five packhorses could carry so much truck. When she finally got to Ike's big workhorses, their hitch felt like it weighed a ton as she wrestled it off them. Then all the livestock required watering, hobbling, and an extra portion of grain since the grass was so sparse.

At one point, Betsy had offered to help with the unloading, but Annie couldn't see the thin, young mother-to-be lifting full feed sacks and crates. Besides, if Betsy had some kind of mishap, Ken would never accept any excuse for Annie's risking his "sweet pea" and her baby.

Despite her aches, thinking about the newlyweds brought a smile to Annie's lips. There was such a charm and sweetness about the love those two had for each other. If only her own sister could have had a little of that with her husband.

Annie shook the vision of her sister's wretched sadness from her mind. Today held enough grief of its own.

Those poor lost children. The sun had long since dipped behind the western ridge, and daylight was beginning to fade. Stretching a stitch out of a back muscle, Annie trudged over to the cook fire. She had worked up quite an appetite, and the food smelled good.

Renate stirred a huge iron pot of gobbler stew with a long wooden spoon, while Betsy stooped down to fry slices of venison in a skillet set on some side coals. Both their faces glowed from the intense heat. Lorna, always one to pick the least demanding chore, came from her wagon with trenchers and pewter cups to add to those already stacked on the almost flat top of a low, table-sized boulder.

"Annie," Betsy called, "the food's about ready. I brought out a cup and trencher for you. Get one and come serve yourself."

That small kindness meant a lot about now. "Much obliged," she said, picking up one.

"Ain't nothin' compared to what you done for Ike and Jigs this evenin'." Taking potholders in each hand, Betsy slid the heavy skillet onto a rock rimming the fire; then she turned to Renate. "Would you go fetch your mama?"

The towheaded girl grimaced. She didn't seem too eager to comply. Still, Renate did as she was told.

While filling her plate, Annie glanced up to where she'd last seen Inga. The woman was still at the creek, staring across the water.

Renate walked down to her and said something Annie couldn't hear. But she didn't need to. By the way the woman pushed Renate away, it was obvious Inga wasn't interested in eating. Renate turned to come back.

"Vait." Inga swung around and strode up the bank. "I come for da blessing of da food." She quickly reached Annie and the others. "Ve pray now for mine Otto. Mine baby."

"Only Otto?" The words popped out of Annie's mouth before she could stop them. The damage was done, so she went ahead and finished what was on her mind. "Don't you care if Isolda comes back, too?"

"*Isolda.* Dat girl I vill punish goot ven I get mine hands on her."

Annie's animosity for the woman multiplied as browbeaten Renate glanced furtively away like a scared rabbit.

Annie looked to Betsy, who always seemed to have the right words in moments like these. Betsy would make the dreadful woman see the injustice of her words.

But Betsy just stood there staring at the ground, as did Lorna. As usual, no one would interfere with the family matters of the Bremmers.

Well, this time someone would. Annie would stand up for Isolda. "I'll make a bargain with you," she said, holding Inga in her gaze. "We'll pray for Otto's safe return *if* you'll pray for Isolda's with just as much care . . . and love."

Inga's eyes flared wide, and her mouth twisted downward. "Vat nonsense. Dead is mine t'ree sons. Only two left haf I, *und* one is lost in da vilderness. He is da last one I vill haf. T'ree sons is dead. I vill not lose dis one, too. Ve pray. *Now.*" Dropping to her knees, Inga immediately began crying out to the Lord in her own language. A long, steady stream of German words followed.

Annie and the others felt compelled to kneel with her. As Annie listened to the emotion in the woman's petition, she began to understand for the first time something of the reason Inga prized

173

Otto so much. He was the final son she would ever bring forth. And as Annie herself had learned, only sons held any lasting worth in a family. But why? Why did it have to be that way?

After several minutes of Inga's foreign pleadings—the only intelligible word being *Otto* sprinkled liberally throughout—her voice croaked to a stop as tears flooded down her cheeks.

Betsy then began. "Dearest God Almighty, we beseech thee to bring our young'uns back to us. They're too little to be lost and alone in the woods at night."

"*Amen.*" Lorna broke in forcefully and rose from the ground, brushing pine needles from her fine linen skirt. "Food's getting cold."

The others regained their feet, but Annie knew that more had to be said. "Not yet." She didn't care how angry Inga became, she was going to pray for what she knew in her heart of hearts was right. Annie closed her eyes. "Father in heaven, when Jesus said, 'Suffer the little children to come unto me,' I know he didn't mean just the little boys. He meant all the children. I pray that Isolda's mama will see that she is a child to be cherished, too. To be loved. Please soften Inga's heart, Father. I ask this in your Son's holy name. Amen."

Annie opened her eyes to find Inga standing over her, glowering, fists knotted and planted on her hips, a face flushed as red as her eyes.

"You stupid girl," Inga railed as Annie quickly came to her feet. "You know nudding. If Gott take Isolda now, she is da lucky one. You t'ink you can come *und* go anyvere you please. Vell, you vill learn—you vill learn. Vomans must learn dey haf no life of der own." She slammed a fist against her own chest. "I am not da cruel mama. Mine girls learn not to vant t'ings. I learn dem for when dey go to da man. Da man, he always do vat he vant. Da voman, she must do all da rest. If da man vant to be kind to her—say sweet t'ings now and den—for dat she can be grateful."

"Oh, Inga." Betsy moved close and took the older woman's clenched fist into both of her hands. "It don't have to be like that. When a husband and wife love each other, they both want to do what pleases the other. I'm as happy as my Kenny is. I am. Truly."

"*Nein.*" Inga ripped her hand away. "I know better. You did not vant to come to dis faraway place where da Indians vill take da hair from da head. *If da volfs and da bears don't kill us first.* You husband, he vant dis, not you. But you must come anyvay."

"You're wrong. I didn't have to come. Kenny left it up to me. But I knew how much he wanted to have his own land and his own business. And I couldn't be happy if I stood in the way of that."

"See? It is da vay I say. Da man always get vat he vant. One vay or da odder." Inga raised a finger and shook it in Betsy's face. "And he puts you *and you babies* in danger. Mine husband, he bring me to America *vere everybody get rich,* he say. He make me leave mine family forever. *For da better life,* he say. Vell, ve are here nine years. Seven ve are da bond servants. Ve vork like slaves. And two more years, Rolf labor for anodder man, many extra hours so ve can save money to buy da land. I take in vashing. Look at mine hands." She spread them out to reveal rough, red palms, one with an open crack in the skin. "But ve never save enough. Now Rolf say ve go to country of da savages. Dere, he say ve haf our land. Ha! I say, ve all be slaughtered like da hogs in November. *Gott vill not protect us.* Mine babies . . . . Gott is—is—taking—" Inga choked, and her body heaved into loud, racking sobs.

Annie watched Betsy pull Inga into her arms. She realized the older woman felt as trapped as she herself had felt before she escaped. Annie also considered the possibility that her own mother might've reacted the same way. Her mother had done no more than sigh sadly when each of Annie's sisters had been married off for profit like soul-less cattle.

But still, Inga didn't have to make her two daughters' lives so miserable in the meantime. "Inga, dear," Annie said, placing a hand on the woman's sturdy shoulder. "Life is too hard already. We shouldn't deliberately make it even harder. Let yourself love your daughters. Maybe they'll be given to men who will love them the way the Bible says to. The way Ken loves Betsy. I've watched them together. He cares for her as much as he does for himself. More."

"Aye, he does," Betsy said softly, next to Inga's ear. "He purely does. And I think your Rolf would love you just as much, if you'd let him."

Betsy made the love between a man and a woman sound so dear. How could Inga resist wanting the same?

How could any woman? How could Annie herself?

But was it really that easy to come by? If so, why had she seen it so rarely?

Inga pulled away from Betsy, her face ravaged, her fair freckled skin blotched and wet with tears. Picking up her apron, she swiped at her eyes. Then, with an unreadable expression, she walked away into the growing darkness, back to the creek, back to her vigil.

Watching the woman go, Annie wondered if anything the others had said had softened Inga in the least. As for herself, she'd been given much to ponder. Today she'd learned she wasn't all that wise when it came to judging others' failings. Especially when she wasn't even brave enough to risk loving or letting herself be loved.

But it was so much safer this way.

17

A short while earlier, Brother Rolf had called for his children, and the joyous sound of their answering cries had reached the men. But only in faint, garbled echoes. From which hollow or ridge they'd come, Ike could not discern. He could do nothing but press on as slowly as before, finding a footprint here, one there.

No longer did any light trickle down to the floor of the forest. Soon a blanket of darkness would completely envelop the trackers. Although Bremmer wanted to keep going, Ike insisted they stop long enough to spark a fire to life and fashion some torches.

Dropping into a stoop, Ike gathered a few sprigs of dried debris and got a small flame going with his pieces of flint.

As he added more kindling, Brother Rolf knelt beside him. The worry in the man's fleshy face looked even worse in the erratic glow. "I try to be da brave man, but vy is Gott making *mit* me dis test? Dis is too hard!" He spoke with passion, but softly, for Ike's ears only. "I t'ink I am doing his vill. I take mine family into da land of da heedens not just for mine own gain, but to bring to dis place da light of da gospel. I am obedient servant."

Ike didn't know what to say. Brother Rolf was supposed to supply him with God's truths, not the other way around.

But the man kept staring at him with pleading eyes.

"Well, Brother Rolf, we do know the children are still alive, so I reckon we'll just have to keep on goin' in faith. You know more about that than I do." He shrugged. "Worry about nothin'; pray about everything."

"*Ja, ja.* Dis is da only t'ing I do all dis day. And now da night is coming. Mine babies is out dere in da dark, mine little *kinders.*"

Ike reached over and squeezed the man's hefty arm. "We'll find 'em. But now I need you to take off your shirt and tear it into strips to make a torch." Ike rose up from the fire. "Ken, you and Wolfie help Jigs find some dried moss."

"You don't really need me out here anymore," Ken said, stepping up to Ike. "I ain't no good at trackin', and since nobody's holdin' the young'uns agin their will, I think I'll just head on back to the wagons. I don't like leavin' my Betsy alone up there on the trace. No tellin' who might come ridin' by. Which way do I go?"

Jigs barked a laugh. "*Which way do you go?* If you don't know, you got no business traipsin' off by yourself. We'd just have one more greenhorn to look for."

"But I've never left Betsy alone at night before."

Jigs quirked a sly smile. "Gettin' lonesome for her, are ya?"

"*No.*" Ken didn't take to smutty teasing. "I mean, sure. But that ain't the reason."

As leader of the train, Ike understood all too well Ken's worry, since the women as well as the lost children were his responsibility. "Annie will be keepin' watch with her Brown Bess. Her and that dog o' hers." Despite the way the widow's obstinacy rankled him, her bravery couldn't be denied. She could always be counted on.

And that was the one thing he admired about her even more than that long, leggy stride of hers.

He knew she'd be sitting alone in the dwindling light this very minute, alert to the night sounds. The thought gave him comfort and made him want to be there with her—the way Ken wanted to be with Betsy, or even just the way it had been the other night when he and Annie had waited together, when the only sound he could concentrate on was the sound of her breathing. "Let's finish these torches. The sooner we have 'em, the sooner we'll find the young'uns and get back to the women."

In a few minutes, they were tracking again with three flames to lead the way. But their progress was far slower than before, one man always staying with the last footprint until another was found. A three-quarter moon moved from behind a ridge and played peekaboo among the upper branches of the trees as it slipped slowly across the sky.

Later more torches replaced the first ones, and still they didn't come upon the children. And never again did they hear their answering cries.

Then Jigs, a few yards to the right of Ike, called out, "Come here. Look at this."

The others were just as curious as Ike to see what Jigs had found. They all converged on Jigs, who knelt near the trail. He held the torch low.

Ike stooped beside him. "Show me."

"Moccasin prints. Large ones here, stepping across the children's."

"Following them?"

"Aye."

"How many men?" Ike started examining them, too.

"Looks like three, maybe four."

Wolfie grabbed Ike's arm. "Then the bad men do have Otto and Isolda."

Ike regained his feet and turned to Brother Rolf. "Only two of the robbers wore moccasins." Indians were following the children. But he didn't have to voice it out loud.

"Come." Rolf shoved Ike ahead of him. "Ve must hurry."

~

Sitting with her back against a fir, Annie caught herself nodding off. She jerked her head upright and listened for any suspicious sounds. In the darkness behind her, she heard nothing but a hoot owl. No twigs snapped. No leaves rustled in the windless night. All she heard was pine pitch crackling in a bonfire built on the trace just above the creek. Even on this muggy night, Betsy and Lorna were keeping it at full blaze, hoping its glow or its reflection on the water would act as a beacon for the men and children.

Annie had taken on the task of lookout and had remained in her hidden spot for several hours now. She grew weary of sitting so long and wondered if the men, too, were now lost—they'd been gone so long. Still sleepy, she picked up her metal cup . . . and found it empty. And worse—she suddenly realized her dog had slipped away while she dozed.

She called for Cap several times, but to no avail.

"Blast that dog!" she muttered under her breath. Then, collecting her musket, she picked her way out of the trees to the huge fire.

"*Wha*—" Lorna leapt to her feet at Annie's sudden appearance. "Oh, it's just you," she said as she sank back onto her stool. "Don't you know it's bad manners to sneak up on folks like that?"

Annie didn't bother to respond. "Have you seen Cap?" she asked, leaning down to pick up the blackened coffeepot, using her skirt to keep from burning her hand.

"No, we haven't," Betsy replied, glancing around from her seat on her stool.

"Probably off chasing some fool possum or something," Annie complained. "Of all nights."

"Have you heard or seen anything out there?" Betsy asked as she rose to bring over another stool for Annie.

"No. But you'd think we would. How far can two little tykes wander, for heaven's sake?" Annie looked past the bonfire but couldn't see beyond the bright glow. "Are Inga and Renate still sittin' down at the ford?"

"Aye," Betsy crooned sympathetically.

"Personally, I don't think Ike should have allowed those foreigners to come with us," Lorna whispered much too loudly. "They're nothing like us. And they have such odd ideas. Can you imagine that woman thinking she's her husband's slave? She's so stupid, she doesn't know he tiptoes all around that temper of hers. A little sweet talk, and she could get anything she wanted from him." Lorna's generous lips spread into a smile. "I haven't met a man I couldn't get to do *my* bidding."

Filling her cup, Annie stared down at the stool Betsy had meant for her. If she sat down, she'd have to endure more of Lorna's prattle. Annie chose to remain standing.

"Lorna, dear, once you and your Noah are wed, you'll feel different. You'll just be wastin' to do for him, just like me and Kenny."

Laughter bubbled out of Lorna, as if the young wife had said something wildly funny.

"Shush!" Betsy whispered frantically as she glanced toward the creek. "You'll make Inga think we don't care about her children."

"I'll try," Lorna giggled. "But you're too naive for words, Betsy." She clapped a hand over her mouth.

Annie turned away. She knew if she didn't leave for her sentinel post this very second, she'd make an insulting remark.

Just as she took the first step, she caught a flicker from a copse of trees bordering the trace. Something metal or glass had mirrored the firelight. A rifle? Or maybe a hatchet?

She never should have left her watching spot. Here in the open

181

she was merely a helpless target, along with the women she'd been guarding.

As nonchalantly as her taut nerves would allow, Annie moved back to the fire and set down the coffee cup, then looked squarely at Lorna. "Keep laughin'. Pretend nothin's wrong."

Lorna stiffened, and instead of laughing, she choked, then went into a fit of coughing.

"Betsy," Annie whispered intently. "Be casual-like. Move your musket onto your lap."

"What's happening? Who's—"

Lorna sprang to her feet, looking this way and that. "Please tell me the men are back."

"No," Annie hissed. "Pretend to get more coffee. We don't want—"

From the dense midnight forest stepped a half-naked Indian, holding a musket.

Lorna let out a bloodcurdling scream.

Betsy's weapon slid from her hands.

There was movement behind Annie. She glanced behind her. It was only Inga. She charged up the bank, with Renate on her heels. *"Ja? Ja?* Is it mine Otto?"

Annie had no time for explanations. Ignoring her banging heart, she kept her eyes on the piercing coal black ones of the Indian, her weapon trained at the center of his bare tattooed chest.

He took a step closer.

Inga stumbled to a halt. Seeing the reason for Lorna's hysterical screaming, she dropped like a rock.

Renate knelt beside her. "Mama! Mama!" Staring at the Indian with terror-stricken eyes, she frantically shook her unconscious mother's shoulder. "Wake up!"

It was pure pandemonium.

Annie knew it was up to her to save them. But if she fired, he'd surely shoot. And if she missed, she knew this experienced warrior wouldn't. She'd be dead, and the rest of the women would be at the mercy of his scalping knife. Inga's prophecy would come true.

Into the light stepped another Indian. He, too, was naked from his waist to the top of his head, except for a long braid hanging down from his crown. He looked even fiercer than the first with two hatchets and a knife hanging at his waist. How many more were out there?

It was so hard to concentrate with Lorna screaming, but Annie knew she had only one shot. It was impossible.

Then she remembered something Ike had said to her the night they argued over the bandits. Lowering her weapon, she shifted it to one hand and swung on Lorna, slapping the girl into stunned silence. Then she forced a smile. "Hungry?" she called to the intruders as she stepped forward. Bringing her free hand to her mouth, she mimicked eating. "Food. We have plenty food."

The two Indians glanced at each other. The one who'd appeared first muttered something to his companion in their own guttural tongue.

The other wheeled around and vanished into the darkness. Where was he going? To fetch more friends? Annie was hard-pressed to remain calm as she repeated to herself, *They got no war paint on. They got no war paint on. . . .*

The first Indian took a few steps forward.

It was just the two of them again. At least for the moment. She watched his hands for any suspicious movement. And all the while she prayed for wisdom. Or God's intervention. *Anything.*

"Bremmer," the Indian barked. He pointed at Annie with his long musket barrel. "You Bremmer woman?"

How had he come by that name? Annie could hardly answer. "N-No." She nodded toward Inga, sprawled in a faint on the ground with her frightened daughter madly shaking her shoulder.

Looking at them, the Indian grinned, his teeth startlingly white

183

against his brown skin. He seemed quite amused by poor Inga's state and started past Annie toward her.

"Please don't," Annie beseeched. If Inga woke with him standing over her, she might actually die of fright. "What do you want with Mrs. Bremmer?"

He turned back to Annie, his smile not completely gone. He began a study of Annie then, looking her up and down.

She willed herself not to flinch as she stared back at his sharply etched yet refined features and repeated, "What do you want with Mrs. Bremmer?"

Shifting his gaze beyond her, he nodded toward the woods from whence he'd appeared.

How many were behind him now? She watched as, out of the trees, came three more Indians. Two carried children. *Otto and Isolda!* Both were asleep. And her blasted dog came trotting along as if not a blessed thing was wrong.

Betsy found her voice. "The young'uns! Inga!" She jumped up. Snatching the handle of a water bucket left near the fire, she ran to Inga and doused the unconscious woman.

Inga came up, spitting and sputtering. *"Vas ist—"*

Renate, dripping from the overflow of the bucket, pulled her mother to her feet. "See, Mama? It's Otto. He's back safe. And Isolda."

"Vere? Vere?" Still disoriented, she staggered forward. Then her fist went to her breast. *"Mine Otto!"*

The Indian holding the little boy lowered him to the ground as Otto rubbed sleep from his eyes.

On shaking legs, Inga went to him. Falling to her knees, she swallowed him in a hug.

Watching Otto grab onto his mama, Annie's heart swelled, and she felt the sting of unshed tears. The children were alive and well.

Her attention shifted to Isolda. Awake now and on her own feet,

Isolda looked warily at her mother and Otto, then melted back against the Indian who'd been toting her.

Placing his hands on the child's shoulders, he urged her to step forward.

But she wouldn't budge.

Annie went to her while keeping a tight hold on her musket—she still didn't quite trust these savage-looking good Samaritans. She knelt before Isolda. "Your mama's not gonna hit you. I promise."

The child's light blue eyes showed white all around. Then, with her chin quivering, Isolda shook her head. "She'll get me. And kill me. And eat me, just like she did Prince."

Is that what the child believed? "Oh, no, sweetie pie. Your mama would never do that." Annie lay aside her musket and held out her arms.

Isolda looked longingly at Annie but remained against the Indian as if moving meant sure death.

"Please let me hold you. I need to know it's really you, safe and sound. And not just me a-dreamin'."

"You ain't dreamin'." Isolda placed a hand in Annie's. "See? It's me."

Annie knew her fingers were trembling as she laced them through the child's much smaller ones, but she couldn't stop the quavering any more than she could stop the tears that had started to trickle down her face. "We was worried about you. We prayed and prayed that God would bring you back to us."

"You did?" Isolda looked amazed. "Even Mama?"

What could Annie say? "Aye. 'Specially your ma."

"Truly?" Isolda leaned past Annie to check for herself. Her eyes widened with fear. "She's coming!" Ripping her hand from Annie's, Isolda flattened herself against the Indian again.

Annie looked over her shoulder and saw Inga walking toward them, her face covered with tears.

Inga balanced Otto on one hip. "Isolda, get avay from dat Indian and come to Mama."

Isolda grabbed his leg and held on, digging in her nails.

Annie heard the Indian grunt as he continued to stand there with utter patience, watching what had to be, for him, a very strange drama.

Inga came alongside Annie. "Vat is da matter *mit* da girl? Is she daft?" She raised a raking gaze up to the Indian's face. "You bust mine baby in da head? *Ja?* Ve see about dat." Inga pulled the clinging Otto's arms from around her neck. Setting him down behind her, she stepped up to the Indian, her hands balled into fists.

She was going to hit the Indian! Annie grabbed Inga's arms from behind. "No!" she said as Inga fought to free herself. "He's done nothin' but bring Isolda back to us. This man is God's answer to our prayers."

Inga stopped struggling. "Our prayers?" she repeated softly.

"Ja, our prayers. But if dis is so, vy does Isolda not come to me?"

Annie sucked in a breath. What would the woman do when she knew the truth? "She thinks you're gonna kill her, then eat her."

In a shocked gasp, Inga sucked in a breath of her own. "Vat? Vere do she get such—" She stopped midsentence. Her tense shoulder muscles sagged. The fight was drained from Inga.

Annie released her arms.

Inga bent down and looked Isolda in the eyes.

Flinching, the child hid her face against the Indian's leg.

Inga reached forth, but her hand stopped just short of Isolda. "Mine little *liebchen,* I don't vant to kill you. I vant to kiss you and hug you and—" she glanced up at Annie and smiled uncertainly through her tears before finishing—"and I vant to tell you how much . . . I luf you."

18

Annie watched as the tattooed red men walked off into the night. In their hands they toted a crock of honey, some of Betsy's dried fruit, and a hammer, along with a bag of iron nails from the Bremmer wagon. As bone weary and shaky as she was, Annie had to smile. Those gifts the Indians had been happy to receive, but not a single bite of the gobbler stew would they eat. After taking one whiff of the cauldron's contents, they'd all grimaced, wrinkling their noses as if it smelled worse than the bear grease they had smeared all over their bodies. Most likely, they weren't used to some of the spices the Germans were accustomed to using.

But all in all, she thought they'd departed feeling well compensated for their trouble. And, of course, *her* compensation had been that they'd brought the young'uns back at all. Indians had been known to take lost or stolen children into their tribes as replacements for their own dead loved ones.

Turning back to the encampment, Annie saw that Inga and her offspring were already bedded down. Since Rolf and Wolfie were not there to put up the Bremmer tents, they all shared one big pallet laid out next to their wagon. And even as warm as the night was, Inga held Isolda close. She hadn't let go of the little girl since she first pulled her away from the Indian.

Lorna's tent hadn't been pitched either, but she'd refused to sleep on the ground without one. A mite snappish since Annie had slapped the hysterics from her, she'd piled her bedding over the load of barrels and sacks in Ike's wagon. Annie knew it couldn't be all that comfortable.

She wished she, too, could climb into bed, but someone had to keep the bonfire going to help the men find their way back, and it was more important for Betsy to get her sleep. Plus Annie knew she was the only one who could actually load and shoot a musket. And who knew what other surprises might be lurking out there in the woods.

But the men shouldn't be too much longer in coming. Shortly after Isolda and Otto were brought into camp, Annie'd fired off both hers and Betsy's muskets. As deep into the mountain canyons as they were, the shots had created an amazing cacophony of cracks echoing back to the women from every direction. The shots would be heard for many miles. Then, within a few seconds, a returning set of echoes had ricocheted back. The men had answered.

Stifling a yawn, she added several hefty chunks of wood to the fire, then went to pour herself that cup of coffee she'd hoped to drink earlier. Stepping with care through the darkness, Annie carried her drink back to her guard post under the tree, with the knowledge that her dog was securely tied to her wagon wheel. This time, he would be in camp to warn her if anything or anyone approached.

Sitting in a spot where she had a good view of the entire camp, she rested her head against the tree trunk and took a sip of the brew. She almost spit it out. It was so strong and old-tasting, it curled her nose as bad as the stew had curled the Indians'. Fortunately, she hadn't offered any of this pot to them. They would've thought she was trying to poison them for sure.

The Indians . . . who would've believed they'd come merely to return the children? After all the horrors she'd heard about them, they had performed such an act of selfless compassion. Perhaps these red men were as human as anyone else. Merely deprived of the knowledge of God.

She remembered the New Testament Mrs. White had given her at their parting. At the end of the book of Matthew, Jesus had told his apostles to go forth and make disciples of all the nations. That must have meant the Indians, too. Perhaps she, like Brother Bremmer, would be part of bringing this new light to these people. What a wondrous privilege that would be.

No, it couldn't be true. She was much too unworthy for such an honor. Hadn't she been hoarding hatred of Inga for days now? And for Ike? And when she saw the Indians, what had her first thought been? To shoot.

Oh, thank you, Lord, that I didn't. They would've surely retaliated, killed everyone in camp or carried them off to their village to pay with a slow, torturous death. What would've become of the children then?

All that horror would've befallen these good people had she fired. Thank the good Lord she hadn't. She'd waited, her heart in her throat, not knowing whether or not she'd made the right decision—one that determined not just her fate but that of everyone in camp. What a horrendous burden that decision was.

Now she began to understand why Ike was always so serious about everything. Why he hadn't let her sway him that night with the outlaws. He'd felt bound to give those men the opportunity to leave in peace for everyone's sake. Yet he *had* taken every precaution possible to protect the people for whom he was responsible. And despite all the shooting, none of them had been hurt. Only one thief had been hit, and her calf, of course. A small price to pay, she now saw, considering the danger of the situation.

Annie owed the wagon master an apology. She'd been more than rude to him that night. Her skin crawled as she remembered how she'd as much as told him his decisions—and worse—his ability to protect her and the camp were useless. She'd attacked his very manhood.

And that was not easily forgiven.

But whether he forgave her or not, she would have to tell him how wrong she'd been. She owed him that . . . and more. He'd taken a chance on her by letting her join the train when most men wouldn't have.

Aye, as soon as he returned, she'd get it over with. Eat some crow.

Annie kept herself awake, sipping on the bitter coffee until it was time to put more wood on the fire. Emerging from beneath the tree with her musket in hand, she saw that the dog, too, had risen. Ears perked, Cap stared into the woods downriver.

It had to be the men.

On the off chance it wasn't, she backed into the deep shadow of the nearest tree and waited, her musket pressed tight against her shoulder, her flintlock cocked. She prayed it would be them. And, if not, that she would know what to do.

Cap's tail began to wag, and he ran to the end of his chain, then began to bark . . . a happy greeting yap.

Still, Annie didn't lower her weapon as she saw the flickering light of torches coming her way. One by one, the flames were snuffed at quite a distance away. If it was their men, why would they put out their torches before reaching camp?

Icy tingles of fear spread through her, out to the finger she hooked around the trigger.

Slowly, silent figures began emerging from the woods. Not in a group, but spread out, their weapons at the ready. And they were naked to the waist! *More Indians.*

These had not come as friends.

What should she do? Her lone musket against all of theirs. Would one shot scare them off . . . or only make them that much more vicious? *Lord in heaven, tell me what to do!*

Even though the dog had not ceased yapping at them, they hunkered low, looking from side to side, as they stepped farther into camp. One moved into the light of the bonfire.

Ike? It was Ike! Stripped to the waist except for the cross strap of his powder horn. And so was Brother Bremmer. Then came Ken and Wolfie. And Jigs.

Annie's knees almost gave way with relief. The awful burden of responsibility, the fear, the uncertainty were over. The men were back. All of them.

"Ike!"

Unable to contain her joy, she dropped her weapon and ran to him.

~

Not knowing if the shots they'd heard were a signal to return to camp or the sounds of an attack, Ike had returned upriver with the men, crossing the treacherous terrain as fast as they could.

Exhausted from the race and fearful of what he and the men might find, Ike was overjoyed to see the women and children, including Otto and Isolda, piling out of their beds, running to greet them with cries of joy. Even Annie. She ran straight for him.

She flung herself at him, almost knocking him off his feet.

But he didn't mind one bit as she wrapped her arms around his neck with such enthusiasm. His own arms pulled her even tighter against him. They were all safe. Folks all around him were laughing and crying and kissing each other all at the same time. Otto and Isolda were back safely and in their pa's arms.

191

And Annie was in Ike's. His lips found hers, and he kissed her with all the relief and passion pent up in him.

When she returned his embrace with equal fervor, his heart almost jumped out of his chest. She'd run to him and no other. Then all else disappeared as their kiss changed to one of tender exploration, their lips moving slowly across each other.

On a long sigh, her arms slid limp from his neck . . . she was as overwhelmed by their coming together as he was.

He held on all the tighter.

Then, suddenly, she wrenched away. "I-I-I'm so sorry. I was just so glad to see you. *All* of you. I don't know what came over me."

"Neither does anyone else around here!" The angry words came from Lorna's mouth as she was being helped down from Ike's wagon by Jigs. "Ike, you don't know what's been going on around here. *That woman,* " she railed, pointing a finger at Annie, "attacked me! And I want her gone from here. Either she leaves this train, or I will!" Lorna grabbed Jigs by the shoulders. "You will take me out of here, won't you?"

What in the world had happened between those two while he'd been out hunting for the children? And Annie—could it be she had run to him, thrown herself at him, just to get him on her side first?

That seemed like something Lorna was more apt to do. Ike took a good hard look at Annie. "You struck Lorna?"

Annie stared back a moment, then giving no defense, just turned and walked away. Back to her own cart, shunning his question as she had shunned him this past week.

The rest of the folks, obviously having heard Lorna's outburst, turned toward them.

"I t'ink ever'body tired," Brother Bremmer said, walking over with Otto and Isolda still caught up in his arms. "Ve go to bed now. Talk about dis in da morning. Ever'ting is better in da morning."

"Yes," Betsy agreed. "We're all real wore out."

"One thing first," Ike said. "Tell us how the children found their way back. They were being followed by—never mind."

"By Indians?" Betsy said for him. "It was the Indians what brought 'em back. Wasn't that nice of 'em?"

"*Ja,*" Inga said, taking her husband's arm. "Dey bring da answer to our prayer. Ve give dem gifts, and dey go avay happy."

"Did they say who they were?" Jigs asked as he exchanged glances with Ike.

"*Nein.* But dey come from Gott. Dat is goot enough for me."

More than good enough, Ike thought as weariness set into every muscle of his body, except for those twisting his gut. "Is that some of your sage spice I smell, Inga?"

"*Ja,* ve got plenty gobbler stew vaiting here for you. Plenty stew."

$\sim$

Annie left Ike to his turkey stew that night and kept a safe distance from him the following morning as the wagon train moved forward. She could do no more than blush whenever he passed by her. How could she defend herself against Lorna's accusations when she couldn't even look at him?

And that wasn't the only time her face turned piping hot. It happened every time the shame of what she'd done flashed into her mind—as it had done no less than a dozen times since she'd risen. Everyone must have seen her throw herself at him. Kiss him like some waterfront wanton. What had possessed her to do such a thing? Even yet she could feel the heat of his *bare skin* beneath her fingers.

But at the time, he hadn't seemed to mind. She was almost certain he'd kissed her back. And with as much eagerness as she had kissed him.

No, that was just foolish, wishful thinking. Most likely he'd just been thrilled that the children were back safe and sound. He would've kissed anyone at that moment. Even her dog, Cap.

193

From the way Ike had looked at her when Lorna accused her of attacking her, Annie saw how quickly he'd taken the raven-haired beauty's side against her. Too bad Lorna hadn't explained why she had to be slapped. But it wasn't in the girl to see two feet beyond her own comfort and pleasure. Why was it men couldn't see past Lorna's outward beauty?

Without Annie's realizing it, Ike was almost upon her, riding up from the rear. He slowed his horse to the pace of her yoked team. Had he come to speak to her about last night? And, if so, which aspect of it? The slap or the kiss?

She couldn't even make herself look up past his shirt to acknowledge his presence.

"Down 'bout half a mile," he said, "we'll be comin' to a river, the French Broad. We're stoppin' there overnight to build us some rafts. Then we'll float on 'em partway down to Henry's Station." His voice was flat, the same as it always was when he wanted to hide his feelings. Not a trace of emotion could be detected. With that said, he nudged his mount into a trot and rode to the head of his pack string and Wolfie, who'd been assigned to keep the horses moving.

How could Ike speak to her so casually after last night? She doubted if she would be able to get a single word past the croaking frog in her throat. But then, it wasn't *he* who had flung himself against *her*.

The return of the embarrassing image caused Annie to crowd closer to her young bull, Ruben, hoping she'd be less noticeable if Ike should glance back at her.

Within a few minutes, Annie was overlooking the widest river she'd seen since leaving the North Carolina lowlands. She was vastly relieved that she and her outfit wouldn't be expected to ford this one. Watching its smooth flow as it curved around the next bend, its banks shaded by broad-leafed trees, she took pure pleasure in knowing the current would be doing the walking for her for a while.

Ike halted the packhorses and came cantering back to Annie on his blaze-faced roan. She desperately tried not to blush as he slowed. Thank goodness, he stopped only long enough to point and say "Take your cart over to that flat" before he rode on by.

She quickly complied, not wanting to give him a reason to come back.

Soon all the wagons were pulled into a circle, and as usual, Inga drove her piglets and goats into the center. But now, for the first time, she gifted Annie with a tentative smile.

That simple friendly gesture meant a great deal . . . a moment to be treasured. Annie gladly waved in return. Despite its disastrous ending with Ike and all, much of last night had turned out fine—real fine.

While Annie unfastened the strap under Ruben's neck, Brother Bremmer walked up beside his wife. Wrapping an arm around her, he kissed her on the cheek.

Inga didn't shoo him away as Annie would expect, but leaned into his side and let him hug her close.

Annie quickly ducked her head behind her bull and swiped at brimming tears. Watching that simple show of affection brought such pleasure . . . and such a terrible longing.

A longing that would only get worse if she stayed with these people. She looked over the low bluff to the river. Only a few more days before they would leave her behind at Henry's Station.

19

Annie hurried to tend her camping chores. There were trees to fell, a raft to build. She had no intention of letting Ike think she was slacking, even if they might never run into each other again once they reached the settlement.

Well, one thing for sure, she thought while hoisting her beehive up a tree, *the livestock will have plenty of grazing tonight.* A whole peck of folks had come this way before them and had created a farm-size clearing, doing the same as she and the men would do today. Stumps littered both sides of the trail all the way down to the river, giving her a fine view. Only the largest trees remained. One now cast cooling shade over her cart. Yes, there was a lot to be grateful for, and she wouldn't let herself think on anything else—in particular, the kiss that still made her lips tingle and her face go red. And still made her mad at herself . . . and at him. How quick he'd been to take Lorna's word, to think the worst of her.

Actually, it was best that it had happened. Too often on this trip, she'd found herself dwelling on Ike Reardon, instead of keeping in mind why she trekked across the mountain in the first place. This trace was supposed to be her rainbow road, taking her to the fabled golden pot that held her dream . . . her freedom.

Hearing the first loud chink of axe to wood, she rushed across the meadow to her wagon, bent on collecting her chopping tools along with her yoked team and lengths of rope needed to drag the logs down to the water's edge. As she neared her cart, she saw Ike still unloading his pack animals. How much lighter the crates looked when he swung one up to sit on his shoulder than when she performed that chore. Her back still ached from moving the crates last night. Yet he lifted and stacked in easy fluid motions—a testament to his lean, fit body.

Suddenly realizing she was just standing there staring at the man, she told herself she should be concentrating on one thing only . . . the fact that she would get to the tree chopping ahead of him.

She found Jigs laying his weight into his axe. As much as he tried to sidestep work, whenever he put his mind to it, Jigs was quick and able.

Seeing her, he stopped midswing and waved her to the side. "The tree's about to go," he hollered.

Annie moved the oxen out of the way until, after a few more chops, the tree came crashing down. Then, gauging the size of the trunk, she headed for another pine of similar circumference.

Jigs called out again. "Did Ike send you out here to bring me your team?"

"No. I brought them out to haul back the logs I'm cutting for my raft."

Jigs grinned that irritating, all-knowing grin. "I see. Plan to build one of your own, do ya? Show us men you're as good at raft makin' as you are at whoopin' up on Lorna."

Anger flaring, Annie realized that Ike wasn't the only one who had believed Lorna's accusation. "I never did any such thing!

Lorna was screamin' her fool head off, so I slapped her. It was either me shuttin' her up or the Indians doin' it."

Chuckling now, Jigs nodded. "So that's the real upshot of it. The lovely Lorna went berserk when she saw the redskins. Well, I reckon we should'a left one of the men here to look after you women."

Annie hated the superior tone of his last words. "Or you men could teach these women how to load and shoot. Give 'em some way to fend for themselves, be it from beast or man."

"Hey, don't get all riled up at me. I don't see nothin' wrong with a woman fendin' for herself . . . or choppin' down trees, if that'll keep her happy. So why don't you clean the branches offen that downed pine whilst I fell another one. You ain't got nothin' agin a little teamwork, now, do you?"

Annie supposed she'd made enough fuss for the moment. "No, long as I get to claim half the logs."

Jigs grinned again. "You are a caution."

She wasn't quite sure what he meant by that, but she wasn't about to ask. Starting with a bottom branch, she braced her foot on the trunk just above it and swung down with her axe.

And, who knew, maybe Jigs would tell Ike why she'd slapped Lorna. At least the business about Lorna could be quickly explained away, unlike that other mortifying thing she'd done.

∼

The raft building went smoothly, and by midmorning the next day, Ike was already floating down the river in the lead. He stood near the front of his flatboat, pole in hand.

Ken stood at the rear behind their two lashed-down wagons and one of the giant workhorses. He held steady the steering beam of the hastily fashioned tiller while Betsy, sitting on a crate, kept herself busy darning one of Ken's oversized socks. Lorna, Ike couldn't see, but he figured she was probably inside his wagon, trying to decide what she'd wear when they rode into the fort. She did like to dazzle the menfolk.

Yes, Ike thought as he looked back at the other two rafts, all was going as smoothly today as the water they floated upon. Upriver a dozen or so yards behind his raft came the next one, carrying the Bremmers' wagon and Annie's cart. Behind them, the biggest one lumbered low in the water. It was manned by Jigs and Wolfie and carried all the animals that couldn't be fitted on the other two.

Quite an impressive little flotilla, Ike thought with a grin. They'd crossed the Smoky Mountains and were now leaving the worst of the trip behind them.

"What's that?" Betsy cried. She hopped up from the crate, eyes wide, and pointed with the threaded needle toward shore.

Ike followed her aim and saw that a great hairy beast had come down to the river for a drink. "Oh, that's a buffalo. They're real fine eatin'. It's a good sign, seein' one. Means we're comin' into the Tennessee Valley."

Betsy stepped gingerly across the lashed logs to reach him. "I heared buffalo meat tastes as good as beef."

She teetered.

He caught her by the arm to steady her. Wouldn't do to have anything happen to Ken's little wife. "Some judge 'em to be better. Once we get to our valley, maybe me and Ken will go hunt us up one. Dress it down and smoke it for winter. Would you like that?"

"Aye, I purely would," she said, straightening the sunbonnet he'd knocked askew. "But there's somethin' I'd like even more." Her last words had an ominous ring to them.

"Oh, what's that?" Ike asked hesitantly. Lorna had taught him to be leery of a young woman's requests.

"I wish you and Annie would make up. I know you're both just a-wastin' to. I saw how you two kissed and hugged the other night before you remembered you was mad at each other."

200

Well, he sure didn't have to go on guessing any more. The whole train had seen him make a fool of himself.

"Now, I know you two ain't been real friendly-like since them outlaws come in and kilt Annie's calf. To the rest of us, that wouldn't mean so much. But you gotta understand, Ike, her bein' a childless widow and all, them animals is all she's got in the whole world. You seen how she dotes on 'em. So if she did anything or said anything outta anger and set you off, well, I think you should ease up on that temper of yourn. Show her you got plenty a God's mercy in you."

"My temper's no worse than anyone else's."

"Good, I'm glad to hear it. Leastwise, since you owe her a heap o' thanks."

"Me?" He glanced back at the Bremmer raft but couldn't see past the covered wagons to where Annie worked the tiller.

"Aye, you. I wager you don't know that Annie unhitched, unloaded, grained and hobbled every single one of your animals the night you were gone, 'sides helpin' me and Renate with ourn."

"She did? With Lorna's help, of course." Even as he said the words, they didn't ring true.

Betsy's gaze faltered. "No, not a'tall. Lorna helped me and Renate get supper, 'cause Inga was takin' on so. All Inga done was stare off into space—when she wasn't a-prayin'. It were kinda creepy, her just standin' on the bank for hours on end, but I reckon if it was my young'uns lost, I'd'a did the same."

At least that was in the past now. "Betsy, I've gotten two versions of why Annie hit Lorna. One from Lorna, and one from Jigs, who wasn't even there at the time. And Annie? She's not talkin' to me about that or anything else. But whatever happened, Lorna is set on havin' me leave Annie at Henry's Station."

"Then maybe you oughtta hear it from me. You see, 'tweren't nobody's fault. When them Indians stepped outta the trees, Lorna took to screamin' her head off. She ain't got no idea how close she

201

come to havin' one of them Indians take a club to her. If Annie hadn't a-slapped her quiet, that one might'a butted her in the head with his musket. And Ike, you should'a seen Annie—the way she stood right up to them Indians. I never seen anything so brave." Betsy placed a hand on his arm. "But even if she didn't act scared in front of them, I knowed she was, 'cause when they lit out, she started shakin' worse'n a eighty-year-old woman. And you seen the way she run to you when you come in." Betsy's lips slid into a sly smile. "And, in case you didn't notice, it was you she went to. Not Brother Rolf or Jigs. You."

"I know that look you're givin' me. You been set on doin' some matchmakin' betwixt us ever since she joined the train." Though he tried to sound serious, his own smile forced its way onto his face as he remembered the kiss they'd shared.

Or had they? Had it just been him kissing her, forcing himself on her?

"And if my matchmakin' don't take hold soon, Annie'll be leavin' this train."

"I haven't told her to leave. Not yet, anyway."

"Well, she told me she was goin' to. And that'd be a pure shame. Annie's the kind of neighbor I'd like to have livin' close by. She's someone I could always count on."

Ike'd had that same thought night before last when he was miles from camp. Betsy was right; Annie staying in the Watauga settlements would be a real loss to his valley . . . her and her cheese and honey. "Maybe I'll speak to Annie about travelin' on with us."

"Better do more than just maybe, and make it soon. Time's a-runnin' out as fast as this here river is."

"Yoo-hoo," Lorna called to Ike from the back of his wagon. "Please be a sweetie and come help me down."

The girl's voice was really starting to grate on Ike's ears. "If you'll pardon me," he said to Betsy. Inhaling deeply, he went to do the gentlemanly thing. Odd how, when he first met Lorna, he'd considered her voice rather musical. Leaning his long river pole on a wagon wheel, he reached up and lifted the girl and her many skirts down from the wagon bed, all the while wondering if his brother Noah would tire of listening to her as quickly as he did . . . or tire of her need to be doted on. He hoped not, for both Noah and Lorna's sakes. Because marriage was for life.

Just the thought of being tied to Lorna for life made Ike cringe.

Lorna held a comb and two brushes. "My hair gets such tangles in it. You'd think some of those pesky squirrels made a nest in it whilst I was asleep. I'm going to brush it out really good; then I'm going to wash it. I want to look my best when we ride into the fort. Let folks get a good first impression of the new mistress of Reardon's Valley. Thank goodness I won't have to worry about a week's worth of trail dust in the meantime. Oh, and would you be a dear and dust off that crate for me?" She pointed to the one he'd scooted out from the rest of the stacked supplies for her to sit on.

Tempted to tell her to do it herself, he decided he didn't want to deal with her wounded sensibilities. Pulling a not-so-white kerchief from his shirt pocket, he swiped across the rough boards as her last words rolled through his brain. The idea of her seeing herself as mistress of the whole valley didn't set well. Not at all. No more than his being her lackey.

Aye, he sure would be glad to turn this one over to Noah.

Lorna eyed the crate warily, then carefully settled her silver gray linen dress, one of many she owned, over it as she sat. "Do you think they'll have a shop with a good supply of ribbons and lace? All these splinters have simply ruined two of my gowns."

"I wouldn't know. Never had much call for 'em, myself." Ike watched worry lines mar her smooth complexion. Making a good appearance was all she ever had on her mind, and, as for the shops she expected to find, there was only the one trading post.

Suddenly Sylvia popped into his mind. Most likely, his former betrothed would have acted no differently on this journey than

Lorna. Both had been raised to expect all the comforts and conveniences of city life. It really wasn't their fault they'd been taught that maintaining their beauty and learning to make pleasant conversation were their primary duties in life. But life on a farmstead deep in the wilderness required far different duties. For the first time he was truly thankful Sylvia had understood that and reneged. Even if Lorna had yet to figure it out.

He wondered if she ever would.

But it wasn't his concern. Noah was a man full-grown, only two years younger than himself. Ike's duty—his *only* duty—was to deliver her safely to his brother.

He retrieved his pole and started for the front of the raft.

Lorna caught his arm. "Have you told her yet?"

"Who? What?"

"That widow—if she even is one. I mean, just look at her. I can't imagine any man willingly taking her to wife. She might not be able to afford decent clothing, but it doesn't cost a thing to do something with your hair. The way she just braids it down her back . . . it looks worse than a horse's tail. And she's got no respect for her betters, *as you've plainly seen.*"

Ike couldn't believe what Lorna was asking. "You want me to tell Annie McGregor to fix her hair different?"

She returned his amazed look, which quickly crumbled into one of irritation. "No, of course not. I'm asking if you've made it clear to her that we're leaving her behind at the settlement."

"Lorna, dear." Betsy's voice came from behind Ike.

Turning, he saw that she'd returned to her own seat, her darning in her lap.

"Me and Ike was just talking about that," Betsy continued. "Have you thought that without Annie, we wouldn't have no honey to put in our tea, no cow's milk? And, Lorna, *hard cheese.* I'll wager there ain't another maker of cheese in the whole over-mountain territory."

Lorna retook her feet and, with lifted skirts, carefully moved toward Betsy, navigating the log deck in her hard-soled shoes. "Yes, but have *you* thought about the fact that, for some smelly old cheese, we'd have to put up with that woman? It's too unpleasant a price to pay. Why, she's no better than some nasty-tempered fish-wife."

The pot calling the kettle black.

Ike intervened. "Lorna, it's a big valley. If the widow comes, I'll see to it that she doesn't settle within two miles of you."

"*If she comes?* No! I will not live within twenty miles of her—a hundred miles. Either she stays behind at the settlement, or I will. And I just dare you to tell Noah you brought *her* home instead of *me.*" She whirled about and stalked toward the aft as quickly as the precarious footing would allow.

The girl had no idea how tempting her dare was. Exasperated, Ike glanced back at Betsy.

She shrugged and smiled that sad smile of hers. "I'll talk to Lorna. I'm sure she'll come around in time."

But did he really want her to?

Or Annie, for that matter. If Annie came to the valley, he knew that, in her own way, she'd be just as big a thorn in his side as Lorna.

Problem was, in that stubborn, prickly way of Annie's, she'd already dug herself in . . . all the way to his heart.

"No, Betsy, don't say anything to either one of them. I'll handle it." *Somehow.*

20

Ike's stomach tightened into a ravenous knot as he inhaled the smell of frying catfish mingled with woodsmoke. It would be a welcome respite this evening from the wild game they'd eaten during most of the trip. He hurried to finish hobbling the last of the horses, feeling more hungry than tired for a change, since he didn't have a pack train to unload.

Heading back toward the tantalizing aroma, he neared the widow's cart and was again reminded of the source of his dilemma—Annie. All day out on the river he hadn't been able to make up his mind about her. She intrigued him, no question about that. But her bullheadedness certainly gave him pause. Too, if she came to the valley, he and the other men would have to raise her cabin and get her set up . . . whether or not she thought she could do it by herself. Was she more trouble than she was worth? He just didn't know. But of one thing he was almost certain: if she settled near him, his life would never again be as it had been before.

Then there was Lorna. Did he want to listen to Lorna harangue him about Annie for the rest of the trip—as she surely would if Annie continued on with them? Ike rubbed the taut muscles at the back of his neck. The decision was no easier to make now than it had been all day.

Passing Annie's chicken cages, he picked up one and set it on a fresh piece of pecking ground as he'd seen Annie do several times each evening. The two plump hens greedily searched the new patch, trying to push each other away. A body'd think they hadn't been fed in a week.

He chuckled at their antics as he moved the next two cages. Betsy was right about the widow. From the constant attention Annie gave her animals, it was evident she cared for them a great deal. He shouldn't blame her too much for her poor behavior and standoffish ways since her calf died.

She hadn't been standoffish, though, when she rushed into his arms. That was a moment he wouldn't soon forget. Especially if Annie had come to him with the sincerity Betsy said she had. Amusement replaced his confusion.

His smile still lingering, he looked out to the river. Yes, this had been a good day. Except for a few rough spots, the rafts had all floated along smoothly. Thank goodness, August was usually a lazy month for the river, he thought, as he came around a cane-brake. The sound of voices drifted to his ears.

"I been thinkin'," Betsy was saying, "that if you don't plan to go on to Reardon Valley, maybe I'll see if Ken will stay around Henry's Station, too."

What? Ike stopped in his tracks. He hadn't brought Betsy and Ken all this way to have them quit him at the first settlement. "If Ike is sellin' land cheap," Betsy continued, her voice carrying across the tall reeds, "I imagine someone there is too. We could buy land next to each other."

"I'd wait on that if I was you." The other voice was Annie's. "Most likely, Henry's Station already has a wheelwright. There probably wouldn't be enough business thereabouts for two shops. Ken might end up doin' what he did in Charlotte. Workin' for the other wheel maker."

"That would be fine, too. That's nothin' to be ashamed of. 'Sides, we'd still be better off than before, 'cause we'd have our own land."

"But Ken won't want to be answerable to nobody else if he don't have to be. He should be able to go where he can be his own man, not stay under someone else's thumb. That can be a terrible thing, Betsy."

"I know you said somethin' like that before. But the same goes for you. What if there's another cheese maker in these parts?"

Ike moved closer.

"Then I'll keep goin' till I find a settlement that needs my cheese and honey."

"So why not just come along with us now? You know we need you." She lowered her voice to a more conspiratorial level. "And, besides, I think Ike is real partial to you."

Ike sucked in a breath. Why did Betsy have to go and say that? Annie would think he'd been mooning over her.

Silence followed Betsy's last words. He could just imagine the shocked expression on the widow's face. He knew he should walk into camp and break up any further talk, but he couldn't quite bring himself to show his face after Betsy's comment.

"Ain't you got nothin' to say about that?" Betsy probed.

Ike leaned toward the sound of the women's voices, suddenly as interested in Annie's answer as Betsy was, though he was beginning to feel a bit like an interloper.

"You're just sayin' that because that's how you want him to feel about me. And even if it was true, I didn't come all this way to gain my freedom only to turn myself over to the rule of another man."

Ike was shocked. What did that woman think marriage was, the joining of a master and his slave? Was that how her first marriage had been? Small wonder she was so standoffish.

Not wanting to hear any more, Ike turned away. But while circumventing the canebrake to the other side of the encampment, one of her statements stuck in his mind. She said she had come on this long arduous journey all alone to gain her freedom . . . which meant she wasn't free when she started out. And that could mean only one thing. She wasn't the widow she claimed to be. She was a runaway wife. And with all the truck she'd brought with her, her husband was bound to show up sooner or later to fetch it *and her* back.

No, that didn't make sense. Brother Bremmer never would have vouched for her if that were the case. Whatever the truth was, the entrapments of marriage were the last thing she wanted. At least with him.

So be it. If she wanted to stay behind at Henry's Station, he certainly wasn't going to interfere with her freedom to make that choice.

~

The next day the river grew too swift and rocky to navigate any farther. Annie was grateful when Brother Bremmer motioned for her to veer the raft to shore. Finding a spot among an array of abandoned rafts already beached next to Ike's, Annie left her position at the tiller and hopped off as Brother Bremmer secured their raft to a tree.

Two strangers stood on a small wooded rise, watching them.

Annie stopped. She'd better go back for her musket.

Five-year-old Otto shot past her, running up the bank.

She tried to catch him, then noticed that Ike didn't seem disturbed. He'd already climbed up to the men's level and strode casually toward them, even before the third raft had pulled in beside hers.

She took a closer look and saw that the strangers weren't carrying weapons. Dressed in the same backwoodsman garb as Ike and Jigs, they grinned and waved a greeting.

Reaching the top of the bank, Annie saw a wagon and a team of horses waiting among the trees. Loaded in the wagon was a stack of logs. The men had come to collect wood from the discarded rafts.

With forestland in every direction, no one would have to drive very far from home for wood. The thought thrilled her.

Without Annie noticing, Inga came up beside her and took her hand to squeeze. "Ve getting close," she said, her voice ringing with excitement.

Annie returned the squeeze. "Aye, appears so." The fact that Inga had made the friendly gesture meant far more to Annie than their proximity to the settlement. Inga was a testament to the wondrous workings of God. The change in her was truly miraculous. It was as if she'd had a whole lifetime of love locked away inside her and only now felt she could set it free.

Little Isolda sidled up beside them and, looking up shyly, took her mama's other hand.

Swallowing down a swell of emotion, Annie reminded herself she mustn't ever try to outguess God again. Or forget. To think that something as terrible as losing the children could turn out to be such a blessing. From this day forth, she would do as the Bible said, pray without ceasing and keep trying to follow where God led. *Not* where her own willful self led.

But at the moment, Annie didn't know which way her heavenly Father was pointing. Was she meant to stay at this first settlement or go on with the others? She was racked with indecision, especially since Inga had become this new loving person. Annie couldn't think of anything she'd like more than to have the Bremmers living on one side of her and the Smiths on the other. And Ike . . . Ike, she couldn't let herself think about him. Or was that where God was leading her? But what of her freedom? *Oh, Lord, you know I can't give that up. I can't. Please, don't ask that. Help me.*

Unable to bring herself to speak openly with the wagon master since the night she'd thrown herself at him, Annie stopped short of her fellow travelers as they all gathered around the strangers. Still, she was close enough to hear the men offer to help them debark their livestock and wagons and then invite the wagon train to their farmstead for the night. Except for a trapper's lean-to she'd seen upriver, this would be the first dwelling Annie had seen since leaving North Carolina. Despite the confusion ruling her heart, her spirit soared.

~

Ike was in a good mood the next afternoon as he followed the trace along the bank of the French Broad. This was his side of the mountains, where folks were judged for themselves, not their property or position. Even as primitive as the Canneys' farmstead was, spending last night with such open-armed and open-hearted people had been a joy.

Ike spotted a big *F* carved in the trunk of a maple. It marked the path leading to the Fitzsimmonses' cabin. Only a couple of miles farther to Henry's Station. Assuming the others would want to know how close they were, he put his fingers in his mouth and whistled for Wolfie.

As the lad came running to take his place, Ike dismounted. "Here, you ride Ranger for a spell. I need to stretch my legs."

He strolled back toward the next oncoming outfit—Annie's.

She avoided looking at him—her usual practice of late—as she pretended to fuss with something on her apron.

And suddenly it came to him. She wasn't angry because he'd kissed her; she was embarrassed because she'd kissed him back. An intriguing thought . . . one that gave a mighty interesting slant to everything. Well, almost everything.

He decided tc speak to her whether she wanted him to or not. "Thought you'd want to know. We'll be comin' into Henry's Station before long. We'll make camp at the fort for the night."

"Thanks much," she replied quickly, her eyes still not quite meeting his as she walked on by.

He really liked this shyness she had about the kiss. It was so quaint that if he didn't know better, he'd think she was still a young maiden instead of a woman married and widowed.

So caught up was he in this new possibility, he could barely concentrate on giving the Bremmers and the Smiths the message as they rolled by.

Then Ike approached his own wagon. "Hey, Terrell," he called to his comrade walking alongside the Clydesdales. "The Fitzsimmons cutoff is just ahead."

Jigs's face lit up. "Great! There'll be music tonight!" He glanced up to Lorna riding on the wagon. "Toss me my flute. I need to get in some practice. The settlement's comin' up."

"Oh, really?" Lorna's hand flew to the ruffle-lined bonnet covering most of her black curls. "Is it a real town? With houses and stores and everything?"

"I reckon you could say that," Ike hedged. "A tradin' post, anyway."

Lorna's hand fell, along with her expression. "What you're really saying is, instead of there being just one log hovel like where we stayed last night, they're going to be clustered in a bunch. Stinking pigsties and all."

Unable to miss Jigs's grin, Ike tried to answer without doing the same himself. "Pretty much, I suppose. Nothin' fancy."

"Nothing fancy? *Plain* would be too grand a word to use for that smoke-blackened cave. Ike, don't lie to me. Are you bringing me to something like that? Some piled-up bunch of logs?"

He was mightily tempted to shout out *yes*, but controlled himself. "Lorna, it'll be some time before enough folks come overmountain to warrant building a sawmill, so you won't be seein' anything but logs in the whole of Tennessee Valley."

Jigs stepped in. "Lorna, you're lookin' at this all wrong. You should think of Noah's land as a new dress you'll be workin' on. You've sewn it together out of some new material—say, a rich emerald velvet. No one else has ever touched it or even seen it 'ceptin' you. Now, it may not be quite a perfect fit yet . . . it needs a tuck here, a bit o' lace there. But you with your keen seamstress's eye can see past all that to what the dress will be once it's all finished."

While Jigs continued to expound with strange gestures as if he actually had a dress on, Ike escaped. For some reason, Lorna's petulance never seemed to bother Jigs. He never took what she said seriously. Ike hoped his brother would be as patient and unaffected.

Lengthening his stride, he hurried down the sloping, rutted trail to reach the front of the train again. As he approached the rear of the widow's cart, he saw that it had stopped. She just stood there, staring ahead.

Was something blocking the trail? Ike quickly caught up with her.

Without taking her eyes from the scene in front of her, she swept her hand out. "Look at that. Isn't it glorious?"

A break in the trees provided an unobstructed view of gently rolling wooded hills sprinkled with lush meadows and sliced by a glimmering silvery ribbon of river.

"Aye," he murmured.

She jumped slightly when he spoke—she obviously hadn't known he was next to her. But she didn't run away as he'd expected.

So he continued. "But it's not half as pretty as the overlook of my valley."

"How could anything be lovelier than this?" Even though she

kept her eyes averted, the woman still couldn't stop herself from contradicting him.

Well, he was no slacker at debating. "If you really want to know, I'll tell you." He pointed to a straight stretch of river. It seemed natural to also put an arm around her shoulder, but that he refrained from doing. "Pretend there's a long wide valley there, spreading out along both banks with grass so tall a man could get lost in it. Where cattle get so fat their bellies near drag the ground. And just off to the right is a small rise with a giant oak shading it. That's where the house will be . . . one with lots of glass windows, so every morning before you start the day, you can sit at the table and survey everything around you. And the best part is knowin' it's all yours."

"Yes," she sighed, "that would be more beautiful." Then, to his surprise, she turned and looked him squarely in the eyes. "If it's as you say, God has truly blessed you, Isaac Reardon. Don't ever forget that."

A body would think she was his mother, and a mere two seconds ago she wouldn't even look at him. "I know that. That's why I asked Brother Rolf to come back with me."

"You're right. Forgive me for lecturin'. And, I reckon, this is as good a time as any to get my thanks said, too. And to admit that you've been right all along. About most everything. I never could'a made it this far without your help. And, most of all, I'd like to apologize for the disrespectful things I said to you the night the outlaws came. I didn't understand how awesome a burden it is to have everyone's lives restin' on your shoulders . . . not until it happened to me when the Indian walked into camp. I came awful close to shootin' him, but I didn't. And I'm afraid I owe that to you as well."

Ike couldn't believe what he was hearing. Annie McGregor eating humble pie? "I was nowhere near camp that night."

215

"It was something you said the night we argued about the out-laws. You said Indians wear war paint if they intend to—"

"Vat is dis stopping?" Brother Rolf yelled to them as his lead team of oxen reached the rear of Annie's cart.

"Oh, just admirin' the view," Ike called, though at the moment, the view was the furthest thing from his mind. He turned to Annie. "I been meanin' to say somethin' to you, too."

"You have?" Those wondrous green-and-gold eyes melted to soft inviting pools.

"About how sorry I was about your calf dyin'."

The invitation in her eyes was withdrawn. "Yes, well, I'd better get my cows movin'." Abruptly, she swung away and, slinging up her whip, she snapped it.

The nearest cow walled her eyes toward Annie, then started forward at a sluggish pace.

But not Ike. He remained where he was, trying to figure out what he'd said wrong this time.

21

As they neared Henry's Station, the trace widened, and on both sides of the river valley, Annie saw that cabins and outbuildings sat in the middle of cleared property. Soon the Reardon party would go on without her and the folks living in these dwellings would be her new neighbors. The thought of meeting so many new people and facing their questions set her on edge.

It was a comfort, though, to see their friendliness, as those who lived near the trail came out of their cabins and in from their fields to wave and call out greetings. The settlers seemed mighty glad to welcome new families to this side of the mountains. She just hoped they wouldn't mind too much having a lone woman come among them.

She placed her hand over the book in her apron pocket to help fortify herself. Her New Testament—the one Mrs. White had given her the day she started on the journey. She'd pulled it from the cart a few minutes ago, along with her bonnet and white shawl collar. Having the Holy Book had given her courage back then, and she hoped it would do the same now. Because this rustic settlement was where she was destined to stay.

She'd thought differently while talking with Ike earlier. For a few moments, she'd suspected he was going to ask her to go on with them . . . that he would give her that sign from God she had found herself hoping for. Only it hadn't happened.

Ike, ahead of her with the string of pack animals, broke out of the trees into brilliant sunshine. Soon she could see a stockade, which occupied the center of a very large clearing. Its gate stood wide open and a person from within started clanging some kind of bell. Their little band of wagons was getting quite a welcome.

About fifty yards from the gate, Ike veered off the path, signaling for her to do the same. Even though the stockade appeared large enough to easily accommodate them, he was apparently having them make camp on the outside.

Annie had to smile as she followed him with her outfit. Ike didn't like being under anyone else's authority anymore than she did.

As the wagons all circled around to make the enclosure Annie had become so accustomed to, she suddenly realized that this would be her last night to spend with these people, and maybe the last time she'd ever see any of them again.

She glanced across the square at Ken and Betsy perched high up on their wagon, their faces flushed with the excitement of reaching the fort. Then Brother Bremmer, standing beside his oxen, drew her attention. She'd come to think of him as the kind of father she'd always wished she'd had.

The minister caught her staring and took a step toward her, then paused. Glancing about him, he called out. "Ever'body, come. Ve t'ank Gott for da safe journey over da mountain."

Jigs shot past Bremmer, heedless of their religious leader's order. Bremmer caught his shirttail and hauled the much smaller man back. "Hold you horses dere, mine friend. Ve pray, den you go visit."

A circle began to form, with Ike being the last one to reach it. Annie hoped against hope that for this one last time he would come stand by her. She couldn't bring herself to be so bold as to ask him to, or to even beckon with her eyes.

But when she ventured a quick glance, he swerved toward her.

Then Lorna called to him, a hand outstretched as she clung to Jigs with the other.

"Let us all join da hands," Brother Bremmer said as he took the hands of his wife and his daughter Renate.

Betsy grasped one of Annie's hands, while Wolfie crowded in next to her and grabbed the other one.

He leaned close. "I'm going to miss you and your Brown Bess a lot."

"Shhh!" Brother Bremmer said, reprimanding his son.

Even so, Annie had to smile. The lad sure did love her gun.

"O Lord of all dat is in heaven *und* eart'," their pastor began. "Ve come to you as humble servants dis day to t'ank you for bringing us safe over da mountain. Ve know you haf come *mit* us ever' step . . ."

He paused midsentence, and Annie glanced up to see a knowing glance pass from Brother Rolf to Ike, one that seemed to be between just the two of them. Ike, too, must share a secret with Brother Bremmer.

". . . even ven I t'ink, maybe, you are not dere," he continued. "Forgive my veakness, and make me into da servant you vant in dis new country." He took a breath. "And now, I bring Annie McGregor before you. She is leaving us here, staying in dis place. She is goot girl. I pray dat you keep her safe. And I pray dis is your vill for her, not chust her going her own vay. Ve ask dis in da name of you Son, Christ Jesus. Amen."

"*Amen,*" Jigs repeated with loud finality. Then, firmly shoving his tricorn down, he took off for the fort with his flute in hand. "Gotta practice for tonight."

Bremmer frowned. "Vat he mean by dat?"

A grin captured Ike's features as he answered, making him all the more pleasurable to look at. "Just that folks round about will come in this evenin' to give us a welcomin' frolic."

"You mean da dancin' and da drinkin' of da hard liquor?"

Ike's grin vanished. He opened his mouth as if to speak. By the way his troubled gaze shot to the stockade, Annie could tell he was having trouble finding the right words.

"Well, it's like this, Brother Rolf," he finally replied. "There aren't too many Baptists overmountain. Mostly Presbyterians and Methodists and some Anglicans who aren't likely to admit they ever belonged to the Church of England. So none of these folks think it's a sin to dance or have a little rum now and then."

"Da dancing is not da sin, nor da bit of rum. But vat it leads to. Ve vill haf no part in da frolic." The brother spoke with finality.

"Brother Rolf," Ike said with measured words, "these folks will be mighty disappointed if we turn our backs on their welcome. They don't have a minister of their own. And since our valley is only three days away by horseback, they'll be wantin' you to come preach from time to time and for marryin's and funerals and the like. You don't have to dance or drink yourself—they won't mind. But, I beg you, don't throw their welcome back in their faces."

"And besides," offered Ken, who'd stood quietly by, "hoppin' around to 'Froggy Went A-Courtin'' ain't never done no harm." He squeezed his wife at his side. "Ain't that right, sweet pea?"

Betsy looked up at her husband. "Aye. Me and Kenny met at a barn-raisin' frolic. It was a real nice night." Her smile said the rest.

The big German puffed up his chest. The muscles in his beefy jowls twitched. He wasn't about to back down.

Inga tugged on the sleeve of his homespun shirt. When he looked down at her, she gave him a rosy-cheeked smile. "Rolf, mine husband, I t'ink tonight ve make new friends. Den ve invite dese new friends to our church meeting in da morning."

Brother Bremmer reared back. "Tomorrow is not da Sabbat'."

Annie tried her hand at convincing him. "These people haven't heard a man of God preach in so long, they won't care what day of the week it is."

The big German released a heavy sigh and rolled his pale blue eyes heavenward. "Very vell, ve go to da frolic, but I keep mine eye on all of you. No drinking of da rum."

Wolfie let out a howl befitting his name and, grabbing Renate's hand, ran toward the folks already strolling out of the stockade to greet the newcomers.

"Vait!" their father called. "Ve need to unhitch da animals!"

"In a minute, Papa. We'll be back in a minute."

Otto and Isolda followed on their older siblings' heels, with Ken and Betsy not far behind.

But not Annie. Before she sought out the storekeeper, she had one more person to thank. "Brother Bremmer, could I have a word alone with you?"

"*Ja.*" His answer came out on a grunt as he watched his children disappear past the sturdy open gate made of long, thick pickets. He then motioned her a few steps away from the others. "Vat is it you need, mine Annie?"

Blocking the afternoon sun from her eyes with a hand, she looked up at her dear benefactor. "I reckon what I want mostly is to thank you. You've been a true friend, even when I wasn't." She still cringed every time she remembered the awful things she said to him the day after her calf died. "And you kept my secret."

"Only so long as it do no harm to da odders. But I t'ink now you can trust dem enough to tell da truth. But, like I say, I leave dat to you."

"Brother Bremmer, do you think because I never told them the truth, God is keeping his truth from me? I can't be sure what God

221

wants me to do. Whether he wants me to go on with you or to stay here."

"Child, do you feel dis secret is between you *und* da Lord?"

"I never even thought about the possibility until just now."

He rested a heavy hand on her shoulder. "Search you heart, Annie. But for now, I tell you vat I t'ink. If you stay here, I vorry about you. Too many mans here vit'out a voman of dere own, and you haf nobody to protect you. *Mit* us, you be safe."

"If here is where she wants to stay," Ike said from behind—he'd been listening—"I'll take her over to the tradin' post and speak to Mr. Keaton about seein' her safely situated."

How long had Ike been standing there? How much had he heard? Did it matter, really—since he was certainly making sure he divested himself of her, right down to placing her in someone else's care whether she wanted to be deposited there or not? If she'd needed any more reason not to go on with him, this was it.

"Yes, Mr. Reardon, I'd appreciate your directin' me to the store-keeper. He and I have business to discuss."

~

We're back to calling me Mr. Reardon, I see, Ike thought as he took Annie's arm. *And what's this about a secret?* What could someone as rigid in his beliefs as Brother Rolf be keeping from the rest of the train and, in particular, from him?

"Ike!" Lorna called out. Tugging at a ruffled undersleeve, she came forward. "You're taking her into the fort and leaving me behind?" The indignation in her voice was evident.

"We have a piece of business to tend. I'm sure Rolf and Inga would be glad to escort you until I'm through."

The narrowing of her violet eyes was her only reply. The girl seemed to have lost all her charm and manners of late.

Turning away with Annie, he made a hasty retreat.

Ike observed that for their arrival Annie had tucked her golden brown braid beneath what seemed to be her only bonnet and put on her collar. Simple and proper. She would fit in real nice with the other women hereabouts. Nothing too fancy about her that would cause envy. Except, maybe, her gold-fringed green eyes.

And another pleasing thing about Annie, Ike mused as she lengthened her paces to match his, was that he didn't have to slow down to accommodate her. Her height lent easily to his. He also noted how slender her upper arm felt beneath his fingers, even with all the work she did. No doubt, her spirit and determination to be free of her shackles carried her through—that same spirit and determination that had brought victory to Washington's ragtag army when they took on the mightiest power in the world.

There was no doubt he admired a great deal about Annie McGregor. Too much for a woman living a lie.

Come to think of it, she'd never actually said she was a widow that first day in Charlotte, any more than she'd divulged anything else about her past. She just said she'd be coming alone. Yet never in all this time had she corrected his mistake. If that, in fact, was the secret. But what else could it be?

And Brother Rolf—was he keeping her secret because her husband was so abusive that she had no choice but to run away? Just the thought that some vile man had laid hands on this fine woman made Ike fighting mad. That husband of hers had better not show up around here and try to take her back.

"Ike, which way?"

At Annie's question, Ike realized they'd entered the gates of the fort and come to a stop. On the parade ground to the right, almost everyone from the settlement was gathered around Jigs and the others, but the trading post was in the opposite direction. "This way," he said, taking Annie with him to the left. He spotted Mr. Keaton on the shaded porch of his store and was grateful to see that he looked fit and sound of limb. Considering their own run-in with

223

the bandits, Ike had often wondered how Keaton and his pack train had fared.

The storekeeper waved to them as they approached. He was clean shaven, wearing a white shirt tucked into breeches. Meeting his knee pants were long finely woven stockings. Buckled shoes covered his feet. Now in his middle years, the man had always made a point of not turning woodsy.

"I see you made it back all right," Keaton called. Then he stepped down from the porch, straining to get a closer look at Annie. "Oh, thank goodness, it's you, Mrs. McGregor. Before I heard it was the Reardon party that come in, I was beginning to think you and your group didn't make it through."

Ike noticed that Annie glanced furtively up at him. She'd been caught in a lie.

"Do come up on the porch and light a spell." Keaton motioned them to a long bench positioned against the log wall. "Everyone else is over with Jigs. He certainly livens things up when he drops by."

Once they reached the top of the landing, Annie pulled away from Ike, but she didn't sit down. She stepped directly in front of the storekeeper. "I must admit, Mr. Keaton, that I was not truthful with you that day out on the trace. No one was with me. I was alone. I'd gone ahead of the Reardon party and was waitin' for them to catch up."

The man's even features took on the look of amazement, but he quickly regrouped and turned to Ike. "You allowed this?"

Annie quickly intervened. "No, of course, he didn't. He knew nothing of my plan."

Keaton raised his thin, graying brows. "I see. Well, God's angels must have been with you, because a lonely trace is rife with all manner of dangers."

"Aye, sir, angels surely must have been keepin' watch. 'Cause they kept me safe till the wagon train caught up. Then these kind people showed me more kindness and charity than my own family ever did."

Another piece to the puzzle that was Annie . . . had her family married her off to someone she detested? Poor girl. Ike quickly added her family to the list of people from whom she needed protection.

Then he remembered the outlaws again. "Annie did us a good turn that more than made up for anything we did for her. She warned us about the lies some backwoodsmen was tellin' when they came into our camp one night. One of them, she said, had been with your pack train—Frank Beckley. If she hadn't, I fear we would've lost more'n one packhorse and a calf."

"Aye, providence was with you. And me, too. My hired hand, Wendell, and me, we smelled a rat when Beckley's two trapping mates showed up outta nowhere. But sounds like we fared better than you folks. From us, they got away with *less* than nothing. By the time the smoke cleared, we found they'd run off, leaving behind one of their horses."

"Did I mention that the horse we lost was one you rented me?" Ike grinned, hoping Keaton was in a charitable mood. "Sounds like a fair trade-off to me, wouldn't you say?"

The storekeeper eyed him, then shrugged. "I was kinda hoping that horse would be pure profit, not a trade-off."

Ike took that for an agreement that Keaton wouldn't expect payment for the stolen animal. "I thank you for your generosity. And I'll return the other four soon as I get my folks settled on their land."

"Speaking of settling," Keaton said, "Mrs. McGregor, are you still interested in buying land hereabouts?"

"Aye," she said in almost a whisper.

Although he'd been expecting it, that one soft reply slashed across Ike's heart like a broadsword. She really would be leaving them. The reality wasn't one he was quite ready to face.

"Just you, alone?" Keaton asked.

She repeated her answer with more force this time. "I'm prepared to set up a cheese-makin' business, and I also have a beehive."

The man's eyes brightened considerably. "I'd be glad to take all you produce from either. Now, as for a piece of land, Captain Maynard up on Dumplin' Creek is willing to part with some of his grant for three dollars American or one English pound an acre."

"Three dollars?" Her dismay was evident in her tone. "Oh, my, I was hopin' to buy ten acres, but at that price I couldn't afford but two. That wouldn't be enough grazin' land for the cows I have now, and one of my cows will calve this fall. And I need room for a cabin and a garden and—"

"That's the price for bottomland along the creek," Keaton quickly amended. "He's selling land in his hills for only a dollar an acre."

"I suppose I could buy on a hill," she said hesitantly. "Are you sure there's no one else sellin' land cheaper than that?"

"I am," Ike found himself piping in. Suddenly it didn't matter that she'd been keeping secrets or that she might still be married. Or how much extra work or even the bother she would be. Or, he thought with a mental groan, how much Lorna would complain. "Annie, come the rest of the way with us, and you'll have everything that brought you across the mountain." For good measure, he added, "And you could still send your extra produce in to Henry's Station whenever one of us comes this way. It's only three days by horseback and five or six by wagon."

"Are you sure you want me?" she asked, all her hopes laid bare in her eyes. The sight did strange things to Ike's insides.

"Yes," he answered with all the conviction he felt. "You belong with us." *Where I can look after you,* he all but tacked on.

"Why don't you sleep on it?" Keaton suggested. "Don't decide on anything right now, except that you'll dance the first reel with me tonight. Once the neighborhood bachelors find out there's an unattached female here, they'll be swarming worse than those bees of yours."

If anyone was doing any swarming around here, it was Store-keeper Keaton. Ike took Annie's arm. "Well, we'll see you tonight, then," he said as he steered her away from the store before she had a chance to accept.

22

"Annie, over here."

Returning from putting her livestock out to pasture, Annie saw Betsy at the Smiths' cook fire, gaily beckoning her with a long wooden spoon.

Despite the fact that Annie had decided to travel on with the train—or rather, *because* she had decided—her mood was quite the opposite of Betsy's and had been since she'd been so rudely whisked away from the trading post. Even yet the memory galled her. The very instant she'd told Ike she'd come with them, he started treating her like she was his property. How humiliated she'd been to be dragged down the steps before she could even give Mr. Keaton an answer to his request for a dance.

Nevertheless, she couldn't ignore the dearest of young women. "Yes?" she called, veering toward her friend. "Do you need something?"

"No. I just wanted to tell you I've made enough food for you, too. I'd like you to join us for your last supper with the train.

'Sides, seein' as how they're givin' us a party tonight, you'll need the extra time to get ready."

Just as Annie started to tell Betsy that she would be going to the valley with them, excited voices drew her attention to the Bremmers' outfit. A large chest had been brought down from their wagon, and Inga bent over it, dragging out clothes, while her children took what she handed them, their eagerness evident in the bright flush of their round Germanic cheeks.

Lorna, who should have been helping Betsy, was nowhere in sight. Annie hadn't seen her since Lorna had returned from the stockade with Inga and Betsy. But no doubt the belle was up in her wagon doing the same as the Bremmers . . . rooting through her never-ending supply of frocks.

All the men, too, were missing, but Annie knew they were still inside the stockade, catching up on the latest news. Ike had gone to join them right after departing the store and ordering her back to the camp.

"You don't need to be out here with all these stray bachelors loitering about," he'd proclaimed, as if she had no sense of her own.

But since the men had been gone for quite a spell, she wondered if the news had been bad, if they were learning more about Frank Beckley and his cohorts or of other brigands that might be lurking on the other side of this most far-flung of the Watauga settlements. Or maybe some not-so-friendly Indians.

She didn't want to think about that tonight. Returning her attention to Betsy, Annie bent over the big kettle, took a whiff and smiled. "Smells like pork."

"Aye. Ken traded for a slab of ham."

"I thank you much for supper. But I don't want to eat off you falsely. As it turns out, land around these parts costs too much, so it appears I'll be goin' on to Reardon's Valley with y'all."

"You don't mean it! Land o' Goshen!" Betsy flung her arms around Annie, dripping spoon forgotten. Finally letting go, Betsy

said, "All the more reason to celebrate. What're you gonna wear tonight? How are you gonna fix your hair for the frolic?"

Betsy's hug had been a real spirit-lifter, but not so her mention of the dance. "I'm not much good at dancin'. Besides, I don't have anything special to wear. I only got two work dresses and one that isn't much better for goin' to church."

"That's no problem. I got a real purty dust cap that I'll make you the loan of. It's got lots of ruffles that are edged with lace my aunt tatted for me. It'll look real sweet, framin' your face. And I have a shawl collar to match. It's long enough to cross in front and tie at the back so's it'll purt'near hide your dress. So you ain't got no excuse not to come. 'Sides, from what I seen of the clothes in these parts, you'll look better'n most."

"Not Lorna."

"No, not Lorna." Betsy's chuckle was light and airy. "Fact is, it's a puzzlement that someone with her looks and advantages would even set foot out here on the frontier. That Noah of hers must surely be somethin' special."

"Actually, he's a lot like Ike," Lorna spoke from behind, catching them off guard. "Just as tall and handsome," she added, as she climbed off the back of her wagon with the most gorgeous gown Annie had ever seen folded over her arm—emerald green satin with a brocaded bodice. Although Lorna had caught them talking about her, she didn't seem perturbed. She just kept on talking as she walked toward a line of rope strung between two wagons. "Except, of course, Noah dotes on me. He'll give me anything I want . . . and that's why I came on this loathsome journey. Had I stayed in Carolina, my father and my brothers would've been hanging over my shoulder day and night, smothering me worse than an old woman. I'll swan, but I don't think they would've stopped even if I'd married one of those clods in our neighborhood." Shaking out the elegant gown, Lorna draped it across the

231

rope to air out. "I just had to get away. And Noah, I know he'll do what's right for me, once I have a chance to talk to him."

Annie couldn't believe that someone as beautiful as Lorna craved freedom as much as she did. Lorna just had a different way of going about getting it.

"If you don't mind my askin'," Betsy said in a quiet tone that didn't sound all that pleased with Lorna, "what do you fancy *is* right for you?"

Lorna didn't seem to notice Betsy's displeasure any more than she noticed that she was actually being civil while Annie was present. Most likely, Lorna still thought Annie would be staying on at Henry's Station. Bareheaded, the raven-haired girl began pulling pins from her upswept curls and dropping them into her already bulging apron pockets. She shot a cursory look to the left and right, then smirked. "If I tell you, promise me you won't tell Ike."

Betsy stared at her a moment. "Not if you don't want me to."

Lorna's lovely features became animated. "Well, Jigs has been talking a lot about New Orleans. He says it's the best port in all the Americas. Just like going to Paris, France. Anything you want to do or buy is there. And he's promised to go along with Noah and me. He says after we get to the valley it's only three days by canoe on to Nashville. And from there we can take a keelboat downriver to the Mississippi. Then it's an easy float all the way south to that French town. Doesn't that sound just the most thrilling?"

Her hair now free of pins, she shook out the thick curls, then looked past Annie and pointed toward a line of trees. "Isn't that the creek over there?" Without waiting for an answer, she started in that direction. "Can you imagine, naming a creek Dumplin? These people are so backwoodsy." She shook her head. "Oh, well, at least there'll be music and laughter tonight."

Neither Annie nor Betsy spoke until Lorna disappeared into the thicket. Then they exchanged incredulous glances.

Betsy's mouth dropped down at the corners. "I'm a-feared Lorna's settin' herself up for a big fall. If Noah is anything a'tall like Ike, he'll never leave his land to go traipsin' off with her. She really needs to be in our prayers. We'll be gettin' to the valley in less than a week. Oh, my, don't the thought of that just make you want to dance." Betsy twirled around, giggling. Then, remembering the long-handled spoon in her hand, she stopped and started stirring the kettle vigorously again.

Tingles chased up Annie's spine. One week! In just one week she'd be standing on her very own land!

"Annie, dear, would you help me get this pot off the fire? It's plenty done, and we need to start gettin' ourselves purtied up."

Bunching up a section of her apron to protect her hand, Annie took hold of one hot handle. "You and Ken go on to the frolic without me. I think I'll stay here, keep watch over the camp."

"Pshaw! That dog of yourn can do a better job at that than you can. Now Annie, you just gotta stop bein' so man-shy. Men ain't no different than us. Some good, some bad, some who yammer on and on, and some quiet like you. From what you told me, I figure you weren't happy with that first man of yours. All you need to do is to find one that's a good fit. That's all. And from where I'm standin', I don't think you got far to look."

"Ike." Annie shook her head. "No. I ain't disputin' that he's real pleasin' to the eye, and when he puts his mind to it, he can say some real nice things. But then he always falls into his true nature, and that's tryin' to lord it over everybody."

"Dear heart, someone has to take charge, or we'd never get nowhere. And I think he's been real nice about it."

"*Nice?* To you maybe. But do you know what he did to me not more'n an hour ago? He flat drug me away from the store. Just took me by the arm and hauled me outta there, whilst Mr. Keaton and me was still talkin'."

"That don't sound like him. What was bein' said?"

"The storekeeper? Oh, he was just bein' neighborly."

233

"How exactly?"

"He was puttin' in a request for the first reel at tonight's welcomin' party. And Ike hauled me away before I even had a chance
to give him my answer. Like anything I have to say don't mean a
thing."

Betsy's generous lips spilled into a grin. "I declare, Annie, don't
you know nothin' about men? Ike weren't bullyin' you; that was
his way of tellin' that other fella to back off. That if he's thinkin' of
shinin' up to you, he'll have to get past Ike first. I told you he's
sweet on you."

Although this wasn't the first time her friend had suggested that
possibility, the thought sent a rush of warmth through Annie's
being . . . starting with her cheeks. "Well, if he is—which I ain't
sayin' he is—Ike should'a given me the chance to speak, because
my answer would'a been no. I only been to a dance a time or two.
I don't even know how."

"Dancin'? That ain't nothin' to fret about." Betsy grabbed
Annie's hand and started toward the back of her wagon. "Just move
your feet to the beat of the music, and follow what the other women
do. Don't you know? The only thing important to them clumsy-
footed men is that you *agree* to dance with 'em. A body'd think
you'd given 'em a feather to sport in their cap, they're so tickled."

Annie regarded her friend with added respect. "Betsy, as young
as you are, how'd you get to be so wise?"

"Me? This ain't me talkin'. I'm just tellin' you what my mama
told me, and her mother before her. Now quit your stallin'. We
gotta do somethin' special with that hair of yourn."

$\sim$

"*Where are those two?*" Ike took another gander over the heads of
the milling settlers, looking out the entrance of the stockade for
Annie and Betsy.

A welcoming speech had been made, and the music had been

playing for some time. He wanted to go check on them, but he'd been occupied with introductions since the Bremmers and Lorna had walked into the fort a half hour ago. Word of the new arrivals had spread throughout the Henry's Station neighborhood like a wildfire since the wagon train pulled in, and folks for miles around were streaming in to meet the newcomers, especially the minister and his wife.

The Bremmers stood on one side of Ike, keeping their blossoming daughter Renate tucked safely between them. Ken was on Ike's other side—Ken, who rarely went anywhere without his bride. Yet Annie and Betsy still hadn't walked through that gate.

"Oh, you know women," he said. "Probably can't get a curl to go just right. My Betsy's determined to turn Annie into the belle of the ball."

"Annie looks just fine the way she is," Ike groused, knowing the men here outnumbered the fairer sex many times over. Lorna had been dancing within the glow of a multitude of lanterns since she walked in and had changed partners with each lively reel. And still there must be a dozen eager bachelors waiting their turn.

Ike glanced out the gate again. He really should go check on Annie and Betsy. Even Lorna, who always took an inordinate amount of time preparing herself, had strolled in with the Bremmers just after the music started.

Playing the lively music were three fiddlers, with Jigs, in his only ruffle-cuffed shirt, piping on his flute. They all sat on a platform held up by barrels, tapping their feet, grinning, and mostly eying Lorna as she charmed all the young men.

No one could deny she was spectacular looking with the strung lantern lights playing off her green satin gown. But to Ike she was like a cut rose or a child's play-pretty. Not someone with whom to build a life.

But Annie, now . . . she was as real as her simple beauty. And, as it turned out, she was free to marry. That thought had recently begun to take hold in his mind.

He'd no sooner left her this afternoon than he'd gone straight to Brother Rolf and put the question to him. Was Annie a runaway wife? And the minister had been just as forthcoming when he flatly said, no, she was not. That she was free to marry anytime she chose.

Ike hadn't ventured to ask about their secret, though. He trusted Brother Rolf completely. If the good man didn't think it impeded her ability to wed, then that was good enough for him. If he looked a hundred years he wouldn't find a woman more suited to frontier life. And she had her own business enterprises to boot . . . ones he would not interfere with as long as she felt the need for her own bit of independence.

"It's about time," Ken said. "The girls are finally coming."

Ike's heart picked up pace as he shot a glance toward the gate. There the two young women came strolling in. To his incredible delight—and utter dismay—Annie looked far more beautiful than he ever thought she could. Tonight, of all nights. Tendrils of curls spilled from beneath a lavishly ruffled white cap, softening to fragile femininity every curve and angle of her face. And those fascinating eyes looked all the larger. The realization he was gawking barely registered.

"Pardon the intrusion, Reardon." One of the settlers, Gilbert Cullpepper, stood in front of Ike with his round little wife. "I don't believe we've met the new minister."

Delayed by more introductions, Ike wasn't able to go with Ken to fetch the women. His intent was to escort Annie into the festivities and to keep her close from that moment on.

But who did he see making a beeline for her? Keaton, the storekeeper.

While Ike tried to concentrate on the conversation buzzing

236

around him, he was far more interested in learning what Keaton was telling Annie . . . or asking her.

". . . and we'll be sure to stay for church service in the morning, Brother Bremmer," Cullpepper's wife was saying.

"Wonderful," Ike concluded before she'd finished speaking. "We'll see you then." And he took off—he could no longer see Annie's face. Keaton had blocked his view.

By the time Ike pushed his way through the crowd to reach them, Keaton was walking away . . . to Ike's profound relief. Annie must have rejected his request for a dance.

Ike stopped directly in front of Annie. Removing his hat, he lifted her fingers to his lips. "I reckon I didn't get to be the first to tell you how beautiful you look tonight."

Annie appeared a bit befuddled. Deftly, she pulled her hand from his. "I, uh—no. I mean, thank you."

"Would you care to dance?"

"I—" She looked around him to the area where folks had formed a long line of couples.

"Ike," Betsy intervened, "Annie's a little uneasy about dancing. She ain't done it in quite a long spell. Why don't you take her over to the refreshment table and get her a cup of punch and maybe just watch awhile."

"*Betsy,*" Annie reprimanded. "It's not polite to—"

"Polite or not," Ike said, "I would be most honored if you'd accompany me. I'm a bit rusty myself." He offered his arm—and a smile.

Annie just stared up at him, speechless.

Was he being too pushy? The look they'd exchanged in the store when she agreed to go with him—had he misread it? Or was he acting too much like a dandified fop?

"Annie, dear, the man is holdin' out his arm for you."

"Oh, aye." She took his arm gingerly, almost as if it might bite.

She was acting mighty skittish. Ike placed his hand over hers,

237

but only lightly. The last thing he wanted now was for her to bolt. "Shall we?"

~

Annie couldn't believe the improvement in Ike's conduct, and his choice of attire couldn't be faulted. A finely woven white shirt complemented his tanned face delightfully and brought out his smile—one he displayed every time he looked at her. His hair he'd taken care to pull back into a smooth queue and tie with a thin black ribbon.

He escorted her through the noisy crowd of people, politely introducing her merely as "Mrs. McGregor, a member of our party," to more curiously staring faces than she could ever remember having seen in one place.

As they bade her welcome, she knew they wanted to question her, so she couldn't have been more grateful when Ike deftly and subtly maneuvered her past them to a long, makeshift table. What a far cry his manners tonight were from his rude behavior this afternoon.

A short but sturdy woman with a long stick stood guard over the table, keeping a horde of children at bay. Annie tried to concentrate on the amazing array of treats. It was hard to believe the number of fried pies and tarts and hoecakes that weighted down the long board, considering the scant notice the women of the area had had.

"Why don't you sample a few things?" Ike suggested, being the perfect gentlemen—with the exception that he stood much too close.

Annie couldn't decide if this was Ike's way of courting her, as Betsy suggested he might do, or was he just putting his best foot forward in front of all these folks? Whichever it was, her stomach was much too jumpy to partake of any food.

The many sounds vibrating the air didn't help: the loud music, a fast tune she'd heard Jigs play on the trail; dozens of folks laughing and talking all at once; young'uns running and screaming; dogs barking; a baby's cry. She hadn't realized how accustomed she'd become to the quiet of the wilderness. This sudden clamor and confusion made it all but impossible to think clearly.

Annie moved to the far end of the table, where a huge cauldron sat, still half full of some sort of fruit drink. An assortment of chipped crockery and metal cups ringed it. Nothing fancy here. But she hadn't come across the mountain expecting to find china and crystal.

And Ike was still right at her elbow. "Mistress Williams," he said to a middle-aged woman who was serving the punch, "if you please, my lady would like some refreshment." He reached past Annie and picked up what looked like the nicest crockery cup and handed it to the woman whose hands, like Inga's, were red from years of washing clothes with lye soap.

But Annie was unable to concentrate on the woman for more than a second. Ike had called her "my lady." *His lady.* Betsy was right! He was proud to be with her. He did think her pretty. Even with someone as beautiful as Lorna there.

She knew her hand trembled when she took the cup from him, and her pulse throbbed at her throat.

He smiled, holding her within the depths of his light hazel eyes. Then his gaze slowly meandered down to her telltale throat . . . and lingered. Finally his attention moved back up to her mouth, then eventually back to her eyes.

She could hardly breathe. She knew he knew how utterly he affected her, and he seemed equally taken with her. His eyes confirmed it.

The night turned a whole lot warmer.

With a flush rising in her cheeks, Annie tore her gaze from his and took a rather large drink from her cup. When he looked at her like that, the very depths of her heart cried out for her to, in truth, be his lady.

She took another swallow. She needed to clear her head . . . a head that needed to remind her foolish heart that, for all the wonderful things she loved about Isaac Reardon, this man, like her father, had to rule all those around him. Why else would he want to start his own town?

23

"Let's skirt the crowd on our way back to the Bremmers," Ike said after they finished their punch.

"That might be wise," she agreed, knowing he was doing the usual—making a decision for her. But she was pretty sure he only meant to please her. And she found herself liking that. Besides, her heart argued, men just naturally wanted to protect *their ladies*. For tonight, anyway, she'd let him.

Moving away from the light and to the outside of the gay but hurly-burly gathering, Annie became aware that Ike no longer held her by the elbow, but had her hand, his fingers intertwined with hers . . . which he held tucked against his chest as they made a wide circle of the festivities.

Through the finely woven linen of his shirt, she could easily feel the beat of his heart. It pulsed at the rate of the fast-paced quadrille now being played and with the same pounding intensity. Was he truly as aware of her as she was of him?

She sneaked a peek at his face. Even in the darkness, his eyes were clearly visible, reflecting the distant lantern light—*and they were looking back at her.* Her own heart tripped, then began to race all the faster.

Unable to take her eyes from his, a moment passed before she realized they were no longer walking, just looking at each other. Slowly, he brought their entwined hands up and gently brushed her knuckles across the supple warmth of his lips.

Nothing could have prepared her for the tingle that shot up her arm and slammed into her already pumping heart. Her legs lost strength. She dragged in a breath. Yet she couldn't bring herself to pull away . . . or to look away.

"I've been thinkin' a lot about you lately," he said, barely louder than the hectic rhythm of the musicians, his breath playing across their hands still so close to his mouth. "I'm real glad you're comin' with us."

She knew she should respond, say something, but everything between her brain and her tongue had turned to mush. All she wanted was for his lips to do to hers what they'd just done to her fingers. She couldn't take her eyes from his mouth, so firm yet how very tender—as she'd just learned.

"Annie," he whispered and lowered those lips to hers. Touching lightly, tracing hers, then taking them in a most stirring way as he pulled her ever closer.

"Ike!" she heard someone call. "There you are."

He groaned against her lips, then placed a hand at the back of her head and gave her an even more urgent kiss before abruptly pulling away.

Leaving her utterly bereft.

"Ike, where you been?" It was Wolfie. He ran to them, along with another lad about his size, panting for air. "We been lookin' all over for you."

"Well, you found me." Ike sounded no more pleased than Annie was. "What's the emergency? Is someone skulking around our camp? What?"

"No, nothin' like that. But I think I found you some more settlers. Newcomb here, says his pa, Mr. Auburn, is looking to move on from Henry's Station. He wants to talk to you."

"Later," Ike said, still hanging onto Annie's hand. "I'll talk to him later."

"But we're leavin' the fort now." Newcomb stepped close. "My baby sister's teethin', and she's taken to frettin'. You gotta talk to my pa now."

"*Ja,* now," Wolfie pleaded. "If they come, I'd have someone my own age to go huntin' with."

Ike sighed, then squeezed Annie's hand. "All right. If you don't mind, Annie, let's go see his pa. Lead the way, Newcomb. Auburn, did you say? I don't believe we've met."

Running ahead, the skinny kid yelled back, "We just got here last week. We took the Wilderness Road overhill from Virginia."

The boys zealously led the way in the search for the lad's father, apparently unaware of the intimate moment between Annie and Ike they'd interrupted. Annie was relieved. She didn't want the whole settlement hearing about her and Ike before she herself could figure out how she'd ended up in his arms so quickly, or had let herself be so thoroughly kissed. Her lips, even now, hummed from the astounding sensation.

By the time they reached the lad's family at their wagon outside the gate, Annie had managed to regain her composure—and some of her sense—though she still allowed Ike to hold her hand and take her wherever he wanted. She couldn't believe how quickly she'd fallen under the man's spell . . . or how much she wished the two of them were still alone, wrapped in each other's arms.

The other Auburn children and their mother were already atop one of the dozen or so wagons and carts parked outside the stockade. In the light of a single lantern hooked on the brake, the woman cuddled a small, whimpering child in her lap.

"Pa! Pa!" the lad called to his father.

Checking one of his team's halters, the slight-built but sinewy man turned around with a scowl on his thin face. "Where'd you take off to? I told you we was goin' on back to your uncle's right now."

"But I had to get Mr. Reardon. He's got good news." The skinny kid grabbed Ike's unoccupied hand and tugged him forward.

The man brushed lank hair from his eyes and sighed wearily. "And what could that be?"

He obviously had no idea what this was about. This was something the boys had cooked up by themselves.

"He's sellin' land for fifty cents an acre," the boy spit out before Ike could get a word in. "Good bottomland. Leastwise, that's what Wolfie says."

The man looked skeptical. "That true, mister? We pulled up stakes and come all the way out here to my wife's brother's, only to find all the decent pickin's was already took."

Ike eased free of the boy and offered his hand. "Name's Isaac Reardon. Me and my brother rode out here three years ago with our veteran's grants. We looked around for quite a spell, but we finally come up with a good-sized valley to file papers on. It's a few days to the west."

"More days of travelin'," Auburn's wife complained from up on the jockey seat.

With four young children and a baby, Annie knew how difficult the trip here must have been. The Wilderness Road that came south out of Virginia was supposed to be more passable than the Watauga Trace, but not by much.

Ike, too, glanced at her with sympathy. "It's about a week farther, ma'am." He turned back to Mr. Auburn. "I'd say we're fifty miles this side of the Nashville settlement on the Cumberland. Our valley's all bottomland that runs along a good-sized fork. And as long as the Indians don't rise up again, we got us an easy river float to take our cash crops to market. All the way down to New Orleans, if you had a mind to."

"You say it's all bottomland?" Mrs. Auburn asked over the noise of her fussing baby. Her interest piqued, she stuck a knuckle in her babe's mouth for her to gnaw on.

Her husband added, "I find that hard to believe. I was told there's nothin' but small coves and vales tucked in the hills 'twixt here and Nashville."

"For the most part, you heard right. But we've walked the length and breadth of our valley, and it runs five to seven miles wide and more'n ten long. We got us a real find."

"And Mr. Reardon is startin' his own settlement there," Newcomb eagerly added.

"That sounds mighty ambitious for a couple of young fellas such as yourselves," the father observed.

Yes, it is, Annie agreed silently. Her reasoning powers were solidly in place now.

But Ike only chuckled. "Aye," he continued. "Not that we started out with that in mind. My father passed on whilst we was away at war, and since the farm went to my oldest brother, our inheritance was the workings for a gristmill. We came overmountain searchin' for a spot along a quiet stream to set one up. But exceptin' where other mills was already operatin', we didn't find a likely place amongst these Watauga settlements. So we had to go farther west, a-lookin'. And now that we found our valley, we need farmers to come and grow enough corn for meal to make the mill worth settin' up."

"And you're askin' only fifty cents an acre?" Looking suspicious, the man cocked his head. "Sounds almost too good. Is there somethin' you're leavin' out? Like, have you got any special rules

245

you're expectin' folks to follow? Like them Quakers do back in Pennsylvania?"

"Not really. Only one."

Aye, Annie thought wryly, *to do exactly as he says.*

Ike continued. "We're hopin' to have nothin' but God-fearin' families."

"Well, we're that. What else?"

"Nothin' else. I figure when folks get settled in, we'll form our own militia in case there's Indian trouble. And if the need arises, I reckon we can elect us a sheriff, too."

"And who's gonna decide that?"

"The landowners, of course. Every man in the valley will have an equal vote. Equal representation, just like we fought so hard to get."

"And you're sayin' you wouldn't feel you had no extra say-so over the valley, you bein' the starter?"

"Only over the land I hold title to. I've had enough of givin' and takin' orders whilst I was in the army. Eight long years of bein' told when to get up and when to go to bed. Where to stand, *how* to stand. I just want to tend to what's mine and live in peace with my neighbors and my Lord."

Annie could hardly believe her ears. Isaac Reardon didn't want to run things. He'd said the words loud and clear. He'd been in bondage for eight years, just like she had. Even if it had been his choice. And now he wanted exactly what she wanted.

Was this God's way of telling her Ike really wasn't the same as her father, that she needn't fear letting him get close?

"When you folks pullin' out?" Mr. Auburn asked.

"Brother Bremmer, our minister, is havin' a church service for the folks hereabouts in the mornin'. So we won't be strikin' out till after noonin'."

"Did I mention I'm a mason by trade? When I build a fireplace, you don't never have to worry about your house gettin' all blacked up with smoke."

"We sure could'a used you last summer when we raised our first cabins."

Mr. Auburn and his wife exchanged nods of assent, and he returned his attention to Ike. "Then if it's agreeable with you, we can be here tomorrow, all loaded up and ready to leave with y'all."

Ike stretched out his hand to the man again and grinned. "We'd be plumb proud to have you." He drew Annie close, including her. Even now, he didn't forget she was with him. "See you folks tomorrow."

Waving good-bye, Annie strolled with him back to the music and revelry, not minding one bit that he'd released her hand to put his arm around her waist. Or that people might notice. God had heard her and shown her that Ike truly was the man for her. And she liked that just fine.

She didn't even mind when Jigs, up on the stage, sent her a bawdy wink when he spotted her snuggled against Ike's side.

She caught sight of the Bremmers and the Smiths seated on one of the many benches lining each side of the dance area. It warmed her heart all the more to see that the local settlers had pulled up stools in front of their friends to sit and chat. From Brother Bremmer's congenial smile, Annie knew he was glad Inga had talked him into coming. Despite the fact that a jug of rum was being passed around among one small cluster of men, everyone else seemed to be having good, clean fun.

"Yoo-hoo, Annie, Ike. Come sit with us," Betsy called, grinning like the cat who had eaten the mouse. She must have figured her matchmaking hopes for Annie and Ike had been realized. She scooted over and patted the spot next to her.

"Do you mind sittin' a spell?" Ike asked, giving Annie's waist a little squeeze. "I'd like to tell the others about the Auburns."

"Not at all," Annie deferred. He'd asked her permission! She took the vacancy next to Betsy.

Ike sat down right beside her . . . and reclaimed her hand, though he directed his conversation to Ken and Brother Bremmer. He had to almost holler above the laughter and music as he recounted what had just taken place with the new family.

A reel was in progress with a line of men facing one of women. Keeping time to the fast tune, the women curtsied, while the men bowed and swung their ladies around, before changing partners and doing the same again. The dancers all looked so merry and sure of themselves, with Lorna the gayest and most confident of them all, her gown mirroring the many lights like a fiery green jewel. And everyone was moving so fast!

Seeds of panic began to take hold in Annie. If Ike asked her to dance, how would she ever keep up?

Betsy leaned close. "Like I said, just step to the beat and do what the other women do."

Annie couldn't take her eyes off of Lorna's flying feet and whirling skirts. "I don't know."

"Ike won't care if you miss a step or two. He just wants a chance to hold you. I told you he was sweet on you." The music stopped just before Betsy said the last few words, and they came out much too loud in the void.

Annie's face flushed fire hot as those next to them turned and stared . . . and smiled.

"Pardon me, Betsy," Ike said with his own knowing grin. "Were you speaking to me?"

Annie almost died of mortification, but Betsy didn't seem the least ruffled. "Why, no, Ike. But I was just fixin' to say it's time you two got yourselves out there for the next dance."

"And I think you're right." Rising to his feet, Ike pulled Annie up without even asking.

She wanted to refuse as he walked her out to where the other dancers awaited the next tune. To run away, hide, anything. But everyone around them was watching.

One of the fiddlers called for couples to circle up. "The next dance," he said, "will be a round."

Ike, right beside Annie, whispered assurances. "This won't be near so hard."

On trembling legs, Annie joined the circle with him.

And straight across stood Lorna . . . Lorna, who would most likely laugh at her awkward attempts.

Annie tried to bolt, but Ike held her fast. Then, moving directly behind her, he lifted up her hands and held them out, imitating the stance of the other couples.

The music started. Annie took a deep breath and thanked heaven the beat wasn't nearly as fast as the last tune.

Ike's breath feathered across her ear as he whispered. "Start with your right foot . . . one, two, three, now."

Annie did as he said, and with him steadying her, she followed the lead of the couple ahead of her. Step, step, hop. Step, step, hop.

She was doing fine, just fine. Still, she felt certain all the other couples were staring. Taking a quick glance around, she found she was right. Noticeably curious about the unattached woman with whom Ike danced, folks smiled and nodded . . . all except Lorna.

She'd spotted them, and the look she gave Annie would've curdled milk faster than vinegar.

Annie missed a step.

"Don't let her fluster you," Ike encouraged. "Forget her. Just have fun."

Glancing back at this man who was swiftly and easily becoming so dear to her, Annie saw in his eyes all the encouragement she needed. This evening had the makings of the most wonderful night of her life, and she wasn't about to let Lorna ruin it.

Together, Annie and Ike finished the round dance, then went on to a reel. By the time the musicians stopped to take a break at the end of the second reel, Annie found herself grinning and laughing as much as anyone else. Thanks to Ike, she'd not only gained confidence in the dancing, but was thoroughly enjoying herself.

Jigs hopped down from the stage and immediately made his way through the throng to them. "I caught both of you laughing," he crowed. *"And at the same time.* What is this world coming to?"

"To exactly what it's supposed to be." Ike, his breath a little labored from all the exercise, draped an arm across Annie's shoulders.

That said it all. Feeling a bit bold in her own feelings, Annie let herself sway against him just enough to let him know she agreed.

"Lorna must be having a night of the first water, too. If ever there was a belle of the ball, she's it. Hasn't missed a dance or danced with the same partner twice."

"Aye, I know," Ike said, the gaiety gone from his voice. "I reckon I better go check on her. Jigs, why don't you keep Annie company till I get back?" He then gave her shoulder a quick squeeze. "I'll brave that mob beating their way to the punch bowl while I'm at it."

"Fetch me a cup, too," Jigs requested as Ike left Annie's side . . . for the first time since she'd walked through the gate.

"Glad to see Ike laughing again," Jigs declared. "He's been in a sour mood since Sylvia Enfield, from up Salisbury way, jilted him. He was supposed to be bringin' her back with him this trip. Just like he's bringin' Lorna for Noah."

Annie's smile fled. "I didn't know that."

"Aye." Jigs lost his own dimples. "She married herself to a fancy house and a prosperous tobacco plantation instead." He ground out the words as if it had happened to him. Then he brightened again. "I'm glad to hear you're goin' on with us. You keep him laughin'. He deserves some good times if anyone does."

Annie supposed this was Jigs's way of giving his blessing to her newfound closeness with Ike. "I'll try."

At that moment, the young man she'd seen dancing the round with Lorna stepped up to Annie. Tall, but not nearly as tall or as well filled out as Ike, he doffed his tricorn, exposing autumn-colored hair and a friendly smile. "Ma'am, the name's Cal, Cal Woods. Miss Graham, over there, bade me to seek you out."

Lorna? Annie instantly wondered what the girl was up to. She did not extend her hand to the simply attired fellow. "It's a plea-sure to meet you, Mr. Woods."

"Miss Graham was kind enough to tell me that not only are you not hitched to anyone—so to speak—but you'll be staying on with us here at Henry's Fort."

"Well, actually . . ." Annie began, glancing to Jigs for support. But he no longer stood beside her. He'd moved away to speak to a couple of giddy young girls barely into their maidenhood.

Annie turned back. "Actually, I'll be going on with the train tomorrow. The price of land here is more than I was prepared to pay, and—"

"I wouldn't be too hasty in my decision if I was you," he inserted. "I'm sure if you just give yourself half a chance, you'll find the other particulars hereabouts more than make up for the expense. And even that I'm sure could be worked out. I'd see to it."

"Mr. Woods, that's mighty kind of you, but I've—"

He caught up her hand and stepped closer. "Lovely lady, please don't cast my offer aside without due consideration. This is an established settlement. Not one that still needs to be hacked out of the wilderness. We got folks of almost every trade here. The onli-est thing we are woefully lacking here is marriageable women. It would pleasure me to no end if you'd stay. And let me come a-courtin'."

The earnestness in his blue green eyes and on his lightly freckled face made Annie uncomfortable. She withdrew her hand as politely as possible. "Sir, I scarcely know your name."

Mr. Woods backed away ever so slightly. "I beg your forgiveness, ma'am. It's just that I wanted to get my bid in first. When the other fellas around here find out you're not taken—"

"But she *is* taken." Ike's authoritative tone boomed forth from right behind Annie.

Startled, she darted a glance over her shoulder. He'd come up so close without her realizing.

Ike took possession of her, his arm wrapping her shoulders as before, only now with definite purpose.

The other fellow wasn't cowed in the least. "That ain't what I heard, Ike. Miss Graham, over there, says she's a free woman. Free to choose whoever she wants."

Ike tensed. His grip on Annie tightened. "You heard wrong, Woods."

Undaunted, Mr. Woods stepped closer. "Well, I think we should let the lady speak for herself."

"She doesn't need to speak for herself. I'm telling you."

Not free to choose? Doesn't need to speak for herself? Annie wrenched away from Ike. Every time she thought she could trust herself to him, he proved her wrong. "Oh, I'm free to speak for myself, all right. And that's the way I intend to remain. *Free.* Good evening . . . *gentlemen.*"

24

Ike jerked awake at the tapping of a woodpecker. He groaned and closed his dry, aching eyes. Between all the noise at the stockade and the bedeviling thoughts of that infernal woman, he couldn't have slept more than an hour all night.

He rolled over, and not seeing the usual circle of wagons, it took a second for him to realize where he was—in the woods. Alone. But he wouldn't have bedded down within sight of that woman last night for all the tea in India. Nor had he been up to answering the questions Jigs would have put to him.

Annie McGregor had not only rejected him in a most humiliating way in front of Cal Woods, but Jigs had witnessed their altercation from up on the platform—and only the Lord knew how many others had, too. That idiotic grin and shrug of Jigs's shoulder when their eyes met across the crowd had told him as much. And more. He'd been jilted. Again . . . for the second time in less than two months.

He still couldn't believe how quickly he'd let himself trust another female after his last put-down. But this time everything had seemed so right. The two of them seemed to want the same thing—to build a new life on their own land. In fact, Annie wanted it so much that she'd actually risked her very safety to come overmountain for it.

The difference between them, though, was insurmountable. What she wanted, she wanted for herself, alone. She did not want to share herself or anything she owned with anyone else.

Or at least not with him.

Oh, she'd forgotten for a little while last night, let him think she really cared. Overcome by gratitude, he supposed, for his offering to sell land to her for a price she could afford. And of course there'd been the music. Music and dancing did have a way of making folks let down their guard. Maybe Brother Rolf was right, after all, about wanting it banished.

No, he couldn't let himself take the easy path and blame her actions on the dancing. He was sure Annie, honestly and briefly, had considered giving up her freedom for him, then decided he wasn't worth it. So be it.

"Enough of this!" Ike threw off his blanket and sprang to his feet. He had too much to do anyway, with starting a settlement, to take on some fickle-minded woman.

He strode down to the creek, and after splashing enough cold water on his face to wake the dead, he snatched up his bedroll and headed back through the trees to the clearing.

Following the creek path, Ike broke out of the woods on the north side of the stockade. He heard the sounds of folks beginning to stir within the standing pikes, then remembered. Several families who lived a good distance from the fort had planned to stay within its walls last night to be here when Brother Rolf preached this morning.

He wondered how many would know about Annie's outburst the night before. Probably every last one of them. And he was in no mood to face their knowing expressions. He'd have to come up with an excuse to stay away from the service . . . one that sounded real plausible.

Giving the stockade a wide berth, he was cutting across the meadow in the direction of his square of wagons when he saw her. Annie. She walked in the direction of her cow, carrying her pail and milk stool. She was bound to see him.

And she was the last person he wanted to see this morning.

But there was no help for it. Even the tree stumps had been cleared for an unobstructed view in case the fort should come under attack.

Annie didn't seem to notice him, though. Her attention trained on her cow, she took long, graceful strides in its direction.

Ike loved to watch her move, her legs outlined by no more than a simple skirt. The morning sun glinted off her loose night braid. Stray strands catching on the soft morning breeze created a golden halo around her lovely, sun-kissed face. He couldn't imagine ever tiring of that sight. He found it even more appealing than the fetching way she'd appeared last night, with the ruffles and soft curls showing off her luminous eyes . . . those eyes that had betrayed how very shy and out of place she felt. And she *had* trusted herself to him for that short while. His instincts couldn't have been that far off.

He swallowed down a swell of loss. He couldn't just stand out here all morning ogling her. He needed to get his own chores done. Be ready to roll out right after the church service and the dinner that would follow it.

He stopped in his tracks. First, he needed to resolve whatever lay between him and Annie. Get things settled once and for all.

"But, Lord, I want to know one thing," he muttered as he started toward her. "Since it was your plan in the first place for a man to take a wife, why did you have to make them so all-fired hard to understand?"

~

Seated on her milking stool next to her cow, Annie saw Ike heading across the clearing, straight for her, with his sleeping gear tucked

255

under his arm. She leaned closer to Queenie, hoping he wouldn't notice her. The last thing she wanted to do was talk to him, or even look at his face, considering her suspicions.

She'd spent most of the night wondering where he'd gone with that bedroll. He'd practically tiptoed into camp to fetch it, then sneaked right back out. Had he found a woman at the frolic who was more congenial? One with a wanton nature, who would let him spend the night with her? Had he kissed her the way he did Annie? And more?

Sufficient reason to keep a safe distance, she'd told herself a thousand times during the night . . . when she wasn't crying out to God for not making it easier to understand his will. Was she destined to always stumble along so blindly? Why couldn't she see more clearly? She'd heard of so many others who did. Like that Englishman John Newton. He'd even been inspired to write that lovely song about how he'd been lost, but now he was found, "was blind, but now I see."

Why not her? Was she even more unworthy than Mr. Newton, a former slave trader? So unworthy that God would leave her to flounder like a fish cast onto the bank?

Mayhap her father had been right to sell her out of the family. Maybe he saw how truly unworthy she really was.

Tears began pooling in her eyes. *You're feeling sorry for yourself again,* she scolded as she rubbed her face across an arm.

The approaching footsteps on August-dry grass crunched ever louder. Ike would be upon her in a second.

And she with tears in her eyes. Taking another swipe at them, she bent into her milking all the harder.

He came up behind her and stopped. "I need to speak with you."

Involuntarily, Annie's back stiffened.

"It's not about last night," he said. Obviously, he'd noticed her reaction. "It's about the land I said I'd sell you in my valley."

The land. Annie let go of the teats and swung to face him. *He was going to revoke his offer.*

"From the look on your face, I'd say you've got me pegged all wrong. As usual."

Annie quickly composed her features. "I'm listenin', Mr. Reardon. What do you have to say?"

"Just that my offer stands. Your milk and bees will be an asset to the valley. The bees for pollinatin' fruit trees as well as for their honey. So, I'm still willin' to lead you there and give you third choice of the land I'm sellin' off—after the Bremmers and Smiths. For fifty cents an acre." He paused. A muscle tweaked in his jaw. When he spoke again, his tone was much flatter. "And as for last night—as far as I'm concerned, nothin' happened between us, not one blessed thing. If that's agreeable to you."

"It's agreeable," she said, not allowing her voice to betray any of the emotions roiling within her. She *would* have her land, but how could he act as if the kiss and the words that had passed between them had meant nothing? It was worse than if he'd raged at her.

"Then it's settled." Without another word, he turned and strode away . . . calmly, casually, as if nothing of any consequence did happen last night.

❧

Church service was held on the same ground where Annie had danced with Ike the night before. Brother Bremmer preached his sermon up on the same keg-supported boards where Jigs and the fiddlers had played their reels and quadrilles. And, same as last night, Annie felt a plethora of curious eyes boring into her from all sides as she sat between Inga and Betsy. She was particularly glad when at long last Brother Bremmer gave the benediction and everyone rose from the stools and benches to set up for the potluck to follow.

"Kenny," Betsy called to her husband as she snagged Annie's arm. "Would you mind fetchin' that gobbler we been roastin' in the pit? Annie and me, we'll get the trenchers and spoons and such."

Like the loving husband he was, Ken gave Betsy a quick peck on the lips, then took off to do her bidding.

Watching him with his young wife hurt so much that Annie wanted to cry. But she wouldn't. "Betsy, dear, I'll help you bring them over; then I'm just going back and rest up a bit before we leave. I must'a eaten somethin' that didn't agree with me last night."

Just then, Lorna, who'd been strolling by on the arms of two young men, halted. Wearing a day gown and bonnet of butter yellow linen with striped ruffles and white lace, she was dressed so grandly compared to everyone else that she looked like a princess viewing her poor subjects. At the moment, a shocked princess. *"Did I hear you say you're leaving? Going on with us? Going to the valley?* But you *said* you were staying here!"

"Land hereabouts is too expensive." Annie hoped that would put a quick end to the very public exchange.

"But I informed several of the bachelors and a widower that you would be staying here," she said with a staged smile. "And truly, Annie, a few of them have some rather lucrative proposals to offer you."

Lorna might as well have been up on the platform making an announcement, considering all the attention she was drawing with her unnecessarily loud words. Everyone stopped talking and just stood there, staring. Thank goodness, Ike was nowhere in sight.

"You needn't have bothered with your matchmaking scheme," Annie said, not even attempting to be pleasant. "I'm not for sale at any price." She swung to face Betsy. "Why don't you have Lorna help you bring over the dishes? Give her hands something to do for a change. It sounds like her tongue could use the rest."

Annie wheeled away but didn't miss Lorna's gasp and her "Well, I *never!*"

She also didn't miss a few rumbling chuckles from the ring of spectators. And for the first time that day, Annie smiled. One small triumph. Knowing that she'd have to ask God's forgiveness, and maybe even Lorna's, tarnished the moment—but not by much.

Heading toward their encampment, Annie didn't get more than halfway across the field before she was again summoned.

"Annie! Wait up!"

She glanced back and spotted Jigs coming after her with two determined-looking men. More of Lorna's doing, she was sure. If she ever got to the quiet peace of her own property, she didn't think she'd ever want to leave it.

Her first inclination was to take off running, leave them to wonder about what kind of a strange person she was . . . something like the way Ike had left her to wonder about him last night when he stole out of camp.

But to her dismay, she wouldn't have that option. Ike stood beside his wagon, grim-faced and watching her. She couldn't afford to show any weakness in front of him now that he'd agreed to sell her the land.

Taking in a lungful of air, she plastered on a pleasing expression and turned to Jigs and the two settlers.

Jigs sauntered up and introduced the two men, with a lopsided grin displaying one of his dimples. Everything was a joke to him.

The shorter one, attired in milled cloth that gave evidence of a certain prosperity, spoke first and fast, as if he were running a race. "I'm the oldest son of my family—the heir," he said, sweeping his tricorn from his head to expose slicked-down blond hair tied at his nape. "We been here three years. We got a hundred and twenty prime acres along the French Broad. Thirty's already under the plow. By trade, my pa's a furniture maker, the only one in these parts, and he's teachin' me all about different woods and glues and varnishes. We already made a few tables and such for folks around here. So as you can see, I got a lot to offer as a husband. I got me a fine future, one that I will be proud to pass on to my own son. And I'm gonna need a wife for that. What do you say?" As suddenly as he'd started, he stopped speaking and waited, his toothy grin expectant . . . as if she couldn't possibly refuse him.

Naturally he had no idea that in recounting his endowments, his boasting about being the oldest son and heir had not been in his favor. Considering the reason she was sold into servitude, it was a real sore spot with her.

Thank goodness the other man filled the void of her silence. He appeared overworked and unkempt, his shirt wrinkled and thread-bare. He, too, made his plea. A pig farmer, he had forty acres with ten in corn and five in sorghum to provide feed for his livestock. As a widower with four children, ages three to eight, and with no other kin in the Watauga settlements, he had need of a mother for his children in the worst way.

Him, Annie pitied. He was in a kind of bondage himself, trying to run a farm and do household chores at the same time. The poor man might be able to manage the cooking and washing. But what would he know about preserving food, making soap or candles, or spinning and sewing? Or the cures for ailments when his babes took sick?

Yes, this one she pitied—but not enough to give up her own dream when it was so close to becoming a reality.

In as polite a manner as possible, she declined both offers. And all the while, she knew Ike watched. She could tell by the way Jigs's gaze danced in his direction every few seconds. To Jigs everything was just one more farce.

But not so with Ike. After her outburst last night, he probably hoped she *would* agree to marry one of these men to take her off his hands, even if it did cost him and his valley her hive of European honeybees.

Well, it wasn't going to happen. She was almost at the end of her rainbow. She wouldn't forfeit her dream now. Not for him. Or because of him. Or anyone else.

25

"Giddyap! Giddyap!" Otto yelled, gallop-skipping along the trail past Annie, whacking his rump as if it were a horse.

Two of the younger Auburn girls chased after him, doing the same. The oldest whinnied, her nut brown braids flying out behind her like two thin tails.

Chuckling to herself, Annie watched from beside her bull. The children topped the gentle wooded rise and "galloped" down the other side.

All that peace and quiet she'd hoped for once the wagon train got under way again certainly hadn't materialized. The quiet part, especially. In the three days since the company had left Henry's Station, the Bremmer and Auburn youngsters had been romping and yelling as if they'd all just been let out of cages. Even this morning's rain hadn't slowed them down.

Too bad Mrs. Auburn didn't have some of that energy. From the look of her, she could use a week's worth of undisturbed sleep and a whole lot more stick-to-the-ribs food. With five children

261

ranging from eleven years to six months, the two oldest being boys, the woman really had her hands full. Perhaps once they got settled she would fare better. At the moment, the poor creature didn't look like she would survive another birth.

Mr. Auburn could end up in the same fix as the poor widower at Henry's Station who'd asked Annie to marry him. She sent up a swift prayer for the man.

Now that really was praying blind, she told herself. She'd probably never know if God answered that plea . . . not *if* but *how,* she corrected. A Bible verse popped into her mind—her recompense for occupying herself these past few days with the memorization of certain verses from her New Testament. *If we ask any thing according to his will, he heareth us: And if we know that he hears us, whatsoever we ask, we know that we have the petitions we desired of him.* Memorizing Scripture had proved the best way to keep her mind off her incessant yearning.

At the thought of Ike, her heart started that hollow, lonesome throbbing. But she had to believe that the Lord knew Ike was not the man for her. She snapped her whip over the cows to speed them up. The sooner they got to the Reardons' valley, the sooner she'd have so much to occupy her that there'd be no more time for thoughts of him.

But was that what she really wanted?

Another verse popped into her head, one she'd learned while staying with the Whites. *Delight thyself also in the Lord; and he shall give thee the desires of thine heart.* The Lord knew she'd tried to delight herself in him, so why was her heart in so much pain over this desire for freedom she'd had for so long?

But is that truly your heart's desire?

The thought came out of nowhere. A stunning thought. Had God just spoken to her? If that were so, what did he mean by it? He knew that for years her deepest longing, the center of her every prayer, had been to live in freedom.

Annie gained the top of a treeless rise along with her yoked cows and abruptly came upon Otto. His back to her, the child stood stock-still in the middle of the trail a scant few feet ahead of her team's hooves. Rushing to him, she plucked him up and set him safely to one side.

As she did, he pointed to the sky. "Look! Look!"

A rainbow after the storm, the second she'd seen since she'd left Charlotte. Was this the sign of a covenant . . . a covenant God was making with her? Was he saying he would give her the desire of her heart?

Even as a sense of joy rose within her, a very real concern emerged. Maybe this rainbow was God's way of telling her he was giving her some other desire, not the land.

Panic taking over, Annie glanced back at the outfit behind her.

How she wished she could discuss her questions with Brother Bremmer. Although she knew what his answer would be—the one that ministers always seemed to give. *Set your sights and your desires on pleasing the Lord, and everything else will fall into place.*

But she knew that if she couldn't have property of her own, a say over her own life, she'd just shrivel up and die. Land could be counted on. It would always be there to provide a home and food and clothing. Why shouldn't she desire her small share of this part of God's creation?

Annie stepped to the rear of the cart and pulled her New Testament from a suspended tote. The answers were here. That's what the men of God always said.

Wolfie, not Ike, came jogging back toward her. "We'll be stoppin' at the bottom of the hill for noonin'," he announced as he sped by.

During the past three days, Ike had managed not to speak a single word to her. And she rarely caught sight of him. Which was just as well, she reminded herself every time she started to weaken.

The final blow was Cap. Her dog deserted her whenever they

263

were on the move. He'd rather spend his time up front with Ike than back here eating dust with her. But she had no intention of going to fetch the traitor.

Once the company settled down for nooning, Annie ate a solitary meal of leftover pancakes and some of the dried buffalo meat she'd bartered for at the fort. She sat on the far side of her cart, finding it harder than ever to be sociable. The Smiths and Bremmers had a tendency to ply her with questions whenever she did mix with them.

Lorna sauntered around the corner of the cart—this one who usually avoided Annie like she had smallpox, or worse, the bubonic plague.

"Afternoon," Lorna said as if she were dropping by for a pleasant chat.

"Afternoon." Employing caution, Annie stood up. She couldn't imagine what the girl was up to now.

Lorna smiled sweetly, dimples denting both cheeks as she smoothed the ruffled tucker of her blue-striped frock.

Annie became more suspicious.

"I just dropped by to tell you—," Lorna said, her words flowing smooth as the green satin she'd worn the other night—"you may think you've won because you're still with us. And you may think you're going to live in our valley. But it's simply not going to happen, my dear."

The delivery may have been courtly, but the words themselves were pure Lorna.

"Ike," she continued, "doesn't have the only say over the property. Noah has just as many rights. And I'm certain I can charm their little brother, Andy, into siding with me, too. So you might as well turn this pile of junk around right now and head back to Henry's Station. Get your sights off of Ike, and marry one of the ignorant clods there."

Annie refused to let Lorna and her nasty words get the best of her. "I do thank you for droppin' by, Miss Graham," she said in her own best English. "Your visits are always like a ray of sunshine on an otherwise dreary day."

Lorna's smile crashed. "I'm not jesting. You'll turn around now, if you know what's good for you. Ike is not interested in unwashed urchins like you, no matter what you think. I'll have you know, the Reardons are the most prosperous farmers in Rowan County. Their uncle is an honored judge. And Will Jr. said his tobacco was looking so prime this year, he's even planning on buying a slave or two. And, surely, Ike has mentioned that his mother is coming out here to live in a few months. Never in a thousand years would she approve of a rag like you. So give it up!"

Despite Lorna's nasty message, Annie actually felt sorry for the girl if she truly believed everything she said. Because Annie knew different. She'd been there when Ike explained the hard truth to Mr. Auburn. "Lorna, I know you find this hard to accept, but you're goin' to be livin' on raw land in a rough wood cabin for a long time to come. Just like the rest of us. Surely your betrothed told you that he and Ike inherited only the innards to a gristmill from their father, along with their strong backs and willingness to work. It'll be years before your Noah will be able to provide you with the fancies you're used to. . . . But why is anything about the valley botherin' you? You said you were goin' to get your husband to take you to New Orleans."

That got a powerful reaction. The haughtiness in Lorna seemed to melt away before Annie's eyes. Annie stared at her for the longest time. Lorna looked as if she'd just been informed that someone very dear to her had died. Finally she spoke. "I hadn't thought things through all that well. Without cash money, we couldn't just take off and go. I'm going to have to wait till Noah's mama comes. She'll bring lots of money with her—I know she will." She glanced about uncertainly. "Or I may have to wait until next year when more folks come to buy land."

Annie couldn't help smiling. "I wish you luck."

"I don't need your luck." The fire was back. "Merely your absence from my presence. Heed my words—go back to your own kind. Oh, I know Ike flirted with you at the frolic, but as you can plainly see, in the clear light of day he'll never consider anyone of your crude sensibilities. Go away!"

As the mean-spirited girl whipped her voluminous skirts around to leave, Annie knew that much of what Lorna said was ridiculous. But not all. Hurtful truth stuck its ugly head up here and there. Still, she would never allow Lorna to glimpse her pain.

Annie put her hand over the New Testament in her apron pocket for strength and comfort . . . and was slapped with the realization that one thing had been left unsaid. Although she hated to, she called after Lorna. "Wait. There's something more I need to tell you."

Lorna stopped and jerked around, her composure fully regained, even haughty.

"I need to apologize for striking you the night the Indians came. I could just as easily have thrown water in your face the way Betsy did to Inga."

Lorna's hands went to her hips. "That's an apology? To wish you'd thrown water in my face instead? I suppose that shouldn't surprise me, coming from such an ignorant wench. I'm amazed your people don't keep you hidden away in a cellar. Or maybe they did. You look like you crawled out of a hole."

Watching Lorna stalk away, Annie shook her head. That girl sure made 'love thy neighbor' hard to live up to.

Annie glanced down at the unfinished meal she'd left on the grass. Ants now crawled in it. Picking up the trencher, she tossed the contents. Let the bugs have it—her appetite was gone.

Instead, she dipped herself a cup of water from the bucket hanging on a cart spike. Her mouth had turned very dry with the thought that Ike's mother would be coming soon. Was Mrs. Reardon cut from the same cloth as Lorna? After getting to know Ike, Annie found that hard to believe. He was so levelheaded.

But maybe he took after his father. After all, Mrs. Reardon *had* blessed the marriage of one of her sons to a frivolous girl like Lorna.

Another very good reason not to succumb to her yearnings for Ike.

∾

The afternoon darkened into evening sooner than usual. A second bank of storm clouds had rolled in from the south, threatening more rain. Camped by a narrow but fast-flowing creek, Annie hurried through her chores. Whenever she passed Ike while putting her animals out to graze, she tried her best to ignore his considerable presence just as he did hers. It was too soon to trust herself to gaze up into his eyes for even the most casual of pleasantries.

After getting her cook fire going, Annie took her bucket to refill. Walking down to the creek, she noticed that dark clouds had gathered again and appeared ready to burst. She hoped they'd hold off until she got her meal prepared. And, she remembered, she still had to dig a trench around her cart to keep the rain at bay.

So much to do every day.

But in four more days they would reach the valley. Only four more days!

Buoyed by that thought, Annie stepped more lightly as she passed through an opening in a thick tangle of berries, while being careful not to catch her already ragged skirt hem on any of the thorns. Or to step on any. Because it had been such a wet day, she'd gone barefoot to save her moccasins.

Reaching the gentle roar of the rain-swollen stream, she took rest in the thought that for the first time since her distasteful conversation with Lorna, she was truly out of sight and sound of the camp. Stretching her weary neck muscles, she stole a moment of peace before stepping cautiously out onto a gnarled sycamore root that stretched into the water. Only four more days.

"There you are."

Her solitary moment shattered, Annie balanced herself on the root and turned to see Betsy. She did her best to put on a hospitable face for her dear friend. "Yes? Did you need something?"

"Not exactly." Surprisingly, Betsy had her own bucket—Ken usually fetched all their water. "I just thought it would be nice to chat a bit."

"Please, Betsy, if this is about Ike and me, I'm really too tired to talk about that now. Besides, I need to get back to my cookin'."

"No, it's not that—not *this* time," she quipped with a grin. "It's just that I'm startin' to worry about Lorna."

"Just startin'?" Annie said sharply, then wanted to bite her tongue. Betsy hadn't done anything to earn her sarcasm.

Betsy didn't seem fazed as she continued. "No, really. The closer we get to the valley, the jumpier she gets. And she's been plaguing Ike with all manner of questions a body'd think she'd already know the answers to."

"Betsy, why are you talkin' to me about this? There's nothin' I can do about her. She's hated me from the day I joined with you folks."

"I don't think she knows what she hates or likes. I saw her come talk to you today. She's never done that before. I hoped my prayin' for her had done some good. Anyway, I was wonderin' if she said anything in particular to you that might make you think she's startin' to look to the Lord for her answers."

"I'm afraid not. She just came to deliver more of her usual threats if I don't leave the train. For some strange reason, she's always seen me as a threat. I think her worst fear is that she might have to call me sister-in-law. But, you're right; she was actin' real nervous. I reckon this adventure she started out on is fixin' to turn into real grown-up life, and that scares her to death. You know, the thought of giving up her red dancin' shoes to become an everyday settler's wife."

"Aye. Ever' chance she gets, she's at Ike or Jigs, askin' 'em what Noah's really like. It seems she only got to know him one month last year whilst he and his brothers come home for a visit. And I don't think she's likin' what they're sayin'. I suspect she reckoned he was gonna whisk her away on some grand adventure. But from what Ike and Jigs are sayin', it appears Noah is as interested in gettin' this new settlement goin' as Ike is. Maybe more so. I do pray Lorna will calm down once she sees her husband-to-be again. She's always bragged on how handsome and dashin' he was when he came a-courtin'."

"Well, I pray Brother Bremmer won't marry them 'lessen she does."

"Speakin' of courtin'—I think that's the problem betwixt you and Ike. There ain't been no time when he could just come by of an evenin' for a little spoonin'."

The peacemaker was turning into a matchmaker again. Annie groaned. "I really got to get back to my cookin'."

"I got plenty extra. Don't fret about that. In fact, don't fret about anything." Betsy's mischievous expression couldn't be missed even in the fading light. "Once we're settled, things'll just take their natural course."

"I thought we agreed not to talk about this. No matter what you say, you can't change things. Ike and me, we're like milk and cream. Oh, when we're stirred together real good, it looks like we'll stay that way, but it only takes a little while for us to be back to our own selves again . . . with him floatin' to the top, tryin' to lord it over me."

"I don't believe that. What I see is a good man simply actin' like a man. The other night he was just protectin' what you let him think was his . . . *whether you thought you needed it or not*. Just like that night when him and the other men took on them outlaws."

Betsy placed a hand over her slightly swollen belly and glanced down. "It's his job to protect his wife and whatever children they have together. Just like it's her job to make a home for him and their children. A place where they can have peace and rest from the trials of the world."

"Betsy, I know you mean well. And, mayhap I will marry one day. But if I do, the man will have to—to . . ." Annie stopped. Taking her hopes there was too painful. "No, I don't think I'll ever marry."

"That would be a real sadness. You'd make a real good mama." Betsy's puppy-dog eyes lent extra feeling to her words. "Well, I reckon I better fetch my water and get back."

"Here, let me." Annie took Betsy's bucket, knowing the greatest sadness of all was that she'd never marry anyone and have children because no other man could ever measure up to Ike—in those things that made her love him. And, heaven help her, she did.

Annie dipped Betsy's wooden container into the water, filling it only halfway so it wouldn't be too heavy. Then, handing the bucket back to the girl, she realized that she too always did what she could to protect Betsy. But unlike herself, Betsy needed to be in someone's charge and just naturally accepted it without question.

"God keep you, Annie," Betsy said with much more feeling than a mere parting remark. Then she stepped across the maze of roots toward the path up the slope.

"You, too, dear friend."

Annie watched her go, knowing that Betsy never saw beyond how things were in her own marriage. She'd undoubtedly had loving parents and now a husband equally so. Her baby would verily benefit from all that love. A wonderful life for a child. Annie caught herself starting to slip into a maudlin comparison with her own childhood.

Not today. She slung her bucket down into the water and came up with liquid almost to the brim. Carefully making her way off the bare root, she started up the path, then paused at the sound of children's laughter.

It came from somewhere just beyond the bankside thicket. "Ring around the rosie, pocket full of posies," they sang . . . that same song that accompanied the game Annie had played with her sisters when she was little. Then came the words "All fall down" and the familiar giggles that always followed.

Betsy was right. Not having children of her own would be a great sadness.

But most things in life came at a price. And freedom had always cost dearly, she knew, remembering the war that had lasted as many years as her servitude. A country ripped apart, thousands of lives lost.

Thank goodness she didn't have to pay for her freedom in Christ as well. Jesus had paid the very great price to purchase her spiritual freedom . . . and even after sacrificing his own life, he still stood ready to give her love and comfort. *And protection.*

Hadn't Ike merely been trying to do the same? Following the example the Lord had set before him?

Had she been the one in the wrong—as Betsy had hinted?

Annie looked around her as her thoughts became clear. Yes, the Lord was always keeping her close. The Bible said so. Putting down the bucket, she withdrew the New Testament from her apron pocket. Where was that passage? "In John, aye. About the middle."

She quickly scanned the pages before the gloaming faded to night, then found the spot where Jesus had said, "I give unto them eternal life; and they shall never perish, neither shall any man pluck them out of my hand."

No matter who else was in her life, Jesus held her close in his hand.

But this was the same Christ who was the head of the church and who said the husband was to be the head of his wife. That was the part that scared her . . . the idea of trusting a man to lead her.

There was the second half of that edict, though. The husband was supposed to love his wife as himself . . . to give her comfort and provision and keep her as safe as if she were in the palm of his own hand. Just like her Lord.

How could she not want that? Ike had as much as offered all this to her, and she'd thrown it back in his face . . . because of faithless fear.

Ike had never been in the wrong. It had been her, always her. He'd just been clumsy. And most likely, even that had occurred because she'd deceived him from the start about what brought her to the wagon train.

Her hope took the wings of morning. Then plummeted. What if Lorna was right? If she told Ike the truth, that her own pa thought she was of so little worth that he'd sold her into servitude, wouldn't that put Ike to wondering about her worth, too?

No, Ike was better than that. The Bremmers had been bond servants, and he treated them with the utmost respect.

The fault lay with her. She was as proud and haughty as Lorna ever thought of being . . . and just as greedy for land as her pa ever was.

Then a most stunning revelation came to her, and she fell to her knees. Didn't the Lord's Prayer say "forgive us our debts, as we forgive our debtors"? What right had she to beg forgiveness of her heavenly Father, when she had long harbored unforgiveness toward her earthly father? As the truth broke through to her stubborn heart, she whispered, "Forgive me, Father, as I forgive my pa."

With her repentance came a peace that flowed through her, holding her within its warmth. She remained in the fullness of that comfort for she didn't know how long, praising her loving, forgiving Lord.

Her knees stiff, she finally started to rise, then paused for one more request. "Father, I know I don't have the right to ask this after I rejected all your and Betsy's attempts to make me see the truth. But would you please give me the right words to say to Ike? And please help him to forgive me, too."

Pocketing her New Testament and her hope, for the moment anyway, she caught up the bucket handle and rose to her feet. Filled with trepidation, she turned toward the path . . . and slammed into a wall of a man.

Terror froze her in place as she stared up into the cold malevolent eyes of the outlaw Frank Beckley.

26

"I got my half all lashed down," Ike called across the wagon to Jigs on the other side.

"Me, too. Just about," he returned.

"For all the good it will do," Lorna groused from the interior, where she was making a bed for herself. "My blankets are still wet from last night."

Ike and Jigs had just tossed Lorna's damp tent over the wagon's bowed cover to give the girl some added protection. And Ike had no doubt he'd be hearing a lot more from her, since a miserable drizzle had been growing stronger for the past half hour.

"You want me to come up and keep you warm?" Jigs called through the layers of canvas.

"No," Ike answered for her. As squirrely as Lorna had been since they'd left Henry's Station, she just might take Jigs up on his offer.

Only four more days, he told himself as he unhooked the spade from beneath the wagon bed. If he could just hold his tongue for four more days, Lorna would no longer be his problem. None of them would. He scraped the debris from beside a wheel, then started trenching and banking. If Lorna thought *she* was going to have a soggy night, she should have the pleasure of spending it down on the ground as he and Jigs would be doing.

Annie McGregor, too, would be lying on damp grass and leaves, but that woman would cut out her tongue before she complained about a blessed thing . . . except about him. Him she'd complained about loud and clear.

Well, he'd be shucked of her in four days, too. And good riddance. This had been a very enlightening trip to Carolina and back. Twice convinced he'd found the woman to share his life, he'd twice been made a fool of. And twice saved, thank the good Lord. Before he ever again thought of marrying, he would have to know his prospective bride inside and out.

He shot a glance over to Annie's cart. No lantern glow had come from her outfit this evening. She must have turned in early. To avoid him, he was sure. All the more reason to dismiss her. No man wanted a surly, pouty wife.

"Ike, Jigs, you come quick! Now!" Brother Rolf ran toward them, a lantern swinging wildly in his hand. Wolfie hurried alongside.

What now? Ike wondered. He leaned the spade against the wheel as Jigs leapt across the wagon tongue to join him.

"Ken! Mr. Auburn! Ve need you, too!" Rolf yelled, breathing heavily. "Ve haf trouble. Da big trouble. Look." He held a scrap of parchment. *"Read."*

Jigs took it from him and slanted it toward the light. "Reardon," he read haltingly, "we have your wife. Bring loaded packhorses to Obed Creek tomorrow one hour after dark. Come alone."

Wife? Ike snatched the coarse paper from Jigs's hand and quickly scanned the message. Though poorly written, with several words misspelled, its meaning was unmistakable. The only ones who thought he had a wife were those useless thieves they'd run off. He glanced toward the cart. "Annie—has anyone seen Annie?"

"I found that paper wrapped around her bucket handle," Wolfie said, his voice shrill with fear.

"*Where?*" Jigs barked at the same time as Ike.

"Down at the creek. Just a minute ago when I went to fetch water."

Fear clamped onto Ike. Annie . . . in the hands of those pirates.

"They come up on us that close?" Ken Smith glanced warily into the darkness.

Ike noticed that both he and Jesse Auburn were now eying the scribbled note, and the women and children were converging with apprehensive faces.

When had it happened? Just now? An hour ago? Ike encompassed them all in his gaze. "Who saw her last?"

"I saw her down at the creek," Betsy said. "Around dusk."

"How long has that been?" Ike asked. It seemed like hours.

Jesse Auburn pulled a timepiece from his pocket. "About thirty, forty minutes."

"That long?" Ike groaned. He glanced around the encampment. "Where's that dog of hers? He should'a sounded a warnin.'"

"We had him off fishin' with us, sir," Wolfie answered in a rush, then cast a frightened glance to his new pal, the oldest Auburn boy. "Cap took off after a possum, and we ain't seen him since."

"He could be gone half the night. We can't wait." Ike reached under the wagon for his saddle.

Jigs grabbed his arm. "You're not thinkin' of settin' out after her now, are you? That's what they're waitin' for. To pull us away from camp, so they can ride in and take what they want."

"And who knows how many men they got with 'em by now," Ken added. "I won't leave here. I won't leave my Betsy here alone."

277

"And you're not going either, Isaac Reardon," Lorna ordered, climbing down from the wagon. "You promised to see me safely to Noah, and that's exactly what you're going to do."

"She's right," Jigs said. "We can't risk it. Besides, the note says they'll trade her back to us tomorrow night."

"But vat about Annie?" Inga asked. "She is *mit* t'ose bad mans all night."

"They already got too big a head start on us," Jigs said. "It's dark, and the rain's washin' away their tracks . . . if they're not wipin' 'em out themselves as they go. We'll never be able to find her tonight."

"You're right," Ken agreed. "We couldn't even catch up to Otto and Isolda in the daylight."

Ike became aware of a tugging on his leggings.

"Don't worry, Ike!" Otto exclaimed in a thin voice. "The Indians! They'll come and save her, just like they did us."

~

The filthy rag stuffed in her mouth and the foul smell of the unwashed hunter holding her flush against him had caused Annie to gag and wretch a number of times. Once again, bile rose in her throat, and again she swallowed it down rather than choke.

And as before, Frank Beckley chuckled at her distress as they rode his tall horse through the rain and the darkness. It was the only sound he'd made since taking her back at the creek.

With the outlaw's rain-dripping body hunkered low over hers to avoid any unseen branches, Annie had no idea where he was taking her. But even if she were able to ask, she probably wouldn't—for fear of his answer. Trapped within his arms, her hands tied by a rope he'd also secured to his own wrist, her panic rose as often as the bile. But she forced that down, too. If ever in her life she needed to keep her wits about her, it was now. As deftly as possible, she worked at loosening her bindings.

Suddenly Beckley reined the horse to a stop.

Had he caught her?

No. Beckley swiveled his torso and looked back the way they had come. Saying nothing, he remained in that position for a minute or so.

Listening for pursuers, Annie was sure. *Oh, God, let them be coming. Ike, please come!* She strained against the ropes all the harder, stopping only when he turned forward again.

He pulled off his floppy hat, shook the accumulated rain from it, then jammed it back on his head. "Well, lassie, looks like we made us a clean getaway. Thought as much. Yer men ain't got no stomach for much but back-shootin'. Didn't even try to chase after us that night we took off with one of yer horses and all them supplies. A bunch o' mama's boys, they is."

He nudged the rangy mount into a walk again, at a slower pace than before. "Yessiree, by George, a clean getaway. But, I swear, it took you long enough to come traipsin' down to that creek. I waited nigh onto an hour. And then that other wench showed up. The mouthy one. For a minute there I thought I was gonna have to knock her in the head to get rid o' her. But she finally lit out on her own."

He'd been waiting just for me? Annie's mind flashed to that first time she saw Beckley on the trail . . . the day he'd stared at her with those sunken eyes, then pointed at her and nodded just before he disappeared around a bend. She'd been afraid of him then. But that was nothing compared to what gripped her now.

"Yep, I come for you, and I weren't takin' nobody else." More words came out on his foul breath. "You and me, we got us a little score to settle. You see, that night when we rode into yer camp, I spotted that shaggy dog o' yourn. So I knowed it was you what fingered us. And ol' Foley, he's purely itchin' to get a-holt o' you, too. Took a bullet clean through his leg 'cause o' yer meddlin'. Yessir, he's gonna be plumb tickled to see you, little lady."

279

Oh, Lord, why now? Why have you brought me to this now?

~

With Rolf's lantern in hand, Ike hurried back to camp after searching both sides of the creek, almost oblivious to the squishing sounds of his soaked moccasins. He'd found the prints of only one man and horse on the far side and had followed them for more than a hundred yards. Deep prints. Rather than being washed away by the rain as Jigs had predicted, the tracks were even more visible because the horse was being ridden double on the rain-softened ground.

The men, toting their long-barreled weapons, met him before he reached the circle of wagons. "You're probably right, Jigs," Ike said. "She was taken by only one man on a horse. No sign of any others."

"So that means his thievin' cohorts is probably out there, watchin' us right now. Chompin' at the bit, waitin' for us to ride out after her," replied Jigs.

"Aye" was all Ike could say. But the thought of Annie with those brigands—he couldn't just sit here and do nothing.

Wolfie wedged himself past the other men, Annie's musket in his hand. "Since you men gotta stay here to protect the camp," he said, his voice as deep as he could manage, "me and Newcomb Auburn figure we'll slide on outta here real quiet and go after Annie ourselves."

"*Nein!*" Rolf scolded. "You are staying here vere I can see you. You understand?"

"If anyone's goin', it'll be me," Ike said, his resolve hardening.

"That's fool talk," Jigs said. "Even if you did catch up to them and shoot it out, you'd only be puttin' Annie's life in danger. They won't kill her as long as she's worth somethin' to 'em." He stepped closer and lowered his voice. "I know what you're thinkin'. We all are. But she's a strong girl, and even if they do decide to have their way with her, it's not as if she's some young maiden, pure as snow."

Ike couldn't believe the man's callousness. Before he could find acceptable words to rebuff Jigs, Rolf pushed his way between them.

"But she *is* da pure maiden. She is not da vidow like you t'ink."

Ike grabbed the big man's arm. *"What are you saying?"*

Rolf winced, but spoke up. "I promised I let her tell you, but. . . . She is not da runavay vife like you t'ink, but da runavay daughter. Her papa bound her out to Farmer Vite ven she is da age of mine Renate."

Ike veered around Rolf. He had to get to Annie *now.* He swung toward his wagon to fetch his saddle.

Rolf kept step. "Da time of Annie's service, it vas done, *und* her papa vas coming to get her *und* take vat da dairyman owes her at da end. Den her papa, he marry her off for profit, like her sisters. She say he sell her once, he not her papa anymore. So she come over-mountain to—"

"Wolfie!" Ike interrupted as he pulled out his saddle from beneath his wagon, the bridle draped over it. He tossed the latter to the lad. "Fetch my horse. Jigs, you and Ken soak some rags in oil and make me some torches whilst I saddle up."

"What for? It's raining." Jigs came toward him. "This is crazy. You'll just get yourself and Annie killed."

Ike grabbed him by the collar and ripped the powder horn and cartridge pouch from around Jigs's neck. *"Make the torches."*

◡

Ike's torch sizzled as a large dollop of water fell from a branch above. Reminded that the rain had stopped just before he'd set out after Annie, he again thanked God. The deep gouges left in the softened earth by the weighted-down horse he followed remained clearly visible.

Leading Ranger up a deep ravine at a fast pace, Ike let no minute go by that he didn't also thank the Lord that the prints continued before him at a steady pace. As long as they did, he knew Annie was safe.

Or had been at the time she and her kidnapper passed where he now rode. He knew he had to be close to an hour behind them. An hour. So much could happen in an hour.

Though the Bible said not to fear, he couldn't help it. Icy fingers squeezed his heart while he scourged himself for having let Annie be taken in the first place. If he'd done as she asked, acted on her information and taken the men prisoner when they'd been delivered into his hands, she wouldn't be at their mercy now.

How she must hate him for his weakness. *And his arrogance.*

He'd been so wrong about her, in so many ways. So very wrong. Now that he knew the truth, so much fell into place . . . all that she'd done and said to him from the moment he first laid eyes on her. Even the fact that she'd let him believe she was a widow was easy to understand. She'd been so vulnerable, yet so valiant. She had to be the bravest person he'd ever met, and he'd come across his share of brave men during the war.

"Keep her spirit strong till I get to her, Lord. Keep her strong. And safe."

She must have been born into terrible poverty for her father to even consider selling her. All she had in the world was that broken-down cart and whatever else the dairyman had been kind enough to give her. Small wonder that the five measly acres she planned to buy meant so much to her.

Oh, he'd known poverty was not something new to her—her homespun clothes attested to that. The fancy dust cap and shawl she wore the night of the frolic he'd recognized as a set Betsy wore their first Sunday on the trail. But he hadn't known the depth and breadth of her destitution. To be sold off like a sack of corn.

And her father planned to do it again.

No wonder she was so fiercely determined. And so bent on being her own mistress. No wonder she'd rejected him so resoundingly.

What a mess he'd made of his attempt at wooing her. He couldn't remember exactly the last words he'd said in her presence, but the gist of it seared his brain. Something to the effect that she didn't need to speak for herself—he'd do that for her.

A sharp, high-pitched cry echoed through the narrow ravine.

Ike stopped, frozen in place. Was it Annie?

Another cry.

No, it was an animal. Closer. Coming from behind.

Ike ran to the rear of his horse and held out the torch, searching the inky darkness.

And out of it bounded Cap. Reaching Ike, the animal collapsed at his feet, panting hard, his tail thumping on the soggy leaves.

Ike's eyes stung with tears as he dropped down and gathered the dog into his arms. "Thank you, God," he croaked, hugging the dog close. "We'll find her now. For sure. We have to."

27

"*I was right!*" the outlaw railed as he reined the leggy horse down a steep bank, perilous in the darkness.

Sucking in a breath, Annie halted her efforts with the bindings. Had he detected her movements?

"I was beginning to think my horse had got hisself lost," Beckley continued. "But the creek's right where I left it. Won't be much farther now. Then you and me can have us some of that fun I been promisin'." A guttural chuckle spewed from his offensive mouth as he rubbed his wiry beard against her cheek.

A shudder convulsed through her.

"I see you cain't hardly wait neither." He squeezed her close with one clublike arm while he nudged the horse across what, in the dank night, sounded like a shallow, rock-bottomed stream. "An' jest wait till the boys see what I brung 'em. You remember the boys, don't ya? Ol' Foley and Colburn? Colburn's a real ladies' man, fancies hisself to be a 'English gent.'" The last words came out in a sneer. "But fer once, I reckon Foley will be happier about seein' a woman than Colburn. Since it's you. Yessir, havin' to stay holed up till his leg heals, he's gonna have a lotta fun lettin' you make up for what yer man done to him. Reardon shot his leg up purty bad."

Panic overtook Annie. She had to get her hand free. Now! Escape before she reached the outlaws' lair. *Oh, Lord,* she cried silently. *Please, don't let this happen. Please, help me!*

"Yessiree, yer gonna be a sight fer sore eyes."

They reached the far side of the creek, and Beckley slammed his heels into the horse's flanks, sending the overburdened animal scrambling up the other bank.

Taking advantage of the jolting ascent, Annie frantically, painfully wrenched and twisted against the bindings she'd managed to loosen on one hand. This might be her last chance.

The horse gave a final lunge to reach the top, and in the same instant Annie's hand flew free. She jerked it back to the other, praying her captor hadn't seen.

Beckley's heavily muscled arms closed tighter around hers. "Girl?" *He'd seen her.*

"Before we get to the cave, tell me what-all yer totin' on them pack animals. I want the boys to know all we'll be tradin' you fer."

Did he actually believe Ike would exchange his pack train for her?

What else could he think? The man thought she was Ike's wife. But she wasn't, and after the way she had treated him . . .

She had to escape now.

Beckley banged his shoulder into hers, hard. Only the fact that his arms were around her kept her from falling off the horse. "I said," he bellowed, "what's on them pack animals?"

The dunce didn't remember she was gagged. She made as much noise as she could past the wad of cloth to remind him.

His wide ironlike body relaxed, and his chest bumped with a sharp chuckle. "I plumb fergot."

Wrapping the reins around the horn, he came dangerously close to her unbound hand.

She curled it tight against the other and prayed.

Again, he didn't notice a thing. He must not think her brave enough—or stupid enough—to try anything. He fumbled a moment with the leather thongs at the back of her head, then ripped them up and off . . . along with some of her hair.

Ignoring the pain, Annie took this last opportunity and freed her second hand.

She had a surplus of telltale rope gathered into her palms by the time he pulled the soggy ball of homespun from her mouth. Taking in a gulp of fresh air, she went into a fit of coughing as the sudden coldness hit her lungs.

Beckley grabbed her arm. "Stop yer hackin' and tell me what-all yer carryin'. Yer man ain't gettin' you back 'lessen it's worth our while. We can always trade you up north to the Shawnee."

Annie stifled a gasp. The man's evil had no end.

"You think we ain't got a right to get back some of what you traitors stole off us?" From the tone of his voice, a body would think he was the injured party. "Listen to me, girly. Hiram Colburn and me had us a real prosperous store. We was makin' a fortune tradin' in beaver pelts and buffalo robes near the Indian town of Tikwalitsi. That is, till you greedy land-grabbers overmountain ruined it all with yer blasted war. Comin' over here, runnin' us franchisers off—and our customers, the Cherokee. Squattin' anywheres you please."

Annie couldn't keep her mouth shut. "You and them Indians were burnin' out whole settlements on land bought and paid for fair and square from the Indians. Killin' innocent women and children in their beds, armed to the teeth by King George's redcoats."

"Well, we was just cleanin' out a few nests of traitors, missy. Just like I plan to keep on doin'. Now, quit your stallin'. We're almost to the cave. What's in them packs?"

Almost to the cave? She had to do something. Now. *"What's that?"* she cried and looked back.

He, too, swiveled to the rear. "Wh-what?"

Swinging a leg up over the horse's head, she tossed away her end of the rope and vaulted off into the inky night with no idea what lay below her.

With a loud curse, the outlaw caught her ankle.

But it didn't stop her. Kicking and screaming, Annie hit a down-hill slope, slick with mud.

He came after her, his fingers digging into her flesh.

⁓

A blood-freezing scream came at Ike from somewhere in front of him, and the chilling cry repeated, echoing over and over in the starless night.

Then silence.

Annie.

"Go, Cap! Faster! Faster!" Slamming his heels into Ranger's side, he sent the horse into a galloping chase after Cap, pell-mell up the forest path. "Go! Go!" he shouted, barely able to make out, by the remains of his second torch, the dog racing ahead of him.

They sped through the darkness for the longest minutes of Ike's life. He heard no further screams. Had Annie's captor knocked her unconscious? Killed her?

Then Ike caught a whiff of smoke. A fire burned somewhere close. It had to be the outlaws' campsite.

He reined in hard. *"Cap, Cap, halt!"* he ordered low, hard, hoping his voice wouldn't give him away before he located Annie.

He swung down before his horse came to a complete stop. Stubbing the flame from his torch, he quickly tied Ranger to a branch, then pulled out his rifle. He prayed he would be able to sneak up undetected.

By the time Ike had lifted the brace of pistols from his saddlebag and tucked them into his belt, Cap came panting back. "Good dog," he whispered. "Now, *sit. Stay,*" he commanded, hoping Annie's pet would obey. He couldn't afford to have the dog tip his hand before he was ready.

Making his way up the narrow, uneven trail in almost pitch dark, it wasn't long before he spotted a glow through the trees. It came from higher up, on the side of the ravine. Climbing toward it, he saw that it came from a cave. Moving closer, he reached a tree a stone's throw away.

Then he realized there was no noise. No sound of a struggle. Nothing. As stealthily as possible, he stepped across the spongy ground . . . until the opening was clearly visible.

Then he heard a rustling.

Ducking low, he waited.

A horse whinnied softly near the cave opening.

Only a horse. He exhaled with relief, then moved forward again.

Just outside the cave, he counted the dim outlines of three horses. So it was only Frank Beckley and his two cohorts. No attack had been planned against the wagon train after all. They had taken Annie merely to hold for ransom.

That eased his mind somewhat. But why didn't he hear anything? Was he too late to save her?

Lord, it can't be so. Father, I pray my powder's dry and my aim is true. He'd have one shot at each of them before he had to reload. *And Lord, I pray that's all it will take.*

Not wanting to spook the horses, Ike stayed a number of yards below the cave entrance and moved across to its far side. He searched the interior as he went, hoping to see Annie safe and unharmed, but he saw only one man. The pudgy Englishman. He sat near the entrance, smoking a pipe and staring out as if he might be on guard. All else seemed calm. Much too calm.

Where was Annie?

Behind him, Ike heard a loud snap.

289

Instantly he dropped to the ground.

More snaps and crunches, growing louder, louder. Not a horse. But heavy. More like a bear. Had one come back to reclaim its den?

Ike wedged between two tree trunks.

Whatever it was lumbered past a few yards from him, breathing hard. Just before it reached the cave, it moved between Ike and the light. It wasn't a bear. It was a man.

The stocky man stumbled to the entrance, one hand on his head. "Colburn! Foley!" he shouted.

Ike noticed that the Englishman was already on his feet. Musket in hand, he stepped outside, reaching the one who'd yelled, just as Foley, the lean, dangerous hunter, limped to the entrance, using his rifle as a crutch.

"My head's a bloody mess," the newcomer whined in a hoarse voice. It was Beckley. "She near kilt me. Just down the hill there."

Foley pushed past the Englishman. "You mean you drug the woman this far and let her get the best of you?"

But what about Annie? Ike wanted to shout. Was she hurt—or worse?

"When your mount galloped in alone," the Englishman said, "we feared you'd been captured or killed."

"Aye," Foley said. "And I figured that horse of yourn was leadin' 'em straight back here to us. Yer lucky we didn't shoot you comin' in."

But where's Annie?

"Those Yankee-Doodles," the Englishman said. "Are they pursuing you?"

"Naw, no more'n they did last time."

"That's a relief. I couldn't decide whether to douse the fire or—"

"Shut yer yappin', Colburn," Beckley roared. "Can't you see I'm bleedin' like a stuck hog? That woman near crushed my skull with a rock. Get me a rag. Then get mounted up and track her down. Don't want to lose that golden goose."

Profoundly relieved that Annie had escaped unharmed, Ike thanked the Lord. But he still had to stop them before they went after her.

Foley turned back toward the cave. "You should'a just slit her throat," he growled.

"Then what would we have to trade?" Beckley retorted. "If we work it right, we can dangle her as bait to get them packhorses off'a Reardon. Then you can take yer meanness out on him 'stead of me for a change, an' we'll *still* have the woman to trade to the Shawnee."

"Not to mention the fair bit of entertainment she will provide in the meantime," the Englishman said, a slow grin plumping his cheeks. "I had better fetch my saddle."

Ike would take great pleasure in wiping that smile from the doughy face. He stepped out from between the trees, a pistol cocked and pointed at each of the two who carried weapons. "No, Colburn, stay where you are. We got you covered. Toss your rifles and come outta there. Now!"

For a second, the three froze in place. Then they turned toward Ike, squinting to see into the darkness.

"Dreadfully sorry, good sir," the Englishman called. "But you seem to have us at a disadvantage. Perhaps you could move into the light."

"I said, drop your guns."

In a flash, Foley swung his rifle up, clicking back the flintlock as he did.

Ike shot first.

As Foley grunted and doubled over, the Englishman fired.

The ball whistled by, slicing Ike's arm. His pistol flew from his hand.

Ike's matching gun sent the Englishman reeling backward, screaming in pain. "My shoulder. He broke my shoulder."

Ike stuffed his remaining pistol back into his belt and grabbed for the rifle he'd left leaning against a tree. When he turned back, Beckley had disappeared. Had he escaped into the cave?

The Englishman, though, had crumpled to the ground and was crying, great racking sobs, preventing Ike from hearing any movements Beckley might be making.

Ike melted into deeper shadows, cocking his rifle. He moved quietly in the direction from which he'd come, changing the angle of his view into the cave as he went. No doubt Beckley would be trying to arm himself.

But where was that reprobate?

Beneath Ike's foot a twig snapped.

He heard the click of a flintlock near the whinnying horses.

Powder flashed.

Growling . . . vicious. Cap.

A bullet splintered a tree branch above Ike's head. Instantly, Ike swung his rifle barrel toward the telltale flash . . . where Cap still snarled and Beckley bellowed. He fired.

The man crashed against the horses.

The animals broke free from their line and galloped away down the trail in a stampeding panic, while Cap continued to growl and snap as if he were warring over a bone.

Good old Cap, who'd disobeyed him . . . *and saved him.*

Beckley, like Foley, was now silent. Only the Englishman continued to make any noise.

Was it over? Had he really disabled them all? Ike couldn't be sure. Moving behind a tree, he unslung his powder horn to prime and reload his rifle.

The wounded Englishman called between sobs to his comrades.

Neither answered.

Even the dog had fallen silent in an eerie hush that was softly broken by the first drops of rain.

Ike knew the danger had passed. The burgeoning heavens no longer needed to be held at bay.

∽

Annie stayed where she was, huddled within the drooping limbs of a scratchy pine. All the shooting, yelling, and yapping of dogs had not fooled her. This was just a ploy of Frank Beckley and his accursed friends to make her think she'd been rescued. They'd even cut their horses loose. Did they really think she was fool enough to walk into their trap?

But at least she knew from their racket where they were . . . much too near. Closed in on both sides by steep rises, she knew she needed to get out of the ravine before the light of morning made her tracks visible. And somehow she had to find her way back to Avery's Trace. God had kept her safe thus far. She had to trust that he would see her the rest of the way.

Nerves raw, she listened a few minutes more to be sure the outlaws hadn't started out after her. Hearing nothing but the gentle rustlings of the forest, she gathered what was left of her courage and crawled from under the tree, asking God for the strength she so desperately needed.

Exhausted from the fear and strain of the past few hours, she found to her dismay that it had started to sprinkle again. More misery for her already aching body.

Then she realized that the patter of the rain would muffle her own sounds. Barefoot and with a bruised hip from diving off the horse, her progress would be slow.

The low rumble of a man's voice came to her through the hollow. "Annie . . . come out. It's safe now."

They were close. Too close. Carefully, she tiptoed across the forest debris until she reached a tree trunk and flattened herself against it. She attempted to hold her breath, to stop her loud panting, but her racing heart needed air.

Crashing sounds came toward her, fast, through the brush.

Stooping, she frantically searched the ground for a stick, a rock. Something! Her fingers latched onto a fallen limb.

Too late. She was knocked over . . . by a hairy beast—a licking tongue, a wagging tail. A whining, clawing dog. *Cap!* Her good and faithful Cap!

Then strong but gentle hands were on her arms, lifting her, turning her. "Annie, Annie. Thank God, I found you."

"Ike . . . oh, Ike." Dissolving into tears, she flung her arms around him and held on tight.

His arms enfolded her, pulling her close, so close he all but surrounded her.

Ike was here. He'd come for her. She was safe.

28

Annie stood safe in Ike's arms, clinging to him for the longest time, breathing in Ike's very presence as the leftover tension within her subsided. He was here. With her.

One big gentle hand smoothed over her hair while the other held her close.

Finally, she felt calm enough to speak. "I didn't hear you and the men ride in, only Frank Beckley's horse racing around out there, except when there was a stampede during the shootin'."

"The horse you heard was probably mine."

"Thank you so much for comin' after me."

He pressed her tighter to him. "Thank you for bein' alive. Beckley's horse went straight to their camp when you made your escape."

"You knew I escaped?" She looked up, but it was too dark on this stormy night to see more than a shadowy outline.

"I overheard Beckley tell the others when he came crashin' in. Nothin' quiet about him."

"But where are our men? Brother Rolf, Ken, Jigs."

"They didn't come. Just me."

"Just you? But all that shootin'—"

"It's done now. You're safe." Ike hugged her tight again.

She pulled back. "But, Beckley and his—there was three of 'em."

"I know."

"You went up agin all of 'em? Alone? You could'a been killed. Are you hurt? Are you hit?" She ran her hands over his face and down to his chest.

"No, not really. I think one of my arms got grazed is all."

"Which one? Let me see."

"It's nothin'. Besides, I'm not ready to let go of you just yet." He drew her close again and moved her beneath a tree, out of the rain. "I was so afraid I wouldn't make it in time."

"But you did. . . . You came, just you . . . for me."

"I couldn't leave you out here with them. Even for one night. *'Specially* not for a night." He cupped her chin. "Annie, you had to know I'd come."

"I just thought . . . after the way I kept tellin' you I could take care of myself. Tryin' to act like I was so tough all the time."

"And you are. The toughest and bravest woman I know. To think, a little thing like you gettin' away from that bear of a man. Crowned him real good, too."

"He was gonna—they were . . ."

His hand moved up to the nape of her neck, and he pulled her into the warm hollow of his shoulder. "I know. But no one's ever gonna hurt you again."

She felt his breath tickle across her hair, then his warm lips as he kissed the top of her head.

"I don't care how much you carry on about it," he continued, "you're stuck with me from now on. I'm not lettin' you out of my sight again."

"You still want me after the awful way I treated you?"

"Just try and get rid of me."

She pulled away, depriving herself of the comfort of his arms. "Ike, I think maybe you should wait before you start makin' promises to me. I've been lyin' to you. Well, not lyin', exactly. But I let you think somethin' about me that wasn't true." She took a breath and spewed it out. "I'm not a widow. I've never been married. I've been in servitude for eight years. I just finished my time, and I was hopin' to go west. Have my own place. I wanted to be able to hold my head up again when I go out and about to church and such. With my own land, folks would start thinkin' of me as a worthy person, instead of someone to be bought and sold."

Lightly, he stroked the line of her jaw. "Annie girl, don't you know? You're the most worthy person I ever met in my life. When Rolf told me your pa sold you off, it only gave me more reason to want to keep you safe with me. You've suffered too much already."

His touch was doing crazy things to her insides, making it hard to think. "Are—are you sure it doesn't bother you? My own pa placed more value on a piece of land than he did on me. And Lorna said your ma would never approve of someone common as me . . . and that was without her knowin' I've been a bond servant."

"Lorna doesn't know my mother. She's a wise lady with a good heart. My mother will love you for what you are, *not* who you were. And so will my brothers . . . but not nearly as much as I do. At least, they'd better not." He chuckled, then turned serious again. "I love everything about you, your graceful ways . . . and your unassumin' beauty. Even that fiercely stubborn streak of independence. But I want you to be as independent as you want. Have your own dairy, keep a hundred beehives if it makes you happy. All I ask is that when day is done and you come home, it's to me. Be with me. Be my wife."

Everything she would ever want to hear him say, he was saying. And he'd risked his life to come for her, a lass whose only value had been the price of her servitude. This must be a dream. She reached up with both hands again, this time tracing her fingers slowly over the angles of his face, letting them linger at his lips. "You really are here, tellin' me all these heavenly things. You did come for me."

"Believe me, no matter how mad I get at you, I'll always come for you. I love you, Annie McGregor."

"Oh, Ike, I love you too. I'll never doubt you again, or question what you're doin', or—"

"Oh yes you will. And I'll probably get my feathers ruffled. But that's all right, because—"

"Because then we'll get to make amends. Like this." Annie rose up on her toes and brushed her lips across his.

"Aye," he whispered on a ragged breath. He pulled her closer. "Like that."

∽

"It shouldn't be much longer," Ike said, raking his whisker stubble across the top of Annie's head as Ranger brought them out of the trees and onto a wide track that showed evidence of wagon travel. "This has to be Avery's Trace, the road to Nashville."

"Which way to our wagons?" Annie asked, looking in both directions.

"Into the sun. We've come onto it a little to the west, I judge."

"It's been hours since dawn. It's at least ten o'clock. Everyone must be waitin', real anxious, for you to return."

"They're worried about you, too. And prayin' all this time for your safety. The men wanted to come with me to find you, but they had to stay put in case Beckley had more men out there, set on raidin' the camp when they left. You are loved, Annie. Don't ever doubt it."

"I—thank you for sayin' that." She snuggled back against his chest again . . . exactly where he wanted her.

The train would get a late start today, but it couldn't be helped. With the rain and bodies that needed burying. Then there was the matter of Colburn. Ike really should have tied the Englishman up before leaving to search for Annie. Now the brigand was wandering around in the wilderness wounded and alone. At least Ike had removed all of the weapons before leaving the man.

Ike felt a twinge of guilt about not spending more time this morning looking for Colburn. He would most likely meet a bad end. But he must have preferred taking his chances against the wolves and bears than being hung from the noose end of a rope. *May God have mercy on his soul.*

At the thought of God's mercy, Ike recalled all he'd been blessed with in the past few hours . . . and was filled with so much joy, even a sleepless night couldn't diminish it. These feelings poured off his tongue as they'd done so many times during those precious pre-dawn hours when he'd held his lady close while waiting for the sun.

"I love you, Annie."

"And I love you," she sighed contentedly without lifting her head, which was pillowed against his chest. It had been a long night for her, too.

Cap, scampering along beside them, barked excitedly several times, then raced ahead up the trail.

"Probably some varmint," Ike ventured.

"Cap!" A child's voice carried through the trees.

Ike's horse whinnied and broke into a trot.

"Sounds like we're back," Annie said almost sadly.

Ike brushed his lips across the tender skin beneath her ear . . . the last kiss he'd probably get for a while. "I'm really gonna hate sharing you with the others again."

She turned her lips to his, and the passion in them told him she felt exactly the same way.

From up the wooded trail, Jigs came walking into view, his long rifle couched in the crook of his arm. Seeing them, he stopped and stared, looking from one to the other as they neared. The worries of last night showed plainly on his face. "Everything's well with you?"

Ike couldn't stop the grin. "Aye. Everything's just fine."

A half-cocked smile meandered into place as Jigs eyed them again. "I can see that."

Annie's neck turned rosy—she was blushing.

Ike liked that. But then, what didn't he like about her? He was smitten, unabashedly.

"It's them!" he heard one of the lads yell as the bowed canvas of a wagon came into view.

In a matter of seconds, their friends surrounded them, all laughing and talking at once. Ken dragged Annie from the saddle and gave her a big hug, then passed her to Betsy.

Ike hated that they'd taken Annie from him so quickly, and though he knew she'd probably balk, he was tempted to tell them to give her back, that she belonged to him. *My Annie!* he wanted to shout, as if he were as young and spoiled as Otto. Ike wasn't merely smitten, he was besotted . . . as besotted with love as Ken was over Betsy. *More.*

The Bremmers took Annie from the Smiths and enveloped her in their own big hearty hugs.

There was nothing Ike could do but wait until this tide of welcomes ran its course, so he dismounted.

As he lighted, Jigs stepped up beside him. "We waited up all night, but no one tried to attack us. I checked the perimeter this morning, and I didn't find any sign of men skulking around out there."

"I know. It was just the three that robbed us the last time. Beckley, Foley, and the Englishman. And we don't have to worry about them anymore."

Jigs's raven brows took flight.

Ike clapped his shoulder. "I'll fill you in later. Right now we could use somethin' to eat. And I could use a shave," he added, rubbing his jaw. It was much too scratchy to be touching Annie's soft skin.

"I can see that," Jigs said, wearing that dumb lopsided grin again. His friend had read his mind. As before.

Ike caught sight of Lorna. She moved up beside Jigs, looking as if she'd spent the entire morning brushing her hair into perfect black ringlets that she'd clustered on each side of her violet eyes.

"Ike Reardon, I hardly slept a wink last night," she complained. "You shouldn't have abandoned us like that. But I see you accomplished your mission. Brought her back again. Though I do believe she would've managed quite nicely on her own. Her kind usually does."

That was the last straw. Not another spiteful word about Annie would he take from Lorna. "You listen here—"

"*Ike.*" Inga's strident voice cut him off midsentence. "Is dis true?" With Annie in tow, she pushed her way between Jigs and Lorna. "Did you spend da night *mit* Annie? Alone under da tree?"

What did she think they'd done, slept on different sides of a mountain? "We didn't have much choice, Inga. We sure couldn't ride all the way back here in the rain."

"Da rain did not stop you from going after her. It vas not too vet for dat." Inga's finger jabbed within inches of his face. "You know you should bring her straight to here. Somet'ing haf to be done about dis. *Now. Rolf?*"

Lorna caught Inga's arm. "You don't seriously expect Ike to marry her, do you? That's ludicrous! She has no reputation to protect. If she were a decent woman, she wouldn't be traveling out here unchaperoned."

"Dis is not for you to say," boomed Brother Rolf as he stepped up behind Lorna. He put his massive hands around her upper arms and lifted her to one side. "Mine Inga is right. Dis is serious business." He turned his penetrating blue eyes on Ike. Squinting, he studied Ike's for a moment. "You haf always been honest and fair. If you say, on your honor, you vas a gentleman last night, I vill belief you."

Ike became very aware that every single person in camp surrounded them, waiting for his answer, even the thumb-chewing Auburn baby. He turned to Annie.

She stared back at him, looking as embarrassed by the insinuations as she was stunned. Then that beautiful gold-rimmed green gaze fled. "I'm sorry. I never expected this. I'm—"

He stopped her with a finger to her lips. "I'm not. I think it's a fine idea. And not because you've been compromised, because we both know you haven't. Marry me because I love you and always will. Marry me. Here. Today."

The blush vanished, leaving nothing but enormous eyes in a pale face. "I—are you sure?"

"That's not the problem. I need to know if *you* will have *me* here today . . . and forever more. Till death do us part."

She searched his face for a long, agonizing moment. Gradually her gaze softened, and the hint of a smile curved her lips. "I will."

Wolfie, at the edge of the circle, shouted out, "Then I pronounce you man and wife."

Laughter erupted all around them, and Ike took that as his cue. He gathered Annie into his arms—where she belonged—and sealed it with a kiss.

Epilogue

The tantalizing aroma of coffee brought Annie awake. She opened her eyes to find Ike kneeling beside her, offering her a steaming cup and a most endearing smile . . . and his silver blue eyes told her everything she ever wanted to know.

She reached for him.

"Hey, watch out," he warned, dodging with the hot brew. Setting it away from the blankets, he leaned over her and planted a good-morning kiss on her lips.

Wrapping her arms around his neck and returning his embrace, she felt lazy and happy and so very safe. Never in her most fanciful dreams had she thought being awakened in the morning by her husband could make a woman feel so complete—the closest thing to what heaven must be like. Again she thanked God for bringing them together. From that moment two days ago when Brother Bremmer had pronounced them husband and wife, she had felt as if she were walking in a lovely dream.

The constant sound of a bawling cow edged its way into her consciousness, eventually bringing her to her senses. Pushing Ike away, she sat up and looked around. They had spread their pallet in a secluded spot. At the edge of a stand of pines, a living wall of berry vines and a small glen separated them from the teasing of the rest of the campers. The mischief in Ike's eyes, though, she didn't mind one whit.

Shielding the sun's rays from her own eyes, she smiled up at him, then it dawned on her. "The sun's already crested the hills, and I'm still abed. Why didn't you wake me?"

"And miss watching you sleep?"

The thought of someone spying on her while she slept made Annie feel uneasy, vulnerable. But only for a second. She and Ike would be watching each other sleep—watching over each other—for the rest of their lives. Indeed, the rewards of loving someone were worth the risk. She touched his cheek. "That's sweet."

Looking most pleased with her and himself, he handed her the cup of coffee.

"Thank you. I feel like such a princess."

"You *are* one. Mine." Picking up his own cup, he sat down close to her.

My, but wasn't this a lovely way to start a morning? Their last on the trail. Ike had said they would be turning south off Avery's Trace before noon, and an hour or so later they'd drop down into his valley. This very night she would be sleeping in her new home!

With almost no warning, Wolfie came tromping through a break in the berry vines. Wearing only her night rail, Annie scarcely had time to grab a pillow to shield herself.

Wolfie didn't bother with amenities. "Ike, Pa says you need to come straightaway."

Ike groaned. "What's the problem?"

"It's Jigs and Lorna. They're gone."

Ike raised a sun-bleached brow. "Are you sayin' that as lazy as Jigs is, he hitched up and started out ahead of us?"

"No, sir. They took two horses and sneaked out in the middle of the night."

~

Ike tossed out his coffee and sprang to his feet. "That can't be true." Jigs was his army pal and frontier partner. They'd faced danger together more times than he could count. Jigs wouldn't betray him like that.

"It is. Papa found a letter. It's got your name writ on it."

Before the straw-haired kid had finished, Ike took off for the wagons. Crossing the meadow, he counted his horses. Sure enough, two were missing—Beaver, one of the bay geldings; and Smoky, Jigs's gray.

At first glance, everything in the camp appeared normal— the women cleaning up after breakfast, the young'uns scampering about. But not the men. They were clustered together, talking.

Brother Rolf broke away from the others, holding a folded piece of paper in his hand. He intercepted Ike. "I go to vake up dat sleepyhead Jigs," he said, offering the missive, *"und* all I find is dis."

Taking it, Ike saw his name scrawled on an outside fold. As he spread out the paper, the other men and now the women converged on him, concern evident on all their faces. He knew he would have no privacy reading it. If Jigs had in fact run off with Lorna, this was a serious matter.

"Read da letter," Inga prompted as she came to stand by her husband.

Still reluctant, Ike knew that whatever was in it couldn't be any worse than what these folks were thinking. He might as well do as she bade.

Looking down, he recognized Jigs's sloppy scrawl. *"Dear Ike,"* he read to the others.

I know this letter catches you by surprise. I knew if I told you last night, you would be honor-bound to stop us. But what I do, I do for you and the valley and most of all for Noah. I want to save him from worse hurt later on. Since she saw her first wilderness cabin, Lorna has been after me to take her and Noah with me to New Orleans. I thought it was just foolish talk, and I did not think much of it. But three days ago, she said she did not want to marry Noah and live in some log hovel. She was going to Nashville to hitch a ride downriver with or without me.

Betsy spoke up. "I can't believe she actually did it. She was always talking such nonsense, but I never took it serious."

"Finish da letter," Brother Rolf grated out. "Then ve talk."

Ike glanced back at the paper and continued.

Lorna is so determined, I knew we would have to tie her up to keep her here. I know you promised her father to keep her safe, so I vow to be a gentleman and see only to her needs until we get to New Orleans. I took two horses. Lorna insisted on taking all her dresses. She plans to trade them to the Indians for beaver pelts to pay her way once we arrive in New Orleans. I will see she gets a good price. The horses I will leave at the Miffin cabin on the fork north of here and take his canoe down to Nashville. I know you will be mad for a while. But try not to hold it agin me too long. It is better she goes now before Noah says any wedding vows with her. He does not need a runaway wife. Your true friend, James Terrell.

Ike's first thought was to saddle up and ride after them—to drag that willful girl back by her curly black hair. "Does anyone have any idea when they left?"

306

Bone-thin Mrs. Auburn moved closer. "The baby woke me up an hour or so after we bedded down, and I saw Jigs and Miss Graham still sittin' at their fire. They probably left after they was sure the camp was settled for the night."

Heaving a sigh, Ike shook his head. "They're probably already on the water, headed downstream."

Rolf's big hand landed on Ike's shoulder. "Four times I talk to Lorna about her walk *mit* da Lord. She never vant to listen. She alvays say she belong to anodder church dat don't ask da personal questions. Dere is not'ing left to do now but pray for her." Rolf gave Ike's shoulder a squeeze. "And dat Jigs, too. Dat one did not even pretend to be da Christian."

"I know," Ike said, looking to the north over the other folks' heads. "And you're right. All we can do now is pray." *And say a prayer for me and Noah, too,* he wanted to say. He had no idea what Noah would do when he found out.

∽

The afternoon was hot and dry for a change, as only mid-August could be. With a corner of her apron, Annie dabbed at the perspiration beading her brow while keeping step with her cows. Today she was in the lead of the wagon train. The packhorses, as well as Ike's Ranger, were strung from the back of her cart.

With Jigs gone, Wolfie had volunteered to drive Ike's wagon, leaving him free to walk at the front with Annie. But for the first time since they married three days ago, Ike was not pleasant company. Rarely speaking the whole morning, he now wore that unreadable expression that had always made her nervous.

Since they'd turned south off Avery's Trace about an hour ago, she'd sensed Ike drawing away from her more with each step that brought them closer to the valley . . . closer to the moment he would have to face his brother. Annie cringed at the thought of Ike's having to tell Noah that he'd lost his brother's intended bride only a few hours short of bringing her to him. That Lorna had run off with Ike's best friend.

Annie wanted to say something that would comfort her husband, but she had no idea what that could be. In fact, even the thought of his needing to be comforted had seemed inconceivable before today. Never had it occurred to her that he would be the one in need.

Nearing the top of a rise, the cows began to slow. Annie cracked her whip above their backs to keep them moving. Earlier Ike had said his valley was only an hour off the trace. Any time now they would be dropping down into it, perhaps even on the other side of this very hill.

Seeing it together for the first time should have been a memorable moment, a day of great joy. Yet all had gone so quickly awry. Ike was deeply troubled, and he was keeping his feelings to himself, hiding his pain . . . doing exactly what she'd always done to protect herself. He was shutting her out.

She looked at Ike again, his eyes turned away, staring off to the side, and suddenly she knew that if they were going to be one as in the Bible, this moment did have to be shared . . . this moment when they gazed down upon the dream that had first brought them together.

Annie walked over to Ike and took his hand, and though he stiffened, she laced her fingers through his.

He turned then and made an effort to acknowledge her gesture. Peering down at her, he smiled—a forced smile.

She wanted to cry for him, for both of them. Instead she squeezed his hand and said something she'd never said unless he said it first. "I love you."

He withdrew his hand from hers.

He was rejecting her?

No. Wrapping an arm around her, he snugged her close against his side. But he still seemed a mile away. "At the top of the knoll,

308

we'll have a clear view of my valley. I hope you like it as much as I do." His voice lacked enthusiasm.

Somehow she had to get through to him. "Wherever you are is where I want to be, whether it's in your valley or anywhere else." She then found herself saying more, a long-remembered quote from the Book of Ruth. "*Whither thou goest I will go; and where thou lodgest I will lodge: thy people shall be my people, and thy God my God.* And, husband, your brother shall be my brother, his pain my pain . . . as your pain is mine."

Ike stopped. He turned her toward him and stared intently into her eyes.

The words had just poured from her. Had she overstepped her bounds?

"You don't know how much I've been looking forward to showing you my valley."

He was talking about his land again, ignoring her words, her offering, as if she'd never spoken. The thought broke her heart as he continued.

"Such a perfect day it was to be. Then to have such a pall hang over it, on this day of all days. . . ." He cupped her head. "And then to hear those words come from you. To have your very soul wrap itself around my heart, to feel it beat as one with mine. What a gift you are. With you at my side I can face anything. Even the wrath of my brother."

Annie drank in the love pouring from his eyes for a wondrous moment before she found her voice. "And you, Isaac Reardon, are the treasure at the end of my rainbow."

Proving that he was, his lips found hers in a long lingering kiss that said more even than his words.

She stepped into his embrace with as much wonder and love as she knew he felt . . . giving herself to him with the same promise.

"Vat is da holdup here?" Brother Rolf's demand gruffly intruded as he strode up to them.

Breaking away from Ike, embarrassed at being caught in such an intimate moment, she saw that her cart had come to a halt, with the pack train behind it, and the Bremmer outfit crowded close.

Ike only laughed. "I was just welcoming my bride to Reardon's Valley. It's just over the hill."

"It is?" A huge grin plumped Rolf's heavy jowls. Swinging around, he trundled fast back to his wagon. "Come! Come, mine *liebchens!* Come see da valley. Ve are here!"

The ardent message was carried down the line, and everyone came running. The children sprinted by Annie and Ike, yelling and laughing, their feet kicking up dust as they ran ahead of their parents.

Ike took Annie's hand. "Come on!"

She hesitated. "Not just yet."

"But I thought more than anyone you'd want to see the valley."

"Oh, I do. Very much. But we have somethin' much more important to do." Annie clasped her hands behind Ike's neck and drew him down until his lips were only a breath away. "We have that kiss to finish."

A Note from the Author

Dear Reader,

It was a joy for me to take this journey to *Freedom's Promise* with such a mix of fictional characters. They became so real and dear to me while I was writing. I do hope you've had as pleasurable and as spiritually uplifting a trip as I had. For me it was particularly meaningful because after the American Revolution my own ancestors traveled from North Carolina to settle in Tennessee country.

I especially enjoyed shaping my characters after reading letters and journals of real women who took such journeys in those long-ago days. In their diaries I read not just about their arduous crossings of rivers and mountains but also about their reliance on the Lord, who traveled with them. When faced with a life-threatening situation, their first response was not to call 911 as most of us would do today, but to call upon the Lord. I hope I've portrayed in some measure their spirit, for these were women who might easily have said, "The Lord is my strength and my song; he has become my victory" (Psalm 118:14, NLT).

I'm having a lot of fun writing the next novel of the series. Noah Reardon tries to turn a backwoods innocent into a Baltimore lady, even though everyone knows you can't turn a sow's ear into a silk purse!

I would also like to extend my special thanks to those of you who wrote to Sally Laity and me in response to our Freedom's Holy Light series. Your thoughtful letters were as much of a blessing to us as I hope our books were to you.

Sincerely,

Dianna Crawford

About the Author

Dianna Crawford lives in southern California with her husband, Byron, and the youngest of their four daughters. Although she loves writing historical fiction, her most gratifying blessings are her husband of thirty-eight years, her daughters, and her grandchildren. Aside from writing, Dianna is active in her church's children's ministries and in a Christian organization that counsels mothers-to-be, offering alternatives to abortion.

Dianna's first novel was published in 1992 under the pen name Elaine Crawford. Written for the general market, the book became a best-seller and was nominated for Best First Book by the Romance Writers of America. Three more novels and several novellas followed under that pen name.

Dianna says that she much prefers writing Christian historical fiction, because our wonderful Christian heritage is commonly diluted or distorted—if not completely deleted—from most historical fiction, nonfiction, and textbooks. She felt very blessed when she and Sally Laity were given the opportunity to coauthor the Freedom's Holy Light series for Tyndale House. The books center on fictional characters who are woven into many of the real-life adventures and miracles that took place during the American Revolution.

The Freedom's Holy Light series consists of *The Gathering Dawn, The Kindled Flame, The Tempering Blaze, The Fires of Freedom, The Embers of Hope,* and *The Torch of Triumph*. Dianna has also authored two HeartQuest novellas, which appear in the anthologies *A Victorian Christmas Tea* and *With This Ring*. Her novel *Out of the Darkness,* published by Heartsong Presents, was coauthored with Rachel Druten.

Dianna welcomes letters from readers written to her at P.O. Box 80176, Bakersfield, CA 92240.

Current HeartQuest Releases

- *A Bouquet of Love,* Ginny Aiken, Ranee McCollum, Jeri Odell, and Debra White Smith
- *Dream Vacation,* Ginny Aiken, Jeri Odell, and Elizabeth White
- *Faith,* Lori Copeland
- *Finders Keepers,* Catherine Palmer
- *Freedom's Promise,* Dianna Crawford
- *Hope,* Lori Copeland
- *June,* Lori Copeland
- *Prairie Fire,* Catherine Palmer
- *Prairie Rose,* Catherine Palmer
- *Prairie Storm,* Catherine Palmer
- *Reunited,* Judy Baer, Jeri Odell, Jan Duffy, and Peggy Stoks
- *The Treasure of Timbuktu,* Catherine Palmer
- *The Treasure of Zanzibar,* Catherine Palmer
- *A Victorian Christmas Cottage,* Catherine Palmer, Debra White Smith, Jeri Odell, and Peggy Stoks
- *A Victorian Christmas Quilt,* Catherine Palmer, Debra White Smith, Ginny Aiken, and Peggy Stoks
- *A Victorian Christmas Tea,* Catherine Palmer, Dianna Crawford, Peggy Stoks, and Katherine Chute
- *With This Ring,* Lori Copeland, Dianna Crawford, Ginny Aiken, and Catherine Palmer
- *Magnolia,* Ginny Aiken—coming soon (April 2000)
- *Olivia's Touch,* Peggy Stoks—coming soon (May 2000)

Other Great Tyndale House Fiction

- *As Sure As the Dawn,* Francine Rivers
- *Ashes and Lace,* B. J. Hoff
- *The Atonement Child,* Francine Rivers
- *The Captive Voice,* B. J. Hoff
- *Cloth of Heaven,* B. J. Hoff
- *Dark River Legacy,* B. J. Hoff
- *An Echo in the Darkness,* Francine Rivers
- *The Embers of Hope,* Sally Laity & Dianna Crawford
- *The Fires of Freedom,* Sally Laity & Dianna Crawford
- *The Gathering Dawn,* Sally Laity & Dianna Crawford
- *Home Fires Burning,* Penelope J. Stokes
- *Jewels for a Crown,* Lawana Blackwell
- *The Last Sin Eater,* Francine Rivers
- *Leota's Garden,* Francine Rivers
- *Like a River Glorious,* Lawana Blackwell

- *Measures of Grace*, Lawana Blackwell
- *Remembering You*, Penelope J. Stokes
- *Song of a Soul*, Lawana Blackwell
- *Storm at Daybreak*, B. J. Hoff
- *The Scarlet Thread*, Francine Rivers
- *The Tangled Web*, B. J. Hoff
- *The Tempering Blaze*, Sally Laity & Dianna Crawford
- *Till We Meet Again*, Penelope J. Stokes
- *The Torch of Triumph*, Sally Laity & Dianna Crawford
- *A Voice in the Wind*, Francine Rivers
- *Vow of Silence*, B. J. Hoff

HeartQuest Books by Dianna Crawford

Freedom's Promise—For the first time in Annie McGregor's life she's free, and she intends to stay that way. After completing her years of servitude to a dairy farmer in North Carolina, she hears there's a man in town looking for settlers to accompany him across the mountains to Tennessee country. Could this be the answer to her prayers?

Isaac Reardon and two of his brothers have spent the last three years staking out a place for themselves in virgin territory and working hard to make it suitable for womenfolk—in particular, two young women who have promised to marry Ike and his brother Noah. Ike returns to North Carolina, intending to collect the two intended brides, a preacher, and any other tradesmen willing to relocate to their new settlement. He is devastated when he learns that his betrothed has married another. And now to make matters worse, he's confronted with a mule-headed tenderhearted young woman who insists on accompanying his wagon train—without a man to protect her along the way.

During their adventurous journey to Tennessee, both Annie and Ike learn that God truly works in mysterious ways, and that freedom's promise holds more than either of them ever dreamed.

A Daddy for Christmas—One stormy Christmas Eve on the coast of Maine, the prayers of a young widow's child are answered in a most unusual manner. This novella by Dianna Crawford appears in the anthology *A Victorian Christmas Tea*.

Something New—An arranged marriage awaits Rachel in San Francisco. But her discovery on the voyage from the Old Country threatens to change everything. This novella by Dianna Crawford appears in the anthology *With This Ring*.

Other Great Tyndale House Fiction
by Dianna Crawford

Freedom's Holy Light series, Sally Laity and Dianna Crawford

The Gathering Dawn—This story portrays the fervor of the growing American Revolution—and the yearning for spiritual fulfillment—through the lives of an Englishwoman and an American patriot.

The Tempering Blaze—Hunted by the British Crown, Ted and Jane Harrington and Dan Haynes must run for their lives, leaving Susannah a prisoner in her own home.

The Fires of Freedom—Hostilities break out between the colonists and the English troops in 1774. Daniel Haynes is arrested and charged with aiding his brother-in-law Ted Harrington in deserting the British army.

The Embers of Hope—The exciting and gripping Revolutionary War saga of love, betrayal, and forgiveness continues when Emily suddenly finds her dreams in ashes and has to struggle for a new life and love.

The Torch of Triumph—In the captivating conclusion to this Revolutionary War saga, patriot spy Evelyn Thomas is taken captive by Indians and has only one hope for rescue—her true love.